Beauty for Ashes

Dorothy Love

Thomas Nelson

Since 1798

Published in Nashville, Tennessee, by Thomas Nelson. Thomas Nelson is a registered trademark of Thomas Nelson, Inc.

Thomas Nelson, Inc., titles may be purchased in bulk for educational, business, fund-raising, or sales promotional use. For information, please e-mail SpecialMarkets@ThomasNelson.com.

All Scripture quotations are taken from the King James Version of the Bible.

ISBN 978-1-4016-5829-8 (custom)

Library of Congress Cataloging-in-Publication Data

Love, Dorothy.

  Beauty for ashes / Dorothy Love.

    p. cm. -- (A Hickory Ridge novel ; 2)

  ISBN 978-1-59554-901-3 (pbk.)

  1. Widows--Fiction. 2. Tennessee--Fiction. I. Title.

  PS3562.O8387B43 2012

  813'.54--dc23

2011046298

Printed in the United States of America

23 24 25 26 27 LBC 5 4 3 2 1

ACCLAIM FOR DOROTHY LOVE

"*Beauty for Ashes* is a touching story about finding joy and healing in the midst of heartache. Set in the small town of Hickory Ridge, Dorothy Love takes readers on a beautifully written journey into the heart of the South during the years that followed the Civil War. As her characters search for healing, they must choose to either cling to the past or trade the bitterness in their hearts for love."

—MELANIE DOBSON, AWARD-WINNING AUTHOR OF *THE SILENT ORDER* AND *LOVE FINDS YOU IN LIBERTY, INDIANA*

"Dorothy Love paints a vivid picture of the post-Civil War south [and] the need to rebuild hope. And she does it beautifully . . ."

—CATHY GOHLKE, AWARD-WINNING AUTHOR OF *PROMISE ME THIS*

"You'll adore this book from beginning to end. The story will capture your heart from the first line. Love uses romance and humor to tell the story of characters who are trying to better their lives and break down barriers."

—*ROMANTIC TIMES*, 4 ½ STAR REVIEW OF *BEYOND ALL MEASURE*

"With well-drawn characters and just enough suspense to keep the pages turning, this winning debut will be a hit with fans of Gilbert Morris and Lauraine Snelling."

—*LIBRARY JOURNAL* REVIEW OF *BEYOND ALL MEASURE*

"Beautifully written and with descriptions so rich I'm still certain I caught a whiff of magnolia blossoms as I read. *Beyond All Measure* is pure Southern delight! Dorothy Love weaves a stirring romance that's both gloriously detailed with Tennessee history and that uplifts and inspires the heart."

—TAMERA ALEXANDER, BEST-SELLING AUTHOR OF *THE INHERITANCE* AND *WITHIN MY HEART*

"Soft as a breeze from the Old South and as gentle as the haze hovering over the Great Smokies, the gifted flow of Dorothy Love's pen casts a spell of love, hate and hope in post-Civil War Tennessee. With rich, fluid prose, characters who breathe onto the page and a wealth of historical imagery, *Beyond All Measure* will steal both your heart and your sleep well beyond the last page."

—JULIE LESSMAN, BEST-SELLING
AUTHOR OF *A HOPE UNDAUNTED*

"Dorothy Love captures all the romance, charm and uncertainties of the postbellum South, delighting readers with her endearing characters, historical details and vivid writing style."

—MARGARET BROWNLEY, AUTHOR OF *A LADY LIKE SARAH*, REGARDING *BEYOND ALL MEASURE*

"Find a porch swing, pour yourself a tall glass of lemonade: [*Beyond All Measure*] is the perfect summer read!"

—SIRI MITCHELL, AUTHOR OF
A HEART MOST WORTHY

For my mother

"To appoint unto them that mourn in Zion,
to give unto them beauty for ashes,
the oil of joy for mourning,
the garment of praise for the spirit of heaviness . . .
that he might be glorified."

ISAIAH 61:3

ONE

Carrie Daly watched a knot of people hurrying past the dress-shop window and tried to think of something—anything—except the wedding. These days, everybody in Hickory Ridge made a point of speaking to her about it. For Henry's sake, she smiled and thanked them for their good wishes, ignoring the creeping dismay at the bottom of her heart.

"Hold still a minute longer, Miz Daly. Almost done here." Jeanne Pruitt, the wife of the mercantile owner and the new proprietress of Norah's Fine Frocks, knelt on the floor to attach the lace trim to the hem of Carrie's dress.

In her stocking feet, Carrie balanced on the small step stool and listened to Mrs. Pruitt's detailed recounting of her recent visit to her sister's place in Muddy Hollow. The new dressmaker wasn't as stylish as Norah had been. She was, however, a magician with needle and thread. The ladies of Hickory Ridge kept her busy repairing seams, restyling old frocks, and occasionally making a new dress from scratch. Now, with a final snip of her scissors, she finished both the hem and her tale and got to her feet. "You're all set, dear. Take a look."

Carrie crossed to the cheval glass in the corner and studied her reflection. The dress, a pale robin's-egg-blue silk, featured wide ruffled sleeves and a neat bustle in the back. A row of tiny mother-of-pearl buttons graced the bodice. It was much too fancy for farm life—once the wedding was over, where would she ever go to wear it?—but Henry had insisted that she have the best. "It's beautiful, Jeanne. You outdid yourself."

"I'm glad you like it. That color exactly matches your eyes." Jeanne's gaze met Carrie's in the mirror. "Things must be busy at the farm these days."

Turning sideways, Carrie eyed the bustle and smoothed it with her fingertips. "Everything's ready except for baking the cookies. And the cake."

Jeanne grinned, revealing a missing front tooth. "Every last soul in Hick'ry Ridge is hankering for an invite to the wedding just to eat a piece of your coconut cake. And to see the Caldwells, of course. I hear they're due in from Texas tonight."

The prospect of seeing her dear friends took Carrie's mind off her apprehensions, if only temporarily. She nodded. "Wyatt sent a wire from Nashville yesterday afternoon. I can't wait. I'm only disappointed they aren't bringing Wade and Sophie."

"It's a long way to bring a little one on a train but I'm sure this won't be their last trip to Hick'ry Ridge." Jeanne folded a scrap of lace and placed it on a shelf. "Wyatt Caldwell may not own the lumber mill anymore, but he can't stop caring about it."

"I'm glad *someone* cares." A tiny frown creased Carrie's forehead, and she absently rubbed the small bony protrusion on her wrist, the result of a fall from the hayloft the summer she turned nine. Hard times at the mill had everyone worried. Only last week Henry had mentioned that orders had slowed to a trickle. And the Chicago Yankees who now owned the place, safe and secure in their distant lakeside mansions, were talking about letting some of the mill hands go. Why Henry wanted to get married now, taking on so much responsibility when times were so uncertain, was the mystery of the ages. But his mind was made up.

Jeanne patted Carrie's shoulder. "Why don't you change out of that dress and I'll box it up for you."

Carrie stepped around a muslin-draped dressmaker's dummy and a scarred pine table laden with fabric samples and pattern books. Behind the folding screen, she shucked out of her new dress, draped it over the top of the screen, and slipped into her everyday green calico.

Jeanne folded the new frock, nestled it into layers of tissue paper, and tied the box shut with a length of yellow ribbon. "There. Hang it up as soon as you get home so the wrinkles won't set."

Carrie picked up her bag, her parasol, and the dress box. The bell above the door tinkled as she stepped out onto the boardwalk. A horse and wagon rumbled past, a sturdy farm girl at the reins. At the far end of the street, on the porch of the Verandah Hotel for Ladies, two residents sat in rocking chairs watching groups of noisy, barefoot boys congregating outside the bakery. Businessmen in dark suits and bowler hats hurried toward the railway station, their valises bumping against their legs. A train whistle blew, two sharp blasts that echoed against the fog-shrouded mountains. Cupping one hand to the dress-shop window, Carrie waved another good-bye to Jeanne and started along the boardwalk to Mr. Pruitt's mercantile, thinking about what she needed for baking the cake. More sugar, a pound of butter, a dozen—

"Look out!" A man's booming voice shattered her reverie. She looked up just in time to see a horse charging toward her, the young woman in the buggy yanking furiously on the reins. The horse was immense, coal black and sleek as an eel. His hooves pounded the street. His legs pumped like pistons. Carrie stood transfixed, clutching her package as the huge beast thundered toward her, scattering a group of farm women outside the post office and nearly colliding with a freight wagon just turning onto the street.

"Whoa," the buggy driver cried, her voice shrill with fear. "Whoa there."

The horse bore down on Carrie. He neighed and reared, his eyes wild with fright, his immense front feet pawing the air.

"Move!" the man shouted. Carrie's feet left the ground as he shoved her aside.

Her shoulder cracked against the boardwalk. Her parasol and the dress box tumbled into the dust.

"Steady, boy." The man grabbed the horse's silver-studded bridle and spoke into the beast's ear. Holding tightly to the bridle, he pressed his head against the horse's neck, speaking so softly Carrie couldn't hear a word. But whatever he said worked. The horse nickered and immediately quieted, his powerful legs quivering. The young woman in the rig buried her face in her hands and sobbed. A crowd gathered, but the horse tamer quickly dispersed them.

Before Carrie could move, the door to the bank flew open and the bank president, Mr. Gilman, hurried outside. "Sabrina?" he called to the weeping girl. "What on earth have you done now?"

"I'm sorry, Daddy." Sabrina Gilman tumbled from the rig, her straw hat askew. "Old Peter harnessed him for me this morning, and I thought I could handle him, but when the train whistle blew he went plumb crazy."

"Old Peter should have known better. I've told you both to stay away from Majestic. He's high-strung and certainly no carriage horse. You could have been killed." Mr. Gilman held out a hand to steady her. "Go on inside and collect yourself."

Carrie felt sorry for the banker's daughter. Her intended, Jacob Hargrove, had abandoned his family farm in search of work elsewhere, and the separation had left poor Sabrina in a state of nervous exhaustion. According to Mariah Whiting, who knew everything that went on in town, Sabrina had become susceptible to frequent fainting spells and bouts of the mullygrubs.

The horse tamer hurried over and helped Carrie to her feet. He touched the brim of his hat in greeting. "A thousand apologies, miss. I shouted a warning, but you didn't hear. Are you all right?"

"I think so." She straightened her hat and reached for her crushed dress box.

"Please. Allow me." He retrieved her box and smiled down at her. Her stomach dropped. Heavenly days, but this man was handsome. He was nearly a foot taller than she, with sun-browned skin, full lips, a straight nose, and eyes so brown they appeared almost black. He stood so close she could see beads of moisture on his brow and a tiny white scar just above his upper lip. Somehow the slight imperfection only increased his appeal.

"You're sure you aren't hurt?" He lifted a brow and studied her.

She brushed the dirt from her skirt and took in his attire—a clean, crisp boiled collar, fine wool trousers that fit him perfectly, and a coat that accented the set of his broad shoulders. Everything about him spoke of gentility and old money. He even smelled expensive.

"I'm quite all right, thank you."

Mr. Gilman hurried over and pumped the horse tamer's hand. "I can't thank you enough for what you did, sir. Sabrina knows better, she's—" He nodded to Carrie. "Miz Daly. My word, are you hurt?"

"I'm fine, Mr. Gilman."

He eyed her box. "I suppose that's your dress for the wedding?"

"Yes."

"If there's any damage at all, you let me know. I'll make it right." He turned to the horse tamer. "I don't believe I've heard your name."

"Griffin Rutledge. Griff to my friends." He winked at Carrie and her cheeks warmed.

"Rutledge," Mr. Gilman said. "You by any chance kin to Charles Rutledge of Charleston?"

"He's my father." Mr. Rutledge's face turned stony, but the banker seemed not to notice.

"Well, well, what a small world, eh?" The banker slapped Mr. Rutledge's shoulder as if they were old friends. "I knew your daddy back before the war. Used to go down to Charleston every February for Race Week. Oh, the times we had with your folks and the Venables, the Hugers, and the Ravenels. Y'all had some of the finest horses I'd ever seen." He studied the horse tamer's face. "I remember Charles's boy Philip, but I declare, I didn't know he had two sons."

Carrie stuck out her bottom lip and blew her rust-colored curls upward. The day was heating up, her shoulder throbbed painfully, and she still needed things from the mercantile. But she stood rooted to the spot, unable to tear herself away from Griff Rutledge. Which made not one iota of sense. What was the matter with her?

Mr. Gilman went on. "What brings you to Hickory Ridge, Mr. Rutledge? I hope you're planning to stay awhile."

"Not long."

The banker looked past Griff's shoulder to the huge horse, now standing placidly in the shade of the building. "Maybe a good business proposition will change your mind. You got some time to discuss it?"

"Not at the moment." Mr. Rutledge made a slight formal bow toward Carrie. "I knocked this lovely woman into the dirt and crushed her dress box to boot. The least I can do is to see her safely to her carriage."

Carrie dropped her gaze. The old rig hitched to Henry's plodding bay mare, Iris, was a far cry from a carriage. But the prospect of spending a few more moments with the courtly Griff Rutledge overcame her embarrassment.

Griff offered her his arm. "Which way, Miss . . ."

"Daly. Carrie." She pointed. "My horse and rig are over there."

He glanced at the dress box. "Do I understand that you're about to be married?"

"Marr—oh. No. My brother Henry is getting married the day after tomorrow. He insisted that I get a new dress for the occasion."

A grin split his handsome face. "Well, that's surely a big load off my mind. There's nothing quite so maddening as meeting the prettiest girl in town only to learn that her heart is already taken."

Carrie blushed. Mercy, but he was forward. Were all Charleston gentlemen so outspoken?

"If your brother's intended is half as pretty as you, he's a lucky man indeed."

Overwhelmed by his sheer physicality and the brush of his shoulder against hers, Carrie went mute.

"I hope your dress isn't damaged," he went on. "I'll bet it's beautiful. Wish I could be there to see you wear it."

At last she found her voice. "You should come. We'd be delighted to have you."

Holy hash! What would Nate Chastain say about her inviting a man to the festivities? More to the point, how would Mary Stanhope react to the news? Henry's bride was not the most accommodating woman on the planet. And she put on airs. No doubt she'd give Carrie a blistering lecture about inviting a total stranger to a wedding. *It simply isn't done.* But it would be worth braving Mary's wrath to see this man again.

"That's the nicest invitation I've received in a while," he said, "but I couldn't possibly impose upon—"

"It's no imposition at all," she said quickly. "It's the least I can do. After all, you practically saved my life."

"Well, when you put it that way—"

"It's to be held the day after tomorrow at the Henry Bell farm.

Just follow the main road a mile or so past the church. The wedding's at half past ten."

He smiled. "Half past ten. The Bell farm. Thank you most kindly, Miz Carrie Daly. I'll see you then."

He tipped his hat and sauntered toward the bank. Carrie climbed into the rig and flicked the reins. Iris plodded onto the road and across the railroad trestle. What in the world had possessed her just now? Everyone in Hickory Ridge knew she and Nate planned to wed . . . someday. Everyone said they were a perfect match.

Nate was a fine man, kind, hardworking and intelligent, well liked in town. Maybe he wasn't the most exciting man in the world, maybe the sight of him didn't exactly make her heart beat faster, but she enjoyed his company. So why couldn't she get the image of Griff Rutledge's handsome face out of her mind?

Halfway home she remembered she still needed flour, eggs, and sugar for the wedding cake.

Griff watched Carrie's rig make the turn at the bottom of the street and whistled softly. What a woman. Hers was not the half-formed prettiness of a young girl, but the full loveliness of a mature woman with all the self-possession maturity brings. Her hair was somewhere between red and gold, the color of a Carolina sky at sunrise. And those eyes—clear and blue as the Atlantic. She smelled good too, like the air after a low country rain. He wondered if there was a Mr. Daly in the picture. Probably so. Women like that didn't stay unattached for long. Just the same, he was glad he'd accepted her invitation. Lately he'd spent far too much time alone.

When the rig disappeared from view, he retraced his steps to the bank. Though he didn't plan on staying here any longer than necessary, if a profitable proposition was in the offing, he owed it to himself to hear the banker out.

The big black colt stood where Griff had left him, tethered to the rail outside the bank. Griff stopped to admire the horse. Everything about him, from his height to the shape of his hindquarters to the proud set of his neck, bespoke quality. Obviously, the banker had spent no small sum acquiring him.

The horse bobbed a greeting and nuzzled Griff's hand as if they were old friends. Griff felt a surge of pride. He had disappointed his father in every way imaginable, but his skill with horses was the one thing Charles Rutledge had been unable to ignore.

"Beautiful, isn't he?"

Griff turned to find the Gilman fellow standing outside the bank, puffing a cheroot. "He is indeed. One of the finest I've seen since the war."

"Come on in." The banker ushered Griff to his private office at the back of the building and motioned him to a chair. He extracted another cigar from the humidor on his desk and held it out. "Care for a smoke?"

"No, thank you." Griff unbuttoned his coat and settled into the leather chair.

Gilman puffed his cigar, sending a cloud of blue smoke curling behind his head. "How's your father these days?"

"I wouldn't know. I've been away from home for a long time. After my mother passed on, I lost touch."

"I see." Gilman eyed Griff across the desk. "What brings you to this neck of the woods?"

"I've a bit of unfinished business to clear up. Soon as it's done, I'm headed west."

"Ah, the lure of California claims another son of the South. Too bad."

"The South we knew is gone, Mr. Gilman. I'm headed much farther west, to New South Wales. A friend of mine went over in 'fifty-eight. Ever since the war ended, he's been after me to come down and take a look."

Gilman frowned. "Australia? What on earth for? All they have there is red dirt and kangaroos."

"I'm told the place is booming since the great gold rush. There's still some gold to be mined and millions of acres of ranch land available. I might try my hand at running a cattle station."

Griff paused and gave free rein to his imagination. What would it be like living amongst a bunch of foreign drovers, fighting off dingoes in the middle of the night?

"Good heavens, man," Gilman said. "If it's a ranch you want, I'll put you in touch with Wyatt Caldwell down in Texas. He sold his lumber mill here in town a few years back, and now he's got one the finest herds of longhorns in the state. There's no need for you to go clear to the edge of the known world."

"I appreciate the offer, but my mind is made up." Griff shifted in his chair. "Maybe we should get down to business."

"Very well." Gilman set his cigar aside. "I'm the head of a committee looking for ways to bring more money into Hickory Ridge. Like a lot of other towns these days, ours is declining, and we have to do what we can to save it."

Griff nodded.

"I expect you heard about that fancy horse race they started in Louisville last spring."

"The Kentucky Derby, yes. Eleven horses in the race this year, or so I heard."

"We can't compete with that, but we've decided to sponsor a horse race of our own this fall. We're inviting the best horsemen from all across the South to come to Hickory Ridge and compete for a thousand-dollar prize. We'll have barbecues, a parade, and a dance." The banker's eyes shone. "Why, it'll be almost like Race Week in Charleston in the old days."

Griff nodded, though in his experience nothing could match the excitement and grandeur of Race Week, when ladies wore their finest gowns and men competed for honors on horseback. Years ago he'd turned his back on Charleston and everything it represented, but he couldn't forget the exhilaration of those crystalline winter days when he'd raced one of his father's sleek Thoroughbreds. The glittering balls when he'd held some of Charleston's most beautiful women in his arms. Then the carriage rides home through the chill evenings, the sounds of soft laughter drifting through the moss-draped oaks lining the streets.

Charleston was a magical place then. But that life was over and done. He eyed the banker across the desk. "Where do I fit in?"

"It's clear that you have a way with horses. And given your background, I'd say it's a fair bet you know something about racing."

Griff nodded. "I've trained and raced horses since I was a boy."

"I need a good trainer to work with Majestic and ride him on Race Day. I'll pay you to train him. And if you win, I'll throw in the prize money to boot."

"I see." A recent run of bad luck, coupled with complications at his bank in London, had rendered him temporarily short of funds. The money he'd put away for safekeeping after the war had been invested overseas and was proving difficult to extricate. "What's in it for you?"

"Bragging rights. And the satisfaction of helping my town onto her feet again. If our race is a success, every business from the mercantile to the inn to the barbershop will benefit. If people have a good time, they'll want to come back to Hickory Ridge next year. Race Day could become an ongoing event, bigger and better every year. One day we might even outshine the Derby. What do you say?"

"I'm intrigued. But I need time to think it over. I haven't yet had a chance to pick up my bags from the train station."

The banker rose. "Fair enough. But don't keep me waiting too long. Majestic's a natural on the track, but he's a handful, and the trainer I hired last fall up and quit on me a few weeks back. It'll take a lot of work to get this colt ready. I want to get him back into training as soon as possible."

"Understood." Griff shook Gilman's hand. "I'll be in touch."

He left the bank and headed for the train station, turning the offer over in his mind. According to the report he'd received two weeks ago from the Pinkerton Detective Agency, the person he'd come here to see appeared to have settled in for a while. He could afford to take his time. If he stayed on in Hickory Ridge until after Race Day, he could sail from San Francisco afterward and arrive in Australia just as spring was unfolding. The most hospitable time of year down there, if the newspapers were to be believed.

At the railway station he claimed his bags from the agent and walked the short distance to the Hickory Ridge Inn. After signing for his room and obtaining his key from the pale-faced clerk, he headed up the carpeted stairs to his room, surreptitiously taking in the gleaming woodwork, wide windows that let in the clear spring light, tasteful paintings adorning the long hallways. He fitted his key into the lock and entered his room. Though the carpet was worn in places and the bed sagged a bit in the middle, the inn was more elegant than he'd expected to find here in the middle of nowhere. He set down his leather bags, opened the curtains, and raised the window, letting in the sounds from the busy street below.

Maybe he would stay awhile. Figure out what he really wanted to do in New South Wales before heading off to the unknown.

He scanned the street. Two gray-bearded men sat on the porch outside the post office, whittling. Farm women in sunbonnets and calico dresses came and went from the mercantile. An empty freight wagon rumbled over the brick street. Outside the bank, Majestic tossed his head and strained in his harness. Griff massaged a knot at the back of his neck. Training that magnificent colt, riding him in front of a crowd sounded more appealing than anything else he'd done lately. That, and attending a wedding as the guest of the lovely Carrie Daly.

He turned from the window and stretched out on the bed, lacing his fingers behind his head. Nothing much excited him anymore. A restless life that took him to every city worth the name had also left him jaded and dissatisfied. But now he found himself looking forward to the prospect of working with Majestic. And to Saturday.

He grinned to himself. How odd that here in Hickory Ridge he'd found the only two things that were beyond his power to resist: a spirited horse and a beautiful woman.

TWO

"Missus Daly?" Libby Dawson bent to retrieve another tray of cookies from the oven. "Mister Henry said for me to ask is you about done with that weddin' cake."

Carrie pushed a wayward curl back under her kerchief and set a heavy pan on the stove. "It's all done but the boiled icing. And the decorations."

Libby transferred the cookies from the baking pan to a blue enameled serving plate. "These sure do smell good. You the best baker here'bouts, I reckon. Better'n the bakery in town is what folks say."

Carrie smiled. "I don't know about that. But I do enjoy baking when I'm not rushed." She looked pointedly at the young woman. "Tell my brother everything will be ready in time."

She glanced at the clock. Though it was only eight o'clock, she felt as if she'd been up all night. At first light she had walked up the trail to the waterfall at the back of the farm and filled a clear glass jar with bright orange butterfly weed, wild iris, and delicate Virginia bluebells. The Dawsons—Libby and her mother, Cleo—had been busy all morning preparing food for the wedding celebration, setting out bowls and platters on the table beneath the hickory trees in the yard. Carrie's bouquet of wildflowers occupied the center.

Carrie stirred the icing until it thickened. While it cooled, she washed and hulled a bowl of plump strawberries and rearranged the cinnamon cookies on their plate. She finished the cake and headed upstairs to dress for the wedding.

She stepped into her new dress and fastened the tiny buttons, pinned her hair, and donned her hat. The little silk toque was several years old now, but thanks to Ada Caldwell's skill and good taste, it was as stylish as ever, and it matched her new dress perfectly.

Eager for Ada's arrival, Carrie peered out the window. Several of Henry's friends from the mill had arrived, including Sage Whiting, the foreman. Sage's wife, Mariah, stood beneath the trees chatting with Dr. Spencer and his wife, Eugenie. An unfamiliar rig drove into the yard and Carrie's stomach fluttered. Had Griff Rutledge arrived? But it was a friend of Mary's who emerged from the rig. Carrie shook off a vague feeling of disappointment. Why should she care whether or not the horse tamer showed up? After all, she was practically promised to someone else.

Carrie turned from the window and gazed around her bright, airy room. Had it really been fourteen years since Frank Daly lost his life at Bloody Pond? Though she had finally made the decision to set aside her widow's black, she missed her husband still.

And she thanked God every day for Henry. Since Frank's death her brother had been her only family. Together they'd added a parlor and a second floor to their family farmhouse, built a new barn and tool shed. Thanks to Henry's extra income working at Wyatt Caldwell's lumber mill, they lived more comfortably than most. Her life wasn't exciting, but she had grown content keeping house for Henry, attending church, reading by the fire on cold winter evenings. Now, everything would be different.

"Carrie?" Henry knocked on her door. "You dressed?"

"Come in."

He entered the room, a shy smile lighting his tanned face. He took her hand and spun her around. "You look pretty, little sister."

She smoothed the folds of the dress. "Jeanne Pruitt did a wonderful job. But honestly, Henry, it's too fancy for me."

"You deserve it. I wanted you to have something nice." He reached into his pocket. "Look what I found."

"Papa's watch fob." She ran her fingers over the worn leather. "I thought it was lost."

"I thought so too, but Caleb and Joe unearthed it, playing in the attic."

Caleb and Joe. Ever since Mary had accepted her brother's proposal, she and her boys had spent nearly every Sunday at the farm, and Carrie always dreaded their arrival. The boys were dirty, noisy, and rude beyond measure. So far, for Henry's sake, Carrie had held her tongue. But once they were all living together, things would have to change. She sighed. Perhaps Henry was right and a man's influence would shape them up.

"Anyway, I'm glad they found it," Henry said. "Ma and Pa were a good match. Maybe it'll bring me some of their good luck."

"I hope so."

He stuffed the watch fob into his pocket. "You know what I was thinking about last night? That summer right after Ma and Pa died, when we were visiting with Aunt Maudie and them and we went swimming one night to cool off. Two stars came out, and Aunt Maudie told us they were Ma and Pa, keeping an eye on us from up in heaven. You remember that, Carrie?"

"Barely. Mostly I remember cousin Althea trying to drown me."

"She was just fooling. Besides, I was right there. I wouldn't let anything hurt you. I still won't. You know that."

She nodded. He had always been her best friend, her protector. She watched her brother smoothing his hair before the mirror. No one in Hickory Ridge, least of all Carrie herself, had ever expected

Henry to wed. After all, he was long past the age when most men had taken a wife. And he seemed content with his lot until the unfortunate day that Mary Stanhope set her cap for him.

"I've been thinking about Ma and Pa a lot lately," he said. "I sure hope they know we turned out all right."

The sound of hoofbeats on the road drew her to the window again. A handsome couple in a gray rig pulled into the yard. The man got out and turned to help the woman out of the buggy. Carrie's heart lifted. After four years in Texas, the Caldwells finally were back in Hickory Ridge.

All thoughts of Mary and her two ruffians evaporated. Carrie grinned at Henry. "Ada and Wyatt are here."

"I reckon we'd best get down there then." He held the door for her.

Their eyes met. Standing on tiptoe, she kissed his cheek. "Good luck, Henry. Be happy."

"I intend to be."

She picked up her fan and raced down the stairs and into the yard.

The other wedding guests swarmed around Wyatt and Ada, offering words of welcome. Bursts of laughter filled the air.

"Carrie." Ada Caldwell broke away from the crowd and enveloped Carrie in a warm embrace. "How *are* you? And what a darling hat." She cocked her head, studying her friend. "It still suits you perfectly."

"I think so too."

Ada looped her arm through Carrie's. "It's so good to see you. You can't imagine how much your letters meant to me. Especially that first year on the ranch. Wyatt was so busy building his herd and getting the ranch going that I hardly saw him. I don't know what I'd have done without your long letters and without Sophie for company."

"I missed you too." Carrie squeezed her friend's hand. "And our quilting circle. Though it was never the same after Lillian passed on." She smiled, thinking of Wyatt's beloved aunt. "So, tell me, is your millinery business still going strong? You've scarcely mentioned it in your last letters."

"I'm afraid I don't have much time for hatmaking these days. Now that Sophie is away at school, Wade takes more of my time. Not that I mind."

"He's a darling boy," Carrie said. "The photograph you sent was quite the talk of the town."

Ada's gaze sought Wyatt in the crowd, standing near the table. A tender smile lit her face. "Wade looks just like his father. They're quite a pair."

Henry stepped off the porch and rang a bell, summoning the guests for the ceremony. Mary Stanhope, who had sequestered herself in Henry's bedroom on the first floor, stepped outside. Widowed years earlier, she was still a young-looking twenty-eight. She wore a dark blue lace skirt and matching blouse. Her blond hair was piled into a mass of curls atop her head and held in place by two silver combs that caught the morning light. Carrie suppressed a sigh. If only Mary's spirit were as lovely as her countenance.

Mary crossed the porch and took her place next to Henry. Her sons, in stiff new clothes and slicked-back hair, stood beside her.

The guests made their way across the yard, the ladies' skirts bright bursts of color against the pale green grass. Ada squeezed Carrie's hand. "We'll talk more after this is over. I can't wait to hear all the latest news."

"All right."

"Carrie?" Ada studied Carrie's face, her wide gray eyes full of concern. "Where's Nate? And why do I get the feeling you're not happy about this marriage?"

"Nate's on his way back from Nashville. He went to look at

some more books. Though I have no idea where he'll put them. His shop is full to bursting already." She glanced toward the road. "I'm sure he'll be here in time for cake."

"You're avoiding my other question. Do you think this marriage is a mistake?"

"It doesn't matter what I think. Of course I want Henry to be happy. He deserves it more than anyone I know. I only wish that—"

"Dearly beloved." Reverend Daniel Patterson, the pastor of the church in town, smiled at the assembled guests. "We're here on this fine spring morning to join Henry Bell and Mary Stanhope in holy matrimony. Anybody has an objection, best to say so now."

Carrie looked up at her brother. Henry winked at her and reached for Mary's hand. The two young hooligans poked each other and giggled. Carrie looked heavenward. Did Henry Bell have any idea what he was taking on?

"There being no objections, we'll proceed. Henry, Mary, hear these words of God." Mr. Patterson opened his Bible and in a strong solemn voice read from 1 Corinthians: "Charity . . . beareth all things, believeth all things, hopeth all things, endureth all things."

Carrie watched her brother's weathered face come alive with hope and promise and regretted her own lack of it. Shouldn't she be grateful that Henry had found love so late in his life? If a ready-made family was what he wanted, who was she to object? It wasn't as if Henry was kicking her out. He expected Carrie to remain in the house until her own wedding day. He'd fixed up a room in the attic for Mary's boys, and Mary would share his room, of course. There was no reason for Carrie to be displaced at all. And with another woman in the house to share the chores, Carrie would have more time for herself. It sounded so pleasant and sensible. Why did she feel so desolate?

"Amen." The preacher closed his Bible and smiled at the

newlyweds. "Those whom our Lord has seen fit to join together, let no one put asunder."

Carrie watched Henry kiss his new bride and said a silent prayer for their happiness. Her sons danced around Henry, yelling, "Pa! Pa!"

"Come on, everybody," Henry called. "Let's eat."

Carrie hung back, allowing the guests to fill their plates, her gaze searching the empty road.

"Carrie?" Mariah Whiting and Eugenie Spencer, her closest friends from church, crossed the yard, carrying plates and glasses.

"You'd better get some food before it's all gone," Eugenie said.

"We'll save you a place over there." Mariah indicated a shady patch of grass near the fence. "Ada's joining us too. It'll be like old times."

"Did someone say my name?" Ada appeared behind Mariah with her plate.

"Let's go sit," Mariah said. "I can't wait to hear all about Texas."

The four friends seated themselves on the grass, their skirts billowing around them, and took up their forks.

"First of all," Eugenie said, "tell us about Wade and Sophie."

"Sophie's doing wonderfully well," Ada began. "Last year she won a prize for a poem she wrote for a magazine. Wyatt was so proud he had it framed and mounted it on the wall in the dining room. Sophie said it was nothing special, but I know she was pleased. She adores Wyatt. Always has." Ada smiled. "At first he wasn't sure about taking her with us to Texas, but neither of us has regretted it for a moment. We think of her as our own."

"Is she hoping to write for the newspapers?" Mariah popped a strawberry into her mouth and closed her eyes, sighing in appreciation. "I remember she was quite taken with Patsy Greer's typewriting machine."

"Perhaps. Last fall she met a correspondent for the Dallas

Herald, Mrs. Aurelia Mohl. Sophie was quite impressed." Ada paused to take a bite of wedding cake. "Of course, Sophie is only fifteen. She changes her mind about as often as she changes her hat. One moment she wants to study medicine. The next, she talks about coming back here to run the newspaper."

"I'm surprised she'd even think of coming back here, after the way the other children treated her."

Ada nodded. "Children reflect the attitudes of their elders. I'm thankful Sophie survived her years at the orphanage. But the experience left her feeling that she has something to prove."

"I admire the child's spunk." Eugenie sipped her lemonade. "Has she had any trouble in Texas because of her mixed blood?"

"No one there knows."

Carrie's eyes widened. "She's passing for white?"

"Yes. Wyatt and I feel it's best. Texas has become such a jumble of people since the war, nobody gives Sophie a second look. She isn't the only one who has crossed that invisible line."

"But, Ada, what about when she grows up and wants to marry?" Mariah's brown eyes reflected genuine concern. "What then?"

"We'll deal with it when the time comes. Perhaps someday people's attitudes will change."

"I doubt it," Carrie said. "Around here, blacks and whites can't even be buried in the same graveyard, much less intermingle on this side of the dirt."

"Ada?" Mariah patted her friend's arm. "How is that baby son of yours?"

"He's just turned two and tags along after Wyatt every waking minute of the day. Which Wyatt encourages, of course." She sought her husband in the knot of men talking with Henry, her expression soft with affection. "He's still beside himself that he has a son of his own. You know how fond Wyatt was of Robbie."

"Robbie still talks about Wyatt." Mariah bit into a cinnamon cookie. "When he has time to talk to us at all. School keeps him busy these days. He wants to read law as soon as he's old enough."

"He'll be good at it," Eugenie said. "My word, but that boy can talk. I remember he used to talk to Wyatt for hours on end."

Ada nodded. "I didn't realize just how much Wyatt wanted a boy of his own until Wade was born. One morning when the baby was about eight months old, I went to feed him and he was gone. The sight of that empty cradle nearly stopped my heart."

"I'm sure." Eugenie nodded, her expression grave.

"I was certain Wade had been kidnapped or a coyote had snatched him. I ran screaming for Wyatt and there he was, on his horse, holding the reins in one hand and Wade in the other. Teaching his son to ride." Ada set down her plate. "I nearly fainted from sheer relief."

Eugenie caught Carrie's eye. "Have you told Ada about you and Nate?"

Carrie felt her face warm. "Really, there's nothing to tell."

"That isn't true." Mariah winked at Ada. "They've been keeping serious company ever since you left Hickory Ridge. The longest courtship in history." She gave Carrie's arm a playful bump. "Everyone can see they're a perfect match. I can't imagine what's holding things up."

"I want to be sure." Carrie scanned the yard. Clearly, Mr. Rutledge wasn't coming. The pang of disappointment that moved through her served only to make her more uncertain of her feelings. If she were truly committed to Nate, why would she care whether or not the horse tamer appeared?

"You're making excuses, Carrie Daly, and you know it." Mariah leaned over and gave her friend another playful nudge. "Every day that you fail to appreciate Nate's good qualities only proves how completely misguided you are."

Carrie smiled at her friend's gentle teasing. "Maybe I am, but

I worry about depending on anyone other than my brother. Times are hard around here lately, and a bookshop is hardly a necessity in a town as small as ours."

Picking up her plate again, Ada finished the last of her strawberries. "I don't blame you for being concerned. The papers are full of stories about the depression."

"It's really bad, Ada." Eugenie shook her head. "I can't remember the last time Ennis actually got paid cash money for taking care of a patient. I don't mind telling you, we've been down to our last dollar more than once. But he won't hear of moving away. Hickory Ridge is our home."

"We noticed a lot of closed businesses when we got here on the train last night," Ada said. "Wyatt was most distressed to see that Miss Hattie's is gone. He was quite fond of her fried chicken."

Mariah nodded. "Miss Hattie's isn't the only one. The *Gazette* folded a couple of years back, just before Patsy Greer's daddy passed on. Business is way down at the mill too. Sage says the demand for timber from up north has leveled off. Wyatt sold out at just the right time."

"I am surprised Mr. Chastain's bookshop has held on," Ada said. Beneath the shade trees, a fiddle player warmed up; the notes danced in the warm air. "Carrie's right. Books are a luxury, after all."

"Nate was smart," Carrie said. "When the university in Knoxville expanded, he offered to handle the ordering of all their books. He's handling orders for Vanderbilt too. I suppose Nate and Jasper Pruitt are faring better than most." She smiled at Ada. "Last week Jasper asked whether you and Wyatt were coming for the wedding. I think he still has a soft spot in his heart for you."

Ada laughed. "Maybe. Ironic that he of all people wound up rescuing me from Bea Goldston's attack."

"I guess you heard about Bea," Eugenie said. "She's—"

"Come on, ladies." Henry jogged across the yard and pulled Carrie to her feet. "Time to dance."

"Later," Eugenie whispered as the four friends were swept up into the celebration.

Wyatt Caldwell, handsome and charming as ever in a pearl-gray suit and matching Stetson, danced first with his wife and then with each of the ladies in turn. Henry did the same until, finally, the last waltz was announced. Then he swept Mary into his arms. Wyatt claimed Ada and the Spencers and the Whitings paired off, leaving Carrie standing alone. A hard lump pulsed in her throat. Why couldn't she belong to someone, someone who would love her the way Wyatt loved Ada? Despite their long acquaintance, she wasn't sure how Nate felt about her, what true happiness was, or where to find it.

The music swelled. Was it true? Was she a fool for postponing her marriage to Nate? She'd always believed that God would lead her to the man he had chosen for her. And she was certainly fond of Nate. She respected him. But the giddy excitement she'd known with Frank, the deep, sweet joy she felt every time he looked at her, was missing. She'd been so young then, so certain that nothing could rob her of happiness. Perhaps mature love was a different thing altogether and it was foolish to suppose she could ever feel that way again. After so great a loss, perhaps nothing was untainted, not even hope.

"Hello? Is this the Bell farm?" A deep voice called out as an unfamiliar rig rolled into the yard. Griff Rutledge jumped out, carrying a small, neatly wrapped package, and made a beeline for Carrie. "My dear Mrs. Daly, I am unforgivably late, and I do apologize. I had the devil of a time finding a rig for hire." He jerked his thumb toward the swaybacked gray mare hitched to a ratty-looking buggy. "A sorrier outfit I have never seen. At any rate, I do hope I'm in time for cake."

He was again impeccably dressed, and he spoke with bemused

confidence and a mischievous gleam in his dark eyes. Carrie was captivated. "Of course there's plenty of cake. Come with me."

"Carrie?" Mary Stanhope Bell marched across the yard, a frown creasing her forehead, the youngest of her two hellions dogging her heels. "Who is this man, and what is he doing at my wedding?"

Carrie made a hasty introduction. "Mr. Rutledge saved me from being trampled by Mr. Gilman's runaway horse yesterday. The least I could do was to offer him some hospitality while he's in town." Seeing the red flush of anger creeping up Mary's neck, Carrie rushed on. "I was certain you wouldn't mind my inviting an extra guest, since I'm the one who handled all the preparations."

"I can see that it was a lovely wedding," Griff said, "and I can't tell you how sorry I am to have missed witnessing the vows. I wish you all the happiness in the world." He bent from the waist and kissed Mary's hand. "And I apologize again for my lateness."

"Well, that's . . . I'm . . . sure you're quite welcome, Mr. Rutledge."

He proffered the package. "Back where I come from, a wedding guest never arrives empty-handed. A small remembrance, Mrs. Bell, for your wedding day."

Clearly flustered, Mary tore open the package. "A silver picture frame." She turned it over in her hands and watched it catch the light. "It's very pretty."

"Perhaps you'll use it for your wedding portrait."

"Unfortunately there is no photographer here in town, and the expense of importing one for the day—"

"I see."

He was so obviously embarrassed at having brought a useless gift that Carrie's heart went out to him. Was it his fault there was no money for photographs? But Mary spoke as if he were somehow to blame.

Mary swept her hand toward the tables. "Thank you for your gift, Mr. Rutledge. Do have some cake."

Carrie showed Griff to the table and handed him a plate. Henry hurried over, and Carrie repeated the introduction. Henry pumped Griff's hand. "Any friend of Carrie's is welcome here, Mr. Rutledge. Please enjoy yourself."

He left to join Mary. Griff bit into a piece of the cake, his aplomb apparently recovered. "Luscious. I've always been partial to boiled icing." He licked his fork clean. "Our old cook Sethe made the best cake I've ever eaten." He took another bite. "Until now."

"I'm better at baking bread than cakes. But I'm glad you like it."

The wedding guests had begun gathering their things, saying their good-byes, offering congratulations to Henry and Mary. Ada and Wyatt spent a few moments with the Whitings and the Spencers before Ada crossed the yard to find Carrie.

Carrie introduced Griff, who bowed to Ada before joining Wyatt and the other men. Ada clasped her friend's hands. "Mr. Rutledge is terribly attractive, isn't he?"

Carrie's stomach jumped. Griffin Rutledge was more than merely attractive, he was—

"But a bit mysterious," Ada said.

"Mysterious?"

"Perhaps it's those dark eyes. I'm not entirely sure. But I am sure of one thing. You're smitten."

Carrie felt her face grow warm. "I'm no such thing. Why, we met only yesterday. Besides, he's merely passing through."

Ada glanced toward the men standing beneath the trees. "From the look on Nate's face, I'd say I'm not the only one with questions about Mr. Rutledge."

"Nate's finally here?" Carrie turned. "I'd nearly given up on him."

"Maybe you'd better go talk to him. He looks perturbed." Ada returned her husband's quick wave. "Wyatt is ready go."

"But you just got here."

"We're staying through next week, maybe a little longer. Wyatt wants to make some repairs to Miss Lillian's—to my house. It has stood empty since we married, but now Wat Stevens wants to rent it out for one of his nephews who recently married."

Carrie frowned. For more years than she could count, Watson B. Stevens had been after Henry to sell some of the Bell land down by Owl Creek. People said he had plenty of money, but that didn't stop him from driving a hard bargain, even cheating when he thought no one was looking. "Better tell Wyatt to collect the rent in advance."

"I will." Ada kissed Carrie's cheek. "I'll see you again before we leave."

"I wish you weren't going back so soon."

"Me too. But Wyatt must see to a shipment of cattle next month, and Sophie will be coming home from school at the end of the term." Ada smiled. "Besides, I miss my son. This is the first time we've left him for so long, and I'm uneasy about it."

"I'm sure he's fine. His granddaddy is taking good care of him."

"Jake spoils Wade silly. But I'm glad our son is growing up with his family. I never knew my grandparents. I've always felt that something important in my life was missing."

Carrie nodded. "But you look better than ever these days."

"Chalk it up to love." Ada paused and nodded toward Nate, who was deep into conversation with Wyatt and Griff Rutledge. A robin sang into the silence. "Don't wait too long, Carrie, and miss your chance at happiness. I nearly lost Wyatt to indecision and doubt, and now I know what I would have missed."

Wyatt ambled over to them, his blue eyes so full of love for Ada that Carrie's breath caught. Would anyone ever look at her that way again?

"Darlin', we ought to be going." Wyatt clasped Ada's hand. "It's a ways back to the inn, and I need to be up early tomorrow." He smiled down at Carrie. "It was a grand wedding, wasn't it?"

Carrie nodded.

"I've never seen your brother so happy. Looks like being an old married man agrees with him already." He offered his arm to Ada. "Ready, sweetheart?"

"I am." Ada patted Carrie's hand. "Think about what I said, all right?"

Carrie walked them to their rig and waved as Wyatt drove away. Nate crossed the yard and slipped his arm around Carrie's waist. "Sorry I was so late. The train was half an hour behind schedule this morning."

"Mrs. Daly?" Griff Rutledge had dispensed with his plate and now he stood before her and Nate, his hat tucked into the crook of his arm. "I'm afraid I must say good-bye. I thank you for your hospitality."

"You're quite welcome, Mr. Rutledge. I'm happy you could join us."

"I'm glad your fancy dress suffered no damage." He grinned. "And I am very glad indeed to have enjoyed the sight of you wearing it."

She smiled, acutely aware of the way his slow gaze traveled over her. What was he thinking? More to the point, why was she responding this way? His frank expression kindled a flame inside her. She looked away, hoping he couldn't see the unsettling effect his very presence had on her. It wouldn't do. Not when she was promised to Nate. More or less.

Mr. Rutledge shook hands with Nate. "Mr. Chastain. A pleasure to have met you, sir."

Nate's expression hardened, but he nodded. "Good-bye, Mr. Rutledge." He turned to Carrie as Griff crossed the yard and climbed into his rig. "I believe I'll head on back to town too."

"So soon?"

"It won't make any difference to you." He frowned. "I agree with Mary Stanhope on this one, Carrie. Why in the world would you invite a man like Rutledge to a family wedding?"

"A man like him?" Nate's attitude made her want to defend their departed guest. "You don't know anything about him."

"He's smooth as spit on a doorknob. The clerk at the inn says he pays for everything in gold. I'd bet my last dollar he's hiding something."

Was it true? Was Mr. Rutledge concealing a secret? Perhaps it was only jealousy talking, as ugly as that prospect seemed. "Oh, Nate, just because he has money and isn't from around here, that doesn't mean he's sinister. But you needn't worry. I heard him tell Mr. Gilman that he isn't planning to stay in Hickory Ridge long. You have nothing to be concerned about."

"That isn't the song he was singing just now."

"What do you mean?"

"Apparently Gilman wants Rutledge to stick around and train his horse for some to-do he's planning for this fall. Rutledge says he's seriously considering the offer." He turned to watch Griff Rutledge's rig disappear down the road.

"Really? He's going to stay awhile?"

He glanced at her. "That's what he said. And I wish you wouldn't look so all-fired happy about it." Nate found his hat and jammed it onto his head.

"Nate. Don't go away mad."

"I'm not mad." He jumped into his rig and flicked the reins. "I'll see you, Carrie."

Mary crossed the yard, the hem of her skirt trailing in the grass. "What happened? Did you and Nate have a quarrel?"

"Mama." Mary's oldest boy, Caleb, raced across the yard, his brother at his heels. "Joe said Carrie Daly is gonna live with us. Is it true?"

"Of course it's true." Mary smiled at Carrie, though there was little warmth in it. "She's your new papa's sister."

Caleb frowned. "But I don't want her to."

Both boys had taken off their jackets. Their boiled white shirts were smeared with dirt, grass stains, and cake icing. "Me either, Mama. I don't want her here." Joe glared at Carrie. "Go get your own family."

Carrie felt her blood heating up. "Henry was my brother long before you were ever born, Joseph. And he will be my brother as long as I live. He *is* my family, and that won't change just because you want it to."

"Just a minute," Mary said. "Don't be cross with him. He's a child."

"He's old enough to know not to be rude."

Mary's face flushed. "This is new to the boys. Joe was so little when my husband died, he doesn't remember Pete at all. They're excited to have a man in their lives. They need time to adjust."

"Mary, honey?" Henry stepped onto the porch. "All right if I send the rest of the food home with the Dawsons? Cleo and Libby have been here all day."

"That's a lot of food to give away," Mary said. "Have you forgotten you have two little boys to feed now?"

"But we need to give them something. They're hungry and dog-tired."

"You paid them, didn't you?"

"Of course. But—"

"You don't want to be too generous with Negroes. They'll come to expect it every time they do the least little bit of work. Besides, Caleb and Joseph love ham. We'll have the rest for supper."

Carrie sent her brother a pointed look. *Stand up for yourself, Henry. This is still your house, your farm.*

"You're right," Henry said. "I wasn't thinking." He grinned and his ears turned red. "I guess I'm not used to being a family man yet."

He stepped back inside, and a few minutes later the Dawson

women came out. They nodded to Carrie and Mary, climbed onto their wagon, and headed for their home in Two Creeks.

Carrie followed Mary and her boys inside. Henry had already shed his coat and tie, and now he helped the boys change their clothes. Mary changed into a simple yellow calico house dress. Settling herself into Carrie's favorite chair beside the window, she took up her fan. "What a day. I declare, I cannot ever remember being so worn out. But it was lovely, Henry dear. Thank you for making it so special."

"I'm glad you're pleased, but Carrie did all the work." Henry winked at Carrie.

Mary's fan moved back and forth, stirring the warm afternoon air. "Carrie, would you bring me some tea? I'm worn to a frazzle."

"Mama?" Joseph raced into the room. "Can me and Caleb go see the horse? They's kittens in the barn too."

"For a little while. But stay close to the house. I don't want you wandering off."

The boys tore out of the house, banging the door behind them.

Mary looked up, brows raised. "Well, Carrie? The tea?"

Carrie sent her brother a withering glance. She was resigned to sharing her home with his new wife and her noisy, rude children, but becoming Mary's handmaiden? Never. Henry cocked an eyebrow at her and began fiddling with his pipe. Clearly he didn't intend to come to her defense. "I'd like to change my dress first, if you don't mind."

Mary flicked her fan. "Please don't be long. I've had a very tiring day."

A tiring day? Carrie almost laughed out loud. While she had rushed about setting up tables, ironing tablecloths, gathering flowers, and baking for days on end, Mary had avoided involving herself in any of the wedding preparations, saying that Carrie was much the better cook. Which was true, but still . . .

With another glance at Henry, Carrie sighed, went upstairs, and changed. Back in the kitchen, she made and served tea while Mary chattered to Henry about the wedding guests and Mr. Patterson's ceremony.

"When he asked for objections, I was afraid you might speak up, Carrie." Mary's eyes glinted with amusement and something else. A subtle challenge?

"I'd never object to anything that makes my brother happy." Carrie drained her cup.

Henry smiled. "The reverend did a fine job, but I miss our country preacher."

"So do I," Carrie said. "But we can't blame Mr. Dennis for moving on to a larger church. Even preachers have to feed their families."

Mary's cup rattled onto her saucer. "The Lord always provides. It was his citified wife who wanted to leave Hickory Ridge. She complained about everything when she came to town."

Henry stretched out his long legs and looked out the window. "Maybe the town will start growing again if Mr. Gilman's plan works out. That Rutledge fellow seems to think the idea has merit."

Carrie was eager for the details of any scheme that would keep Griff Rutledge in town, but Henry rose and said, "I'll go round up the boys. They can help with the chores before supper."

Mary finally got to her feet and went reluctantly to the kitchen to help Carrie prepare supper from the wedding leftovers. Afterward, Henry brought in water to heat for washing up. Mary helped the boys get ready for bed and settled them into the room Henry had fixed for them in the attic. Feeling like a third wheel, Carrie made coffee, and they sat on the front porch watching night come down. The spring breeze stirred the yellow jasmine growing on the trellis beside the porch. Night birds called plaintively in the trees. Carrie sipped her coffee and fought a wave of melancholy. How was it possible to be sitting here with two other people and still feel utterly alone?

At last, Henry stood, knocked the ashes from his pipe, and reached for Mary's hand. "I reckon we'll say good night, Carrie."

Mary blushed and nodded to Carrie. "Good night, sister. We'll see you in the morning."

Henry planted a kiss on Carrie's hair. "Thank you. Everything was delicious. I appreciate it."

"You're welcome." For so long, it had been her and Henry against the world, and now another woman had taken first place in his affections. Of course she was happy for him, but a hole had opened up in her life. Nothing could ever be the same.

Carrie mounted the stairs to her room and closed the door. The window was open to the cooling night air and to the sounds of the birds settling into the trees. She turned up the wick in the lantern, washed her face and hands, and changed into her nightgown. Taking her Bible from the table beside her bed, she read from Psalms until her mind and heart calmed. She closed her eyes. *Help me, Lord, to love Mary and her children. Give me the grace not to resent them. I ask you for Henry's happiness. He deserves it, after looking after me for most of his—*

A hard thump overhead followed by a bloodcurdling scream pierced the silence, destroying her serenity. Below her she heard Henry's startled voice, and Mary's, and then their footsteps pounding up the stairs, past her room, and upward to the attic. Carrie set aside her Bible and threw on her dressing gown. She took up her lamp, opened her door, and peered down the dark hallway.

Henry came down the narrow staircase holding a sobbing Joseph in his arms. Mary followed, holding Caleb by the hand.

"What's the matter?" Carrie asked.

"Nightmares," Mary said.

"No, Mama," Caleb said. "It weren't no bad dream. Me and Joe was both wide-awake, and then we saw 'em."

"Saw who?"

"Robbers. Three of 'em. They came right through the winder. I shoved Joe to the floor, and he hid under the bed, but they almost got me."

Joseph whimpered and wound his chubby arms around Henry's neck.

"There now, Joe," Henry said. "You're all right, boy. There are no robbers way out here."

"They are so," Caleb said. "Mama, please don't make us go back up there. It's too dark, and I'm scared."

"Come on," Mary said. "You can stay with Mama and Papa tonight. We'll figure out something else in the morning."

Carrie returned to her room and tried to recapture the sense of peace prayer always brought her. But she couldn't forget the way Mary had looked at her just now. She had the feeling that whatever the "something else" was, it wouldn't be good news for her. She climbed into bed and extinguished the light.

THREE

"Could you finish these for me, Carrie?" Mary set the rolling pin aside and brushed flour from her fingers. "I haven't felt well all morning."

In the week since the wedding Mary had come up with a thousand excuses rather than help with chores. So far, making biscuits was her only contribution. Now apparently the poor dear wasn't even up to rolling out dough for their midday meal.

Carrie bit back a refusal. Last Sunday's sermon had been about serving others, being the hands and feet of Christ. How could she refuse to follow his perfect example?

"In a minute." She shifted the heavy bucket of water she'd just drawn from the pump and headed for the stove.

"Mama, look what we found." Caleb yanked the door open and rushed inside. "Ain't he a beauty?"

Carrie dropped the bucket and let out a loud scream. Water poured over her shoes and soaked the hem of her skirt. "Get that snake out of my house this instant."

"For mercy's sake, calm down, Carrie," Mary said. "It's only a common garden snake. It's harmless. I figured a farm girl like you would know that."

"I don't care. I want it out. Now."

Caleb stood there, letting the lime-green snake wind through his fingers. He turned his freckled nose up at Carrie. "You can't tell me what to do."

Henry came in with a load of wood for the cook stove, Joseph at his heels. "Mary, honey? What's all the commotion? What's going on here?"

"Your sister had a screaming fit because Caleb brought in a little-bitty snake." Mary set the half-empty pan of biscuits in the oven and slammed the door. "I realize she hasn't spent much time around little boys, but honestly, she simply must adjust. She's making my children fearful. I won't have it."

Henry sighed and dumped the wood into the box. "Just give her some time. This is a big change for all of us."

"Excuse me, Henry," Carrie said. "I'd appreciate it if you'd stop talking about me as if I'm feebleminded or not even in the room."

"Now, Carrie, don't get your dander up." He motioned for Caleb to take the snake outside. "I'm simply trying to make peace in the family."

"We're not a family."

Henry picked up her overturned water bucket and set it on the table. "You know that isn't so."

"A family takes care of each other. Accommodates each other. But the only one who has been doing any accommodating around here is me." Carrie turned away and busied herself with setting out their glasses.

Mary spun around, her calico skirt swirling, and took a stack of plates from the shelf beside the sink. She plopped them onto the table, fetched a pot of coffee from the stove, and tossed a bowl of diced potatoes into the skillet. "Don't bother yourself about these potatoes, Carrie. I'll accommodate you and fix them myself."

Henry cleared his throat. "You'll never guess who showed up at the mill yesterday." He sat down at the table, poured himself a cup of coffee, and opened the Knoxville newspaper that had arrived at the post office on Thursday. "Wyatt Caldwell stopped by. I think he misses the mill, despite loving his ranch down in Texas."

"Really." Mary salted the potatoes and flipped them with her spatula. Steam wafted through the room. "Was his fancy stuck-up wife with him?"

Carrie bristled. Mary Stanhope found some reason to dislike everyone. "If you think Ada is stuck-up, then you don't know her at all."

Through the kitchen window, she watched bright-blue morning glories trailing along the backyard trellis Henry had made for her birthday last year. Caleb and Joseph, bareheaded and shoeless, were chasing the chickens around the yard. "Ada Caldwell is one of the kindest, most tenderhearted women I've ever known."

"Oh, that's right. I forgot she made you a hat for free when you finally decided to throw away your widow's weeds. No wonder you think she's something." Mary slid the sizzling potatoes onto a platter and brought them to the table. "Lady Bountiful, spreading her gifts around Hickory Ridge. I imagine she got a boatload of free advertising for her hat business out of that little gesture."

"Maybe. But that isn't why she did it." Carrie stared at Henry, feeling heartsick and bewildered. How had her sweet brother, the very soul of kindness, wound up with such a hateful, bitter bride?

Mary took the biscuits from the oven, piled them on a plate, and placed it on the table in front of Henry. "Sit down, Carrie."

"I'm not hungry."

"Sit down anyway. There's something Henry and I want to talk to you about."

"I'll stand." Carrie folded her arms and leaned against the sink.

"Suit yourself. Henry? Sweetheart?"

Henry set down his paper and looked up at her, questioning.

"This might be a good time to talk to Carrie. While the boys are outside."

"Oh. Right." Henry buttered a biscuit and took a bite. "Well, you see, Carrie girl, Mary . . . that is, the both of us, were wondering if you would mind swapping rooms with Caleb and Joseph."

"What? You mean move into the attic?"

"Maybe not forever, but until they get used to living here."

"But that room is so small."

"Exactly." Mary stirred cream into her coffee. "It isn't large enough for two active boys, and they need to be closer to me at night, so they won't be scared. Whereas you—"

"I won't do it." Carrie plopped into her chair and faced her brother across the table. "Henry, you can't expect me to give up my room. All my things are there. My books, my journals, the few things I have that belonged to Frank."

The door flew open. Caleb and Joseph raced through the kitchen, laughing and shoving each other. "Go on, Joe," Caleb yelled in a voice that shattered Carrie's last nerve. "I dare ya."

Joseph reached into his pocket, drew out the snake, and tossed it at Carrie. "Gotcha."

The snake slithered across the pine floor. Carrie grabbed the boy and held him fast. "How old are you anyway, you little heathen?"

"Five and three quarters." He stared up at her, his pale blue eyes bright and defiant.

"You pull a stupid stunt like that again and you won't see six." She shook him, hard. "Do you understand me?"

"You can't tell me what to do. You're not my ma. You're just a dried-up, mean ol' widder woman, and—"

Carrie slapped him, hard. A red handprint rose on his cheek, and he buried his face in his mother's skirts, his shoulder heaving. She stared, horrified and dismayed at her loss of control. How could one small boy cause so much trouble? "I'm sorry, Joe. I didn't mean it."

Mary shoved away from the table and scooped up her son, her eyes blazing. "If you ever hit my boy again, Carrie Daly, so help me, I'll—"

"Now, Mary." Henry got to his feet. "Let's all settle down here."

"*You* can settle down, Henry Bell. I will not have anyone hitting my children."

"I apologize," Carrie said. "It was wrong of me to strike him. I lost my temper."

"You should know better." Mary sent Carrie a murderous glance and handed Joe her handkerchief.

"Joe should have known better than to toss a snake at her," Henry said. "And he shouldn't have talked to Carrie like that. Boys should be brought up to respect their elders. Especially womenfolk."

"He's just a little boy."

"That's no excuse. Where did he get a notion like that anyway?"

Mary blushed to the roots of her hair, but she stood her ground. "Whose side are you on anyway, Henry?"

"There's no call to be taking sides, sweetheart."

"Don't call me sweetheart. Not if you're going to let that sourpuss sister of yours force my children to sleep in a dark attic where they're scared out of their wits and then beat them for playing a harmless joke." She began to cry. "I thought you loved me. I thought we'd be happy, but now I feel like this was all a big mistake."

She set Joe on his feet and led him from the room. Caleb balled his fist and socked Carrie squarely in the stomach. "That's fer hittin' my little brother and makin' Ma cry."

"Go upstairs, Caleb," Henry said. "And do not come out until I tell you to."

"I ain't going up to that old attic. No, sir. You can beat me till I'm dead and I won't go."

"Then you can muck out the barn. Stay there until I come for you."

"You mean shovel horse apples?"

"Somebody's got to."

"Why me?" The boy folded his arms across his chest.

"Because you live here now, and everyone has to pitch in."

"Carrie Daly don't shovel horse—"

"Carrie takes care of the house. Shoveling manure is a man's job. Go on now."

"But I ain't had my—"

"You can eat after you finish."

Caleb stomped off.

"I'm sorry he hit you, sister," Henry said. "Are you all right?"

He looked so defeated that Carrie's heart twisted. "I'm sorry too. I shouldn't have let Joe make me so angry."

"Joe had it coming. Mary says both the boys have been hard to handle all their lives. I thought it would make a difference, having a man around and living out here instead of that cramped rented room in town, but I don't know. Maybe I bit off more than I can chew."

Mary came into the kitchen, her eyes red from crying. "Joe's asleep. Poor child. He's tuckered out from all this fussing and fighting. It can't be good for him."

"It isn't good for anybody." Carrie poured herself a cup of coffee. "I've had quite enough of it myself. I'm going up to my room."

"Oh, I put Joe in there," Mary said. "He's getting so big I couldn't carry him all the way up to the attic. He loves that room already. I promised it to him. I hope you won't upset him again over it."

"You had no right to make such a promise."

"Carrie?" Henry looked at her with such a mixture of hope and resignation that she averted her eyes. Maybe she owed him this chance at happiness after all that he had done for her.

"Fine. Take it. Take everything."

Griff flicked the reins and urged the old nag along the dirt road. This morning's visit to the banker's elegant house just outside town had put him in mind of his Charleston days and whetted his appetite for training Majestic. Once Gilman coaxed the horse from his stall, Majestic had seemed to remember Griff, and Griff had come prepared. He'd handed the horse a carrot and rubbed the big colt's neck while Majestic chomped and swallowed his treat.

Then Griff climbed the fence and entered the pasture, letting the horse get used to his presence and his scent. Majestic, nervous at the unknown, shied away when Griff approached too closely. It would take several more visits before he could actually begin the training. Only when he had gained Majestic's trust would he attempt to saddle him. Too soon and the horse might go barn sour, making training all the more difficult.

Griff breathed in the damp air and thought of home. In the old days, at this time of year, Sethe, the family's cook, and Leah, his mother's favorite servant, would pack up their plantation house on the river. The entire household would then begin the eleven-mile trip to the Rutledges' cottage on Pawley's Island, there to pass the summer until the danger of malarial fever was over.

He still remembered those boyhood treks to the island, traveling by rowboat and by land. His mother complained of the heat and the discomfort of the journey, but to him summers on the island were a magnificent adventure. His first sight of the rolling waves, the brilliant blue sea stretching to the horizon, always exhilarated him. Even now he could almost taste the salt on his lips and the musky tang of oysters roasted on a fire-lit beach.

As he grew older, he accompanied his father to Charleston on business trips, learning the intricacies of planting, harvesting, and selling the rice they grew in vast fields along the Pee Dee River and the values his father insisted upon instilling in him—pride, duty, the unbreakable code of Southern honor. His father had never wavered from that code, despite the war that had transformed the city, and all of South Carolina, into a ghost world.

When he chafed at the unwanted lessons, preferring his horses and stables over everything else, his mother encouraged him to be patient. "God trains us with patience and gentleness, just the way you train these colts," she said one day after a particularly loud argument. "Try to understand your father, Griffin, and honor him as our Lord commands. He may not always show it, but he loves you, perhaps more intensely than any of the rest of us."

Griff took off his hat and wiped his forehead. Rounding a bend in the road, he spotted a woman marching ahead, arms swinging, a straw hat perched precariously on her head. There was something oddly familiar about the sway of her hips, the set of her shoulders. He drew alongside her.

"Mrs. Daly?" Saints in a sock, but she was a sight for sore eyes, even with that ferocious scowl on her face. "What are you doing way out here?"

Carrie pushed her hat to the back of her head and fixed him with a determined look. "Running away from home."

She looked so young and vulnerable he couldn't suppress a smile. "Without the requisite bundle of clothes and victuals for the road?"

A tiny smile tugged at her mouth. "I left in a hurry."

"So it seems. Dare I ask why?"

"It's intolerable. I'm on my way into town. I have a friend there who will help me move my things."

"So you're serious about quitting the farm."

"Yes, sir, I am. Serious as a boil on the—never mind. Let's just say I'm never going back there. Once I retrieve my possessions, that is."

"I'd be happy to help you. Save you a trip all the way to town and back again."

"Would you?" Without waiting for an invitation, she climbed into the rig beside him. "I can't take many of my things. The rooms at the hotel are quite small. But I won't leave behind my mother's walnut chest or my books and clothes. Or my good umbrella."

He glanced at her. "Of course not. It's true the rooms at the inn are a bit lacking in the size department, but it's clean and quite comfortable."

"Oh, I'm not staying at the inn. I'm headed for the Verandah Ladies' Hotel. I made some inquiries at church last week, but I didn't make my decision until today."

"I see." He turned the rig around and they headed for the farm.

"I know the hotel is an awful wreck, but the plain truth is that I have only a bit of money saved and I can't afford the inn. I'm counting on Mrs. Whitcomb—she runs the Verandah—to let me help with serving meals and cleaning up to help cover my expenses."

"Cooking and cleaning in a derelict hotel? I don't know you very well, but somehow I want better things for you."

"Me too, but it's the best I can do for now. At least I won't have to deal with Mary's two ruffians tossing snakes in my lap and hitting me. I won't have to listen to her incessant complaining about all the work of running a farm." She fanned her face, which, he couldn't help noticing, was a charming shade of pink. "If she hates farm chores so much, she should have stayed on at the telegraph office."

He nodded. "The grass is always greener, as they say."

A short time later they arrived at the farm. Mrs. Bell was in the garden gathering strawberries in her apron. A cool mist had moved in from the mountains, and a breeze shivered the flowers blooming on the trellis. Griff tethered the horse and helped his passenger from the rig.

"Right this way." She led him through the parlor and up the stairs to her room. While he wrestled the walnut chest down the stairs, she tossed her clothes, books, and journals into a battered suitcase. She retrieved her small travel satchel, her hat box and umbrella, and met Griff in the yard.

Perspiring from the exertion of carrying everything down from the steep stairs, he wedged the chest onto the seat between them and set the suitcase on top. He mopped his forehead and tucked his handkerchief into his breast pocket. "We'll be a tight fit, Mrs. Daly, but I don't mind if you don't."

Mary Bell rounded the house, her apron full of strawberries, and stopped short. "Carrie? You're leaving?"

Griff touched his finger to the brim of his hat. "Mrs. Bell."

She ignored him and glared at Carrie. "You're taking all your things?"

"Not all my things. Half of this farm is still mine. But there's no room at the hotel for everything." She set her hatbox into the rig. "Joe and Caleb can have the room you promised them."

"If you're going to run out on us like this, you might at least wait until your brother gets back from the fields and say a proper good-bye. You owe him that much."

"I'm sure you'll be only too happy to tell him where to find me." Carrie climbed into the rig so quickly that the wheels creaked.

Griff climbed in beside her and picked up the reins. "Good-bye, Mrs. Bell."

"Wait." Mary crossed the yard to where the rig stood beneath the trees. "You've made your point, but you can't go through with this, Carrie."

"Why not?"

"Well . . . because. You know how much there is to do around here, especially with Henry working part-time at the mill. I don't know how to milk the cow or work that infernal cook stove. And who's going to help with the washing and all?"

"I suppose you'll have to figure it out. Teach your boys to do the milking and such. I would advise Caleb not to punch Miranda in the gut while he's milking her, though. She's liable to punch back."

Mary dropped her gaze. "I'm right sorry about that. But Henry punished him for it. You can't still be mad about that."

Taking up her shawl, Carrie nodded to Griff. "Let's get going. I want to be settled before dark."

"All right, you win." Mary stamped her foot. "Since you're making such a fuss about it, I'll let you have your room back. The boys can bunk in with Henry and me until we can figure out something else. I never dreamed you'd cause such a ruckus."

"And I never dreamed I'd be set upon with snakes and fists and ordered about like some hired girl. There's room in a house for only one mistress, and since you are Henry's wife, I must be the one to go."

Mary clutched her apron. "If you won't stay on my account, think of Henry."

"I am thinking of him. He deserves to come home to a peaceful house. Now he can."

She nodded to Griff. He snapped the reins, and the rig rolled down the lane.

FOUR

Carrie watched the farmhouse grow smaller and smaller, floating in the mist like something in a dream. Memories rattled around in her head like marbles in a glass jar—long evenings before the fire reading aloud with Henry, cold mornings in the barn, milking Miranda while a litter of warm gray kittens tumbled about her feet. She remembered the summer Henry saved enough to take her to Nashville on the train. The spring morning she'd looked up from her knitting to find a bearded and bent Uriah McClain at her door, come to pay a condolence call on his best friend's widow nearly ten years after he lost his leg and Frank lost his life at Shiloh.

She and Uriah had talked for hours, reminiscing about happier times. Despite their shared sorrow, Uriah's visit had been a balm to her soul, a blessing connecting her, however briefly, with her lost love. She could never thank Mr. McClain enough for returning Frank's personal effects. Even now, they were the most precious of her possessions.

"Are you all right?" Griff glanced at her from beneath his mist-dampened hat brim. "You want to go back? It isn't too late to change your mind."

"I'm fine, and I won't change my mind."

He laughed and then instantly sobered. "Forgive me. I don't

mean to make light of your troubles. You sounded so determined just now, you reminded me of myself in my younger days. My father always said I was stubborn as a Missouri mule."

She frowned. "That isn't a very flattering comparison."

"Between you and me, or you and the mule?"

She couldn't help laughing. Griff Rutledge certainly had a way of seeing the humor in any situation. One of many qualities she was coming to appreciate in him.

At last they passed the train station, quiet now in the late afternoon light. Griff turned onto the main street and guided the rig past the Hickory Ridge Inn, the barbershop, and Nate Chastain's bookshop. A line of buggies and wagons waited outside the mercantile. Scents of cinnamon and baking bread wafted from the bakery across the street. Sheriff Eli McCracken glanced up from his conversation with the postmaster as they drove past. He nodded to Carrie and touched the brim of his hat before resuming his conversation.

Griff drew up front of the Verandah. "Go ahead in. I'll see if I can find someone to help me unload. That walnut chest is heavier than I thought. I'd hate to drop it and damage it."

He helped Carrie out of the rig. Taking up the small bag that held her essentials, she went inside. Behind the rough pine reception desk in the parlor sat an olive-skinned woman wearing a dark green silk dress that exactly matched the color of her eyes. Her glossy black hair was swept away from her face with two tortoise shell combs. She turned a deck of cards, one card at a time, her slender wrist and bejeweled fingers working in rapid synchronization.

Carrie stared. Who was this exotic-looking creature, and what on earth was she doing in Hickory Ridge? Had Mrs. Whitcomb converted her genteel old wreck of a hotel into a gambling parlor? Carrie shifted her bag to her other arm. "Good afternoon."

The woman's hands stilled. She glanced up, a question in her eyes.

"I'm looking for Mrs. Whitcomb."

"You and me both, honey. She promised to fix the leak in the roof over my room, but she took out of here awhile ago and hasn't come back."

"Do you know where she went?"

"No idea." The woman gestured toward the threadbare sofa in the parlor. "May as well get comfortable. It might be awhile longer before she gets back."

"I don't believe we've met. I'm Carrie Daly."

Carrie paused, waiting for the woman to introduce herself, but she merely smiled. "Well, Carrie, if you want my recommendation, room number seven at the end of the upstairs hall is your best bet. It leaks, of course. They all do. But it's the quietest spot in the house and Mrs. Whitcomb just put in a new bed yesterday. Mrs. Athison passed to her eternal reward night before last and Mrs. W's been cleaning up a storm ever since."

The front door opened, and Nate Chastain walked in with Carrie's suitcase.

"Nate?" Carrie frowned. "What are you doing here?"

"I was just about to ask you the same thing." He thumped her suitcase onto the floor.

She peered past his shoulder. "Where's Mr.—"

"Mr. Gilman waylaid him in the street. They're talking horses. I happened along, and he asked me to help a lady moving in." Nate shook his head. "I sure never dreamed it'd be you, though. What on earth happened, Carrie?"

"It's a long story."

The woman in green dealt herself another hand. "You movin' in here for good?"

"For the time being, yes."

"I suppose you know this is a ladies-only establishment, Mr. . . . ?" She smiled up at Nate.

"Chastain," Nate said.

"Mr. Chastain." She favored Nate with another smile. "I personally think that having gentlemen around elevates the atmosphere of a place quite considerably. Mrs. Whitcomb, unfortunately, does not share that view."

She turned her extraordinary gaze to Carrie. "And what's your name again, honey?"

"Carrie. Mrs. Daly."

"Oh. *Mrs.* Daly. Is there a Mr. Daly somewhere?"

Carrie briefly closed her eyes and massaged the knot at the back of her neck. Hunger gnawed at her stomach. The woman's flirtatious manner with Nate was getting on her nerves. "Mr. Daly is lying in a hero's grave at Shiloh."

"Oh." The woman blushed. "I'm so sorry." She laughed, a bell-like sound. "Seems I'm always opening my mouth and sticking my big ol' foot right into it."

Nate smiled. "Don't worry. I find genuine curiosity in a woman quite attractive."

"Do you? Well, Mr. Chastain, I am so pleased that you feel that way, because I find I am quite curious about you. And about all of Hickory Ridge."

"I figured you must be new in town," Nate said. "I own the bookshop here, and I don't recall seeing you before today."

"I've been so busy ever since I got here that I haven't ventured out much. But I do intend to pay you a visit very soon."

"Splendid." Nate blushed. "If you'll tell me what sort of books you like, perhaps I can have some suggestions ready for you."

Carrie glared at him. Good gravy. Nate was grinning like the proverbial cat that ate the canary. She dropped her satchel onto the floor with a resounding thump. "Yes, please do tell. Who are your favorite authors, Miss . . . forgive me. I didn't catch your name."

"Well . . . I . . . that is, I like most every kind of book that ever was written. I am quite certain that whatever you choose for me, Mr. Chastain—"

"Nate, ma'am."

"Nate. I'm sure whatever book you choose will be just perfect."

"Yes, Nate knows books better than anyone in Hickory Ridge." Turning to him, Carrie continued, "Would you mind seeing to the rest of my things?"

"Oh. Right. Got so busy talking that I almost forgot."

He hurried outside. Minutes later Carrie's belongings and her mother's walnut chest lay in a jumble in the hallway outside room seven. The woman in green went downstairs to resume her solitary card game, leaving Nate and Carrie alone in the dim, chilly hallway.

"You're sure you want to stay here, Carrie?" Nate looked around. "The place is almost deserted."

"Mrs. Whitcomb says there are five ladies living here besides me. Two of them are ancient sisters who live on the third floor by themselves. She said they never come downstairs, not even for meals."

"Sounds spooky." He paused. "What made you mad enough to up and leave home?"

"I can't talk about it now. I'm too upset."

A headache was forming behind her eyes. Carrie massaged her temples. "I don't mean to be so cross. I'm tired. And that woman downstairs . . ."

"Jealous of her?" he teased.

"Of course not. Why should I be? She's beautiful, no question. But the way she flirted with you and called me 'honey' and the fact that she knows how to deal cards makes me wonder what kind of person she is. Did you notice that she took pains not to tell us her name?"

"Well, it'll come out soon enough with you living under the same roof." He squeezed both her hands. "I ought to get back to the shop. Those books that came in today won't sort themselves."

"Thank you for helping me. I'm sorry Mr. Rutledge left the job to you."

Nate nodded. "I hope you won't regret leaving the farm. But if it's too awful here, you can always go home."

Together they walked down the creaking wooden staircase and to the door. Carrie peered onto the empty street. Apparently Mr. Rutledge had driven away without even saying good-bye. She thanked Nate again and watched him leave.

"All settled?" the woman asked when Carrie returned to the parlor.

"As settled as I can be until Mrs. Whitcomb arrives to give me a key."

The woman fished a key from her bodice and pressed it into Carrie's hand. "Use mine. They're all the same. A fact I discovered last week when I came home late and went into poor Mrs. Athison's room by mistake. Was she ever surprised."

She laughed, her green eyes dancing, and Carrie found herself laughing too. The woman was so charming that it was hard not to like her, despite the fact that she was a terrible flirt and perhaps too flamboyant to be completely respectable.

The door opened, and two women of about Carrie's age came in arm and arm, pink-cheeked and laughing. One of them hurried across the room and handed the woman a small package. "For you, Rosaleen, for getting me out that jam last night."

So that was her name. Rosaleen.

"That's real sweet of you, honey, but really, you didn't have to. I'm glad I came along when I did." Rosaleen turned to Carrie.

"Lucy was coming home from Mrs. Grayson's last night, and a couple of men from the sawmill started giving her a hard time."

"They were drunk." Lucy removed her hat and shook out her hair. "Scared me half to death. Rosaleen here told them in no uncertain terms to leave me alone. Thank goodness they listened."

"It saddens me to think that sort of thing happens in our little town," Lucy's companion said. "Hickory Ridge has always been a decent kind of place." She bobbed her head at Carrie. "I'm Rachel Ryan. You must be Carrie. Mrs. Whitcomb said you'd asked last week about renting a room, but she wasn't sure if you really meant to."

"I *wasn't* sure, until this morning." Carrie smiled at the women. "I'm happy to meet you."

"Likewise." Lucy tossed her hat onto the sofa in the parlor and unbuttoned her jacket. "I'm exhausted. If anyone ever asks you to look after a passel of kids, Carrie, run as fast as you can in the opposite direction. It's the most thankless task on this green earth."

"Lucy looks after the widow Grayson's children," Rachel said. "Seven of them in all, and every last one of them younger than six."

"Twin boys were put on earth to make death seem more attractive." Lucy flopped onto the sofa beside her hat. "I swear if I have to haul them out of the river one more time, I will lose what little mind I have left."

"At least your situation is temporary." Rachel patted her companion's shoulder. "Just think. This time next year, you'll be married and on your way to Montana."

"I can't wait. Blue skies, mountains, and nobody for a hundred miles except for my Jake and me." Lucy grinned. "And nary a Grayson in sight."

The pendulum clock on the wall behind the desk emitted six

soft chimes. Rosaleen set down her deck of cards. "I don't know about y'all, but I am about to perish. I say we raid the kitchen and forget about Mrs. W. It seems like she's gone for good."

"She'll be back," Rachel said. "I owe her for two weeks' rent."

"Any news from Sam?" Rosaleen asked.

Together the four women walked down the long hallway and into the kitchen.

Rachel shook her head. "No good news, anyhow. His letter last week said there might be a job for him in North Carolina. He says jobs are so scarce we can't afford to be choosy, but I don't know. North Carolina's such a long ways from Mama and them."

Rosaleen nodded. "Homesickness is a bad affliction, but eventually you get over it."

She rolled up her sleeves, took a stack of plates from the pantry, and peered into the icebox. "Looks like there's some cheese and some leftover beans . . . and some pie."

"What kind?" Lucy rummaged in a drawer for forks and set them onto the table with a clatter.

"Hard to tell." Lifting the pie pan from the icebox, Rosaleen set it on the table and bent to take a whiff. "I'd say it's the remainder of last Sunday's cherry pie, but that's only a guess."

"Tell me again why we put up with this horrible food." Rachel plopped onto her chair.

"Because it's cheap." Rosaleen scraped the shriveled pie pieces into a pail beside the door. Taking a heavy black pot from a shelf above the stove, she dumped the bowl of beans into it and stoked the fire. When the beans were hot and bubbling, the women made a meal of them along with wedges of cheese and hunks of cold cornbread.

"Somebody ought to go upstairs and get the Provost sisters," Rachel said, "but I am too tired to move."

"They hardly ever eat," Lucy told Carrie. "I don't see how they stay alive."

"Jasper Pruitt at the mercantile gives them candy every time they go in there," Rachel said. "That's how. No wonder they're never hungry for beans and corn pone."

Carrie stole a glance at her surroundings. A chipped cookie jar and a couple of worn cookery books sat on a shelf beneath the one grimy window. A couple of earthenware pitchers lined up next to the water pump. A metal washtub beside the door held wood for the cook stove. An open cupboard door revealed an assortment of pots and bowls, plates, and cooking utensils.

She pushed away her half-empty bowl of beans. They were too salty by half and gritty to boot. Despite her misgivings about the hotel, she looked forward to putting decent meals onto Mrs. Whitcomb's table.

The front door opened and slammed shut, then the hotel proprietress stuck her head into the kitchen. "Carrie. So you decided to make the move, I see. You got a little something to eat?"

"Very little," Lucy grumbled. "Beans and corn pone again."

"The pie was ruined," Rachel said. "It's a wonder we don't die of the epizootics from eating rotten food."

The proprietress ignored that remark and beamed at Carrie. "Sorry I wasn't here when you arrived. I had business at the bank, and it took longer than I expected. Did you get settled in all right?"

"I gave her room seven," Rosaleen said. "The one with the fewest rats and the fewest leaks in the roof."

"And the best bed," Lucy said. "I should have moved in there when I had the chance."

"Too late now." Rachel rose from the table and set her bowl on the counter. "I'm going up to my room."

"Me too," Lucy said. "Tomorrow is another exciting day with the Grayson gang."

"And I need my beauty sleep." Rosaleen cleared the table and set a kettle of water on to heat. She hauled the dishpan from the cupboard and set it on the table. "As soon as I finish these dishes." She shrugged. "At least the extra money comes in handy."

"But I thought—" Carrie frowned.

Mrs. Whitcomb sat down heavily. "When you asked me after church last week about moving here, I wasn't sure you were serious."

"I wanted to stay at the farm, but in the end, I couldn't. We talked about my working for you, and—"

"I'm nearly broke, Carrie. I expected Mr. Gilman to approve another loan. I was there all afternoon, jawing about it, but he won't budge."

The kettle whistled. Rosaleen pumped some water into the dishpan, then added the boiling water. The plates clattered against the metal as she scrubbed them with a faded blue rag.

"Hard times seem to go on and on," Mrs. Whitcomb said, "and for the life of me I do not know where it all will end or what's to become of any of us." She patted Carrie's hand. "Don't worry, I promised you a place to stay, and I intend to live up to it. We'll manage somehow."

Carrie climbed the stairs to her room and sat on the creaky bed. What would become of her indeed? Only last month, her life had been unfolding in its predictable pattern. Now her world had tilted beyond recognition.

A huge brown roach crawled over her shoe. Carrie shuddered. She regretted her own impulsiveness. It was terribly ungrateful of her to have run off without even saying good-bye to Henry, but this morning's argument with Mary had been so contentious that she could not abide another minute in that house.

She rose and unpacked her suitcase. Nate was wrong. No matter how bad things got at the Verandah, she would not go back to the farm.

She'd made her bed, as Granny Bell used to say. Now she'd have to lie in it.

FIVE

"You're sure you've done the right thing, Carrie?" Nate led her through the maze of books, papers, and shipping crates to his desk at the rear of the bookshop. He motioned her to the seat beside the window, lowered himself into his chair, and took up his pipe. His gray cat, India, hopped onto the desk to greet Carrie before settling into her favorite spot on the windowsill. "Moving off your brother's place . . . I don't know. It seems awful drastic to me."

"I had no choice. Mary made it impossible for me to have a moment's peace. Her boys are undisciplined and rude, and she took over the house and ordered me around as if I were nothing more than hired help. She's imperious and, I hate to say it, lazy. She doesn't know how to run a farmhouse and has no intention of learning. And she'd argue with a signpost."

He nodded. "I had a few disagreements with Mary when she ran the telegraph office. She isn't the most pleasant sort, is she?"

Carrie snorted. "About as pleasant as an eyeful of cinders. For the life of me, I don't understand why Henry chose her."

"Don't fault your brother for taking a chance on happiness." He gazed out the window, his mind clearly a million miles away. "A man gets to be a certain age, and he sees his life slipping away.

All his hopes going by the wayside. To salvage something of his dream, he quits looking for perfection and settles for something more attainable."

For some reason, she found his words irksome. "And is that what I represent to you? Something attainable?"

"You know better than that. As far as I'm concerned, you're about as perfect as a woman can get. Smart, sweet-natured, and pretty too. Why, just looking at you is like being outside on the finest summer's day." He smiled. "Except that you are more lovely and more temperate."

Carrie blushed, her irritation forgotten. "You've been reading those poetry books again."

"Guilty." He puffed his pipe to get it going. Behind his gold-rimmed spectacles, his gray eyes were serious and kind. "I'm sure it wasn't easy getting along with Mary. Every woman wants to feel in charge of her own home, I reckon. What does Henry have to say about all this?"

"He's caught in the middle, trying to keep the peace among all of us. I hated making him feel guilty for wanting the same things I want—a home, a family. And aside from all the other indignities, they were going to move my things into a cramped room in the attic so her children could have my room. It's the only place I've lived since Frank died."

"A long time."

"Yes." India vaulted into her lap, and she stroked the cat's soft hair. "Maybe Mary's right. Maybe I'm too old and set in my ways."

His eyes twinkled. "Not too set in your ways to marry me, I hope."

"We've been over all that."

"That we have, my girl. I'm sure I don't know why you keep putting me off." He waved his hand around the cluttered shop that smelled faintly of musty books, ink, and pipe tobacco. "Just think. All this could be yours. What woman wouldn't jump at the chance?"

Carrie smiled. It was an old dance between them, this dithering about their future. Would Nate actually go through with a wedding if one day she dropped her objections and said yes? He was, after all, nearly forty and, like her, set in his ways. Perhaps the notion of marriage was more attractive than the reality of it.

"You know how deeply fond I am of you and how much I enjoy this shop," she said. "But I want to be sure that marriage is the right thing for both of us."

Smoke curled from Nate's pipe and drifted toward the pressed-tin ceiling. "I can appreciate that, but we're neither one getting any younger. I want a wife and children before I'm too old to appreciate 'em."

He made it sound as if any woman capable of fulfilling his wishes would do. A pang shot through her. She cared for Nate; at times she convinced herself she loved him. Certainly she admired his intelligence, his kindness, his gentle humor. He would be a wonderful father. The children of Hickory Ridge adored him. He always had time to read a story or show them a sleight-of-hand trick that left them gaping in wonder and clamoring to know how it was done. She could imagine a life with him, a life of quiet contentment. Maybe that was the best she could hope for now. And yet . . .

Nate glanced around the cluttered bookshop. "You could help me out here," he blurted.

"What?"

"Since Mrs. Whitcomb can't hire you, I'll pay you to assist me."

"Nate, I—"

"Just look at this place. It's a disgrace. If folks had another bookshop close by, they'd never darken my door." He set down his pipe. "Not that too many folks have been coming around lately anyway. If this depression doesn't end soon, I don't know that I can continue to hang on."

She saw how much that prospect hurt him. Books were his passion.

"What about your college accounts?"

"Barely keeping me afloat for now. The locals don't come around anymore. Nobody has money for extras like books. And with only three trains a week, the business I'm getting from travelers is not enough to take up the slack."

"Then I can't let you spend money on me. I'm grateful, from the bottom of my heart. But I wouldn't feel right, taking your money at a time like this."

He drew her to her feet. "I must go. I'm expecting a shipment of books this afternoon. Meanwhile, I hope you'll reconsider my offer of employment."

Carrie stood on tiptoe and kissed his cheek. "Thank you, but I'll get by."

He sighed. "I sure hope you know what you're doing, going off on your own like this."

She blew out a long breath. "So do I."

He walked her to the door and opened it, jingling the little bell. Somewhere far off a dog howled with such mournfulness that Carrie was assailed with doubt and longing. She missed the farm and the life she'd left behind. And now she'd turned down a chance to earn her keep. Had she made the right decision?

SIX

Carrie woke to sun pouring in her window and the sound of hoof beats in the street below. Leaving her bed, she crossed to the window and peered out in time to see Ada Caldwell emerging from her rig.

She dressed and grabbed her straw hat, hastily pinning up her hair as she descended the creaky staircase. She glanced into the kitchen, where Rachel and Rosaleen sat at the table. The smells of boiling coffee and burned biscuits filled the air. Torn between happiness at seeing Ada and complete mortification to be found living in such a shabby place, she hurried along the threadbare carpet and opened the door for her friend.

"Carrie?" Ada swept into the parlor and peeled off her gloves. "I stopped by the farm this morning, only to be told that you've moved here."

Carrie nodded. "The Verandah isn't much to look at, but the other residents are kind. Not a one of them has tossed a snake into my face, punched me in the stomach, routed me from my own bed, or ordered me about like a servant."

"Oh my dear, was it really as bad as all that?"

"I'm afraid so."

A burst of laughter from the kitchen punctuated her words.

Carrie fiddled with the ribbons on her hat. "I'd offer you some coffee and biscuits, but I'm afraid they aren't very—"

"Nonsense." Ada looped her arm through Carrie's. "Let's buy something decadent from the bakery and go to the park. I haven't been there in ages."

Carrie hesitated. A morning in the park with her friend was much more appealing than sitting in the parlor watching Rosaleen deal her cards, each one falling onto the table with a little slapping sound. But her finances didn't allow for bought baked goods.

"My treat," Ada said. "Come on."

They left the hotel and crossed the street to the bakery. Ada chose a couple of small strawberry tarts, and they set off. The bright spring sunshine and Ada's company acted like a tonic on Carrie's spirits. She laughed along with her friend as Ada described her son's antics and Wyatt's efforts at teaching Sophie to fish.

Ada tethered the horse at the rail and led the way across the pale grass to the gazebo. Opening the bag, she handed Carrie a tart, then bit into her own. "Now, tell me," she began, "what's holding up your nuptials to Nate Chastain?"

Carrie blinked. Had Ada always been so blunt? Maybe that was what life on a rough-and-tumble ranch did to a person. She brushed crumbs from her skirt. "I'm not sure I can put it into words. I have prayed to know whether Nate is the one God has in mind for me, but I honestly don't know the answer."

"Does Nate love you?"

"I think so, in his own fashion. But sometimes he seems so keen to be married that I think any woman will do."

"Do you love him?"

"I thought I did—until Mr. Rutledge arrived. But now I am more confused than ever."

Ada's lovely gray eyes widened. "Surely Mr. Rutledge hasn't declared himself already?"

"Good heavens, no. I've spoken to him only twice . . . well, three times counting the day he saved me from being trampled. But there's something about him, Ada. I think about him more often than I should. I can't explain it really."

"What does your brother think of all this?"

"I haven't spoken to him since the day I moved out."

"Oh, Carrie. I understand Mary Stanhope can be most difficult, but I hate to see anything come between you and Henry." Ada placed a hand on Carrie's arm. "Can't you forgive Mary and make your peace with the situation? Our Lord requires—"

Carrie nodded. "I know what I'm supposed to do, but it isn't that easy." She bit into her tart and watched a noisy blue jay darting in and out of the trees. "I don't blame Henry. He's entitled to a life of his own. And he's caught in an impossible situation, trying to please both Mary and me. I'm not angry with him. But I can't go home and allow Mary and her rude children to rule my life either."

"Of course not." Ada polished off her tart and wiped her fingers on her handkerchief. "Perhaps after some time has passed, you can have a talk with them. Give Mary another chance."

Carrie shrugged.

"Does Nate know about all of this?"

"Yes. He hasn't said much, but I feel he disapproves too." Carrie got to her feet. "It's all a big mess. I don't know what's right anymore."

"I know how you feel. When Wyatt first proposed I was terribly confused, even though I loved him more than anything." Ada put an arm around Carrie's shoulder. "I nearly lost him because of my own fears. Pray about this, my dear, and then have the faith to act."

"I have prayed about it. But I feel more uncertain than ever." A gust of wind loosened the ribbons on her hat, and she reached up to retie them. "Maybe I'm asking God the wrong questions."

"Sometimes I feel that way too," Ada said. "That's when I pray the prayer that never fails: Thy will be done."

"Maybe."

"It would break my heart if you lost your chance at happiness."

Carrie swallowed the hard knot in her throat. What would bring her true happiness? Would she even recognize happiness if it came calling?

Ada consulted the tiny gold watch she wore in a chain around her neck. "I should get back. I promised Wyatt I'd be packed and ready by four o'clock."

"You're leaving today?"

Ada nodded. "This evening."

So soon? Carrie felt like bawling, but she kept her voice light. "You'd better write to me. I can't wait to hear what Sophie is up to and how Wade liked staying with his grandpa."

They crossed the park, climbed into Ada's rented rig, and returned to the Verandah.

"Good-bye, Carrie." Ada squeezed Carrie's hand. "Nate is a good and decent man, but all men have their limitations. It isn't in their nature to postpone their desires indefinitely." Ada smiled. "Don't make him wait too long."

Carrie got out of the rig. "Thank you for the tart. And the advice."

Ada waved, turned the rig, and headed down the street to the Hickory Ridge Inn. Carrie shaded her eyes and watched her friend drive away. Was Ada right? Was she in danger of losing her chance at happiness? She tried to imagine herself as Mrs. Nate Chastain, but it was Griff Rutledge's face that rose in her mind.

Ridiculous. She shook off the preposterous thought and climbed the steps to the hotel.

Griff finished a breakfast of eggs, grits, and biscuits and downed his second cup of coffee. He shaved and then donned the gray wool suit he'd sent out to be freshened. He tucked the report he'd received by wire into his pocket and descended the stairs just as an attractive woman in a stylish feathered hat entered the lobby. He nodded, then stopped short. "Well, hello. It's Mrs. Caldwell, isn't it?"

She looked up, startled. "Mr. Rutledge."

"How kind. You remembered. Wasn't that wedding something? I can't remember the last time I saw such a beautiful cake."

"Mrs. Daly is an accomplished baker."

"So I gathered." He bowed. "It was lovely seeing you, Mrs. Caldwell. Please forgive my haste. I'm late for an appointment."

She nodded.

Leaving the inn, he crossed the street and hurried past Gilman's bank, the bookshop, and the mercantile, which was already buzzing with customers. At the entrance to the Verandah Hotel, he paused to collect his thoughts. When it came to doing business with a man, he considered himself a master. Women, however, were a different matter entirely.

He opened the door and went inside.

SEVEN

She sat in the parlor dressed in a bright yellow frock that contrasted with her dark hair, so engrossed in her game that she hadn't heard his approach. On the table in front of her, next to a chipped coffee mug, a deck of cards fanned out. Watching her nimble fingers flip the cards, Griff felt as if no time at all had passed since their last encounter. He doubted she even remembered.

"Hello, Rosaleen." His voice echoed in the empty room.

Her hands stilled. "Griff."

Her head came up. Her lips curved into a sardonic smile. "I figured you'd find me sooner or later. But I didn't expect it would be here."

"You didn't make it easy for me."

She shrugged. "A girl has to make a living. After what happened in New Orleans—"

He tamped down his anger. "I wouldn't bring up New Orleans if I were you."

She tossed the cards onto the table. "Want some coffee? It's bitter as sin, but—"

"No thank you."

"A brandy then. I think Mrs. Whitcomb has some around here somewhere."

"I don't drink in the morning. Quit stalling. You know why I've come."

"Yes, Griff, I believe I do." She sashayed over to him and planted a firm kiss on his mouth. "Aren't you going to say a proper hello? It's been a long time."

"Yes. Much too long." He drew a paper from his pocket and handed it to her. "Recognize this?"

Her eyes clouded. "You know I do. But surely you aren't going to hold me to that silly old IOU."

"Why shouldn't I?"

"Because I'm poor as a church mouse and you have plenty of money." She handed the paper back. "You won't miss this paltry sum at all."

"I had money, but there was a war. You might have heard about it."

"That's ridiculous. Your family still owns the plantation on the river and that beautiful old house in Charleston, not to mention all the money you earned from—"

"Why, you little minx. How is it that you know so much about my holdings? Have you been checking up on me?"

"No. Well, maybe a little. But, Griff, don't be mad."

He laughed. "I'm not mad. I admire your acumen. But the fact remains that you owe me money. Quite a lot of money. And now I need it."

"Well, I don't have it." She swept one arm around the room. "Do you think I'd be living here if I could afford anything better? And you've obviously been checking up on me too."

He didn't deny it. "What in the Sam Hill are you doing in a town like Hickory Ridge? Far as I can tell, there's not a gambling house between here and Nashville."

She sent him a mysterious smile. "There is if you know where to look."

"Nevertheless. I know you. You didn't come all this way to cheat the good people of Hickory Ridge out of a few dollars. There's some other reason you're here."

She glanced away. "What if there is? It has nothing to do with you."

"You're right. It doesn't." He caught her chin in his hand. "All I want from you is my money. And soon."

"All right. I'll get your blasted money." She grabbed a handful of cards and flung them at him. "You're certainly no gentleman, Griff Rutledge."

"And you, Miss Dupree, are no lady."

Carrie stood transfixed at the top of the stairs. After bidding goodbye to Ada, she'd gone back upstairs to tidy her room. She'd left it just in time to hear Rosaleen's voice . . . and Mr. Rutledge's raised in anger. Obviously they knew each other, a fact that shouldn't bother her in the least. But it did. She felt disappointed. Maybe even jealous, which was even more ridiculous. Griff Rutledge was a stranger just passing through Hickory Ridge. She had no claim on him whatsoever.

The door slammed shut behind Griff. Carrie squared her shoulders and hurried downstairs. Rosaleen was on her hands and knees in the parlor, picking up her cards.

"Need some help?" Carrie retrieved the jack of diamonds lying beneath the side table.

"Thanks. I've got it." Rosaleen got to her feet, and Carrie saw tears standing in her eyes.

"Are you all right?"

"Fine." Rosaleen straightened her blouse and sniffed. "Just a misunderstanding with an old friend."

"Mr. Rutledge?"

Rosaleen's eyes went wide. "You know him?"

"Not really." Carrie explained the nature of their acquaintance. "I recognized his voice just now, that's all."

"I hope we didn't disturb you." Rosaleen dropped the stack of cards onto the table and looked up, her expression troubled. "How much did you overhear?"

"Only the barbs you traded as he was leaving."

Rosaleen seemed relieved. "He didn't mean it. Nor did I. We've always been—"

The door flew open and Lucy Whitcomb rushed in, her skirts blood-soaked, a small, golden-haired girl lying limp in her arms. "Quick, I need bandages."

"What happened?" Carrie touched the child's face. It felt cool and dry beneath her fingers.

"I—I turned my back for half a minute." Lucy gulped air, stifling her sobs. "She picked up the ax and accidentally cut her foot. Please help me. I'm afraid she's bleeding to death."

Mrs. Whitcomb rushed down the stairs. "What's all this commo—oh my heavens, that poor child. Rosaleen, don't just stand there, go find Dr. Spencer."

Lucy's voice trembled. "He's out at the Rileys' place. I couldn't think where else to bring her."

"Put her on the sofa," Mrs. Whitcomb said. "And for heavens' sake, Lucy, bear up. Carrie, bring a basin of water and that can of powdered alum from the kitchen."

Carrie hurried to pump the water, her heart twisting with worry and pity. Poor child. Poor Lucy. What would happen to her, to her future, if the little girl died? More importantly, how would Mrs. Grayson ever cope with such a horrific loss?

She returned to the parlor with the alum and the water. Rosaleen was busy tearing an old sheet into long strips. Mrs. Whitcomb held smelling salts beneath the child's nose. The little girl revived and whimpered as Mrs. Whitcomb bathed the deep, ragged cut and poured the alum into the wound. Rosaleen paled and rushed from the room.

Carrie smoothed the child's hair off her face and murmured to her while the hotelier bound up the cut. Lucy, as white-faced and shaken as her charge, took a piece of candy from her pocket and offered it to the child. The little girl licked the candy, fat tears sliding down her cheeks.

Lucy collapsed onto the sofa beside the child, her shoulders sagging. "Thank you for your help. I was so scared I couldn't even think."

"You did all right," Mrs. Whitcomb said. "I raised six boys of my own," she told Carrie, "and one or the other of them was always getting hurt." She patted the little girl's shoulder. "This cut looked worse than it really is."

The little girl turned her teary eyes on the hotelier. "I gots Miss Lucy's dress messed up."

Lucy cradled the child. "Oh, honey, it's all right. Don't worry about that."

"Mama is going to be awful mad," the child said.

"No doubt," Lucy muttered. "How will I ever find another job?"

"It was an accident," Mrs. Whitcomb said, "pure and simple. And you got help for the child right away. I'm sure I don't know what more the child's mother can expect."

"I should have paid more attention," Lucy said. "But the children are so noisy and energetic, it's more than I can handle." She brushed her hair off her face. "I must go. I left the oldest boy in charge of the others, and there's no telling what trouble they're into by now."

She settled the little girl on her hip and headed for the door. "Tell Rosaleen I said thanks for her help too."

Mrs. Whitcomb looked around. "Where is Rosaleen? She was here a minute ago."

She followed Lucy out onto the porch. Carrie gathered the rest of the bandages and the tin of powdered alum and carried the pan of bloody water to the back door to empty it.

Rosaleen sat on the back steps, her arms looped around her drawn-up knees, sobbing as if her heart had shriveled to nothing and blown away.

"Rosaleen?" Carrie dropped onto the step beside her. "Are you all right?"

Rosaleen shook her head and waved her away. Carrie rose and went back inside. Perhaps Rosaleen was upset over her meeting with Griff Rutledge. Perhaps her tears were the result of seeing the little girl in so much pain, though her anguish seemed deeper than that. She wept as if grieving for one of her own.

EIGHT

"Carrie?" Rosaleen poked her head into kitchen where Carrie was busy kneading bread dough. "Mr. Chastain is waiting for you in the parlor."

"Nate's here?" Carrie felt a stab of guilt. In the weeks since moving to the Verandah, she'd hardly seen Nate. True, he'd been busy, but she should have made more of an effort. After all, it wasn't as if she had anything to do aside from reading, moping, and waiting for letters from Ada.

She dusted the dough with flour, covered it with a towel, and set it in the pan to rise.

"There you are." Nate rose as she entered the parlor, a smile creasing his round face. "I'd about decided you'd left the country. Figured I'd best check and see."

She grinned. "Still here."

He squeezed both her hands, and she squeezed back. It was good seeing him. Why had she neglected him these past weeks? From now on, she'd pay more attention to him.

"I was hopin' I could take you down to the bakery for a sweet"— his gaze swept over her flour-smudged face—"but I reckon that wouldn't be much of an occasion for you."

She dabbed at her face with her handkerchief. "I've been baking bread this morning."

He nodded. "Can we take a walk?"

"I'll get my hat."

She ran up to her room to retrieve the straw toque Ada had sent her last summer. Draped in soft pink satin and trimmed with a small nosegay of white chenille flowers, it made her feel happier just to wear it. She returned to the parlor to find Nate handing Rosaleen a stack of books.

"Why, Mr. Chastain, how positively wonderful of you. I can't remember having received a more thoughtful gift." Standing on tiptoe, Rosaleen kissed Nate's cheek.

Carrie watched his face turn beet red. Land's sakes, but Rosaleen was the boldest woman in the entire state. Carrie herself would never engage in such a public show of affection, and she and Nate were promised to each other.

"Carrie." Rosaleen held up the books. "Look what Nate brought. Isn't he the most wonderful man?"

"Yes." Carrie looped her arm through his and smiled up at him. "Simply wonderful."

Nate blushed again—he never could cope with her teasing—and escorted her onto the street. They skirted a couple of farm women who had stopped to chat outside the post office and headed down the road toward the park.

"What have you—" he began.

"I'm sorry I've—" she said at the same moment, and he laughed.

"Ladies first." He squeezed her hand. "What were you about to say?"

"Only that I'm sorry I haven't been to the bookshop much lately."

He smiled. "I've missed you. India has too."

Carrie smiled at the mention of his beloved cat. "I should bring her some catnip next time."

"Have you been out to the farm to see Henry?"

"No." She took her fan from her reticule and fanned her face. "I've wanted to, but I can't face Mary and those boys."

"Don't you think you should?"

"I'm the one who was wronged, Nate."

"Because Henry chose to make himself happy?"

She stopped in the road, one hand on her hip. "You know better than that. I'm truly glad he's found love. But Mary Stanhope has no use for me. And honestly, the feeling is mutual."

"You surprise me, Carrie. I never figured you for the type of woman to hold a grudge."

"I'm not holding a grudge. I simply don't belong at the farm anymore. Besides, Henry comes into town every week to shop at the mercantile. He knows where I am, if he wants to see me."

"Well, one of you has to make the first move. You can't let this go on. What if something terrible happened to him? You'd live with the guilt forever. Is that what you want?"

"Of course not. But nothing's going to happen."

"Oh, so now you're God. Now you can predict the future."

She stopped to stare up at him. "What's the matter with you today? Did you come to see me just to start a disagreement?"

They reached the park. He plopped down beneath a towering hickory tree and patted the ground. She sat down beside him.

"I apologize. I don't mean to be cross with you. But I'll admit I have been feeling peevish lately. I don't like the way that Rutledge character looks at you. Just yesterday he stood outside the post office and followed your every move, all the way to the mercantile. Don't tell me you didn't notice."

"I noticed. But you shouldn't worry about it."

As soon as the words left her mouth, she was assailed with guilt. She *was* attracted to Griff Rutledge despite herself. Did it show?

"Are you sure about that, Carrie? I saw the two of you that day at the wedding. And then you asked him to help you move."

He pulled at a blade of grass. "Something as important as that, I figured you might have asked me about it."

"It was entirely coincidental. I happened upon him on the road and acted on impulse. I was so upset, I wasn't thinking about who should do the honors. I only wanted out from under Henry's roof as soon as possible."

"I guess I can understand that. But maybe you ought to know, some folks are wondering about Rutledge and what all went on before he came here." His gray eyes sought hers. "I don't want you to get mixed up with the wrong sort of people."

"I'm not mixed up with anyone. Mr. Rutledge and I have spoken only a few times since Henry's wedding."

"If you say so." He leaned against the trunk of the tree and squinted at the patch of sky above them. "I sure do feel bad for Henry and the way things have turned out. I don't like seeing the two of you at odds. Nothing this side of heaven is more important than family."

Did Nate honestly think she didn't already know how precious a family could be? She missed Henry terribly. And she felt guilty for storming off the way she had—or she would if she allowed herself to think about it. A rush of anger at Mary Stanhope displaced her sadness. Why did Mary have to be so judgmental? So thoughtless and demanding? If Henry had to marry at this late date, why couldn't he have found someone sweet and thoughtful, someone like Ada Caldwell?

". . . anyway, that's my idea. What do you think?"

She blinked. "Sorry. What?"

"I offered you a job again. While you were woolgathering just now, I was explaining that I've bought out a store in Saint Louis. The inventory will be here on the train next week, and I'll need help sorting it, marking it for sale and such. You've seen my shop. It's all a-jumble."

"I won't argue with you there." She smiled, her thoughts of

Mary forgotten. "Even so, there's something about it that makes me feel good from the moment I step inside."

"Wish I knew what it was. I'd bottle it like snake oil and make a fortune."

She caught the look of worry in his eyes. "You told me weeks ago that business is bad. What in the world are you going to do with even more books?"

"I don't rightly know. But it seemed too good a bargain to pass up. Enrollment at the college is up this year. The students will need books. And I'm counting on the Race Day visitors to buy them too."

"Then the town council approved Mr. Gilman's plan?"

He nodded. "They took a formal vote Tuesday night. Mr. Gilman is beside himself because Rutledge is sticking around to ride that black colt of his." Nate paused. "So will you help me with the shop? I can't pay much but—"

"Of course I'll help, but I won't charge you a cent."

"We've been over all that. I wouldn't feel right not paying you when you need the money." He took her hands and smiled into her eyes. At moments like this, she truly loved him. Loved his quiet affection and innate goodness. What more could a woman ask for? Ada was right. She was a fool for putting him off for so long.

"Maybe you can save the money for your trousseau," he went on. "I hear ladies like to buy all sorts of fancy things when they're going to be married. In a way that'd be like giving the money back to me. When you finally set a date."

She blushed. "All right. Thank you, Nate. I *can* use the money. And I would like something more constructive to do than listen to the gossip at the hotel."

He rose and helped her to her feet. Tucking her hand into the crook of his arm, he led her back to the road. "I'll let you know when the books get here. In the meantime, I hope you'll think about what I said and talk to your brother."

Griff climbed the fence and dropped to the ground. Majestic snorted and lifted his head at the sound, but he didn't shy or run. With slow, deliberate movements, Griff unwound a light lead, and the horse trotted over. Griff grinned and rewarded him with an apple and a pat on the neck.

Resting his head against the three-year-old's hard, warm neck, Griff breathed in the smells of horseflesh and manure and fought another wave of homesickness. By now the summer social season in Charleston would be well underway. Garden parties, beach picnics, Sunday walks in White Point, and the endless round of gentlemen's sporting outings had never much appealed to him, but he'd feigned interest for his father's sake. Not that it had made any difference in the end. He and his father were simply too different. Still, he felt a powerful longing for his roots, ambushed by his long-denied need for a home.

He thought of Carrie Daly. Every time he caught a glimpse of her coming and going from the post office or the mercantile, something about her touched a chord in his heart. How would it feel to hold her silky hair in his hands? To hear her bright laughter? He worried about her. She had seemed so bereft the day he helped her to leave the Bell farm. He knew all about family estrangement, and it wasn't something he would recommend to anyone.

He wasn't sure why Carrie's situation mattered so much to him. After all, he'd be gone from Hickory Ridge once the race was done. Once he'd collected his money from Rosaleen.

Rosaleen. One thought of her, and the peace of the warm summer afternoon vanished like a dream. He could certainly use the money that was still in limbo in London, but he wasn't exactly destitute. It was the principle of Rosaleen's unpaid obligation that gnawed at him. The way he saw it, people ought to keep their commitments. He saddled the colt, slipped a bridle over Majestic's head, and led him out of the corral and into the Gilmans' side meadow.

If he knew Rosaleen Dupree, she wouldn't merely hand over the money. She'd want to play cards for it. And there had been a time when he'd have been only too happy to oblige her. He'd grown up in a city where everyone gambled and no one was thought the worse because of it. But he'd long since lost his taste for cards and for women like her.

What he hadn't lost, though, was a deeply ingrained sense of right and wrong and an even deeper aversion to being played for a fool. He swung into the saddle and nudged Majestic into a brisk trot. If settling an old score meant spending time in places he'd rather not be, dredging up old memories better forgotten, so be it.

NINE

Dozens of books, still in their shipping crates, filled every nook and cranny of the cluttered shop. Where on earth would she put them all?

Carrie pried open a crate of history books and stacked them on a splay-legged table beneath the window. India jumped into the window, and Carrie stopped her work to run her fingers over the cat's smooth back.

Despite the dusty clutter, working in Nate's shop lifted her spirits. Bright sun streamed through the window. The scent of pipe tobacco, old leather, and the strong coffee he brewed in the store room; the squeak of the pine floor beneath her feet; and India's throaty, contented purr filled her with a sense of peace.

She pried the lid off another crate of history books, noting titles about the diminishing buffalo herds on the western plains and the founding of the Women's Christian Temperance Union. A hefty volume caught her eye: *The Old Regime in Canada*. She flipped the pages and skimmed a few random passages. Perhaps she should buy it for Henry. He loved history, loved to read, though he'd never had a chance to finish his schooling.

After their parents and Granny Bell died, he and Carrie lived with a cousin in Maury County, where Henry did well in school.

But he'd been determined to hold on to the family farm in Hickory Ridge. So as soon as he was old enough, he brought Carrie home. And over time, he'd learned how to do everything on the farm. He planted by the signs as Granny had taught them. Potatoes and carrots went into the ground during the dark moon; corn, tomatoes, and beans in the light. He could mend a broken plow, a leaky roof, a downed fence. He took pride in knowing there was nothing he couldn't fix.

Carrie sighed and set the book aside. Despite his skill, Henry couldn't repair the rift between her and Mary, a rift that had spilled over into his relationship with Carrie too.

The door opened and Nate came in, his arms weighted with another crate of books. Behind him, the driver of the freight wagon plopped yet another crate onto the pine table Carrie had just finished dusting.

The driver pulled a sheet of paper from his pocket and handed it to Nate. "That there's the last of the load, I reckon. How do you want to settle this bill, Mr. Chastain?"

Nate set down his crate and mopped his brow. "Just a minute. I'll get the cash box." He retrieved it from beneath the counter and paid the driver. "Appreciate your help."

"Anytime." The driver folded the bill and shoved it into his pocket. "You and Mr. Pruitt over at the mercantile are just about the only cash customers I've got left."

"Things have gotten worse and worse here ever since seventy-three," Nate said, "and unfortunately, I don't see how they're going to improve."

Carrie closed the cash box and put it away. "I suppose we're all counting on the horse race this fall to liven things up."

The driver nodded. "Everybody's talking about that new fellow riding Mr. Gilman's horse. Folks say he won Race Week nearly every year, back in South Carolina. He was some hero, all right."

He scratched his head. "Hard to fathom why a city fellow like that would come to a quiet place like Hickory Ridge."

Nate pried the top off another crate. "If you ask me, it takes more than winning a horse race to make a man a hero."

"Right enough, I reckon. I'll be seeing you, Mr. Chastain." The driver tipped his hat to Carrie and headed for the door. "Ma'am."

When the door closed behind him, Carrie joined Nate at the table and began lifting books from the crate, dropping them onto the counter with more force than was necessary.

"Whoa, there," Nate said. "What's got your petticoat in a twist?"

"I don't know what you mean."

"You're cross as a wet hen."

"I'm not cross."

"Could have fooled me." He set the last of the books on the counter and shoved the crate aside. "It was because of what I said about Rutledge, wasn't it? I don't know why you're always defending him."

"Maybe because you're forever criticizing him. You don't know the first thing about him."

"Whereas you know everything there is to know about the mysterious Mr. Rutledge."

"I don't know much more than you do. But I believe in giving people the benefit of the doubt. Mr. Rutledge has done nothing to deserve your ill opinion of him."

"And nothing to earn such admiration from you." He studied her face. "At least nothing I know about."

"What's that supposed to mean?"

He held up both hands, palms out. "I'm sorry. Let's not fight. I'm dog tired, and there's so much more to do."

"You're right." As much as she resented his attitude toward Griff Rutledge, she understood Nate's concerns for his shop. She hated seeing him so worried. And he was paying for her help, after all.

"I'm sorry too." She indicated a stack of law books she'd shelved earlier that day. "Those won't sell to anyone except maybe the men at the college. I was thinking we should set up a textbook section in the back, by the storeroom, and use these front shelves for the more popular books." She indicated a stack of novels by Jules Verne, Mark Twain, and Bret Harte. "All of these are new, within the last two years."

He nodded. "Good plan."

"And there's something else. I want to start a ladies' book discussion society."

"A book—what?" He took off his spectacles and cleaned them with his handkerchief.

"They're very popular in Memphis these days. I was reading about it in the paper only last week. A group of ladies meets once a month to talk about the books they've read. The article said the discussions are quite lively. And the meetings stimulate a lot of interest in books. Perhaps our society will encourage more customers to come in and look around."

"And what will they use for money, even if they find a book that suits their fancy?"

She pointed to an assortment of books stacked in the far corner. "Those odds and ends have been sitting on the shelves for years. We should offer them at a bargain price. Put a sign in the window and invite people in to browse. Even if they sell for only a dime, that's a dime more than you're earning while they sit here collecting dust."

He grinned, admiration and hope shining in his eyes. "Mercy's sakes, where did all these ideas come from?"

"I want the shop to succeed. It would break my heart if it closed. Yours too."

He thought for a moment. "All right. Go ahead and organize your book society. Who knows? It might be just the ticket to get things moving again."

She clapped her hands and stood on tiptoe to kiss his cheek. "I was sure you'd say yes. Come and see what I've done with the old storeroom."

She took his hand and led him to the small space at the rear of the shop.

"Holy cats." He looked around, clearly surprised at the changes she made.

She had brought in the rocking chair from the front room and placed it next to the small window overlooking the railway station and the mountains. A couple of plump pillows in shades of pink and blue were stacked on the floor next to a basket brimming with children's books, including a leather-bound volume of fairy tales and an elaborately illustrated copy of *Two Hungry Kittens*. "It's for the children of my book society ladies," Carrie said. "They can read and play in here while we talk."

"They'll enjoy it, I'm sure." He squeezed her hand. "Thank you, my love. I only hope—"

The bell above the door jingled. "Hello? Is anyone here?"

Carrie's heart stumbled. "Mr. Rutledge?"

She and Nate returned to the front of the store. Nate nodded. "May I help you?"

Griff smiled. "Actually it's Mrs. Daly I came to see. They told me at the hotel that you're working here now."

Carrie rubbed the bony protrusion at her wrist. "Yes. I—that is, Mr. Chastain bought out another store, and I . . ."

Heavenly days. Why did being around Griff Rutledge make her feel as tongue-tied as a silly schoolgirl? "I'm helping to organize things."

"And doing a fine job of it from what I can see." Griff swept his arm past the tidy shelves and her hand-lettered signs organizing the books by subject, from Architecture to Zoology.

She blushed, pleased at his compliment, and hoped Nate didn't notice the color rising in her cheeks. "There's still a lot to do, especially now that I intend to start a book discussion society. The shop is keeping me very busy these days."

"Not too busy to accompany me to the Gilmans' place tomorrow, I hope."

Nate frowned. "Whatever for, Mr. Rutledge?"

"I thought she might like to see how Majestic's training is coming along." He turned to Carrie. "He's settled down considerably since the day he nearly ran you down."

"Oh, I would like—"

"She doesn't have time. Unlike other people who gallivant around the county at will, we have a job to do here." Nate grabbed a dust rag and attacked the same counter Carrie had polished earlier in the day.

"Of course," the horse tamer said. "But all the same, I think the lady should make up her own mind."

Carrie swallowed her growing irritation at Nate. How dare he speak for her as if she were a child? But it wouldn't do to make a scene. She smiled at Griff. "Mr. Chastain is right. I'm afraid I'm much too busy at the moment. But I hope you'll visit the shop again and let us know how Majestic is getting on."

"Wait till you see him race."

"I'm looking forward to it. As we all are in Hickory Ridge."

"Well then," Nate said. "If there's nothing more we can do for you, Mr.—"

"I'll be on my way." Griff offered her a slight nod. "Another time perhaps, Mrs. Daly."

He let himself out.

Nate pulled out his pocket watch. "It's nearly five. There's not much more we can do until I finish building the new shelves you wanted."

"Fine." Tamping down her irritation, she snatched up her

reticule and the list of books she'd compiled for the discussion group.

"Carrie? What's the matter?"

"You shouldn't have spoken for me. I'm a grown woman, capable of making my own decisions."

"You wanted to go out to the Gilmans' place with Rutledge?"

"The only horses I've ever been around are farm horses. I don't know the first thing about training racehorses. It would be fun to learn something new, that's all."

"And fun learning it from Griffin Rutledge, no doubt."

"Now that you mention it, yes. I've never met anyone from Charleston. I enjoy talking to him."

Nate grabbed the cash box and shoved it into the safe by the back door. He spun the dial and drew the curtains closed. "I thought we had an understanding."

"This has nothing to do with us." Even as she spoke the words, she was filled with doubt. Was that really true? To hide her confusion, she rummaged in her pocket for her room key.

"Tell you what," Nate said. "Go ahead and keep company with that reprobate if you want to. I don't care anymore."

"Thank you for giving me permission."

"If you loved me, you wouldn't have to think twice about turning down his invitation."

"Does loving one person mean having to cut everyone else out of your life?"

"No, just other men who have an obvious interest in you. If you're starved for conversation, talk to Mariah. Or the women at the Verandah."

"I assure you, Mr. Rutledge has no romantic interest in me whatsoever. And even if he did, nothing would come of it. He doesn't intend to stay here long."

"People change their minds."

She pressed her fingertips to her tired eyes. "Please don't be cross with me, Nate. He was only being polite."

Nate jammed his hat onto his head. "Go ahead and pretend that's true if it makes you feel less guilty."

He motioned her out the door and locked the shop.

Griff reined in his hired horse and peered at the crude wooden sign nailed to a tree beside the road. Beneath the tangled undergrowth, a narrow rutted lane led deeper into the thick stand of timber. The bloated carcass of a possum lay rotting just beyond the intersection.

Griff looked around. This was the road to the gambling hall in Two Creeks? He urged the horse onto the path. A couple of miles farther on, the road widened to reveal a row of shanties on either side. Boarded-up windows, half-naked children running wild, a knot of old men smoking on a collapsed front porch bespoke the coloreds' plight. He could imagine that what little money found its way to Two Creeks quickly found its way out, tucked into the pockets of cardsharps and con men.

At a bend in the road, he crossed a wooden bridge spanning the wide creek and saw the gambling house, a ramshackle, tin-roofed affair perched on stilts above the sluggish brown water. A couple of horses stood tethered at the rail out front. A rig he supposed was Rosaleen's waited at the side door. He reined in, dismounted, and pushed through the door.

The air was still and thick with tobacco smoke and the smell of unwashed bodies. An ebony-skinned man behind the bar looked up, nodded, and went back to polishing a shot glass. At a pine table in a corner, two men sat drinking and talking, their hats pulled low, hiding their faces.

The side door opened, and Rosaleen swept in. Dressed in a dark blue satin dress and feathered hat, she put him in mind of an exotic flower growing in the midst of a weedy patch.

"Griff. You came. I wasn't sure you would."

"I said I'd be here." He motioned her to the table. "Sit down. Let's get this over with."

She perched on the chair, opened her reticule, and took out a new deck of cards. "I expected a bigger crowd than this. Shall we ask those two gentlemen to join us?"

"It won't be much of a game otherwise."

He watched her stroll to the other table. She bent and whispered to one of the men. The two got up and followed her back to Griff's table.

"Gentlemen," Rosaleen said, "this is Griff Rutledge, one of the best card players between here and New Or—um, Texas."

The taller of the two nodded and sat down across from Griff. "I heard about you. You're the feller intendin' to ride some fancy horse in that race this fall."

"That's right." Griff eyed Rosaleen as he shuffled the deck and cut the cards. "What's your pleasure, gentlemen?"

"You ever played triple-draw poker?" The other man's chair scraped the wooden floor as he sat down.

Griff kept his expression impassive. "A time or two. Deuce to seven?"

"Fine by us."

Griff dealt the first hand. The Negro barkeep wandered over with four glasses. Without even tasting the liquor, Griff knew it had been watered down. In the past he'd have insisted on a decent shot of liquor, but along with his loss of interest in gambling, he'd lost his taste for strong drink too. He waved away the drink and took up his cards. Across from him, Rosaleen studied her hand and chewed her bottom lip.

"I'll take two cards." Her rings flashed as she tossed away her unwanted cards and scooped up the ones Griff dealt.

"How about you gentlemen?" he asked.

"Gimme two," said the taller one.

The other one shook his head. "Reckon I'll keep the ones I got."

After several rounds the taller gambler tossed his cards onto the table. "I'm out."

"Me too." The other one tossed his cards onto the table and shook his head. "If it weren't for bad luck, I'd have no luck at all."

The door opened and two colored men came in, laughing and joking. They stopped stock-still at the sight of Rosaleen, their expressions full of curiosity. Griff knew how they felt. The first sight of Rosaleen was bound to throw any man for a loop.

Griff tapped his cards and raised a brow. "Miss Dupree? You in?"

"Just a minute. I'm thinking." She drummed one finger on the table.

He tamped down his impatience. "What'll it be?"

"I believe I'll raise you." She opened her reticule and tossed another bill onto the table.

"You're sure?"

Her emerald eyes flashed. "Are you going to play or talk?"

The taller of the gamblers leered at her. "If you ain't a pistol. Why I bet you'd be——"

"Pardon me, sir. You're interrupting the lady's concentration." Griff tossed another ten dollars onto the table and watched her eyes go wide. She was definitely in over her head. He almost felt sorry for her, until he remembered how they'd arrived at this point in the first place.

She slumped in her chair and tossed her cards onto the table. "All right, Griff. You win."

He raked the pile of cash to his side of the table and pocketed it without counting it. "Get your things. I'll ride along with you, see you safely back to town."

She eyed the lanky gambler, who had returned to the bar for another drink and was now studying her intently from beneath the brim of his hat. "I think I'll stay awhile."

He grasped her arm. "You'll do no such thing. You're coming with me. You don't belong to that life anymore."

"Maybe I do." Her voice wobbled. "Maybe that's all I'm meant for. Anyway, I have no choice now. I'm broke, and I have to pay the rent somehow."

"Where have I heard that story before?" Griff felt a tightening in his chest. For years he'd thought about how satisfying it would feel to collect this debt—fit retribution for her having played him for a fool. But somehow all he felt now was pity and sadness. And self-loathing that he had raised the stakes when he was certain she held a losing hand. He drew a wad of bills from his pocket and pressed them into her hand. "Here's your rent money."

"I don't want it. I'm sick of being beholden to you, of being tracked down like I'm a criminal or something."

"Consider it a gift. As of right now, your debt is canceled."

"But you said you needed the money."

"It turns out I don't need it as much as I need my self-respect." He waved one hand around the sleazy gaming house. "I can't leave you here. You ought to take that money and buy a ticket on the next train out of Hickory Ridge."

"I'm not leaving town." She stuffed the bills into her bodice and picked up her reticule. "Not until I find what I came here to find."

TEN

Her stomach taut with nerves, Carrie slid her key into the lock and entered the bookshop. Today was the first meeting of the ladies' book discussion society, and she'd been awake all night worrying about it. Would anyone actually attend? She'd posted notices at the mercantile and the Hickory Ridge Inn and invited everyone at the Verandah—Mrs. Whitcomb, Lucy Whitcomb, Rachel Ryan, Rosaleen, and even the elderly Provost sisters who spent their days sequestered on the third floor. She didn't expect the ancient ones to actually attend, but she couldn't be impolite and not invite them.

It was disappointing that Lucy would not be able to leave the Grayson children long enough to attend, but at least the young woman had kept her job. Carrie liked Lucy's ready laugh and sharp mind. Her intelligence and patience would make her an excellent teacher. If the Hickory Ridge school reopened before Lucy headed for her new life in Montana, Carrie intended to recommend her for the post.

She set a basket of freshly baked cinnamon rolls on the counter and went to the back room to make coffee. Nate had left everything ready for her. The coffee grinder and a sack of beans waited beside a jug of fresh water and the blue enameled pot that was kept filled any time the shop was open.

She ground the beans and dumped them into the pot, lit the stove, and set the pot on to boil. She set out a saucer of milk for India and opened the curtains to the bright August sunshine. Through the dusty window she watched the activity on the street. A few farm wagons waited outside the mercantile. Mr. Gilman, in a gray striped suit and felt bowler, arrived for his morning shave at the barbershop. Molly Scott, the mayor's wife, hurried into the dress shop and came out almost immediately with a box tucked under her arm.

Watching her, Carrie's eyes welled up suddenly, remembering their conversation at the Founders Day picnic back in July. Mrs. Scott had confided that her newly married daughter was expecting a baby. Carrie offered congratulations, but her insides burned with envy. All her youthful dreams had been so simple—a home, a husband, children to guide and to love. How had such modest aspirations eluded her?

True, Nate said he wanted to marry her. But the longer she delayed setting a date, the more uncertain of her feelings she became. These days she and Nate seemed always to be at cross purposes. Perhaps it was a sign they weren't truly meant for each other. But if they weren't, what other chance did she have for happiness? Would she end up old and alone, living out her days at the Verandah like poor Mrs. Athiston?

The bell above the door sounded, and Rosaleen and Mrs. Whitcomb arrived together. Carrie pushed back her dark thoughts and put on a welcoming smile.

"You've been busy, Carrie." Mrs. Whitcomb looked around the tidy shop, at the gleaming woodwork and neat rows of books. "The last time I was here, the place was a mess."

"That's why Nate hired me."

Mrs. Whitcomb plopped into one of the chairs Nate had brought over from his house for the occasion. "I'd say he got his money's worth."

"Where *is* Mr. Chastain this morning?" Rosaleen purred. She flipped open her fan. "I haven't seen him since he brought another stack of books to the Verandah last week. I declare that man knows about every book that ever was written. I find every single conversation with him utterly fascinating."

Carrie rolled her eyes toward the flyspecked ceiling. Rosaleen hung on every word Nate spoke, feigning interest in every book he mentioned. It was annoying as mosquitoes in July, but Nate seemed to revel in the attention. Couldn't he see through that woman?

"I'll tell him you said so." Carrie shelved a couple of books Nate had left on the table. "Or you can, when you drop in to pay your bill."

"My . . ." Rosaleen's eyes widened. "But I thought, I mean, weren't the books a gift?"

"One or two, maybe, but not all of them. The bookshop must turn a profit, you know."

The aroma of the coffee drifted through the sunlit shop. Carrie raised the windows and peered out at the street. Where was everyone? She had at least expected her friends from church to come. Given the sporadic nature of services these days and the demise of the quilting circle, surely Mariah and the others were starved for somewhere to go and someone to talk to.

"Carrie?" Mrs. Whitcomb blotted her face with her handkerchief and flipped through a book of poems. "Despite this heat, that coffee sure smells inviting."

Carrie turned from the window. "I'll pour some. And I made rolls this morning too."

"I thought I smelled cinnamon when I woke up this morning." The hotelier smiled. "You're welcome in my kitchen anytime, Carrie Daly, as long as I get first claim on the leftovers."

Carrie went to the back, poured coffee, and uncovered the plate of rolls, trying not to feel disappointed at the poor turnout. Well, this was the first meeting, after all. And a book society was a new idea that perhaps took some getting used to. If only Ada Caldwell were here. Ada was a voracious reader, forever writing to Carrie about whatever book she happened to be devouring at the time. And Lillian—she would certainly have livened things up. Wyatt Caldwell's late aunt had an opinion about everything, and she hadn't been shy about sharing any of them.

Carrie served the refreshments and picked up her copy of Thomas Aldrich's *Marjorie Daw and Other People*, which featured the cleverly written short story that the Memphis book club ladies were raving about. Written in the form of letters between a Mr. Flemming and his friend, Mr. Delaney, it was a delightfully humorous meditation on just how easy it was to become enamored with the very notion of being in love. It was just the sort of story to get the ladies talking.

The shop door opened, and a woman in a yellow calico dress swept in, her parasol dangling from one arm. "Is this the ladies' book discussion society?" she trilled. "I'm not too late, am I?"

Carrie looked up. Her stomach clenched.

"Hello, Mary."

✑

Griff dismounted and led Majestic around the pasture, delaying permission for the horse to return to the barn. Majestic's time around the training track was getting better and better. But Griff had noticed that the minute he slid from the saddle the horse headed for the barn, eager for his work to be done—a habit Griff intended to discourage. From his pocket he produced a carrot for Majestic and continued a slow circuit of the pasture while Majestic munched contentedly.

A blue jay sailed into the trees, calling noisily, its sapphire-colored wings shimmering in the light. Majestic blew out and snorted. Griff patted the colt's sleek side. "All right, boy. We'll call it a day. You've earned it."

He dropped the reins, turned his back on the horse, and clicked his tongue. Majestic responded with a soft whinny and walked along beside Griff.

Griff grinned. One of the things he loved most about

Thoroughbreds, aide from their trainability and desire to run, was their affinity for people. He and Majestic were coming to an understanding. They would make a fine pair come Race Day.

The scent of late-summer leaves drifted across the pasture as he and Majestic neared the barn, triggering a memory of a summer in Charleston when he was a boy, abed with aching lungs and a raging fever. His mother had bathed his forehead with rags wrung out in cold water and read all his favorite stories, though he was so sick he heard them only dimly through his febrile fog.

When his fever finally broke, Charlotte Venable Rutledge dropped to her knees beside her son's bed, sending up prayers of thanksgiving for his deliverance. The next week, as Griff regained his strength, she read stories from the Bible. Noah and the Ark, David and Goliath, and Jonah and the whale had been his favorites. Later he'd read the story of Jacob and his immediate attraction to the beautiful Rachel, an attraction so strong he'd worked seven years for a chance to claim her.

He'd thought of that story last week when he stopped by the bookshop and spoke with Carrie Daly. Griff wasn't much of a believer in true love, certainly not in love at first sight. But he couldn't deny he felt something powerful pass between him and the lovely Mrs. Daly every time they met.

He shook his head. So what if they were attracted to each other? There was no future in it. He was headed to Australia. He'd heard that she was headed to a life with the bookseller. Besides, the moment a man fell in love, complications set in, and he was in no mood for complications.

⁓

Carrie forced a smile. "Come in, Mary. You're not too late."

Henry's new wife swept into the bookshop and looked around.

"Oh dear. I'm not the only one who showed up, am I? Oh, how mortifying for you, Carrie."

Mrs. Whitcomb drew herself up. "Mary Stanhope. Did you mistake me for a piece of furniture? You most certainly are not the only one. Me and Rosaleen can hardly wait for the discussion to begin." She winked at Carrie. "The two of us, plus Carrie, of course, are charter members of the Hickory Ridge Ladies' Book Society."

Carrie could have hugged the older woman. She grinned at Mrs. Whitcomb.

"Charter members?" Mary perched on the edge of her chair and arranged her skirts.

"It's a very exclusive group," Rosaleen put in. "By invitation only."

"I'm sure. But I'm family, so of course I'm charter too." Mary snapped her fan open and motioned to Carrie. "Mercy, it's hot! Still, that coffee smells good. And the cinnamon rolls. Bring me some, please."

Carrie poured the coffee and passed the plate of rolls to her sister-in-law, striving to maintain a firm rein on her temper. Mary had usurped her home and her brother. Wasn't Carrie entitled to anything of her own?

She opened her book and read the opening pages. Rosaleen laughed at the description of the hapless Mr. Flemming slipping on a lemon peel and of his doctor's dire assessment of the poor man's mental state.

"The best part is Mr. Delaney's descriptions of Marjorie," Mrs. Whitcomb said when Carrie finished her reading. "I like the way he described her as 'enchanting in the summer twilight.'" She let out a hearty laugh. "I realize Marjorie is only imaginary, but it still makes me jealous. I don't reckon I've ever once been called enchanting."

Mary frowned. "Let me get this straight. There really *was* no Marjorie Daw? She was just a made-up lie?"

"I wouldn't exactly call her a lie," Carrie said. "She was more of . . . an invention, to keep Mr. Flemming's spirits up while his broken leg healed."

"Well, I think it's a stupid story." Mary opened her bag. "The announcement said to bring your favorite book, so I brought this—"

"Excuse me, Mary, but I was here first." Mrs. Whitcomb fished a book from her bag and set on the table. "Any of you read *Lady Audley's Secret*? My sister down in Georgia sent it to me, and I must say I found it quite sensational."

"In what way?" Carrie sipped her coffee and sent the hotelier a grateful smile. The woman had certainly put Mary in her place.

"Imagine a woman who seems a perfect wife and mother," Mrs. Whitcomb said, "but she winds up a bigamist and a murderer. Shocking."

"To say the least." Rosaleen's fan stirred the hot summer air.

"This Lady Audley, for her own selfish reasons, abandoned her own child." Mrs. Whitcomb shook her head as if the story had come straight from that morning's newspaper. "Disowning a child is worse than murder if you ask me."

Rosaleen blanched and got to her feet. "Perhaps she thought she was doing the right thing! Perhaps she had no choice. People ought not to form opinions about others until they have all the facts."

Thinking of Griff and of the way some people in town judged him, Carrie nodded. "I couldn't agree more."

"Thank you, Carrie." Rosaleen turned back to Mrs. Whitcomb. "It's easy to say what someone else should or shouldn't do, but it's harder when you are the one who must decide."

"No need to get all upset," Mrs. Whitcomb said. "Land's sakes, Lady Audley isn't real. She's merely a character in a silly novel."

"Would anyone like more coffee?" Carrie rose to refill their cups. The train whistle pierced the silence.

"That'll be the eleven o'clock from Nashville." Rosaleen retrieved her parasol from the pine table by the door. "I'm expecting a package that should have arrived last week. I must go and check with the station agent."

"I should go too," Mrs. Whitcomb said, "in case there are any ladies arriving on the train who need a place to stay." She patted Carrie's shoulder. "I had myself a right good time today, Carrie. That Marjorie Daw is some story. I can't wait to read the rest of Mr. Aldrich's book."

"I'm glad you enjoyed it." Carrie gathered the coffee cups and folded the blue-and-white striped towel she'd used to cover the rolls. "I had fun too."

"What about me?" Mary looked up at them. "We haven't talked about my book yet."

"Next time," Mrs. Whitcomb said, "it'll be your turn to go first."

"But—" Mary held out her book, urging the older woman to take it.

Rosaleen hurried to the door. "Carrie, I'll see you back at the Verandah."

The two women left the bookshop, jingling the bell above the door as they went.

"Well, I have never been so embarrassed in my life." Mary tucked away her book and followed Carrie to the back of the shop. "First, you invite that unsavory Mr. Rutledge to *my* wedding. Then you show up with him to move out of the house, which was mean of you, considering the amount of work there is to do every day. Then you move to that dingy old hotel. And now you're socializing with Mrs. Whitcomb and that . . . that . . . *woman* as if she were a respectable sort."

"Rosaleen is quite a flirt, granted, but she is respectable, as far as I can tell."

"As far as you can tell? And what do you know about such women, Carrie? You've hardly set foot out of Hickory Ridge."

Carrie emptied the grounds from the coffeepot and set it back on the stove. "Whereas you are a woman of the world."

"Well, I—I've been to Memphis, and Knoxville once, and . . . well, lots of places."

"Good for you. Excuse me." Carrie busied herself wiping a shelf that didn't really need it. Otherwise she might actually strangle Mary Stanhope. Bell. That her beloved Henry had actually married this harridan hit her again like a punch to the stomach.

"If you won't do it for me, do it for the boys."

"What?" Carrie's hands stilled. She stared at Mary, at her milky face and pale eyes. "What are you talking about?"

"What I'm talking about," Mary said with exaggerated patience, "is stopping this silly stunt you've pulled, move back to the farm where you belong, and stop embarrassing us."

"Us?"

"Henry and me. We want the boys to have a chance to be somebody in this town. It won't happen if you keep on acting like this. Living at the Verandah, working as a common shop girl, associating with that empty-headed Rosaleen."

"She may dress fancy, but that doesn't mean she isn't smart."

Mary sighed. "It is possible, I suppose, that the woman's brain is a veritable storehouse of knowledge, but the way she acts, who can tell? And anyway, I'm less worried about her than about your keeping company with Mr. Rutledge."

"Keeping . . . ?" Carrie laughed. "I'm not sure where you're getting your information, Mary, but I assure you I am not keeping company with him."

"This is Hickory Ridge. People talk."

"When they'd be better advised not to."

Mary shrugged.

"The way things are going, by the time Joe and Caleb are grown, Hickory Ridge will be a ghost town and all your efforts will be for naught." Carrie pointed her finger at Mary. "You'd better hope people come here to watch Mr. Rutledge ride that horse. You'd better hope that they spend lots of money while they're here and that some rich businessman decides he'd like to set up shop here." Frowning, she peered at her sister-in-law. "Are you angry because we didn't discuss the book you brought?"

Mary began to weep. "I couldn't care less about your stupid book society. I only came here to talk some sense into you, but I should have known you'd be mean and unreasonable. I swear, I don't see how your brother turned out so sweet and kind, and you're so . . . so . . ."

Carrie folded her arms and leaned against the book shelves, waiting for the waterworks to subside.

At last, Mary sniffed and fumbled for her handkerchief. "Go ahead then. Do what you want. But Henry and I will never speak to you again."

"Don't presume to speak for my brother. Except for the short time I was married to Frank Daly, Henry and I have been alone in the world, dependent on each other since we were children. Blood ties are thicker than water and always will be." She shoved a book onto the shelf. "And I would appreciate it if you'd stop paying attention to idle gossip. A lady's tongue should be an influence for good. Nothing positive can come from speaking ill of others."

Mary reddened and snapped her reticule shut. "I have to go. And don't expect me to come to the next meeting of your pathetic little book society. I wouldn't step foot in here again if you paid me, and neither will any other respectable woman in Hickory Ridge." She laughed. "One old woman, one of questionable character, and you. Charter members. What a joke."

Mary flounced away, her fan dangling from her wrist, and slammed the door on her way out.

ELEVEN

"Thank you for your purchases. Please call again on your next trip to Hickory Ridge." Carrie smiled at the well-dressed man and his little girl and handed them their wrapped packages. The gentlemen had chosen a book of poetry and a handsome edition of Mr. Dickens's *A Tale of Two Cities*. His daughter selected *Little Women* and *Snow-Berries: A Book for Young Folks*. Clutching her package to her chest, she smiled up at her father with such complete delight that Carrie couldn't help smiling too. No wonder Nate loved bookselling.

The pair left the shop. Carrie returned a couple of books to the shelf, finished arranging the flowers Lucy had picked from the Verandah's back garden, and regarded the results with a contented sigh. She could imagine a life here with Nate and their books. And running the shop made her feel useful again.

Sunlight streamed through the front window, casting a warm glow over the burnished wooden counter and the tidy rows of books. India jumped onto the counter, nearly overturning the vase of fragrant pink roses and bright yellow daisies. Carrie nuzzled the cat. "Mrs. Nathaniel Chastain. What do you think, India?"

The cat blinked her amber eyes and mewed. Carrie laughed. "So you approve?"

Carrie mopped her face and downed a glass of water before

returning to her work on Nate's ledger. Maybe he was right and it was time to go after what was attainable. Set a date for a wedding and stop wishing for the moon.

The bell above the door sounded, and Nate came in. He tossed his hat onto the table beside the door and looked around, shaking his head in wonderment. "Every time I come back in here, I am amazed all over again." He leaned over and kissed her cheek. "You've done a fine job with the shop. The flowers sure do gussy up the place."

She nodded. "But my ladies' book society wasn't as successful as I hoped."

"Give it time. That was only your first meeting. Mrs. Whitcomb sure enjoyed it. Miss Rosaleen too. She told me so just this morning."

Carrie arched her brow. Lately Nate seemed to be spending a lot of time at the Verandah, even when Carrie was busy at the bookshop. "You took some more books to her?"

He blushed and raked one hand across his beard. "Well, yes. She's new in town and doesn't have many friends." He headed toward the back of the shop to help himself to coffee. "Some people look down on her, I reckon, because of the fancy way she dresses and her skill with card games and such."

True enough. Hadn't Mary Stanhope practically called Rosaleen a loose woman? Still, Carrie didn't love the idea that Nate had appointed himself as her welcoming committee.

"Miss Rosaleen seems to enjoy the books so much." He reappeared with cup in hand. "Just this morning we were talking about—"

Carrie sighed. Enough about Rosaleen. "Nate?" She put a hand on his arm. "I've been thinking, and there's something important I wish to discuss."

He grinned. "What a coincidence. I was just about to say the same thing. I'm on my way to the bank, but I stopped in here to ask you something."

"What is it?" She set India on the floor.

"I'm going to Chicago for a few days, and I was wondering if you'd take care of the shop while I'm away. I'll pay you for the extra hours." He sipped his coffee.

"That isn't necessary. I love working here. I'll be glad to look after things. When are you leaving?"

"This evening, actually. On the six o'clock train."

"This evening? So suddenly?"

He nodded. "Things happened rather fast. I'm on the way to the bank to withdraw some funds. I should be back on Monday." He set down his cup and took both her hands, the familiar kindly expression shining in his eyes. "You will always have a part of my heart, Carrie girl. Don't ever forget that."

Alarm bells rang inside her head. This almost sounded like a final farewell. Was Nate gravely ill and on his way to see some specialist in Chicago? Suppose he was dying? If only she had taken Ada's advice instead of waiting so long to accept his proposal. At least they might have had a few years before he . . .

She squeezed his hands. "And you are dear to me too, Nate. But . . . is anything the matter? Are you all right?"

"Better than I've been in quite a while." He retrieved his hat. "After I stop at the bank, I must go home and pack. Can you close the shop for me this afternoon?"

Dazed by the sudden turn of events, she merely nodded.

At the door he turned back to her. "My lands, I almost forgot. What was it you wanted to talk about?"

She shook her head. "It can wait till you get back."

"All right then. See you Monday."

Carrie watched him jog across the street, tipping his hat to everyone he met until he reached the bank. He didn't *seem* sick at all. In fact, he looked downright giddy. Surely he wasn't planning to buy out another bookshop. She'd sold only a few of the volumes he had bought in Saint Louis.

Something was afoot. But what? What on earth had gotten into Nate Chastain?

～

The shriek of the six o'clock train sounded in the streets as Carrie prepared to close the shop for the evening. Though she was still unsure about her future with Nate, knowing he was aboard that train, headed for Chicago, left her feeling bereft. She set the cash box inside the wall safe in the back, twirled the dial, and picked up her hat and keys.

She was about to close the front curtains when a movement caught her eye. Someone was coming toward the bookshop. Her heart drummed against her ribs as recognition dawned. Henry.

Until that moment she hadn't let herself think about how much she had missed him. True, they'd run into each other a few times at the post office and the mercantile, but their conversations had been stiff and superficial and exceedingly brief. A gulf had widened between them, and neither she nor Henry seemed to know how to breach it. Tossing aside her keys, she wrenched open the door and threw both arms around her brother.

"Hello, Carrie." He smiled, and she noticed new worry lines at the corners of his eyes. Had she been the one to put them there? Did he hate her because of it? She felt as if she were ten years old again and about to be chastised for losing his prized fishing pole. And she hated that feeling of being on the outs with him.

"Could I come in?"

"Of course." She stepped aside and held the door open.

His gaze swept over the shop. "Looks real good, honey. I heard Nate has practically turned the place over to you."

"He hired me to get things organized."

"Mary said you started some kind of a ladies' book club too."

"I tried." She motioned him to a chair by the window. "Apparently there aren't as many book lovers in Hickory Ridge as I imagined."

"Times are hard. Most folks are too busy trying to survive to sit around discussing the latest novel."

His sharp words pricked her heart. Why couldn't Henry, above all others, understand what she wanted to accomplish? Still, she was glad to see him. Despite her growing contentment with her new life in town, a part of her missed the farm. Could she somehow make things right again?

She took the chair next to his. "How are things at home? How did our garden do this year?"

"Pretty good." Henry leaned forward in his chair, his hands clasped, "We had a lot of corn and tomatoes." He shook his head. "It very nearly overwhelmed Mary. And . . . well, that's why I'm here, Carrie Lou."

She sat up straighter. Any time Henry used her middle name, something was terribly wrong. He'd called her Carrie Lou when their parents perished, when Granny Bell died, when word about Frank Daly came from Shiloh. Her heart kicked. "What is it?"

"The sawmill owners showed up last week and let most of the hands go. Including me."

"Last week? And you didn't tell me?"

"I'm telling you now."

"But—"

"Would it have mattered? You've been furious with me ever since the wedding."

She dropped her gaze and smoothed the folds of her skirt. It was true that she hadn't completely forgiven him for not standing up for her against Mary's attacks. Had her brother chosen anyone else in Hickory Ridge for a bride, she would have welcomed a new sister with open arms, but Mary was too overbearing, too full of airs.

Carrie still didn't understand Henry's attraction to the woman.

And those ruffian sons of hers were the devil's own spawn. How could he bear their noise, their constant whining demands? Even so, her heart ached for Henry. He had a family to support, and now his job was lost. "I don't mean to blame you. It isn't your fault that Mary Stanhope and I are like oil and water. And I'm terribly sorry about the mill. I know you must be worried."

He nodded. "I've tried to find a job here in town, but so has every other mill hand. There's not enough work to go around."

He raked a hand over his tired face. Carrie noticed for the first time that his hair was thinning. Both she and Henry were getting older. Time was rushing by, and it would be a sin to waste it. She and Mary would never be friends, but for Henry's sake she would visit the farm now and then. On Sundays, perhaps, after church. Once she and Nate were married, Nate's natural affinity for people and his gift for storytelling would act as a buffer between her and Mary. It wouldn't be easy, but she owed it to Henry.

Henry focused his gaze on the shelf of books behind her. "I'm leaving Hickory Ridge."

She stared at him, thunderstruck. "Leaving? But how can . . . why?"

"Sage Whiting says the railroad companies in Chicago are hiring men to work in the train yards, unloading freight. He says it's worth a try." Henry's voice cracked. "Easy for him to tell me to go, since he's kept his job for now."

"Then Mariah won't have to leave Hickory Ridge." As worried as she was about Henry's going, she felt relieved that she wouldn't lose her friend too. Even if Mariah had made herself scarce lately. "I will miss you every single day, but maybe it's for the best. Mary Stanhope doesn't know the first thing about running a farm. And you know how she covets fancy dresses and pretty things."

He nodded and sent her a rueful smile.

"Her aspirations are too big for a place like Hickory Ridge.

Just the other day she told me how hard she's working to make sure her boys get on in the world. I know you hate the thought of moving away, but they'll have many more opportunities in Chicago."

Henry rose and began to pace. "Have I been a good brother to you, Carrie?"

"What kind of a question is that? If you hadn't taken care of me after Mama and Daddy died, there's no telling what would have become of me. And when Frank was killed—"

"I need your help."

"I'm not sure how I can help in this situation, but—"

"As much as I want to, I can't take Mary and the boys with me. There isn't enough money for four of us to travel all that way, and even if I could afford the train tickets, where would we live?" His shoulders sagged. "Besides, it could take as long as a month to get hired—if I get hired at all. Hundreds of men are competing for the same chance. I need you to come home, Carrie. To help Mary and look after the farm."

Her stomach clenched. "Move back and live under the same roof with her and those rude boys of hers? You saw how they treated me, and you didn't do much to defend me."

"We got off to a rocky start, all right, but Mary is sorry for everything. She told me so herself."

"Oh, I'm sure she's sorry. Sorry that she's going to have to stop acting like the Queen of Persia and actually get her hands dirty keeping the farm going."

"It may be only for a few weeks. If I don't get the job—"

"Henry, please. I'm not ungrateful for all you did for me when we were children. I'd do most anything for you, in fact. But I have a life of my own now. True, I live at the Verandah, but it isn't so bad once you get used to it. I get along with the other residents. Mrs. Whitcomb is almost like the mother I never really had. And . . .

well, I've decided I've put Nate off long enough. As soon as he gets back from his trip, I'm setting a date for our wedding."

His eyes widened. "Are you? I'm glad of that. Nate is a good man. But you've waited years to marry. Can't you wait awhile longer?"

"I've only recently realized that Nate and I are perilously close to passing the prime of our lives. Every day that goes by is time we can never get back. I've spent all this time putting off my future, wondering whether something better might be around the next corner. But now—"

"You're refusing me. After all I've done for you, you're too busy with your own life to help your only blood kin when he needs it the most."

"You make me sound cruel and uncaring."

He clenched his jaw. "How else would you describe it?"

"Henry, if there is anything else I can do, anything at all, I will do it gladly. But—"

"You don't have to say anything else. I understand." He went to the door.

She followed him. "Please don't go away angry with me. I can't bear it."

"I'm not angry." He jammed his hat onto his head and wrenched the door open. "I'm disappointed."

Tears rolled down her face. Already her heart ached with grief for the loss of the vital bond that had existed between them. "I'm sorry."

"Congratulations on your forthcoming wedding. I hope you and Nate will be very happy."

"You will come to the ceremony?"

"Not likely. I'm leaving soon as I can find somebody to help Mary with the farm. Good-bye, Carrie Lou."

She watched through the window as Henry climbed onto his

wagon and drove away. At the same instant, Griff Rutledge emerged from the mercantile, his arms laden with packages, and started up the street.

Despite her sadness at losing Henry, the sight of Griff made Carrie's nerves jump. Watching his purposeful strides as he headed for the Hickory Ridge Inn, she felt the odd quivering in her insides returning. Something about him made her feel alive, excited, filled with possibility. She started after him, then chastised herself and sat down again. She was about to marry Nate. These inexplicable feelings for Griff simply would not do.

Finally she put on her hat, took up her keys again, and locked the shop. Regardless of Griff Rutledge's unsettling effect upon her emotions, her mind was made up. She was through with waiting for perfection. She'd settle down in Hickory Ridge with Nate. Forget all about the horse trainer, his soulful eyes and charming smile, and the way he made her feel.

TWELVE

Following the pungent scent of boiling cabbage and the rattle of silverware, Carrie headed to the kitchen. Mrs. Whitcomb stood over a bubbling pot, steam fogging her spectacles.

"Carrie. Looks like it's just you and me for supper tonight," she said. "Pull up a chair."

Carrie swept aside a deck of Rosaleen's cards and sat. "Where is everybody?"

"Rachel got a letter from her husband in North Carolina. He found a job—finally—and has sent for her. She tore out of here like the place was on fire."

"I don't blame her. They've been apart a long time."

"Too long. They say absence makes the heart grow fonder, but I don't think so. Even the best of marriages can come undone when people are apart too long." Mrs. Whitcomb ladled the cabbage into bowls and pulled a pan of cornbread from the oven. "Anyway, Rachel went down to Jeanne Pruitt's dress shop to pick out a new traveling dress, and Rosaleen went with her. They're going to the bakery later to buy a cake to celebrate."

Carrie picked up her spoon. "That's odd. When I passed the dress shop just now, I could have sworn the place was dark."

Mrs. Whitcomb sat down and dipped a piece of cornbread

into the soupy cabbage. "Maybe Rachel and Rosaleen are already at the bakery. Personally I hope they bring a peach pie instead of cake. I love peach pie, and the season's almost over. It's Lucy's favorite too."

Carrie tasted the cabbage and wrinkled her nose. Bland as dirt. If only she'd had time to bake a pan of biscuits or a blackberry pie. She reached for the pepper and shook a generous amount into her bowl. "Where is Lucy tonight?"

"At a meeting down at the town church. They're talking about the Christmas pageant."

"I miss having the pageant at our church. It's one of the things that makes Christmas real to me."

Mrs. Whitcomb buttered another piece of cornbread. "Remember the year Mrs. Lowell's orphans sang carols? That was the year it snowed knee-deep to a tall Indian."

Carrie grinned. "I remember. Wyatt Caldwell proposed to Ada that night on a sleigh ride to the top of Hickory Ridge. Can you imagine anything more romantic?"

"Wyatt Caldwell always had a flair for the dramatic. He was very lucky it snowed enough to get that sleigh of his out. I always felt the Lord himself had a hand in that." Mrs. Whitcomb chewed and swallowed. "I sure do miss having him around town."

"I miss Ada something awful." Carrie gave up on the cabbage and pushed her bowl away. "I doubt she and Wyatt can make another trip for a wedding so soon after Henry's."

Mrs. Whitcomb grinned. "You're getting married at last? Are you fooling me, girl?"

"I'm serious. Nate has been after me forever to set a date, and I've decided it's time."

"Oh?" The hotelier's brow went up. "I don't suppose your decision had anything to do with the amount of time he's spent hanging around here, talking to Rosaleen."

The niggling thought that Nate was getting too friendly with Rosaleen had in fact crossed Carrie's mind, but she refused to give it any credence. "Rosaleen is not Nate's kind of woman."

An explosion of laughter escaped Mrs. Whitcomb's lips. "If that's what you think, you've got a lot to learn about men."

"Aunt Maisy?" Lucy called. "Anybody home?"

"In the kitchen." Mrs. Whitcomb hove to her feet to serve up another bowl of cabbage.

Lucy came in, frowning. "For mercy's sake. Cabbage *again*? Hello, Carrie."

"Maybe you'd rather waste a dollar and have dinner at the inn," her aunt said.

Lucy tossed her hat onto the back of her chair and plopped down. "Yes, I would love that, but every dollar I save brings me that much closer to my Jake and Montana." She took a bite of cabbage and made a show of swallowing it. "I'm eating this cabbage for a good cause."

Between bites, Lucy filled them in on plans for the Christmas pageant. "Reverend Patterson is asking Mariah Whiting to play the piano again this year." She picked up the pepper shaker and doctored her bowl of cabbage. "That is, if the Whitings are still in town by Christmas. Mr. Patterson said the mill owners let most of the men go last week, but they kept Sage on for now."

The cabbage sat like lead in Carrie's stomach at the reminder of Henry's plight and her refusal to move back to the farm. She walked over to the slop pail and dumped her bowl of cabbage into it. "I've had a long day. I'm going to bed."

"Don't you want to wait and see what Rachel and Rosaleen bring from the bakery?" Mrs. Whitcomb peered out the window. "They should be here any minute."

"I'm not very hungry."

"Go on to bed," Lucy said, waving her spoon at Carrie. "If what they bring is any good, I'll save you some."

In her room, Carrie got ready for bed and opened her Bible, but the words blurred on the page. Guilt and confusion knotted her stomach. Was she wrong to want happiness for herself? Wrong to marry Nate when she felt something—she wasn't certain just what—for Griff Rutledge? Her attraction to him made no sense at all. They were practically strangers, and he was merely passing through. What was the point of wanting what could never be hers?

⁓

Griff led his hired horse into the livery and handed the reins to the proprietor, a skinny fellow with a scraggly beard and piercing black eyes. "Thank you, Mr. Tanner. I'll see you tomorrow."

"Sure thing, Mr. Rutledge." Tanner spat a stream of tobacco juice into the street. "Will you be wantin' her again tomorrow?"

"I expect so." He nodded toward the chestnut mare. "You might check her left back foot. She seemed to be favoring it some on the way home today. Shoe might be a little loose."

Tanner nodded, scratched his belly, and jerked his thumb toward the front of the livery. "Didja see my new sign?"

Griff leaned back to read it. "Excelsior Stable, H. Tanner, Prop. Horses, Buggies, Hacks, and Harnesses for sale or rent. Horses boarded by the month, day, or single feed. Hack, horses, and Careful Driver available at rates to suit the times. That's quite some sign, Mr. Tanner."

Tanner spat again. "Charlie Blevins over at the mill made it for me. Cost me an arm and a leg, but I figgered it might be worth advertisin', with folks coming into Hickory Ridge for Race Day."

"Let's hope for a good turnout."

"How's the trainin' going?" Tanner removed the mare's bit and saddle and led her into a stall. "That black colt of Mr. Gilman's sure is a beauty."

Griff nodded. "He is. He's a challenge, though. Some days he spooks easily, and others he thinks he's in charge."

"You'll get that notion out of his head," Tanner said. "Folks say you're the best horse trainer in the country."

"I've my share of successes." Griff touched the brim of his hat. "I'll see you in the morning."

Leaving the livery, he jogged across the street and headed for the inn. Exhausted and grimy after a long day with Majestic, he looked forward to a bath and a hot supper. He pushed open the door and crossed the carpeted lobby to retrieve his room key.

The clerk handed him the key and a couple of letters and inclined his head toward the sitting area just off the lobby. "A visitor for you, Mr. Rutledge. He's been here most all day. I offered to send somebody out to Gilman's to get you, but he said he'd just as soon wait."

Griff tucked the mail into his breast pocket just as the man rose from his chair and crossed the lobby.

Griff regarded his younger brother with a mixture of astonishment and annoyance. "Philip."

Key in hand, he turned and headed for the stairs. "How long has it been? Five years? Six?"

"Closer to eight." Philip matched his steps to Griff's as they ascended the wide staircase. "You're looking well."

"Thanks, but I'm sure you didn't come all this way merely to remark upon my appearance."

"It's Father. He's quite ill. His doctors think it's his heart."

They reached the landing. Griff fitted his key into the lock. "I very much doubt that, old boy. Our father's heart is his least vulnerable spot."

He opened the door and motioned Philip inside, noticing that his brother had put on a bit of weight. His hair was graying too.

Perhaps the rigorous duties of a proper Southern gentleman were wearing him down. "How in the Sam Hill did you find me anyway?"

Philip frowned. "A Mrs. . . . . Gilbert?"

"Gilman."

"That's right. Anyway, she wrote to Mrs. Pinckney that you were here, acting as somebody's horse trainer." He grinned, revealing a glimpse of the sunny child he'd once been. "You know how the Charleston grapevine works. Mrs. Pinckney told Mrs. Allston, who told Mrs. Ravenel, who told me."

"I see." Griff tossed aside his key.

"Look, I know you're angry that Father plans to leave everything to me, but can you honestly say you want it? Especially now when all of South Carolina is still a ruin?" Philip plopped into the chair by the window. "The house in town is in dire need of a new roof, and the gardens have fallen into such a state, I can only be thankful Mother is not there to mourn them. You wouldn't even recognize the plantation. One of the winnowing houses is nearly down. The trunk gates are all broken. I'd sell, but who would buy it? There's no one to work it. It's worthless in its present condition."

Griff took the other chair and gazed out the window. His father's house in the city, spacious and elegant as it once had been, held no special charms for him. But the rice plantation on the Pee Dee was the site of the few truly happy memories from his growing-up years. The thought of that property passing out of Rutledge hands left him feeling unsettled. He toyed with a coin and set it spinning on the polished desktop. "No doubt River Place is a ruin after all these years. But by the saints, Philip, it's our family's ruin, and I expected to have some say in what happens to it."

Philip scratched his head. "Well, this is a surprise. First time I've seen any hint of sentiment from you."

"I always loved River Place more than anywhere else. Except Pawley's Island."

"Father sold the island cottage right after Mother passed on. He said it was a business decision, but I think it was too painful for him, holding on to the place that was Mother's favorite."

Griff smiled, remembering. "Even as she complained mightily about the inconveniences of getting there."

Philip looked around the hotel room, and Griff saw it through his brother's eyes—the genteel shabbiness, the quaint, small-town attempts at elegance. "So this is where you're hanging your hat these days." Philip shook his head. "What's the matter? The cards are not falling your way?"

"I'm just passing through. After the horse race I'm off to try my luck in Australia. Ranching maybe."

"You? A rancher? You'll last all of ten minutes."

"Maybe. But it's no concern of yours."

Philip glared at him. "All I care about at the moment is Father. I see now that I shouldn't have come all this way to talk to you. Your heart is as unyielding as ever."

"A wire or a letter would have done just as well."

"I doubted you'd bother reading it. Aunt Alicia said her last three letters to you were never answered. It broke her heart."

"I'm very sorry for that. Aunt Alicia was a great lady. Aside from Mother, the greatest."

"You shouldn't have ignored her because you hate Father."

"I don't hate him. We simply never understood each other. It's best for both of us this way."

"I'm sorry to have troubled you. But I thought you should know Father is dying."

Griff shrugged. "We're all dying, little brother. Some of us faster than others, but dying nonetheless."

Philip's gaze hardened. "Do you ever let anyone into your heart, Griff? Or are you this unfeeling with everyone?"

Griff thought of the night in Two Creeks when he had forgiven

Rosaleen's debt. He had felt sorry for her, wanted to protect her, despite her duplicity. And Carrie Daly—that woman had somehow managed to lodge herself in his heart—not that his attraction to her was going anywhere. He was quite capable of tender feeling, even when there was no future in it.

Philip stood, rattling the coins in his pocket. "So long as I'm delivering family news, there's something else you ought to know. I've asked Susan Layton to marry me, and she has accepted."

"You don't say." Griff laughed. "So, Father and Thomas Layton will have their way after all. I suppose when one's aim is to join two parcels of land, any Rutledge will do."

"That isn't fair, Griff. I happen to think very highly of Susan. She'd have made a fine wife for you, as I know she will make for me."

Griff leaned back in his chair and laced his fingers behind his head. "When's the happy day?"

"We haven't set a date. Susan wants to spend this winter with her cousins in Atlanta. We'll pick a date after Christmas. Not that it will matter to you."

Griff rose and offered Philip his hand. "I wish you and Miss Layton every happiness."

"I'm sure we will be." Philip consulted his pocket watch. "I still have time to make the last train. I can see my own way out."

Waves of guilt and regret pushed hard in Griff's chest. He clasped the younger man's shoulder. "Despite what you might think, I'm very glad to see you. And I apologize for sounding so harsh. It took courage to come here, knowing how I feel about everything. And, of course, I most sincerely hope for Father's recovery. Please tell him I said so."

Philip nodded and headed for the door. "Take care of yourself, Griff. Send me a letter from Australia. I promise not to return it unopened."

Griff parted the curtain and watched Philip hurry toward the railway station. Remembering their shared childhood he felt, despite the bad blood between them, a stab of affection for his younger brother. The news of their father's failing health and of Philip's impending marriage filled him with unexpected sadness.

Through the window he watched the banker lock the door and hurry to his waiting rig. Across the street, Mrs. Daly exited Chastain's bookshop.

He resisted the urge to go after her. Her intended, Mr. Chastain, had made his contempt for Griff quite clear. As drawn to her as he was, Griff didn't wish to cause Mrs. Daly any trouble.

He let the curtain fall and opened a letter from his friend in Australia. Warren had filled several pages with descriptions of his work at the seminary and a recent trip to the seaside, but the minister's glowing report failed to cheer him.

He tossed it aside.

How on earth had he wound up so utterly alone?

Carrie locked the bookshop and hurried along the street toward home. The last few days at the Verandah had been strange indeed. Though Lucy and Rachel had been much in evidence, Rosaleen seemed always to be somewhere else. On Sunday, while Rosaleen apparently slept in, Carrie attended the town church with Lucy. She liked the way Daniel Patterson wove a poem or the words of a hymn into his message and the quiet way his wife, Deborah, welcomed her with a nod and a smile at the beginning of the service. Though Deborah always slipped away as the benediction was read.

After church Mrs. Whitcomb joined them for an afternoon in the park. That night Carrie had heard footsteps in the corridor and the closing of doors, but neither Rosaleen nor Rachel had called out their customary good night. Perhaps they'd feared it was too late and they would wake her.

This morning she'd been the first one up and out the door. Nate was due home on the afternoon train, and she wanted the shop to look perfect. She puttered around dusting shelves that were not really dusty, going over the accounts that were already up-to-date— each transaction recorded in her own neat script—and hoping for customers. Helping them with their reading selections would surely make the time pass faster. But the shop remained empty all morning, the afternoon came and went, and still Nate hadn't returned.

Passing the mercantile on her way home, she nodded to a couple of women just exiting the store, their arms laden with packages. Surely Nate would return in time for dinner. Perhaps they'd splurge and go to the inn for steak and potatoes and his favorite lemon pie. Afterward she'd surprise him by setting a date for their wedding. Imagining his look of happy surprise brought a smile to her face. Now that she had made up her mind, let go of her girlish fantasies, she was eager to set her plans in motion.

She entered the Verandah just as the evening train arrived, the sharp sound of the whistle reverberating in the quiet streets. She called a greeting to Mrs. Whitcomb and mounted the steps to her room with the odd feeling that something was amiss. The hotel was too quiet—no muffled talk coming from the room of the Provost sisters, no Lucy pounding down the stairs, no Rosaleen dealing cards in the parlor. It was as if the entire place was holding its breath.

She shook her head to clear her apprehensions. She was merely overly excited, maybe even a bit nervous, awaiting the chance to tell Nate of her decision. When he got back, the old hotel would breathe again.

She tidied her hair, splashed a bit of lavender water onto her neck, and sank into her chair beside the window. The smell of boiling turnip greens and frying fatback drifted up the stairs, reminding her that she hadn't eaten anything since her two biscuits with jam at breakfast. Her stomach rumbled, but the prospect of more of Mrs. Whitcomb's food wasn't enough to rouse her from her chair.

Shouts and footsteps sounded in the street below. A woman laughed. Someone began singing loudly and slightly off key. A glass shattered. Carrie parted the curtain. Mill hands, no doubt, with a little too much liquor in their bellies.

Then the Verandah's front door crashed open, and Mrs. Whitcomb let out a surprised yelp. Carrie rushed down the stairs. When she reached the landing, she stopped stock-still, her skirt swirling about her ankles. She clutched the newel post, her heart kicking.

Nate Chastain strode into the foyer. Behind him, wearing a shimmering pink dress and a triumphant smile, stood Rosaleen.

THIRTEEN

Griff scrawled his signature at the bottom of the bank draft and sealed it for mailing. The Pinkertons' fee for finding Rosaleen had taken a healthy bite from his funds, and in the end he had forgiven the debt he'd come here to collect. What was the matter with him? Maybe he was losing the granite-hard resolve that had for so long served him well.

He collected his gloves, hat, and a couple of the sugar cubes he kept as special treats for Majestic. The train whistle emitted two short blasts, and he thought again of his brother's surprise announcement. Though marrying anyone merely to increase the Rutledges' land holdings was utterly ridiculous, he envied Philip. His brother would have a family. Somewhere to belong. Everything Griff had rejected in order to pursue life on his own terms.

He hadn't thought of Susan Layton in years. She wasn't a beauty. Her chin was too weak, her eyes too round and too prominent. But she had a trim, womanly shape, a sweet disposition, and a ready laugh. Like most young girls of her class, she'd been educated in the finer points of etiquette. She knew which fork was for pickles and which for fowl and how to chatter on for hours and hours about nothing more consequential than the weather. She had been taught to refrain from expressing her opinions, to be subservient to her man, dutiful in every way. Philip would have little cause for complaint. But what on earth would the two of them talk about?

He picked up his key and headed for the door. When his father had first broached the subject of Griff's marriage to Susan, Griff simply had not been able to imagine twenty, thirty, perhaps forty years of sitting opposite her at the dinner table with little more to say than "pass the salt" and "do you suppose it might rain?" He wanted a woman who shared his curiosity about the world, who knew what she thought about things and wasn't afraid to express it. Someone as open, as warm, and yes, as headstrong and opinionated as Carrie Daly.

He grinned to himself. She'd held her tongue when Nate Chastain had spoken for her that day in the bookshop, but just barely.

Even if she weren't promised to the bookseller, though, he had little to offer her. It might be months, a year perhaps, before things were sorted out at his bank in London and he had access to his funds. In the meantime, all she could look forward to was life in a series of hotel rooms, their fortunes dependent on whatever job he could find to supplement his dwindling bank account. She deserved better that that. Much better.

Downstairs, he nodded to the room clerk and headed for the post office. Maybe it was for the best. Maybe his father was right and Griff was not the marrying kind.

⁓

"Carrie girl."

Carrie stood still as death on the landing, staring down at Nate and Rosaleen. Above her, the ancient Provost sisters peered over the stair railing, each of them clutching a fan, cheeks bulging with dips of snuff. One of them rasped her name, but she had gone numb.

Mrs. Whitcomb hurried into the parlor, wiping her hands on her apron, her eyes hard as stones. "Rosaleen Dupree, where in the world have you been?"

Rosaleen laughed and tucked her hand into the crook of Nate's arm. "I've been to Chicago. And it's Mrs. Chastain now."

"Good heavens. You're married?"

Carrie sank onto the carpeted stair and wrapped her arms around her knees. The room swam before her eyes. Nate, married? To Rosaleen? It couldn't be true. And yet there he was, blushing and laughing as his new wife teased him before turning her attention to Mrs. Whitcomb, regaling her with details of the train trip, the ceremony in the judge's study, and their brief honeymoon stay at an elegant Chicago hotel.

Nate climbed the stairs and sat down beside Carrie, bringing with him the scents of cologne and whisky. He reached for her hand, but she pulled back as if the touch of his skin would burn her. How could he claim to have loved her and still be so careless of her feelings?

Humiliation, regret, and profound sadness overwhelmed her. Lately she had felt adrift in the world, with Nate as her only real tether. Now that tether had snapped. Yet who was to blame except her? If only she'd taken Ada's advice and married Nate when she had the chance.

"I know you're shocked," Nate said, his voice low. "And I'm awfully sorry to break the news like this. I'd planned on being back here sooner, having some time to talk to you before we made our announcement. But we were delayed in Chicago and—"

"You don't have to explain."

"Yes, I do. Please try to see things from my side. Lord knows, I don't want to hurt you. You're the finest woman I've ever known. But I've wanted a wife and a home of my own for the longest time, and it seemed like you weren't ever going to be ready."

She traced the dark floral pattern on the carpet with her

fingers. She had been ready to name a date, but what good would it do to tell him now? She studied his face, so dear to her and, at the same time, unknowable. She would have wagered her very life on his affection for her, but in the end he hadn't loved her enough to wait until she was sure.

"Carrie?" Nate's expression was a mixture of sadness and uncertainty. "Say something."

"I'm . . . stunned. I thought you loved me. I never dreamed you could change your allegiance so easily."

He blushed. "It caught me by surprise too."

Mrs. Whitcomb and Rosaleen headed for the kitchen. For several long minutes Carrie sat beside Nate, listening to the street sounds and the tapping of a tree branch against the parlor windows. Now that reality was slowly sinking in, she felt oddly calm and resigned. Maybe God had another plan in mind for her, one that didn't include a husband and a home. Just last week Reverend Patterson's sermon had been about surrendering to God's will. His way was surely the best. And yet, she was a flawed mortal who wanted what she wanted. And what she wanted always seemed to lie just beyond her reach.

Nate cleared his throat. "You're a fine woman, Carrie. But Rosaleen came along, and we got on so well together that it just seemed like it was meant to be, and . . ."

She laid a hand gently on his arm. "Congratulations, Nate. I truly hope you'll be happy. You deserve it."

"You're not angry with me?"

"I suppose I can't blame you for giving up on me." She managed a wan smile. "I'm confused. About a lot of things. But I'm not angry with you. What good would it do?"

He relaxed then. "I'm glad."

"I am surprised that you went all the way to Chicago when Reverend Patterson could have married you right here."

"That was Rosaleen's idea."

"I'm sure."

"She wanted a nice honeymoon away from people who might gossip about the two of us. How sudden it was and all."

"Don't think people won't talk now. They will. But you mustn't let it ruin your happiness."

Nate squeezed her hand. "I've never had a better friend than you."

"I feel the same. Maybe we were meant to be friends and not husband and wife."

"I sure hope the two don't turn out to be mutually exclusive. I reckon it'd be hard to go through life married to someone you didn't like." He shifted his weight on the narrow stair. "This doesn't have to change things at the shop, you know. You can go on working there, just as before. Only now we'll have Rosaleen to help too."

Carrie stared at him. It was the situation with Mary Stanhope all over again. Husbands and wives building their lives two by two, and Carrie the odd one out. "I don't think so," she said. "Having two women in charge of anything never works out very well."

"But Rosaleen doesn't know anything about running a bookshop. I thought you could teach her."

"You can teach her what she needs to know."

"What about your ladies' book society?"

"It wasn't much of a success." The realization still stung. She felt as if the women of Hickory Ridge had rejected her, not just her idea.

"But it might catch on," Nate said, "if you stick with it."

Just then Rosaleen crossed the parlor and hurried up the stairs, her pink skirts rustling. She nodded to Carrie and smiled at Nate. "I'm going up to pack the rest of my things. I won't be long."

Nate beamed at his bride. "Take your time, my dear."

Though Carrie was quickly becoming resigned to the situation, hearing Nate's endearment and seeing the adoring way he and

Rosaleen looked at each other was more than she could take. She got to her feet. "I must help Mrs. Whitcomb."

He rose. "Carrie—"

"I left a few of my things at the shop. I'll get them in the morning."

"I know this has been a shock. But I wish you'd take some time to reconsider."

"I could think on it a hundred years, but I won't change my mind."

"How will you earn a living?" Nate asked.

"I still have a few dollars. Now that Rosaleen won't be living here, perhaps I can work for Mrs. Whitcomb. She plans to fix the place up before the Race Day visitors hit town. She'll need help with scrubbing floors and washing curtains."

"Such work is necessary, but it's a waste of your intelligence."

She shrugged. "It's honest labor, no different than working the farm. Besides, with so many people around here out of work, I'll be thankful to have anything."

"True enough, I reckon. I heard your brother went up north to look for a job. How's he getting on? Any luck?"

Rosaleen appeared above them dragging a battered trunk and a smaller suitcase. "Nate honey, can you give me a hand?"

"Coming, sweetheart."

Nate bounded up the stairs, grabbed the luggage, and bumped it down the stairs. Rosaleen followed. When she reached Carrie, she put one arm about Carrie's shoulders and whispered, "I'm so sorry."

"Are you?" She and Rosaleen weren't exactly friends, but Carrie still felt betrayed. Had Rosaleen talked about her to Nate? Had they laughed about her together? Did Rosaleen feel sorry for her, the jilted would-be bride, or did she feel only triumph at having so easily stolen Nate away?

Carrie watched them leave the hotel. Arms akimbo, Mrs. Whitcomb turned to Carrie. "If this isn't a fine kettle of fish. I can't imagine what in the world possessed Nate Chastain. I thought the two of you were . . ."

Carrie shook her head. If she tired to speak, she might cry. And what use were tears?

"It don't make a lick of sense if you ask me." Mrs. Whitcomb made a *tsk-tsk* sound. "Well, I reckon it's not for me and you to figure out. God moves in mysterious ways, and this marriage surely must be the mystery of the ages."

Before Carrie could reply, Rachel Ryan hurried into the hotel, her eyes shining. "They did it. They actually eloped, and nobody suspected a thing."

Mrs. Whitcomb frowned. "What do you know about this deception?"

Rachel grinned. "It was just about the most romantic thing I ever heard. I had to help. So I made up the story about needing a new dress to cover for Rosaleen while she caught the train. It wasn't easy, slipping in and out all weekend, pretending she was here when she really wasn't. But we fooled everybody."

"You certainly did." Carrie turned. "Excuse me. I'm going up to my room."

"What's the matter with . . . oh mercy." Rachel clapped one hand over her mouth. "Carrie. I—you must feel simply awful! I never meant to—" Red-faced, she turned and fled.

"You haven't had any supper, Carrie." Mrs. Whitcomb put one arm around Carrie's shoulder. "I made a fresh batch of biscuits, and there's some ham left over from yesterday."

"I'm not hungry."

"Listen to me. This has been a shock, no two ways about it. But you must put your trust in the Lord. He always knows what's best for us, child, even when we think we know better."

"I know that." Hadn't her long-departed grandmother said the same thing?

Granny Bell had rarely ventured from her mountain cabin on the far side of Muddy Hollow. Small, wiry, and tough as a pine knot, she'd never learned to read or write, but she'd been a wellspring of common sense and unshakable faith. *"The Lord knows what he's doing, girl. He's the One that sees the big picture. Best wait on him to make the path clear."*

Carrie shrugged. Her own path seemed murkier than ever now.

"Please excuse me." She climbed the stairs to her room just as the train whistle shrieked. She sank onto her bed and closed her eyes. Henry was gone, swallowed up in the grit and noise of Chicago, and angry with her. And now Nate was lost to her too.

How much more disappointment and sadness can I take, dear Lord? If you have something better in mind, could you please let me in on it?

And soon?

FOURTEEN

In the small storeroom at the back of the bookshop, Carrie found an empty crate. She carried it to the front and set it on the counter. The sun came up, sending shafts of late August light through the closed curtains. Outside, except for the occasional passing rig or wagon, the street was quiet.

Moving quickly around the now-familiar shop, Carrie gathered the personal items that had accumulated since she'd come to work here—a lace fan, an umbrella, a chipped coffee cup. She intended to be long gone before Nate and Rosaleen arrived. Seeing the two of them together would be too awkward. It would hurt too much and feel like an intrusion upon their newly wedded bliss.

India vaulted onto the counter and poked her nose into the crate, meowing loudly. Carrie scooped up the cat and nuzzled her face. "I know, sweet girl. I'll miss you too."

Setting India on her feet, Carrie packed away the list of books she'd planned to recommend to the book society and a small leather-bound journal she'd been too busy to keep. India followed, mewing, her tail straight up in the air.

Carrie took one last look around, feeling as if she were once again leaving home, giving up something she'd had a part in building. Of course she could visit the shop anytime, but it would never be the same.

"Good-bye," she whispered to India. She lifted the crate and carried it outside, closing the door behind her. Blinded by tears, she ran smack into a man hurrying along the street, a bundle of clean laundry tucked beneath his arm.

"Oh, I'm so sor—mercy's sake. Mr. Rutledge."

The horse tamer touched the brim of his hat and smiled down at her. "Good morning, Mrs. Daly. You're up and about early."

She shifted the crate. "I'm moving these things to the Verandah."

"Is that so? It seems that every time we meet, you're moving somewhere." He grinned. "The proverbial rolling stone."

Her breath caught. Heavenly days, why did he have to look so utterly charming at such an early hour? The attraction she'd felt for him from the very beginning rushed over her like a rogue wave. Carrie felt herself smiling. "It does seem that way."

"Allow me." He reached for her crate and placed his bundle of laundry on top.

"That's kind of you, but I can manage."

"I'm afraid I must insist. How would it look if people saw me letting you tote your own things?"

"Very well. If it's a matter of preserving your reputation."

He threw back his head and laughed. "I'm afraid it's much too late to worry about my reputation. I'm a lost cause."

Carrie studied him as they started down the street. There seemed plenty about him that was worth saving, from his genuine concern for others to his way with horses and his impeccable manners. Not to mention his good looks. But Mr. Rutledge seemed resigned to his fate, cheerful about it even. Perhaps he cultivated his role as a charming rogue. Perhaps, deep down, he reveled in it, preferring isolation and disapproval to being merely ordinary. And Griff Rutledge was about as far from ordinary as a person could get. Whatever his motives, the fact remained: when he was around, she couldn't look away.

They reached the mercantile just as Jasper Pruitt came out with his broom, a wet rag stuffed into his back pocket.

"Good morning, sir." Griff nodded to Jasper.

The storekeeper narrowed his eyes and frowned at Carrie before spitting a stream of tobacco juice onto the street. He swept the sidewalk in front of his store, took the rag from his pocket, and washed the window till it gleamed, all without saying a word.

"You see?" Griff shifted the crate in his arms as they continued toward the Verandah. "Folks around here don't like me very much. Even the storekeeper disapproves."

"Don't judge everyone by Mr. Pruitt," Carrie said. "It takes him a long time to warm up to strangers."

They neared the barbershop and the bank. Mr. Gilman arrived just as they were passing. He jumped from his rig, tethered his horse at the rail, and waved Griff over.

"How's Majestic doing? I meant to get home in time yesterday to see you work him, but I got tied up here. Good morning, Miz Daly."

"Mr. Gilman." Carrie glanced down the street toward the bookshop and the sheriff's office at the opposite end of the street. All was quiet at the bookshop, but Eli McCracken reined in, unlocked his office, and disappeared inside. Two men waited outside the livery. Tantalizing smells emanated from the bakery. Everyone had something important to do, someplace to be. Except her.

". . . will be fine by Race Day," Griff said. "A bucked shin is common in young horses that aren't fully grown and are being trained heavily. I may have pushed Majestic a bit too hard."

"But he will be all right?"

"Absolutely. I've been resting him the last few days, working the soreness out. In another day or two he'll be fit as a fiddle."

The banker nodded. "I'm counting on you, Mr. Rutledge.

Only yesterday I received a telegram from the Winstons over in Lexington. Arthur Winston intends to enter Bold Prince in our little race. It would give folks quite a thrill if Majestic could beat that Kentucky Thoroughbred."

"I'll do my best."

A train chugged into the station, the engine heaving and hissing. A cloud of steam billowed upward into the trees. Mr. Gilman checked his pocket watch. "Reckon I ought to get to work. My teller's out with the grippe today. Good day, sir." He tugged the brim of his hat. "You too, Miz Daly."

Moments later Carrie and Griff reached the Verandah. Mrs. Whitcomb was up; the smells of coffee and fatback permeated the air. Footsteps, followed by girlish laughter, sounded overhead. Lucy and Rachel were awake too. Carrie dreaded facing them, but where else could she go?

"Where do you want this crate, Mrs. Daly?" Griff smiled down at her, his gaze full of admiring interest.

"The parlor will be fine. And thank you for your help. It was very kind of you."

"No trouble at all." He set the crate on the floor by the staircase. The parlor clock chimed the hour. "I suppose you'll be getting back to the bookshop. I understand you've become indispensible to Mr. Chastain these days."

Before Carrie could reply, Rachel and Lucy pounded down the stairs. They barely nodded to Griff before Lucy blurted out, "Carrie. I can't believe Mr. Chastain has up and got himself married. You must be heartbroken, you poor thing."

"So," Griff murmured. "That's why you moved your things."

"The nerve of him, running off like that and leaving you in charge of his store while he cavorted in a fancy hotel with his new wife." Lucy's eyes flashed. "I cannot believe someone as refined as Nate would marry a woman like Rosaleen."

"Rosaleen?" Griff barked the word, causing Carrie to jump. "The bookseller has married *Rosaleen Dupree?*"

Rachel gave an emphatic nod that sent her curls dancing around her face. "They eloped to Chicago. I helped."

"Saints in a sock." Griff shook his head before bursting into laughter. "The old girl has done it again."

"Done what again?" Rachel asked.

"Never mind. If you ladies will excuse me, I must be going." He nodded to Carrie and started for the door, shaking his head and muttering to himself. "Rosaleen, Rosaleen, what in the world are you up to now?"

FIFTEEN

Griff wiped sweat from his forehead and shaded his eyes against the brilliant late-August light. In the distance, a thick layer of gray-blue clouds hung like smoke above the mountains. The forested hillsides were a smudge of amber and green, a precursor to autumn color. An old ache rose in his chest, a longing for autumn in the Carolina low country, when the spartina grass undulated in the marshes like fields of wheat and the breeze off the Atlantic turned sharp and cool. Maybe the folks down there were already thinking ahead to their Race Week too.

Did they still hold such events? Probably not. He hadn't much of an idea what life in Charleston entailed anymore.

Leaning against the fence, Griff watched Majestic trotting through the pasture. The soreness he'd worried about had healed. Tail swishing, Majestic raced around the pasture, tossing his head as if he hadn't a care in the world. Griff blew on the tin whistle he'd bought from the mercantile. The resulting blast was not as loud as an actual train whistle, of course, but he hoped the sound would acclimate Majestic and cure the horse's skittishness in town. There was nothing worse for a rider than a mount who spooked at the starting line.

The sound of horses' hooves drew his attention. Carrie Daly

guided her rig along the road, her copper-colored hair beneath her smart straw hat shining in the light. He waved, and she drove up the long curving lane to the Gilmans' place.

Griff mopped his face with his handkerchief and ran his fingers through his windblown hair. "Mrs. Daly. What a wonderful surprise. What brings you all the way out here?"

She halted the rig and stepped out, smoothing her skirts as she crossed the short distance between them. "You do, Mr. Rutledge."

His brows went up. "Me?"

She nodded. "Some time ago you invited me to watch you training Majestic, but then I was not at liberty to accept. Now I am."

"I see." He stuffed his riding gloves into his back pocket. "This wouldn't have anything to do with Mr. Chastain, would it?"

Her eyes flashed. "Of course not. I've been curious about that horse ever since he nearly ran me down. So I rented a rig from Mr. Tanner's livery and came out to see for myself how you tame such a high-spirited mount."

Griff tried but failed to hide a smile. "The same way one tames a spirited woman, I reckon. With infinite patience and affection."

Carrie frowned. "Is that how you think of the fairer sex, Mr. Rutledge? As beasts to be molded to your will?"

He grinned. "Begging your pardon. A poor choice of words." His gaze traveled to the pasture, where Majestic stood cropping grass. "I'm about to give him some practice running with other horses." He gestured toward his own horse standing placidly at the gate. "Perhaps you'd like to ride with me."

He watched the color creeping into her cheeks. Was it wishful thinking? Had he embarrassed her with his comment, or had she taken a liking to him?

"I haven't ridden much since I was a child, and then it was only our farm horses. Maybe I'd better sit here and watch."

"Sit and watch? Now, there's a way to waste a perfectly good life. Where's your sense of adventure? It isn't that hard. Besides, you'll be riding behind me." The wind lifted her curls and set the ribbons on her hat to dancing. He couldn't help noticing how young and vulnerable she looked. "I won't let you fall, Carrie."

Her eyes widened at his use of her Christian name, and he was struck anew by her loveliness. Did she know how appealing she looked in her plain blue dress and straw hat, the sun lighting her face?

"I don't mean to be presumptuous," he went on, "but we have known each other for some months now. And I like the sound of your name. It reminds me of Carolina."

"My formal name is Caroline Louise. After my two grand-mothers. Henry's the one who first called me Carrie."

"Would you mind so much if I called you Carrie as well?" Mercy, but she smelled good—like fresh bread and fancy soap. And summer flowers. Jasmine maybe. He fought the urge to kiss her.

"I'd like that. If I may call you Griff."

"Please do." He tucked her arm through his, and they crossed the shady road to the gate where his horse stood. Griff gathered the reins, swung into the saddle, and reached for her hand. "Put your left foot—no, your other left foot—into the stirrup, and I'll help you up."

She managed to get a foothold and reached for his hand. He helped her up, pleased that she hadn't hesitated to swing her right leg over the saddle. She settled against him, her warmth pressing into his back. He turned his head to look at her over his shoulder. "All set?"

"I think so."

"Put your arms around my waist and hold on tight."

He kicked the horse into a gentle canter, and they crossed the meadow. Majestic lifted his head and danced sideways as they approached.

Griff slowed his horse to a walk and stopped alongside the black horse. "Easy there, Majestic. Easy now."

He leaned out and took Majestic's bridle, drawing the two horses closer together. Majestic blew out and shook his head. Griff laughed softly and rubbed Majestic's muzzle. "That's right. You've met Delilah here, haven't you, boy? You think you can take her in the quarter mile?"

Majestic stood still, muscles quivering beneath his velvet black hide. Griff felt Carrie's arms stiffen against his back. She was as skittish as the horse. "Relax, Carrie," he said, his voice low. "Don't be nervous or you'll spook him. He'll think you're afraid."

"I am afraid," she whispered. "It's a long way to the ground from up here."

He nodded. Keeping a firm hand on Majestic's bridle, he turned both horses until they faced a small pond at the end of the pasture. "We're going to start slow, then let them run. Hold tight."

He kicked Delilah into a canter. Majestic shied, then steadied and galloped alongside, his thick mane flowing behind him. Carrie leaned forward, both arms clamped tightly around Griff's middle, her cheek resting against his back. Griff urged Delilah on. The horses flew across the pasture, clouds of gray dust rising up around them. Consumed with an unexpected rush of joy, Griff laughed out loud.

Too soon, they reached the pond. Griff reined in, but Majestic suddenly wheeled and bumped them, sending Delilah scrambling for purchase on the pond's muddy edge. Instinctively, Griff twisted in the saddle to calm Majestic, and he felt Carrie losing her grip. "Hang on."

"I can't!"

He grabbed for her hand, but she slid sideways off the horse and landed with one foot in the pond. Her straw hat rolled across the grass and came to rest in a patch of tall grass. Griff dismounted and bent over her. "Are you hurt?"

"Only my pride." She sat up. "I'm a little winded is all."

He helped her to her feet, embarrassment and guilt coursing through him. Why had he been so stupid, wanting to show off for her? "I never should have talked you into this. I'm terribly sorry."

"I'm not." Carrie laughed and retrieved her hat.

He grinned, relieved. "You aren't angry with me?"

"Heavens, no." She brushed the dirt from her skirt. "This is the most fun I've had in years."

He picked up the reins and led the two horses toward the barn. With every step, Carrie's wet shoe squished, sending her into peals of laughter. Griff laughed too, wishing this moment never had to end.

He led Majestic into his stall and gave him a bucket of water. "I'll need to look after them in a minute, but I'll see you to your rig first."

Together they crossed the gentle slope leading to the hitching rail. He watched as Carrie took in the sweep of green pasture behind white fences, the towering trees dotting the broad lawn that led to the Gilmans' house. She turned to him, her lips slightly parted, her eyes bright. "Isn't this a wonderful place?"

"You've never been out here before?"

"Only in passing from time to time. I really never noticed how beautiful it is. I can imagine how lovely it would be to live here. Can't you?"

He studied her face. Was she fishing for clues, assessing his potential as a husband? After all, that cad Chastain had broken her heart. And the honest truth was, Carrie Daly was no longer a girl. He looked past her shoulder to the barn, now bathed in late summer sunlight. "It's a pretty place, all right. Good as any, if a man is the settling-down sort. But that isn't the life for me."

"I see."

Was she disappointed, or was he flattering himself? "I guess I was just born restless, Carrie. My father tried to settle me down.

I was in and out of boarding schools until I was nearly grown. But I always found some way to get myself dismissed."

"You're not the scholarly type then."

"Oh, I liked the classes well enough. And I made some good friends along the way. It was the rules and expectations I couldn't abide. I like to come and go without explaining myself to anyone."

She looked up at him, an odd light in her eyes. "What are you running away from, Griff?"

"Is that what you think?"

"It's what it sounds like to me."

"Well, you're wrong about that. I want to experience as much of life as possible, so I won't have any regrets when the candle finally burns down and flickers out. That's easier to do when other people aren't depending on me."

They reached the road. He helped her inside the rig and handed her the reins. "If you promise to come back, I'll—"

He broke off as another rig rattled along the road.

Carrie turned. "It's Mrs. Spencer and Mariah Whiting. I wonder what they're doing out here."

"They're probably wondering the same thing about you."

Mrs. Spencer halted the rig in the road. "Carrie Daly? I thought that was you, but then I said to Mariah, surely—"

Carrie hid her mud-caked shoe beneath her skirt and straightened her hat. "Hello, Eugenie. Mariah."

Mariah nodded, her expression wary.

"You remember Mr. Rutledge. You met him at Henry's wedding."

"We remember," Eugenie said.

Griff nodded and crossed his arms, waiting as Mariah took in Carrie's dusty skirt and hastily tied hat. "Mrs. Spencer, Mrs. Whiting. A pleasure seeing you both again."

"Carrie," Mariah said at last, "Do you think it's proper, being out here alone with someone we hardly know?"

Griff didn't wait for Carrie's answer. He smiled at both women and said, "I don't blame you for being concerned about your friend, but I assure you nothing untoward happened."

Eugenie sniffed. "I don't wish to be rude—"

"Then don't be." Carrie picked up the reins and smiled at Griff. "Thank you for the riding lesson, Mr. Rutledge. I quite enjoyed myself."

SIXTEEN

The flour bin in the Verandah's kitchen was nearly empty. Carrie sprinkled a scoop onto the wooden pastry board and made a mental note to remind Mrs. Whitcomb to buy more. After church last Sunday, Reverend Patterson had asked for volunteers to bake bread for several farm families who were having a hard time keeping food on the table, and Mrs. Whitcomb had signed her up. She finished kneading the dough and set it aside to rise. She'd have preferred being asked outright, but she was too grateful for something useful to do to make a fuss about it. Without her work at the bookstore, she felt aimless and unsettled.

At least there was plenty to do around the hotel, and she was grateful for the modest pay Mrs. Whitcomb offered. While she waited for the dough, she tidied the kitchen, filled the oil lamps, and swept and dusted the parlor. When the dough was ready, she lifted it from the yellow crockery bowl, punched it down, sprinkled on more flour, and picked up her rolling pin, Granny Bell's voice a whisper in her ear.

"Baking bread is a lot like growing your faith in the Lord, Carrie Louise. You mix together the best ingredients you can find and wait for the mixture to mature, but it's the heat of the oven that makes dough

into something of worth and of substance. The same way the tribulations of this world mature a person's faith."

Carrie fitted loaves into greased pans and placed them in the oven to bake, wincing as a sore muscle protested. The morning after her ride with Griff, she had noticed a fist-sized bruise ripening on her thigh. Now it was fading, but the soreness remained. Still, the exhilaration of flying along the pasture aboard Griff's horse, her arms wrapped around his firm middle, had been worth every bit of discomfort, even worth Mariah's disapproval. She'd needed that brief respite from the tribulations of her own life.

She wiped her floury hands on her apron and wandered toward the front of the house, thinking of everything that had happened since Henry's wedding. Was Granny Bell right? Could God use her hurts and disappointments to mold her into a woman of substance?

The clock in the parlor chimed. Lucy Whitcomb, hat in hand, slid down the banister and landed with a thump on the hallway carpet. She grinned at Carrie, a playful look on her face.

"It's a trick I learned from the Grayson kids. But don't tell Aunt Maisy. She'd have a conniption fit." Lucy retrieved her hat from the rack in the corner. "She thinks I should behave like a lady."

Carrie fought a stab of envy. Despite the difficulty of looking after so many children, Lucy seemed to be enjoying her life. Never in her own life had Carrie felt young and carefree.

"I'll show you how it's done sometime," Lucy said. "But not today. I'm already late. Save me a piece of your wonderful bread, all right?"

"It's for—"

"Charity. Right. Never mind." Lucy donned the straw hat and tied the bright green ribbons in a saucy bow beneath her chin. "I'm sure Reverend Patterson appreciates your help." She sighed. "If things don't improve around here soon, I'm not sure Aunt Maisy can afford to keep this place open. We may wind up needing charity ourselves."

She waggled her fingers and left, the screen door slapping shut behind her.

A rectangle of early September sunlight filtered through a chink in the heavy parlor curtains. Pushing them aside, Carrie stared onto the busy street, her thoughts a-jumble. If the Verandah closed, where would she live? What if Henry found work in Chicago? Would he sell the farm, leaving her without any place to hang her hat? Or suppose he left it all in her hands. How would she manage the plowing, planting, harvesting all alone?

Across the way, a man in a felt bowler entered the bank. Two mill hands emerged from the bakery carrying white paper sacks. Outside Jasper Pruitt's mercantile, a drayman halted his freight wagon just as Mariah Whiting came out, her arms full of packages.

Carrie felt a stab of guilt. She shouldn't have spoken so sharply to Mariah and Eugenie that day at Mr. Gilman's place. Despite their evident disapproval, she wanted their friendship. She glanced at the clock. The bread wouldn't be done for another few minutes. She took off her apron and hurried out the door.

Outside Jeanne Pruitt's dress shop, she caught up with her friend. "Mariah?"

The mill foreman's wife turned. "Oh. Hello, Carrie."

Mariah's brown eyes, usually so warm and alive with light and affection, were wary. She turned to study the dark green dress displayed in the shop window.

"I saw you coming out of Mr. Pruitt's just now, and I came to apologize." Carrie laid one hand on Mariah's arm. "I didn't intend to speak so harshly to you and Eugenie the other day. I don't know what possessed me, really."

"Eugenie and I know very well what possessed you. And we're very concerned about you." Mariah whirled around, her skirts sweeping the sidewalk. "Mr. Rutledge is not a proper gentleman."

She glanced at two women coming along the street and lowered her voice. "His brother came here to visit him, all the way from Charleston, and Mr. Rutledge turned him away. His own kin. What's worse, they say he frequents that disgusting gambling house down in Two Creeks."

Carrie fought a stab of disappointment. She didn't want anything to mar her impression of Griff. "Are you sure? You know how people love to gossip."

Mariah nodded emphatically. "I know all too well how folks like to gossip. That's why Eugenie and I are so worried about you. We don't want you to ruin your reputation by keeping company with the likes of Griff Rutledge." She patted Carrie's arm. "Even if the gossip about him isn't true, after Race Day he'll be gone, and then what? If you insist on consorting with him, no respectable man will want you."

"It doesn't matter. I've given up on finding love."

Mariah's expression softened. "You're still in shock about Nate and Rosaleen. But that's no excuse to take up with Mr. Rutledge. This obsession with him is quite unlike you, Carrie."

"I know. I don't understand it myself."

"You need to pray about this, my dear, and wait upon the Lord."

"I do pray. Every day. But sometimes I wonder whether God is listening."

A rig clattered along the road. The train whistle shrieked.

"Sometimes he seems remote to me too." Mariah nodded to a farm boy who passed them on the sidewalk. "All those years ago, when our little daughter drowned, I felt as if he'd abandoned me. But his love is constant, so it must be us mortals who move from beneath his wing."

Mariah shifted her packages to her other arm and peered up the street. "Here comes Sage. I shouldn't keep him waiting. He worries about the mill every moment he's away from it."

Carrie nodded. "I'll see you at church on Sunday."

Mariah waved and hurried down the sidewalk. Carrie watched Sage stow her packages inside her rig. They drove away. Carrie headed back to the Verandah, her thoughts racing, her feelings a mix of shock and disappointment. She hadn't known about Griff's visits to the gambling house. No wonder people were talking. On the other hand, according to the books she read, gambling among prominent men was an accepted practice in the Carolinas. Or at least it had been before the war, when slaves did all the work and there was nothing else to occupy a gentleman's hours. Was it Griff's fault if some folks in Hickory Ridge didn't realize that?

Anger propelled her along the dusty sidewalk. How dare anyone judge her? Head down, she stomped past the barbershop just as the door swung open and a man hurried out.

"Whoa there, Miss . . . well, hello, Carrie."

Griff, smelling wonderfully of bay rum and shaving soap, smiled down at her. "We seem always to be running into each other. Literally."

She returned his smile, stunned at how happy she was to see him. At how quickly the sound of his voice lightened her glum mood. She loved the sound of her name on his lips, his broad, confident smile and dark eyes.

He offered his arm. "Where to?"

"The Verandah. I've six loaves of bread in the oven."

He grinned and brushed one finger across her cheek, sending nerves skittering along her spine. "That explains the smudge of flour."

Heat suffused her face. "I saw a friend on the street and wanted to catch her before she got away. I should have checked my mirror first."

"Mrs. Whiting, wasn't it? I saw her through the barbershop window."

"Mariah, yes. We've known each other for years."

"And she warned you not to get mixed up with the likes of me."

"No, she was—"

"It's all right. I'm used to being new in town—an unknown quantity, so to speak." He nodded to a couple of men who passed them on the sidewalk. "And she's right, you know." His dark gaze sought hers. "The last thing I want to do is make you unhappy, Carrie."

Her heart stumbled. Something was growing between them, something that made her feel beautiful and alive. How could he dismiss that so easily?

They reached the Verandah. He paused, one foot on the bottom porch step. "So long as we understand each other, I would like very much to have the pleasure of your company. How about another riding lesson sometime soon?"

Suppose, in the end, he disappointed her? Shattered her heart? At least she would have a few weeks of happiness.

She smiled up at him. "I'd love to."

SEVENTEEN

Carrie slid into the back pew of the red brick church and peeled off her short lace gloves. The meeting was well underway. Up front Eugenie Spencer was speaking to a small group of women perched side by side in the first pew like birds on a wire. Through the open window came the clopping sounds of horses' hooves and the squeak of the drayman's wagon. In the hawthorn bush beside the window, a cardinal sang.

". . . will need several ladies to take charge of the decorations this year," Eugenie said. "Mariah has agreed to help and to play the piano for the Christmas Eve service."

The ladies bobbed their heads in silent approval. Sitting alone in the back pew, Carrie couldn't help noticing how many of their hats were Ada Wentworth designs, couldn't help wishing Ada were here now.

Molly Scott, the mayor's wife, spoke up. "I reckon I can get Hiram to chop us down a Christmas tree when the time comes. And I can help with the decorations too." She shook her head. "I sure do miss the orphans. Mrs. Lowell had 'em trained into a right nice choir."

"Whatever happened to those children?" Rosaleen asked.

She was seated near the front of the church next to Deborah

Patterson, the minister's wife. Colored light from the stained-glass window above the pulpit played upon Rosaleen's dark hair. Today she wore a simple ivory muslin frock sprigged with pink rosebuds and a matching shawl. Even in the unadorned gown, she was easily the prettiest woman in the room. No wonder she had turned Nate's head.

"Some growed up and left and some of the little ones found homes is what I understand." Molly twisted around in her pew to face Rosaleen. "When the money dried up, Mrs. Lowell had no choice but to shut the doors. She moved to—"

"Ladies." Eugenie tapped the podium to get their attention. "We're off the subject here. Now, who else will volunteer for the pageant this year? There are costumes to sew, and there's lots of baking to be done. It's September already. Christmas will be here before we know it."

Jeanne Pruitt from the dress shop and Sarah Broome, the pale young woman who had taken over operation of the telegraph office from Mary Stanhope, raised their hands. Carrie raised her hand too. Baking was the one thing she was good at.

Eugenie glanced around and scribbled in her notebook. "Jeanne and Sarah, I appreciate your help."

Carrie frowned. Hadn't Eugenie seen her hand in the air too?

"And now to Race Day," Eugenie went on. "I've asked Mrs. Gilman to speak to us about that."

The banker's wife, clad in yards of dark-blue silk, a glittering pin on her shoulder, rose and made her way to the front of the church. "Ladies, unfortunately we've had a setback. The printing company in Knoxville we hired to make fliers for the event has temporarily shut down."

"Oh dear." Mrs. Patterson spoke for the first time, startling Carrie. Usually, the minister's wife spoke not a word and left church as soon as the Sunday sermon was concluded. Mrs. Whitcomb said Deborah was unsuited for the role of pastor's wife, but Carrie liked her calm expression and gentle smile. Maybe Mrs. Patterson was painfully shy. Or drained of energy after her weekly visits to the sick and the indigent.

"We have no way of knowing when the print shop will reopen," Mrs. Gilman went on. "I understand they're waiting for a new part for the steam press. With our event only a month or so away, we can't afford to wait to get the word out. So we need every one of you to make and distribute signs all over Hickory Ridge. Send a copy to your friends and kinfolks living elsewhere. The more people who know about Race Day, the larger the potential crowd, and the better for our town." She looked around the room. "I'm sure I don't have to tell you how much everyone is counting on its success."

Rosaleen stood, rustling her muslin skirts. "My husband will take some copies to Knoxville for us when he goes to call on the university. And well, I know I'm new here and all, but I'd be willing to meet the incoming trains and personally invite visitors to come back for Race Day."

Molly chewed her bottom lip. "A one-woman welcoming committee? I'm not sure about that, Miz Chastain. Some folks might not think it's proper."

"I'll make copies for Sage to post at the mill," Mariah said. "For the few men who are left."

Carrie thought of Henry. There hadn't been a solitary word from him since he'd left for Chicago. Surely he knew by now whether or not he would find work in the rail yard. Surely he'd written to his wife. Was he all right? How was he getting on in the steamy, dirty city? Desperate as she was for word from him, she would not beg the information from the insufferable Mary Stanhope.

Mrs. Gilman handed out a sample flier. "Use black ink, ladies. It'll show up better. Be sure to finish them and post them no later than the fourteenth. That gives folks a month to make plans to watch Majestic run the race."

"What about the other horses?" Mariah asked. "Has anyone heard anything about that?"

"My husband is taking care of that," Mrs. Gilman said. "Two gentlemen from Maryland are bringing horses, and so is Mr. Vaught from over in Maury County. Colonel Bruce of Kentucky is planning to attend too. The colonel is an expert on the Thoroughbred pedigree. He even published a book on it a couple of years back. They say he owns a mare that goes all the way back to the very first Thoroughbred champion in the 1700s. But he won't be bringing her this year. She's about to foal."

Molly Scott nodded. "I reckon it's good for business to have competition from all over, but Hiram is betting on that Rutledge feller to ride Majestic to victory."

Carrie suppressed a smile. Any mention of the magnificent horse and his trainer made her insides soften. She would bet on Griff too if she were a betting kind of person. Griff's way with horses was something rare and magical.

"Well then." Eugenie stood. "I believe this concludes our meeting. Let's all go home and get to work. Hickory Ridge is depending on us."

With a rustling of bustles and petticoats, the women rose, chattering all at once. Carrie slipped out the back door, intending to speak to Eugenie about baking sweets for the Christmas celebration. Though bread was her specialty, baking cookies was a part of the tradition she had long shared with Henry and her friends. Now, more than ever, she needed a familiar ritual to cling to.

Besides, the doctor's wife had been known to flout convention herself. Hadn't she attended births in Two Creeks when others were afraid to venture so far from town? Surely she wouldn't hold Carrie's friendship with Griff against her.

"Carrie?" Rosaleen swept into the aisle and placed one hand on Carrie's arm. "May I ask you something?"

Carrie nodded, one eye on the open doorway. Eugenie and Mariah walked out together, the wide brims of their hats touching as they talked.

"What in the world is an account receivable? Nate told me to go through a ledger and add them all up, but I'm not sure what I'm supposed to add. I don't want to ask him. He already thinks I'm dumb as a fence post."

Well, what had he expected? Anyone who spent more than ten minutes with Rosaleen would realize the woman was in no danger of being mistaken for an intellectual. Still, Carrie couldn't very well let her muddle a business Nate had spent years building.

"Accounts receivable is the list of people who owe the shop money for books they have ordered or already received. The universities are the largest accounts, but you should check Mr. Gilman's too. He orders a lot of books from Nate and pays up when they arrive. If you add all those amounts together, you'll know how much income to expect at the end of the month."

"Oh, is that all there is to it?" Rosaleen frowned. "Why didn't Nate say so instead of giving it some fancy name? Accounts receivable. My word."

"I must go. I need to speak to Eugenie."

"I'll walk out with you."

They left the church and stepped into the bright sunshine. Eugenie—and everyone else—had gone.

"Oh dear. I'm sorry I held you up," Rosaleen said. "Walk over to the bakery with me, and I'll buy you a cinnamon bun. Make it up to you."

"Thank you, but I should be getting back to the Verandah soon. I promised to help Mrs. Whitcomb with supper tonight. She hasn't been feeling well lately."

"I wondered where she was today." Rosaleen snapped open her parasol. "You're absolutely sure you don't want a cinnamon bun?"

"I'm sure."

"Suit yourself." Rosaleen started down the road.

Feeling suddenly bereft, Carrie stood in the shade watching a wren flitting in and out of the nest it had made in the hollow of a tree. Maybe she'd skip the Christmas celebrations this year. By then Griff would be gone. Unless Henry came home, there wouldn't be much to celebrate anyway.

"Sweet, isn't she?"

Carrie spun around. "Mrs. Patterson. You startled me."

"I'm sorry." The minister's wife walked over to a small wooden bench set beneath the trees. Carrie noticed for the first time that she walked with a slight limp and that her left arm hung useless at her side. But her face was radiant, her smile genuine. "I love watching the wrens. So industrious. Please . . . join me for a moment."

Carrie sat down.

"You're Mrs. Daly."

Carrie nodded.

"I've seen you in church for the past several weeks. I meant to welcome you sooner."

"Thank you. I enjoy your husband's sermons quite a lot, and now that I live in town, it's more convenient to attend church here." She brushed at a cloud of gnats forming around her head. "I love our county church, but we haven't had a regular pastor since Mr. Dennis moved away. We have the circuit rider from time to time, but it isn't the same."

"No, it isn't. I'm always sad when a church loses its leader." Deborah Patterson paused and studied Carrie's face. In the trees above them, a blue jay squawked. The little wren ducked into her nest. "But that isn't why I waited for you today."

"Oh?" Carrie rubbed the coin-sized protrusion of bone at her wrist and watched the sunlight dappling the ground.

"I saw Mrs. Spencer ignore your offer to help bake."

Carrie shrugged. "I seem to be out of favor with everyone these days."

"Because of Mr. Rutledge."

"My word. Is there anyone in town who doesn't know that I speak to him now and then?"

A smile lit Deborah's face. "Apparently not. Forgive me for asking, but are you sure you know what you're doing?"

"I'm not sure of anything, other than that my life is a terrible mess."

"I've been praying for you," Deborah said quietly.

"Why?"

"Because I can sense your uncertainty. You want to please God. You want to be happy. You're not sure whether one precludes the other."

Carrie didn't try to hide her surprise. How could this woman see past her troubled heart to her very soul? She nodded.

"Our Lord delights in our joy. You say your life is a mess, and maybe it is, but he can bring order out of chaos and turn the worst suffering to his good. But you must be willing to surrender everything into his safekeeping."

The bony spot on Carrie's wrist throbbed. Her head pounded. She stood. "I must go."

"Because the thought of complete surrender frightens you."

"Because I'm late. I was due back at the hotel an hour ago."

Deborah clasped Carrie's hand. "Stay a moment longer. I want to tell you something."

The headache worsened. "You've given me quite a bit to ponder, Mrs. Patterson."

"Please call me Deborah. After all, I'm not much older than you."

"But the reverend is—"

"Ancient?" Deborah laughed. "Everyone remarks upon the difference in our ages, but we have a very good marriage, Daniel and I." Her expression softened. "He saved my life."

Deborah patted the bench and Carrie sat down again, one eye on the lengthening shadows. If she didn't get back to the hotel soon, supper would be delayed. She couldn't afford to anger Mrs. Whitcomb, whose various ailments had put her in a bad mood lately.

"It's no secret my arm doesn't work," Deborah began. "And I walk with a limp. But I—"

"Yes. And I'm so sorry. But—"

"Another time then." Deborah patted her arm. "Don't be late on my account."

Leaving Deborah sitting on the bench, Carrie hurried toward the Verandah and tried to put the unsettling conversation out of her mind. Was Mrs. Patterson right? Was she afraid of turning everything over to God? Afraid of praying, "Thy will be done"?

She reached the main street just as Mariah got into her rig outside the mercantile. Carrie hurried over. "I'm glad I caught you. I volunteered to bake for the Christmas celebration but Eugenie didn't see me."

Mariah sighed. "Listen, Carrie, I am very sorry for this rift between us. Eugenie cares for you, truly she does. And so do I. But the way you're mooning over a stranger, a gambler we hardly even know . . . well, it's destroying some people's good opinion of you. And you seem not to care in the least."

"But you welcomed Rosaleen Dupree with open arms, and you don't know her either."

Mariah picked up the reins. "Not exactly open arms. We all know the kind of woman she is . . . was. And she's too flashy by half. But we must try to forgive her past and encourage her nobler impulses. For Nate's sake."

"If she's respectable enough for him, then she's acceptable to everyone else. Is that it?"

"Carrie, keep your voice down." Mariah glanced around. "I wish you'd married Nate when you had the chance, instead of thinking you were too good for him."

"I never thought I was too good for him. I only wanted to be happy."

Mariah hesitated, then reached into her leather pouch and pulled out one of the Race Day fliers. "All right. Why don't you make some fliers for now, and we'll see what happens after Race Day." She sighed. "Perhaps by then you'll come to your senses."

Carrie stuffed the flier into her pocket and watched Mariah drive away. Was Mariah right? Was she throwing away her life, ruining her good name, when nothing lasting could come of it?

A blob of black ink mushroomed over the Race Day flier she'd just finished. Crumpling the ruined page, Carrie tossed it onto the table, capped her inkwell, and stared out the window. On the corner, Mariah and Eugenie were deep in conversation, the brims of their fall hats shadowing their faces. Moments earlier, Rosaleen, clutching a handful of papers, had sashayed by in her pink wedding costume on her way to the train station. Clearly the new Mrs. Chastain cared not one whit for Molly Scott's opinion.

Carrie rose and went to the kitchen to check on the bread dough she'd left rising on the counter. Everyone else had a role to play for Race Day, and she was relegated to the sidelines because of her friendship with Griff. She hated being at cross purposes with Mariah and Eugenie, and yet she could not walk away from Griff even if she wanted to. She didn't understand it, really. Why did she always want the thing she could never have? She returned to the parlor and flopped onto the dusty sofa.

Here lately, she'd spent a lot of time thinking about the choices she had made. Mrs. Whitcomb had counseled her not to give up hope, and she hadn't—not totally, anyway. But time was slipping past, and still God was silent.

Lucy Whitcomb slid down the banister and picked up the shawl she'd left on the bottom stair last night. "Where's Aunt Maisy this morning?"

"At the mercantile, buying cleaning supplies." Carrie swept her arm around the dusty, cobwebbed room. "This place needs scrubbing top to bottom before Race Day—in case the inn fills up and the Verandah must accommodate an overflow crowd."

The girl shuddered. "How can you stand it? The very thought of washing windows and scrubbing floors makes me break out in hives. I'd rather spend a week in purgatory with the Grayson twins."

Carrie stifled a grin. "And who's going to scrub your floors in Montana?"

Lucy shrugged. "Want to meet Rachel and me for a sweet at the bakery?"

"I don't think so, but I appreciate the invitation."

"I heard about what the other ladies are saying about you and I don't think it's fair." Lucy circled the room, evidently looking for something. "Mr. Rutledge seems perfectly lovely, and I don't see why you can't see him if you want to." She spotted her reticule tucked beside the sofa and picked it up. "If they want to be mad at somebody, they should be mad at Rosaleen for stealing Nate from right under your nose."

Carrie rose and placed one arm around the young girl's shoulders. "Thank you, Lucy. But a man can't be stolen away unless he wants to be."

Lucy took an apple from the bowl on the side table and polished it on her sleeve. "Ma'am?"

"Mr. Chastain and I were great friends, but in the end we didn't love each other enough for marriage." She smiled. "My granny used to say that the only thing worse than being alone is being married to the wrong man."

Lucy bit into the apple. "All I know is, if anybody tried to take Jake away from me, I'd claw her eyes out."

The ink had dried on the Race Day fliers. Carrie gathered them and set them on the table.

"I can put one of those up on the Graysons' barn if you want," Lucy offered. "It's on the main road, and everybody passes by there sooner or later. Mrs. Grayson says—"

"Carrie Daly! Carrie Daly!" A voice, urgent and high pitched, preceded its owner into the Verandah's front parlor. Caleb Stanhope, Mary's older boy, stumbled in, his hair plastered to his head with sweat, his face red with exertion. "Mama said to give you this letter right away. She said it's a matter of life and death."

Lucy stuffed a Race Day flier into her reticule and headed for the door. "I must go. Tell Aunt Maisy that Rachel and I will be late for supper tonight."

Carrie nodded and looked down at the red-faced boy. "Now what's this about life and death?"

He shoved the letter into her hands. "Fer mercy's sake, just read it."

Carrie sank onto the sofa in the parlor and opened the note. She skimmed it quickly, then read it a second time more slowly, swallowing the sudden churning in her stomach.

"Well?" Caleb stood over her, the expression in his eyes a mixture of fear and expectation. "Are you going to help us or not?"

EIGHTEEN

"She asked you to do *what*?" Nate leaned back in his chair, his pipe clenched in his teeth.

Carrie watched a cloud of blue smoke encircle his head. "She wants me to move back to the farm."

"I'm sure she does. She's made no secret of her disdain for farm life." Nate shook his head. "I have a lot of respect for your brother, but for the life of me I can't figure out why he thought Mary Stanhope was marriage material."

She felt a sudden stab of anger. Though she had entertained those same thoughts herself, she didn't want anyone, not even Nate, to criticize her brother's choices. "Some people might wonder the same thing about you and Rosaleen."

"Touché." He set his pipe on the corner of his desk. "What are you going to do?"

Carrie shrugged. She'd tried to see a way out of the situation, but the truth lodged like a stone in her shoe: she had no good choices, only painful ones.

"I wouldn't blame you if you said no," Nate said.

"There are special circumstances. Mary is . . . with child and—"

"Already?"

She nodded. "Dr. Spencer has ordered her to bed until the child is born."

Nate counted on his fingers "When will that be?"

"Late February, Mary thinks."

"Does Henry know?"

"I'm sure she's written to him. But even if he could arrange for Mary and the boys to go to Chicago, the doctor wouldn't allow it." She gazed out the window. "This child is my brother's first. Given Mary's delicate constitution, maybe his only one. After all he has done for me, I must do everything possible to see that the baby comes safely into the world."

"I suppose so. But I sure do hate to think of your spending the winter out there with only those two little boys to help run the place."

"Before he left, Henry told me he planned to hire someone to help with the heavier tasks, but I don't know whether he found anyone. Most of the men in Hickory Ridge have gone to look for work elsewhere."

"Hard times, all right. But my daddy used to say that nothing lasts forever. Good times eventually end, but so do the bad times. Hickory Ridge will recover from this, you'll see."

"I hope so." She paused. "I came to ask you to help me move my things back to the farm."

Nate sent her a quizzical look. "Rutledge isn't available?"

"It shouldn't matter to you now."

He blushed. "You're right. But I still care a great deal about what happens to you. I want you to be happy."

Her irritation transformed into a rush of affection for her old friend. "I know you do. And I wish the same for you."

India jumped into his lap, and he stroked her from head to tail. "Can I ask you something? Does Rosaleen seem . . . a bit secretive?"

"I couldn't really say. I didn't see much of her when she lived at the Verandah. But I do know that she and Mr. Rutledge knew each other before they got here."

He took up his pipe, looking thoughtful. "Doesn't that seem odd to you, that the two of them would end up here at the same time? After all, Hickory Ridge is off the beaten path, as they say."

"Maybe." She paused, remembering. "Rosaleen said a strange thing to me the night you came back from Chicago. She said, 'I'm so sorry'".

"Doesn't seem strange to me. She knew we were courting. I guess she felt guilty about coming between us." He puffed on his pipe. "Despite what some folks think of Rosaleen, she can be tender-hearted. And she was impressed with your book discussion society. I suppose she hated hurting your feelings."

"Perhaps." Carrie rose. "I must go. I promised Mrs. Whitcomb one last batch of bread before I leave."

"Soon as Rosaleen gets back from the train station, we'll hitch the wagon and come for you. Rosaleen doesn't like to be on the road after dark." He shook his head. "I declare, that woman sure is skittish. Almost like she's looking over her shoulder, waiting for somebody."

"You could ask Sheriff McCracken to look into it. People still talk about how he tracked down Charlie Blevins for terrorizing Ada and burning the Spencers' chicken coop."

"But how would that look? A newly married man checking up on his beloved?"

Carrie had no answer for that. Instead, she placed a hand on Nate's arm. "Thanks for helping me out. I'm grateful."

He nodded. "Always happy to help you, my dear. Save me a loaf of that bread, all right? Rosaleen is a pretty little thing, but she can't cook worth spit."

They headed for the front of the bookshop, and he waved a hand toward the shelves. "You might want to take some books with you to the farm."

"I expect I'll be much too busy and too tired to read."

"Still, I don't like to think of you out there with nothing to occupy your thoughts. You may as well take whatever suits your fancy. Lord knows I'm not selling many of them these days."

Carrie looked around the shop. How she would miss the neat rows of books, the tables laden with magazines and newspapers, the smells of lemon wax and Nate's pipe tobacco. India's warm weight in her lap. "Maybe I will take a few, if you're sure you don't mind."

She chose a couple of new novels, two histories, and a biography she'd wanted to read. At the last minute she added a Horatio Alger tale, a book of fairy tales, and the copy of *Two Hungry Kittens* to the pile. Perhaps those books would occupy Mary's boys in the evenings, affording her a few moments of peace.

"Leave them on the counter," Nate said. "No use toting them all the way to the Verandah. I'll box them up and bring them when we come to pick you up."

Nate's wagon jostled over the rutted road. Next to him, Rosaleen, decked out in a parrot-green silk frock, drew a delicate embroidered shawl about her shoulders and turned around to smile at Carrie. "Saints in a sock, but it's chilly today."

"You all right back there, Carrie?" Nate asked.

"Fine." But her insides were taut with apprehension and bitterness. Only months ago she had embarked upon a new life, one that allowed her to do as she pleased. But God had seen fit to send her back to where she came from. *Why?* she had asked in her nightly prayers. *What am I to learn, Lord, from this experience?*

Nate flicked the reins. "Let me know if you want to stop and rest a minute."

"I will." The whole situation seemed strange and awkward, but he acted as if it was natural to be driving along with the woman who had promised to marry him and the one who actually had.

Carrie inhaled the fresh September air and looked out at the distant mountains. The trees already wore a few splotches of red and gold, mixing with the green. Flocks of birds darted through the wisps of fog collecting in the cool hollows. Perhaps none of this was God's doing and everything happened by chance. If so, then why pray at all? Regardless, she had agreed to look out for Henry's family. She would see it through.

They passed the country church, and Carrie felt a pang of homesickness for the days when Pastor Dennis preached every Sunday and the quilting circle met to sew and share the latest news from Hickory Ridge. Now Ada was in Texas with Wyatt. Mariah was barely speaking to her, and Lillian Willis rested in the grave-yard. So many losses piled one upon the other left her feeling numb.

Another few minutes' journey brought them to the farm. Despite her fears, Carrie's heart lifted at the sight of the white clapboard house with its long, deep porch and shuttered windows. Behind the house, surrounded by a picket fence, sat the neat barn she and Henry had raised only three years before. The garden was another story. The remnants of the summer produce lay in a brown tangle overgrown with weeds.

Nate brought the wagon to a stop in the yard. Caleb and Joe ran out to meet them. "Carrie Daly!" Joe shouted. "Make Caleb give me back my slingshot."

Carrie closed her eyes and stifled a rebuke. This endless petti-ness was what she had to look forward to for the foreseeable future. She lacked the patience for it. Maybe God was right to deny her a chance at motherhood.

"Where's your mother?" Carrie asked the older boy as Nate lifted her from the wagon.

Caleb stared at her with a mutinous look on his face. "It's *my* slingshot. I made it by myself. It isn't his."

From her perch on the wagon seat, Rosaleen frowned at the boy. "That's no way to treat your only brother, young man."

"Who asked you?" Caleb balled his fists.

"Caleb," Carrie said quickly, "help me with these boxes."

"I've got them." Nate set her few belongings on the porch and went back to wrestle the walnut chest up the stairs. A few minutes later he returned, pink-faced from exertion.

"I reckon that's everything." He patted her shoulder. "You're all set."

"Thank you, Nate. I appreciate your help."

"Thanks for the bread."

"Yes, Carrie," Rosaleen said. "I'm sure we'll enjoy it. I myself am hopeless in the kitchen. Why, I can barely boil water." She sent Nate a wicked grin. "But then, you didn't marry me for my culinary skills, did you, sugar?"

Nate blushed. "We should go. It's a ways back into town. You take care of yourself, Carrie. If you need anything—"

"I said stop it." Caleb twisted Joe's ear and shoved the younger boy to the ground.

Carrie marched over to them and grabbed each of them by the collar. "Both of you listen to me. This behavior will stop at once."

"Or what?" Caleb's face was red. His breath came out in little gasps. "You can't do nothing to us. You're not our mother."

"Proof that God is real," Carrie muttered.

Rosaleen laughed. "Oh my word, Carrie, you've got your work cut out for you here."

Nate bent down until his face was even with the two boys. "You boys remember the day that Henry married your mama?"

Joe nodded vigorously. "The cake was really good."

Nate smiled. "Yes, it was. But I'm remembering something the preacher said about loving everyone in your family. Being kind to them." He waved a hand. "Miz Daly here is your aunt. She's given up her own plans to come back here to look after you and your mama. That means you have to respect her and do what she says."

"Even if she's wrong?"

"She's a smart woman. I don't reckon she'll be wrong too often. But I'd say yes, even when you think she's wrong, you still have to mind her. Not because she's bigger than you and can take a switch to your hides, but because you're a family."

"Fine," Caleb said. "But I am still keeping my slingshot."

Nate fished a coin from his pocket. "I'll pay you to make another one for your little brother."

Caleb reached for the coin. "Deal."

"Not so fast." Nate's fingers closed over the coin. "How do I know you'll keep your promise?"

"You'll just have to trust me, I guess."

"Ah." Nate straightened. "The way you must trust your Aunt Carrie to do her best by you. See how it works?"

Caleb kicked at a dirt clod. "I reckon so."

Joe tugged on Nate's leg. "It's not fair. I want a dime too."

Carrie sent Nate a helpless look and massaged the throbbing at her temples.

"Well, sir," Nate said thoughtfully. "I'm not in the habit of giving out free money. The way I see it, a man ought to earn his pay."

"I can earn it," Joe said. "What do I have to do?"

Nate looked around. "Let me see. First off, I reckon you could help your aunt tote that valise up to her room."

"All right."

"And after that, maybe you could fetch a bucket of water from the well. And bring in some stove wood so she can fix supper."

The little boy frowned. "That seems like a powerful lot of work for only a dime."

"Times are hard," Nate told him. "Take it or leave it."

"I'll take it, I reckon."

"Good lad." Nate tossed both the boys a coin and climbed onto the wagon. "We'll see you, Carrie."

"'Bye, Carrie," Rosaleen trilled. "Good luck."

Joe ran to the porch and grabbed Carrie's valise. "Mama said you can have your old room back, on account of me and Caleb are used to this place now, and we growed up and we ain't afeared of robbers no more."

Despite herself, Carrie smiled. "I'm glad you aren't afraid anymore." She picked up the box of books Nate had given her. "Can you hold the door open for me?"

"All right." Joe held the door, then dragged her valise into the front hallway and peered into the box. "What's in there?"

"Some books from Mr. Chastain's shop."

"Anything good?"

"I suppose that depends upon what you like to read."

"Oh, I ain't learnt to read yet, on account of there's no school here anymore. But I know my letters and everything. And I'm real good at listening to stories. Mama used to read to me, but now she's too sick." He bumped the valise up the stairs and opened the door to Carrie's old room. Joe shook his head. "I swear to you, Carrie Daly, I ain't never seen so much puking in all my born days. Why, some days she—"

"That's enough, Joe. I can well imagine." Carrie set the books on the floor beside the bed and opened the window. Her prized morning glories had died. Wispy brown vines drooped from the trellis in the yard.

Joe joined her at the window. "I told her she shoulda watered 'em, but she was too sad when Pa first left, and then she got sick."

"It doesn't matter anymore." She turned from the window. "Let's see what we can find for supper."

Griff led Majestic into his stall and removed the tack. The horse nickered and nuzzled his trainer, looking for the sugar cubes Griff kept in his pocket.

Griff grinned and gave Majestic his reward. "Good boy."

He took his time brushing the horse, enjoying the cool quiet of the autumn evening and the companionship of the magnificent animal. He ran his hands over every inch of the horse's flesh, teaching Majestic to trust his touch, feeling for anything that might cause discomfort. He checked each hoof for signs of abscesses. They could form fast if foreign matter became lodged in the horse's shoe.

Majestic quivered and jerked and Griff found the culprit—a small stone that had worked its way beneath the curve of the shoe. Griff dug it out with a hoof pick and made a mental note to check the hoof again before tomorrow's ride. With only three weeks to go until Race Day, he didn't want to risk even the slightest injury that might hamper the colt's chances.

He bent to retrieve his brush, and the telegram he'd received earlier in the day fell from his pocket. There was still room aboard the *California Queen*, the ship's agent in San Francisco had wired, leaving for Australia on the first of November. A ticket would be held for him until mid-October.

He stuffed the wire back into his pocket and filled Majestic's feedbag with oats. Amazing how quickly a man's priorities could change. He'd come here intending to collect a debt and move on, but now he felt strangely connected to Hickory Ridge. He wanted to win the race not for the thousand dollars in prize money, but because the people here needed something to cheer about. Something to hope for.

And Lord help him, he hadn't been able to stop thinking about the widow Daly. The news that she had decamped from her hotel and returned to the Bell farm left him feeling lonesome. Until she left, he hadn't realized how much he'd come to count on seeing her leave the Verandah each morning with her basket of fresh bread for the church charity, her reddish curls shining in the morning light. She was a sight for sore eyes, all right, lovely in a quiet, refined kind of way. The polar opposite of the brash and beautiful Rosaleen.

He frowned. What on earth had the new Mrs. Chastain come here to find?

She was up to something. He could feel it in the same way he could feel when an opponent was holding a winning poker hand. But Rosaleen never did have an ounce of patience. She'd tire of life in Hickory Ridge before too long, and then she'd be gone.

The bookseller wouldn't know what hit him. Poor devil.

NINETEEN

Carrie rifled through her box of books and handed Joe the book of fairy tales.

"I must see to your mother for a while. Pick out your favorite picture, and after supper I'll read you the story."

The child's eyes lit up, and he favored her with an impish grin. "How about two stories?"

"Just one, Joe. I'm very tired."

He took the book and settled himself on the stairs outside Carrie's room. Relieved that he hadn't made a fuss, she watched him thumbing through the pages. Perhaps he would turn out all right after all. Caleb, however, so angry and defiant, seemed destined for Eli McCracken's jail.

Carrie went downstairs and knocked on Mary's door.

"Come in."

She entered the room and was nearly overcome by the sour smells of urine and vomit. Piles of dirty laundry lay in the corners and beneath the grimy, cobwebbed window. Mary was in bed, a pale blue coverlet pulled up to her chin.

"I heard you arrive," Mary said, "but I didn't feel like getting up."

Carrie scooped a pile of dirty laundry off the chair and sat down. "There's no sense in asking how you feel. It's obvious."

"I don't understand it. I was never this sick with either of the boys."

"Does Henry know?"

"I wrote to him a couple of weeks ago, but I haven't had a reply. Your brother is not much of a correspondent."

"But he is all right? He's found work?"

"At the rail yard. He says the pay is pretty good, but the work is worse than farming." Mary managed a wan smile. "And that's saying something. Farming must surely be the most difficult job on earth."

"At least you have the hired man to do the heavy chores."

Mary looked away.

"Mary?" A wave of uneasiness moved through Carrie. "Henry did find someone? Before he left, he told me he intended to."

"Oh yes, he found someone, all right. But the man was utterly useless, and bad tempered as well. He got angry with me because I asked him to do a few simple things here in the house."

"Like what?"

Mary waved one hand. "Well, once I asked him to sweep the floors, and once to do the washing. But he said that wasn't what Henry hired him for, and he refused to do it. I put up with his nonsense as long as I could, but last week I fired him."

"You what?"

"I let him go."

Hot tears built behind Carrie's eyes. "You let him go. With winter coming on."

"I knew you'd come back, and the ten dollars a month Henry was paying him can be used for better things."

"What if I had said no?"

"I knew you wouldn't." Mary's pale gaze held Carrie's. "You may hate me, but you love your brother."

"I don't hate you. And I do love him. But I can't run this place alone. Even when Henry was here, we hired help from time to time."

"Oh. Well, how was I to know that? If you had stayed to help me instead of running off with that Charleston gambler—"

Carrie ground her teeth. "I did not run off with him. I decided to leave this house, and he helped me move."

"I heard you were seen at the Gilmans' place riding horseback with him, and not sidesaddle either. And that every time he sees you on the street he makes a beeline for you."

"We enjoy each other's company, what little there has been of it." A fly buzzed about Carrie's head. She waved it away and fought a bout of nausea. "How can you live in this filth?"

"It isn't my fault that I'm sick."

Carrie stood. "Tomorrow I'll start cleaning up around here. For now, the boys need to wash up and have supper."

Mary nodded. "All of a sudden, I'm hungry too."

"At least we won't starve. Henry said the garden did well this year. What all did you put up?"

"Put up?"

Carrie rolled her eyes. Lord, but the woman was dense. "The vegetables. Corn, peas, tomatoes, beans. You preserved them, right?"

"Well, I didn't know I was supposed to. Besides, I thought Henry would be back for me by now. I thought that we'd move to Chicago and live in a decent house and the boys could go to school. I didn't plan on getting a baby so soon and being sick." Her bottom lip trembled. "Everything has gone wrong, and you're blaming me."

She covered her face and sobbed.

Carrie felt the last of her patience waning. "For goodness' sake, Mary, stop bawling. It won't solve anything."

"See? You're mad at me. And so hateful."

What was the point of arguing? Carrie turned on her heel. "I'm going to make supper."

In the kitchen, every plate, pot, and pan was caked with dried food. Flies buzzed about the table. The water bucket and the wood box were empty. Truly, it was a wonder they weren't all dead from living this way. Had anyone been feeding the animals and milking the cow?

She went to the foot of stairs and called, "Joe Stanhope."

"Yes'm?"

"Time to earn that dime Mr. Chastain gave you. I need wood and water."

"In a minute. I ain't picked out my story yet."

"If you're interested in supper, you'll do it now."

He clattered down the stairs and grabbed the water bucket.

Carrie started clearing the table. "Where's Caleb?"

"I dunno. He don't stay around here much these days. Mama has to yell and yell to get him to come in at night."

"Well, I'm not going to yell for him. If he wants to sleep in the woods, I don't care. But if you happen to see him, tell him I need a lot of firewood. Tomorrow is wash day."

"Yes'm."

When Joe returned with wood and water, Carrie lit the stove, heated water, and washed and dried the dishes. In the icebox she found a few eggs and a blob of rancid butter. She rummaged for lard, salt, and pepper, and cobbled together a supper of fried eggs, fried potatoes, and coffee. She made a tray for Mary and sent Caleb to deliver it.

In a moment he was back. "Mama says anything made with lard makes her stomach hurt worse."

"I'm sorry to hear that, but until I can churn some fresh butter, lard is all there is. This place is a disaster."

"You were supposed to stay and help us. But you ran away."

Carrie suppressed an angry retort. What good would it do to argue with an eleven-year-old? "Sit down, Caleb."

She joined the two boys at the table. "Now, can either of you say a blessing for our food?"

Joe shook his head, but Caleb said, "I learnt one at school 'fore it shut down."

"Excellent. Let's bow our heads."

Caleb bowed his head and cleared his throat. "Past the teeth and past the gums, look out stummick, here it comes."

Joe giggled.

Caleb poured himself a cup of coffee and sent Carrie a defiant look.

She returned his hard gaze. "I doubt very much that you learned that from your teacher."

"Never said I did." He stabbed a forkful of potatoes from the serving platter and shoveled them into his mouth. "I said I learnt it at school. Jimmy D. Washburn taught it to me."

"Well, it's not the sort of blessing we say in our home. Now put your fork down and bow your head. You too, Joe."

She offered a quick blessing and passed the food around the table. Both children ate as if it was to be their last meal on earth. Joe wolfed down his eggs and potatoes and ran his finger around the rim of his plate, scooping up the last bite.

Carrie's heart twisted. The poor child was half starved. In the morning she'd see about baking some bread. The massive washing awaited, but somehow she must find time for a trip to the mercantile too.

Caleb shoved his plate away and stood. "I'm going outside."

"Please clear your plate first, Caleb."

"That's woman's work."

"Very well. But if you leave it there you will not get any breakfast in the morning."

He went still and she held his gaze, regretting the need to threaten hunger to make him obey. But something had to be done. The boy was too stubborn to listen to reason.

Wordlessly he picked up his plate and with exaggerated slowness, dropped it into the sink. Then he walked out the back door.

"Do I get my story now?" Joe scooped up his plate and took it to the sink.

"As soon as I wash up these dishes."

His grin warmed her heart. He stuck around while she heated water on the stove and washed and dried the dishes. Clearly Joe missed his mother's companionship. He kept up a constant stream of chatter and questions until she felt her head would explode. But at last, after she'd read the story of Jack and the beanstalk, he staggered up the stairs to the attic bedroom.

Darkness fell. Carrie lit the lamp in the parlor and went to check on Mary, who had fallen asleep, one leg protruding from the coverlet. Mary looked so thin and sick that Carrie couldn't help feeling sorry for her. She closed the window against the cool night air and went up to her own room. She lit the lamp and looked around. Someone, Joe most likely, had made an attempt to tidy things up. The pillows had been fluffed. A single daisy in a glass of water rested on the night table.

Overwhelmed with conflicting emotions and the sheer enormity of the job in front of her, Carrie dug her Bible from her bag and opened it at random, but it was impossible to concentrate. Closing her eyes, she prayed the simple prayer Granny Bell had taught her, the one that never failed to bring comfort when she was facing a difficult task. *Father, have mercy. Grant me the grace to do what I must do.*

The front door crashed open, and Caleb pounded up the stairs. *Lord, help me deal with this child. And please keep Henry safe.*

She washed up, changed into her nightgown, and slipped into bed, exhausted but determined. Somehow, she would hold this farm and this family together until Henry could come for them. She closed her eyes.

Then she smelled smoke.

TWENTY

Shoving down a rise of panic, Carrie threw her shawl over her night-dress and ran barefoot down the stairs. Through the kitchen window she spotted a faint glow near the toolshed. Something was definitely burning. Water bucket in hand, she rushed out the back door and across the yard. Smoke rolled from the roof of the shed. Flames licked at the eaves. A narrow trail of fire snaked across the weedy grass.

She tossed the bucket of water onto the smoldering wall of the shed, sending a cloud of acrid smoke curling into the sharp night air. But the grass still burned. She ran to the watering trough beside the barn, scooped out a bucket of water. Heat scorched her face as she doused the flames. Sparks glittered and went out. Only when the last of them smoldered and died did she realize the bottoms of her feet were blistered. She hobbled back to the house.

The lamp in Mary's bedroom flickered and then Mary herself appeared in the darkened hallway, her hair disheveled, her eyes wide and questioning. "What are you doing up? What happened?"

The fear and anger Carrie had kept at bay while she doused the fire came roaring back. She dropped the bucket onto the floor and sank onto the bottom stair. She fought to control her quaking voice. "What happened, Mary, was that your son tried to burn the place down."

"My . . . you mean Caleb?"

"I heard him running up the stairs just before I smelled smoke. One wall of the toolshed was already on fire when I got out there. Another ten minutes and it would have been lost, and the fire might have spread to the house." She got to her feet, wincing as pain shot through her.

"Where are you going?" Mary pushed her unruly hair off her face.

"To get Caleb, of course, and make him answer for this dangerous and irresponsible behavior."

"He's my son. He'll answer to me."

"Then discipline him."

"I will, if he's to blame." Mary leaned against the door frame. "You've never liked him, and now you're jumping to conclusions."

"What other explanation could there be?"

Mary shrugged. "Maybe it was some stranger off the train."

"A complete stranger who, for no reason, decided to come all the way out here to start a fire?"

"I don't know. Maybe it was Jimmy Washburn. He and Caleb are always getting into scrapes. Maybe they had a fight and Jimmy wanted to get even."

Carrie clenched her teeth to stop a torrent of furious words. How could Mary be so naïve? Couldn't she see that Caleb was headed for big trouble? It was almost as if she loved Caleb more because of his willful nature. But maybe that was what mothers did—defended their young in the face of irrefutable evidence. Even in the midst of her outrage and exhaustion, Carrie envied Mary the unconditional love she felt for her child. A kind of love she herself might never know.

She went to the kitchen for some lard to sooth her blistered feet. Up in her room, she soaked her feet in cool water from the ewer, dried them gingerly, and applied the lard. She turned up the wick in her lamp and examined the soles of her feet. Her skin was red, but at least it wasn't broken. Defeated and bone weary, she was unable to stop a rush of bitter tears. How on earth could anyone get along with Mary and Caleb?

They were part of her family now. Christ commanded her to love them. But she felt so overwhelmed and confused that she didn't even know how to pray about it. How could God help her if she didn't even know what exactly it was that she needed or how to ask him about it?

"The Holy Spirit talks to God for us, when we can't find the right words." So said Granny Bell as she lay dying in her little cabin in Muddy Hollow, when grief had stopped the words in Carrie's mouth. *"The Good Book says the Spirit makes intercession for us with groanings that cannot be uttered."*

For the second time this long night, Carrie found herself in prayer before falling into sleep—a prayer without words.

In the morning, moving gingerly on her sore feet, she made flap-jacks with the last of the flour. The boys devoured them, even though there was no butter or molasses. Caleb took his plate to the sink and headed outside.

"Where are you going?" Arms akimbo, Carrie blocked his path.

"Mama told me to draw you some water for doing the washing. I already brought the big kettle into the yard. And I brought some wood for the fire."

"Speaking of fires." She pinned him with a hard stare until he blinked and looked away.

"It was an accident. I already told Mama I'm sorry."

"You should be. You could have burned the house down last night, Caleb. And then what would we do?"

"You wouldn't care." He crossed his arms over his thin chest. "You don't like us."

"What I don't like is the way you are behaving. I'm doing my best to help your mother and look after this place. I would appreciate it if you wouldn't make my job any harder than it is."

Joe let out a loud burp. "Carrie Daly, is there any more flapjacks?"

"I'm afraid not, Joe." She looked around the bare kitchen. "Not until I can make a trip to the mercantile."

"Can I go?"

"We'll see. For now, I need you to go upstairs and bring down everything that needs washing. And that includes your—"

"Carrie?" Mary's voice was sharp enough to shatter glass. "I need you. Now."

Caleb went outside, letting the door slap shut behind him. Carrie shooed Joe up the stairs and hurried to Mary's room. "What is it?"

"These . . . buttons. I can't reach . . ." A soiled nightdress, stinking of sweat and vomit, lay in a heap on the floor. Mary struggled to get into another one.

"Here." Carrie fastened the buttons and helped Mary to the chair by the window. "Sit here while I strip the bed."

She removed the dirty linens and fluffed the feather mattress. "Where do you keep the clean sheets?"

"In the trunk. But there aren't any clean ones. I—I got behind on the washing."

An understatement if there ever was one. "Then the bare mattress will have to do until the laundry's done."

Mary glanced out at the bright sunlight streaming through the trees. "It's such a beautiful day. September is my favorite month. Maybe I'll sit here for a while and read. Doc Spencer said I could, if I'm careful."

"I made flapjacks." Carrie bundled the dirty laundry. "You should eat something."

Mary lifted one thin shoulder. "I don't really want to."

"For mercy's sake. I don't really want to be here cooking and cleaning and doing washing and looking after your rowdy boys. But I'm here—because of that little baby that's coming. That baby who is a part of my brother. You're his mother. Think of him for a change. If you care nothing for your own health, at least have the grace not to deprive the child of his."

Tears welled in Mary's eyes. "I'm sorry. I guess I never considered it that way."

"I'll be back."

Carrie took the laundry out to the back porch. To her surprise, Caleb had stacked the wood for the fire and set the laundry kettle on top. Now he was busy filling it with water from the well.

She lit the fire to start the water heating and went inside to prepare Mary's plate. While Mary picked at her food, Carrie went out to milk Miranda, grateful that at least the animals hadn't been neglected. Caleb apparently had remembered some of Henry's lessons.

She set the milk in the spring house to cool. When the wash water was hot, she added the clothes, tossed in a hunk of lye soap, and stirred the bubbling cauldron with the wooden laundry paddle, lifting steaming skirts, drawers, shirts, and bed linens into the clear rinse water.

She set Joe and Caleb to wringing out the clean clothes while she stirred another load. It was noon before everything was washed, rinsed, wrung out, and pegged to the clothesline to dry. Carrie raked her hair from her face. Her dress was damp and wrinkled, her hands raw. The soles of her feet burned. She massaged the ache in her shoulders. Oh, for a bath and a nap. A glass of lemonade and a quiet hour in the company of a good book.

"Carrie Daly, I'm hungrier than a grizzly bear," Joe said. "What's for dinner?"

"Yeah." Caleb squinted up at her. "We've been working like a couple of slaves all morning."

"Go check the henhouse. Maybe there are some eggs. And we have milk."

"Eggs again?" Caleb frowned, but he headed off with his brother.

Watching them cross the sunny yard, their arms swinging, Carrie felt a wave of compassion for them. It couldn't be easy, growing up without a father's guidance. She rounded the house and sat on the steps to cool off. A lazy breeze drifted across the porch. A flock of chickadees winged across the meadow. She closed her eyes. *Please, Henry, we need you desperately. Please hurry home.*

The next thing she knew, someone was gently shaking her shoulder. She started and gasped. "Mr. Rutledge."

"Sleeping beauty." He touched the brim of his hat and smiled his rogue's smile that never failed to make her weak in the knees. "Pleasant dreams, I hope."

She got to her feet and smoothed her hair, hating that she looked so unkempt. What must he think of her? "I finished the washing, and I must have dozed off." She looked around. "The boys—"

"Are happily occupied with Majestic. I may never be able to pry him from their grasp."

Carrie looked past his shoulder. Caleb and Joe stroked the black colt's forehead, talking softly to him. Majestic stood perfectly still, his magnificent tail swishing at a cloud of flies.

"What are you doing here?" Carrie smoothed the wrinkles in her dress.

Griff grinned. "That's not the most gracious greeting I've ever had."

"I'm surprised to see you is all. What brings you all the way out here?"

"Majestic needed a change of scenery. And I heard that you ended your exile and moved back here, so I came to see for myself."

"I didn't want to, but Mary is quite ill, and my brother is working in Chicago, so—"

"I admire you, Carrie. I'm afraid I lack your sense of duty."

"You'd do the same for your family."

"Maybe." He looked around. "Any chance you could slip away and go riding with me? Just for a little while?"

"I wish I could. But I must make a trip to the mercantile. I'm out of everything, and the boys are ravenous."

He laughed. "Reminds me of myself at that age. I could eat half a dozen eggs for breakfast without blinking an eye."

"Carrie!" Caleb shouted as Joe let out a scream. "Joe fell off the fence."

Carrie and Griff rushed across the yard. Joe was sitting up, but a deep gash had opened on his forehead. Blood trickled into his eye. He was gasping, trying not to cry.

"I wanted to ride Majestic," he said. "I stood on the fence to jump into the saddle, but I missed."

"Here." Griff knelt beside Joe and pressed his clean white handkerchief to the gash. "Hold it there for a minute, son, and the bleeding will stop."

"It hurts."

"I know it does, but you'll feel better soon. I promise."

Carrie rubbed the bony spot on her wrist and watched a red blob form on Griff's pristine handkerchief. How much trouble could two small boys generate? Why did Joe have to get hurt when there was still so much to do? She'd cry too if it would do any good.

Griff lifted Joe and carried him to the porch swing. "You sit right here, my friend, and your brother will fetch you a drink of water. Won't you, Caleb?"

"Yes, sir. I'll be glad to." Caleb headed inside.

Carrie blinked. Was this the same rude, rebellious child who defied her at every turn? Griff Rutledge evidently had a way with boys as well as with horses.

Griff checked the gash on Joe's head. "There now. The bleeding's just about stopped. You'll live, my man."

Joe grinned.

Griff folded his handkerchief and stuffed it into his pocket. "If you'll make up a list, Carrie, I'll be glad to fetch your supplies from town."

"I wouldn't want to trouble you."

"No trouble at all. I'm glad to be of service."

"Thank you. I would hate to leave with both Joe and Mary feeling unwell."

She went inside for pencil and paper and a few minutes later handed Griff a long list. "Ask Mr. Pruitt to put these things on my bill."

"Back before dark." He swung into the saddle.

"You'll stay for supper?" Carrie asked. "It's the least I can do."

"Appreciate the offer, but I doubt your sister-in-law would be pleased to see me. I sure would like to take you to supper at the inn sometime, though."

Filled with heat and an inexplicable lightness, Carrie nodded. But then reality intruded. Her future spooled out in front of her, an endless procession of dreary days that left no time for even the simplest pleasures.

Would she ever have a life of her own?

TWENTY-ONE

The smell of baking bread and the spill of bright October sunshine coming through the kitchen window brought Carrie a rare moment of contentment. Until she remembered the reason for the three loaves of bread just coming out of the oven. A frown creased her brow.

"What's the matter?" Mary shuffled from her bedroom to the kitchen, one hand pressed to the small of her back, and sat down heavily at the table. "You look like you're angry at the whole world."

Carrie set the last of the loaves on the windowsill and tossed her towel onto the counter.

"I told you. We're almost broke. Another week, and the cupboards will be bare again. And I hate asking Mr. Pruitt for more credit."

"I thought Mr. Chastain paid you to work in the bookshop. Surely you haven't squandered it all."

"Paying rent at the Verandah took nearly everything I had."

"Well, that was foolish of you, wasn't it? To pay rent to live in that rat's nest when you had a perfectly good home right here."

Carrie removed the loaves of bread from the pans. "You know full well why I didn't stay."

"Because of the boys and that silly snake?"

"It went a lot deeper than that." Carrie took off her apron and hung it on the peg beside the door. "Is there anything you need, Mary? I must get ready and take this bread into town."

"A fool's errand, if you ask me. Do you really think you'll sell it, with the bakery standing right there in the middle of town?"

"Two of the loaves are promised to Mrs. Whitcomb. She says my bread is much better than the bakery's. I'm planning to give the other one away."

"Give it away? When we're down to our last dollar? What kind of sense does that make?"

"Race Day is coming up in two weeks. Jasper Pruitt is planning on making up lunchboxes to sell from the mercantile. If he likes this bread, maybe he'll place an order."

"Which is all well and good, but what about when Race Day is over? Assuming anyone even shows up for it. Who'll buy your bread then?"

"I don't know. Perhaps we will have heard from Henry by then."

"But what if we don't? You should have planned for this from the first."

Carrie whirled around. "*I* should have planned? If you had put up the summer crops like you were supposed to, we wouldn't be in this mess."

"Don't yell at me. It's bad for the baby."

Carrie spun on her heel and headed up the stairs. Joe was sitting on the top step, the book of fairy tales open on his lap. He looked up with a gap-toothed grin. "Carrie Daly, can you read me a story?"

"Not now, Joe. I must go into town."

"Can I go with you?"

"Not this time."

"Can I go on Race Day? I want to see Majestic win. Griff says he runs like the wind."

Despite her irritation with Mary and her worry, she couldn't help smiling. Joe Stanhope had a way of charming her out of her darkest mood. "Mr. Rutledge says there are four other horses who may be just as fast. Majestic might not win."

"He will. You know why? Because Griff is the best trainer in the whole world."

Carrie opened the door to her room. Joe jumped up and followed her. "Griff said some trainers force their horses to obey, but he says it's better to show the horse what you want and reward him when he gets it right. He believes in natural horsemanship. He says—"

"Joe?" Carrie put a hand on the boy's shoulder. "I'm in a hurry. Maybe we can talk more when I get back. For now, why don't you go play with Caleb?"

"He don't like to play with me. He thinks I'm a baby."

Carrie pinned her hair and picked up her hat and shawl. "Well, he's wrong about that. You aren't a baby at all."

Joe grinned, his eyes shining. "I'm a better shot than Caleb. You just wait till I get my new slingshot. I'll show you how good I can aim."

He followed her down to the kitchen and watched her wrap up the bread, still warm from the oven. She set the loaves into her basket and checked on Mary, who was sleeping soundly, fists curled to her chest. Then she went out to hitch Iris to the rig. "If I'm not back by five, remind Caleb to milk the cow."

"Yes'm."

"And feed the chickens. Caleb forgot yesterday. If we don't feed them, they'll stop laying."

"Yes'm. And don't worry about Mama. When she wakes up, I'll get her some water or something."

"Good. I appreciate it."

She climbed into the rig and set off through the crisp fall afternoon. The trees formed an arch above her. Sunlight filtered through the branches, throwing coins of gold on the fallen leaves swirling across the road. Despite her money woes, the beauty of the afternoon and the rare solitude brought her a sense of peace.

Too soon, she entered town. She halted the rig outside the Verandah and went inside to find Mrs. Whitcomb on a ladder in the parlor, washing windows. The rug was rolled up in a corner. Newly washed curtains flapped on the line behind the hotel.

The hotelier climbed down and tossed her wet rag into a bucket of soapy water. She wiped her hands on her threadbare apron and eyed Carrie's bread basket. "Please tell me those loaves are mine."

"Two of them are. The third is a sample for Mr. Pruitt."

"Well, I'm about to starve. I've been up since dawn working on this old place. No amount of scrubbing can make up for plain old decrepitude, though." She led the way to the kitchen and motioned Carrie to a chair. "I reckon I should have sold this place when my husband died, but he set such store by it, I never had the heart to get rid of it. The old girl sure could use a coat of paint, but I can't afford it."

"Maybe you'll fill up for Race Day."

"Not likely to have too many ladies traveling alone to watch a horse race. Reckon I might have to lower my standards and let the men in here." She sliced the bread and set out a jar of blackberry jam and a crock of butter. "How about some tea?"

"I'd love some."

Mrs. Whitcomb set the kettle on to boil and took two cups from the cupboard. "I'm glad to see you, Carrie. Things haven't been the same since you left. Lucy misses you too. I guess you heard that Rachel Ryan left town last week."

"No, I don't get much news out at the farm." Carrie spread jam onto the bread and took a bite.

"Rachel's husband finally got a job at that pencil factory in North Carolina, and last Saturday he showed up for her, out of the blue."

"I'm sure she was happy about that."

"Yep, and I'm happy for her too, although her leaving means another empty room to fill. Once Lucy's gone west, it'll be just me and the Provost sisters rattling around in this old shell of a place." Mrs. Whitcomb made the tea and sat down opposite Carrie. "I was over to the bookshop last week. Not that I can afford to buy anything these days, but I like to look."

Carrie stirred her tea and smiled. "I know what you mean."

"Nate's right worried about Rosaleen."

"Oh?" Carrie recalled her last talk with him about his new wife, but it wasn't something to share with Mrs. Whitcomb.

"He says she's been actin' kind of strange. Writing letters to people he never heard of and poking around the town hall. Betsy Terwilliger said Rosaleen came into the mayor's office last week, wanting to know if they still had copies of the *Hickory Ridge Gazette*." She shook her head. "Can't fathom what anybody would want with old newspapers."

"Maybe she wants to learn more about the town, now that Hickory Ridge is her home."

"Maybe. But land's sakes, if that's all it is, why don't she stop all that mysterious detective work and just ask somebody? Mayor Scott has been here forever. He could tell her anything she wants to know."

Carrie finished her tea and stood. "I must go. I want to catch Mr. Pruitt before he leaves for the day."

Mrs. Whitcomb pressed a handful of coins into Carrie's hand. "For the bread. Can you make two loaves again next week?"

"Of course."

"I'll let you know if I need extra for Race Day."

Carrie let herself out and hurried to the mercantile. Jasper Pruitt was standing in the back, cutting a length of fabric for a woman wearing a wide-brimmed yellow hat. While he tended to his customer, she perused the shelves. Even though it was only October,

Jasper had already ordered a few extra things for the upcoming Christmas season. On a high shelf sat a shiny red top, a wooden train set, and a brightly painted clown bank whose open mouth served as the coin slot. Any of those toys would delight Joe and Caleb. Maybe enough money would arrive from Henry before Christmas to make such a gift possible.

Jasper lumbered to the front of the store, shears in hand. After his customer had gone, the package of fabric neatly wrapped in a brown paper bundle, he turned to Carrie. "What can I help you with?"

She set her loaf of bread on the counter. "I brought you a sample of my bread. Made fresh this morning."

"How come?"

"I heard you're planning to offer lunchboxes on Race Day. I was hoping you'd buy the bread from me."

"And why would I do that when the bakery's right across the street?"

"Mine is made in smaller batches, so the quality is better." She slid it toward him. "Please try some."

He tore off a hunk and chewed. "It's tasty, all right. But I kinda feel an obligation to the bakery." He ate another piece, the crumbs falling into his beard. "Besides, the people in town for Race Day will be gone in a day or two. It don't make good business sense to spend more for a temporary product."

"I see your point." She paused. "The truth is, Mr. Pruitt, that I desperately need the money. My brother has found work in Chicago and we expected he'd send money by now, but it hasn't arrived. I was hoping to earn a little money until it does. Otherwise, I'm afraid my bill here will grow even larger."

He frowned. "You don't owe me a dime, Miz Daly."

"But that's impossible. Mr. Rutledge was in here only a few weeks ago and—"

"Paid cash money for the whole lot of it."

"Griff—Mr. Rutledge—paid my bill?"

"Yep. It was quite a big one too."

"We were out of everything at the farm. Mary let the summer garden go to waste, so I had to buy more than usual. But I had no idea Mr. Rutledge paid. He didn't say a word about it."

The storekeeper's small, round eyes bore into hers. "That horse tamer's gone sweet on you, I reckon."

Carrie's face burned. What would people say if they knew Griff Rutledge was supporting her family? Mariah and Eugenie would never let her live it down. To them it would be practically as bad as living in sin. "It was kind of him. But I intend to pay him back every cent."

"By selling bread, one loaf at a time?" Jasper's expression softened. "Listen, Miz Daly. I know you've got your pride, and it's an admirable thing. But everybody in Hickory Ridge is barely hanging on these days. You baked bread for the church charity when you were stayin' at the Verandah. Ain't that right?"

"Yes, but—"

"And you helped make quilts for them orphans back when Miss Lillian was alive."

"I was happy to do it."

"Sometimes it takes as much grace to accept help as it does to give it." He returned the half-eaten loaf to the basket. "Why don't you take this on home to Mary's boys and stop worrying about that gamblin' man."

Leaving the mercantile, Carrie glanced up the street toward Nate's bookshop. How was he getting on? She missed Nate's keen intelligence, quiet wit, and warm smile . . . and their lively discussions about books and politics. Why couldn't they have gone on being friends, without the question of marriage intruding? Why hadn't he been enough for her?

Sabrina Gilman emerged from the post office in the company of a young man Carrie didn't recognize. Dressed in a pink-and-white striped frock and a straw boater trimmed in pink ribbons, Sabrina looked impossibly young and happier than Carrie had seen her in a while.

The young man took her arm as they crossed the street to the bakery. Sabrina leaned into him, whispering, and Carrie's heart seized at the memory of Frank and their early days together. Even after the passing of so many years, she remembered his shy smile, the joyous procession from his family's house to hers on their wedding day, his tentative tenderness on their first nights as husband and wife. The plans they'd made for the future, whispering together in the dark.

So many dreams, snuffed out in an instant at Bloody Pond.

She loaded her supplies onto the wagon and drove home through the waning afternoon. An unfamiliar rig was parked in the yard. Joe and Caleb were nowhere to be seen. Carrie frowned. Those two were never around when she needed them.

She unloaded her supplies and headed inside. Deborah Patterson met her on the porch. "Hello, Carrie. I was afraid I'd have to leave before I could greet you." She held out her good arm. "Let me help you with those."

Carrie handed her friend a tin of tea. "Thanks."

They carried everything into the kitchen. Carrie noticed a tea tray and two cups on the table.

"I made tea for Mary," Deborah said. "She's sleeping now, poor thing."

Carrie nodded. "I wish I knew what was wrong with her."

"Perhaps she's heartsick." Standing on tiptoe, Deborah put away a sack of sugar. "Sometimes a sickness of the spirit is worse than a bodily affliction. There's more tea if you'd like some."

"That sounds good." Carrie looked around. "Where are the boys?"

"Mary gave them permission to go fishing. It isn't natural for them to spend so much time indoors." She poured two cups, and they sat at the table. Deborah stirred sugar into her tea and smiled. "My mother, rest her soul, always said I should have been born a boy. She tried to teach me sewing and fine needlework, but when I was Joe's age, I spent more time swimming and chasing fireflies and climbing trees than with needle and thread."

Before she could stifle the impulse, Carrie glanced at her friend's useless arm. How could Deborah have managed such rigorous activities with only one arm and a damaged leg?

Deborah sipped her tea. "I wasn't always this way. I had a normal childhood until my mother died. I was only nine."

Carrie nodded. "I was five when my parents died of yellow fever."

"It's horrible, isn't it, being deprived of a mother so young. My father couldn't take it either. He took to the bottle after that, and drink made him mean. My older brother ran off at fourteen and left me alone to deal with Daddy."

Deborah shook her head. "I did everything I could not to rile him, but the least little thing would set him off. If I served his breakfast on a chipped plate, if I burned the biscuits or forgot to bring in the laundry, he beat me until he passed out."

Carrie thought of her own parents, who had shown her and Henry nothing but kindness. She'd been blessed, had taken the blessing for granted. Her heart broke for Deborah. How could a father show such cruelty to his own child? How could Deborah bear the memory of it? "You don't have to tell me any more."

"I want to." Deborah patted her hand. "The week before my seventeenth birthday, Daddy left early for town and told me not to forget to bring the cows in from the pasture. The day was stifling hot, so after I finished cleaning up the house I got some cool water from the spring and sat for a while on the front porch just listening to the cicadas. Andrew Porter, the boy who lived on the next farm over, came riding up the road and stopped for a drink of water. I told him it was almost my birthday. He laughed and said a girl turning seventeen ought to have a present. He took me into town to get a hair ribbon."

She smiled. "Up to that time it was the only present I'd ever received. After Andy dropped me back home, I got Mama's mirror down and pinned the ribbon in my hair one way and then another."

Deborah paused, a pained look in her eyes. Carrie stole a glance at the minister's wife. Had she stopped for breath . . . or to gather the courage to remember what had happened next?

"The next thing I knew it was dark and Daddy was back. Too late I remembered about the cows. I ran out the back door to the pasture, but he caught me by the hair and dragged me into the barn. He stripped me to my chemise and beat me until I fainted. When I came to, I was covered in my own blood and chained to the anvil he used for making horseshoes."

Carrie stared, horrified. "Oh, Deborah. I had no idea. You must have felt terrified, and terribly alone."

"Terrified, yes. I knew Daddy meant to leave me there until I died. By then death would have been welcome. But I didn't feel alone. Not for a single minute. Because I knew our Lord could see me. He knew where I was and the trouble I was in, and that was when I learned the beauty of surrender. For two days I lay there in my own blood and waste and waited for him. I was ready if he wanted me. But if not, if there was still work on earth he wanted me to do, I was ready to do that too."

Carrie sat transfixed by the power of Deborah's story and the breathtaking certainty of her friend's faith. "How did you escape?"

"Andrew came by looking for me and noticed that my daddy was all scratched up. He figured Daddy had been after me again, so he looked for me until he found me. Eventually my bruises and cuts healed, but my broken foot never mended properly, and my arm was so damaged from being chained up . . ."

She looked past Carrie's shoulder to the yard beyond. "That was when I met Daniel. He and his wife, Cordelia, had a little church in the hills above Cool Hollow. I couldn't go back home, so they took me in and took care of me. I stayed with them until Cordelia died. Later Daniel and I married. We've been together since."

Shaken to her core, Carrie only nodded. "I admire your certainty. But I don't see how—"

"It isn't complicated at all, once you make up your mind to surrender your all to him. Despite my infirmities, I'm happier now than I've ever been." Punctuating the end of her story with a brief nod, Deborah rose. "It's getting late. I should be going."

"Thank you for visiting Mary."

Deborah smiled. "It was you I hoped to see. Will you be at church on Sunday?"

TWENTY-TWO

"See how he's pinning his ears back?" Griff grinned down at Carrie and gestured to Majestic. "That tells me he's heard me, but he's decided to ignore me. That won't do. Even a small infraction must be corrected. Otherwise, he'll get to thinking he's the one in charge."

Carrie perched on the fence and listened, fascinated, as Griff explained the finer points of horse training. Part experience and part intuition, Griff's ability to communicate with Majestic seemed nothing short of magical. She watched the way he moved to reassure the horse, tugging gently on Majestic's bridle until the horse lowered his head and emitted a deep, fluttering breath through his nostrils.

"That's right," he murmured to the horse. "There we go." He swung into the saddle, an expression of triumph and pleasure lighting his tanned face. "Now he's relaxed. Be right back. "

He nudged the horse into a smart canter and then, at the far end of the pasture, into a dead run. Leaning forward over the horse's neck, he urged Majestic on, and the colt thundered past the gate, his dark mane flying, his hooves sending up dirt clods that peppered Carrie's skirt. She didn't care. Being with Griff, watching him doing the work he loved, was a pure joy.

She owed this rare pleasure to Deborah Patterson, who had

returned this morning for another visit with Mary. Despite her admiration and growing affection for Deborah, Carrie was discomfited by her friend's knowing look. Was Deborah waiting to hear that Carrie had given up her struggles and surrendered her all to God? It wasn't that she didn't want the kind of peace such deep faith would afford. It was simply that, after so many losses, she lacked the courage to trust, to lay everything at his feet.

She had hurried through serving tea before leaving to take Griff up on his standing invitation to visit the Gilmans' and watch him train. With Race Day now only a week away, she wouldn't have many more chances to spend time with him. Last week when he'd talked about how much he loved the Gilmans' place, its graceful house and endless pastures set against the dramatic backdrop of the Smoky Mountains, she'd felt a flicker of hope. If only he might stay and settle down in Hickory Ridge. But what could a struggling southern Appalachian town offer a man like him? In a week's time, maybe two, he'd be gone, and today would fade into nothing more than a bittersweet memory.

She shaded her eyes and watched Griff make the turn at the top of the rise. He slowed to a trot and, after a couple of laps around the pasture, halted in front of her. "I think he's ready."

He slipped from the saddle and offered Majestic an apple. The horse chomped it and let out a long whinny that made Griff laugh. "See? He knows he's ready too."

Carrie smiled at his boyish enthusiasm. "Joe is thoroughly convinced you'll win."

Griff wiped his brow with his sleeve. "We've got a chance. Yesterday I had Gilman help me measure Majestic's stride. Best I can calculate, it's nearly twenty-three feet."

"I assume that's good."

"It's exceptional." He opened the gate and they headed for the barn, the big colt plodding confidently between them. "Average on a Thoroughbred is twenty feet. I've heard the horse coming from Kentucky has stride of almost twenty-two." He reached up to rub Majestic's face. "My boy here should be able to take him. As long as he stays focused. I'm taking him to town every day next week so he can get used to the sound of the train whistle." He smiled. "We can't have him knocking down any more pretty ladies."

Carrie smiled back at him. "I'm glad you were there that day."

"So am I." He dropped the reins and took both her shoulders, turning her gently to face him.

Her heart sped up. Her mouth went dry as sand. Clearly he was going to kiss her. And heaven help her, she wanted it. Even though the memory of it, after he was gone, would break her heart clean in two. "Griff—"

He drew her close, slid one arm behind her back, and brought his lips to hers. She was lost, unable to control her reaction to him. Longing moved through her, warm and slow as molten lead. The attraction she'd felt for him on their first meeting sparked within her. She parted her lips for his kiss, and the very air around her seemed to shimmer with promise. Feeling suddenly vulnerable and unsettled, she pulled away. "I should go."

"I know," he said, his voice rough with emotion. But he held her a moment longer before helping her into her rig. "Meet me in town for dinner tomorrow. The cook at the inn makes a mean venison stew."

"I can't. There's no one to stay with Mary and the boys. Come to dinner at the farm. Six o'clock."

A rueful smile lit his face. "Mary Stanhope won't like that one bit. You know she won't."

"The farm was my home long before it was hers. I'm there because she begged me to take care of her. And besides, after your generosity in lending me money for the food bill, she's hardly in a position to criticize my choices."

"I've told you it was a gift, Carrie, not a loan. But in any case, I accept." He leaned in and touched his forehead to hers. "I can't wait until six. How about five?"

"Five is even better."

He nodded. "Majestic needs tending. I'll see you then."

Griff watched her rig disappear at the end of the Gilmans' lane, the memory of her kiss foremost in his mind. Picking up the reins, he led Majestic to the barn, removed the horse's tack, and picked up the currycomb. Majestic snuffled and nodded as if he approved, causing Griff to laugh out loud. He couldn't remember the last time he had felt so content. Holding Carrie, her soft lips clinging to his, had kindled feelings he'd supposed were gone forever—hope, peace, maybe even the promise of happiness. And to think he had met her by pure chance. If he hadn't been in town to settle things with Rosaleen, if Majestic hadn't spooked at the precise moment Carrie emerged from the dress shop . . .

He finished with the currycomb and gave Majestic a bucket of oats sweetened with molasses. Of course he believed in God. He'd never have made it through the war otherwise. But he'd never really believed in miracles . . . until now. Who could have predicted that his life and Carrie's could so quickly become entwined?

He mucked out the stall, filled Majestic's water trough, then mounted his rented horse for the ride back to town. The cooling breeze and the crackle of falling leaves reminded him that the ship's agent in San Francisco awaited his reply. Soon he'd have to decide whether to book passage for Australia.

The lure of the unknown was still a powerful force inside him. And yet the prospect of endless freedom at the bottom of the world somehow seemed far less attractive.

"Did the Yankees shoot at your boat?"

Carrie poured more coffee and smiled at the look on Caleb's face. The boy leaned both elbows on the table and gazed up at Griff, his expression one of pure awe. Supper was over, and for the last hour Griff had regaled them with stories of his days captaining a blockade runner out of Charleston harbor, delivering cotton to Nassau and Havana and bringing back medicines, ammunition, and clothing for the Confederates.

"We got shot at a time or two, but the *Nightingale* was specially built for the job I had to do," Griff said. "She sat low in the water, and she was painted gray to blend in with the color of the sea and the fog. On a moonless night I could sail right past the Union ships and they never even saw me."

Joe laughed. "I bet you were the most famous captain in South Carolina."

"I don't know about that. Captain Wilkinson of the *Robert E. Lee* ran the blockade more than twenty times, delivering cotton to Nassau. Everyone admired his bravery. And his luck."

"I bet he got paid a lot of money for that," Caleb said. "I bet he made millions."

"Did you make millions too?" Joe popped a crust of bread into his mouth and looked up at Griff.

Mary frowned at her son in a way that made Carrie's stomach hurt. "People of quality never talk about money, Joe."

"That's all right." Griff smiled at Carrie and leaned back in his chair, completely at ease in the small, warm kitchen. "Not to contradict your mother, Joe—she has a right to bring you up however she sees fit—but I am not offended in the least. In fact, the subject of my fortune was the talk of the town for quite some time. Still is, among certain of my acquaintance."

"What about the smoke?" Caleb asked, and Carrie saw that he had been working out the details of Griff's adventures in his head. "From the engines, I mean. How come the Union ships didn't see it?"

"That's a good question, Caleb. I like a man with a head on his shoulders."

Carrie studied the older boy. He seemed intrigued, maybe even flattered, but not as easily won over as his younger brother. Caleb Stanhope sure was a hard nut to crack. If Griff, with his easy charm and adventurous past, couldn't win Caleb over, no one could.

"Anthracite coal," Griff said. "It burns without making smoke. Soon as I could see the light on Fort Sumter, I'd cut the running lights, cover the binnacle and the fireroom hatch, and blow the steam off under water."

Joe grinned. "Like when you take a bath in the tub and you—"

Caleb gaped at his brother and fell off his chair laughing.

"Joseph Stanhope, that's enough." Mary blushed and swatted the boy's leg.

"I should go." Griff stood. "I've kept you up far too long. Thank you for the hospitality of your home, Mrs. Bell."

Mary offered him a curt nod.

"And thank you, Mrs. Daly, for the fine dinner. Every bite of it was outstanding."

Carrie fought a nearly unbearable urge to touch him. The more she learned about Griff Rutledge, the more she hungered to know. She smiled, acutely aware of his intense gaze. "I'm glad you enjoyed it."

She walked him to the parlor, where he retrieved his hat and coat.

"Will I see you for the race next Saturday?" he asked, his voice low.

"I hope so. It depends on how Mary is feeling."

He nodded. "Wish me luck."

"You know I do."

A shout and a clatter from the kitchen shattered the quiet. She closed her eyes. Mary had been in a foul temper all day. The best thing to do was clean up quickly and put the boys to bed. Their noise and their constant needs seemed to worsen their mother's mood. And when Mary wasn't happy, no one in the house could breathe easy.

"Go ahead," Griff said. "Look after them. I can see myself out." She watched him cross the yard and mount up.

In the kitchen, Mary was banging pans into the soapy dish-water, a grimace contorting her thin face. Joe and Caleb had gone to fetch water and firewood.

"You shouldn't be on your feet, Mary. Doctor's orders. I'll take care of the dishes."

"I wasn't sure you could tear yourself away from the charming Mr. Rutledge long enough to handle your responsibilities." Mary wiped her hands on a kitchen towel and draped it over the pie safe. "My lands, the way you've thrown yourself at him is a disgrace."

"Thrown myself at him?"

"You were mooning over him all during supper. And whispering with him in the hall just now. And he was nothing short of a criminal during the war."

"A criminal? The government paid men to do his job. It was just as important as taking up arms and shooting people." Carrie tied an apron over her dress, rolled up her sleeves, and banged a few pans of her own. "If men like Griff hadn't brought in weapons, General Lee's army would have been in even worse shape."

Mary looked up from the plate she was scraping. "Don't use that sainted man's name in the same sentence with Griffin Rutledge's. It's sacrilege." She stalked to her room and slammed the door shut behind her just as Joe walked in with an armload of firewood. Caleb, toting two buckets of water, was right behind him.

"All the chores are done, Carrie," Caleb reported. "I brought Miranda up from the pasture. Looks like we might have frost tonight."

Stunned by his unusually helpful attitude, Carrie smiled. Maybe she should try Griff's training methods on the boy. "That was good thinking. I appreciate it."

He set the water on the table beside the door. "Me and Joe was wonderin' if you'd take us to the race on Saturday. I sure would like to see Mr. Rutledge ride that horse."

Ah. That was the reason he'd suddenly turned so helpful. "I'm not sure we can go," Carrie told him. "Who would look after your mother?"

Caleb's face darkened. "We can't do anything fun 'cause she's always sick. But yesterday when the preacher's wife came, she got all dressed up and had her tea and acted like there was nothing wrong at all."

Carrie turned away and concentrated on wiping the plates. "Well, you know how your mother likes to do things the right way."

He leaned against the table, sloshing the water. "Come on, Carrie. Can't we go, even for a little while?"

TWENTY-THREE

Carrie set Mary's breakfast tray on the table by the bed and opened the curtains, letting in the pale autumn light. Red and gold leaves drifted from the trees lining the road. In the distance, geese winged over the fog-shrouded mountains.

"What time is it?" Mary stirred and sat up, blinking.

"Almost seven."

Mary yawned and picked up her cup. "I'm so tired all the time."

"That's to be expected at this stage. Or so I'm told. Mariah said she had a lot more energy after the first few months."

"No. This is something else." Mary sipped her tea and buttered a biscuit. "Sometimes I'm afraid there is something terribly wrong and the doctor is keeping the news from me."

Carrie felt an unexpected surge of compassion for her sister-in-law. It couldn't be easy, being so sick and separated from the man she loved. "I'm sure Dr. Spencer wouldn't do that. He's always been the practical sort." She indicated Mary's plate. "He wants you to build up your strength for the delivery."

Mary ate a forkful of eggs and wrinkled her nose. "Too much salt."

"The boys want to go to the race tomorrow," Carrie said. "But I'm not sure I should leave you here alone."

"Caleb has been nagging me about it ever since Mr. Rutledge

came to supper. And Joe hangs on the man's every word. He's very proud of the tiny scar he got from trying to mount that horse. He tells me over and over how Mr. Rutledge carried him to the porch that day."

"They miss having Henry around."

"Me too." Mary's cup clattered onto her saucer. "Oh, if only I weren't having this baby, we could all be in Chicago by now."

"But you wouldn't trade this child merely for a chance to live in the city?"

Mary dabbed her lips with her napkin and smiled a you-don't-know-anything smile. "Henry told me a thousand times how much you wanted a family. But it isn't as idyllic as you think. Of course I love your brother and my boys. But sometimes I envy your freedom."

Freedom? Carrie almost laughed. Wasn't she tied night and day to this farm and this frail, flighty woman and her children, responsible for their every need? "I suppose it's natural to imagine that other people have the better situation. But I'd gladly trade whatever freedom you think I have for a husband and children of my own. It's all I've ever really wanted."

"Because you've been taught to believe it's what you should want. Personally, I think a woman's life should be about much more than looking out for a man and a passel of children, though of course it's very convenient for—"

"Mama?" Joe burst into the room. "Can we go to the race? Did Carrie Daly ask you if we could go?"

Mary sighed and closed her eyes. "We were just discussing it."

"Oh good. Wait till I tell Caleb."

Carrie put a hand on the boy's shoulder. "Just a moment. Your mama hasn't said yes yet. Why don't you go feed the chickens. See if there are any eggs today."

He frowned. "Jumping junebugs. We've been talking about it all week. How long does it take to say yes?"

Mary leaned over and squeezed his hand. "Go on, son."

When Joe ran outside, Mary said, "I think you should take them. They've had a lot of bad things happen, losing their real daddy when they were only babies and then Henry leaving so soon. They ought to have some good memories of their childhood." She set her tray aside, rattling her cup. "And you're dying to go anyway, to see the magnificent Mr. Rutledge."

"But we'll be away all day. Will you be all right?" Carrie picked up Mary's tray. "I could send word down to Two Creeks, see if Libby Dawson can stay with you."

"I don't want a colored girl prowling around in my house."

"Libby is very reliable. She looked after Wyatt Caldwell's Aunt Lillian lots of times, and the Dawsons were here for your wedding."

"Yes, cooking and serving food. That's different." Mary sat up, fluffed her pillow, and fell back against it. "What if I had to vomit . . . or worse? What if I needed help getting to the chamber pot?"

In a flash of understanding, Carrie realized Mary Stanhope Bell was more terrified of looking weak, of being beholden, than she was of anything else. That anyone, even Libby Dawson, should see her as less than in total command was more than she could bear. No wonder this pregnancy was such a trial to her. No wonder she bristled so when Carrie didn't follow her advice or her orders.

"If you can be back before dark, I'm sure I'll be all right." Mary gestured to the newspaper that had arrived in last week's mail. "If I feel up to it, I may catch up on my reading." She smiled. "It might be rather nice, having a day to myself."

⌒

By the time Carrie rose the next morning, Caleb and Joe were already up and dressed. The wood box in the kitchen was full, as were the water buckets. On the table, three clean plates and three forks waited.

Joe tugged on her arm. "Hurry up, Carrie Daly. Let's eat some breakfast and get going. I don't want to miss a minute of Race Day."

Carrie tied an apron over the dress she'd bought for Henry's wedding. Griff had seen her in it before, of course, and it was too fancy even for today, but it suited her coppery hair and blue eyes, and she wanted to look her best for him. She sliced the bread she'd baked yesterday, set out jam and cheese, and poured milk for the boys. They downed their food like prisoners at a last meal, but her stomach was so knotted and jumpy she couldn't swallow a single bite.

She wanted Griff and Majestic to win the race. And she wanted him to stay—but that would take a bona fide miracle. *Please, Lord. If it's all the same with you, find a way to keep Griff Rutledge in Hickory Ridge.*

She made a tray for Mary, filled a water pitcher, straightened Mary's coverlet, and emptied the foul-smelling chamber pot. Mary moaned and stirred, her broomstick-thin arms thrown across her face.

When Carrie finished hitching Iris, and the boys were aboard, she went inside to wake her sister-in-law. "We're leaving now. Is there anything you need?"

Mary grunted and sat up. "Maybe my knitting?"

Carrie handed her the small ball of yellow yarn and her needles. "We'll be back before dark."

"Oh, and maybe another glass of milk. If it isn't too much trouble."

Suppressing her irritation, Carrie fetched the milk and escaped before Mary could think of other things she needed. She handed Caleb the lunch basket she'd prepared for them, climbed onto the wagon, and picked up the reins. "Well, boys, we're off."

"I can't wait to get to town," Caleb said. "I'm getting some candy at the mercantile with the dime Mr. Chastain gave me. I've been debatin' all morning, and I still can't decide between peppermint sticks or sarsaparilla."

"Caleb made me a darn good slingshot, Carrie Daly," said Joe, producing it from his pocket. "Last night I run off a possum with it."

Taking a small, smooth stone from his pocket, he fitted it into the slingshot and drew it taut. The rock sailed across the road and thudded against the fence railing.

Carrie grinned. "That's a powerful weapon, all right. But you must be careful, Joe. Don't aim it at anything you don't intend to hit."

"No, ma'am, I won't." Joe held tightly to the side of the wagon as they left the farm behind and rounded a curve. "Carrie Daly, is your brother ever going to come back home?"

"Of course he is—when your new sister or brother is born. Then I suppose you'll all be moving to Chicago."

"I hate Chicago," Caleb said.

"How do you know? Have you ever been there?"

"No, but I've seen pictures. All it is, is a buncha big ol' buildings. There's no grass or cows or trees."

"Their city parks are full of grass and trees," Carrie told him. "And there's a big lake for boating. And a train station that's a hundred times bigger than the one in Hickory Ridge. I think it sounds pretty exciting."

As they passed the country church, the wagon jostled over a stretch of rutted road, nearly upending their lunch basket. Joe set it to rights.

"I don't care if they have a million trains," Caleb said. "They's no mountains or hollers or fishin' creeks or nothin'. No sir, I'm stayin' right here."

"But we don't even have a school here," Joe said. "I want a school.

Mama says if we stay here we'll always be poor as church mice. She says we'll never become men of quality."

"Becoming a man of quality has everything to do with character and very little to do with where one lives," Carrie said. "We have plenty of men of quality right here in Hickory Ridge. Dr. Spencer and Mr. Chastain are two of the finest men I know."

"And Mr. Rutledge," Joe said.

Carrie blushed. "Yes. Mr. Rutledge too."

At last they arrived in town. Wagons, horses, and rigs of all descriptions lined the main road. Crowds of people moved along the sidewalks, admiring the displays in the store windows. A knot of people crowded into Nate's bookshop. Through the window, Carrie spotted Nate and Rosaleen talking to a customer. She caught Nate's eye and waved. He smiled and nodded before going back to his customer, but she watched him a moment longer. Had his reservations about his new wife been resolved? She drew up next to a fancy rig and tethered Iris.

"Can I go to the mercantile?" Caleb jumped off the wagon, landing with a thump.

The owner of the rig parked next to her appeared, carrying a tripod and camera. He placed a set of glass plates into the rig and tipped his hat. "Morning, ma'am. That's a pretty dress you're wearing. How about a picture of you and your handsome boys? It'd make a nice souvenir."

He handed her a business card. "George Platt's the name. Just off the train from Buffalo, New York. Portraits are my specialty."

"Thank you, but I don't think—"

"She ain't our mama," Joe said. "She's ain't no real kin at all."

Tears sprang to Carrie's eyes. She thought of Henry, so far from home and most surely lonely for his new life and his new family, which had been sundered almost as soon as it began. She couldn't really afford a portrait, but . . .

"It's only a dollar," the photographer said. "And if you aren't completely satisfied, your entire fee will be cheerfully refunded."

Carrie felt her resolve weakening. So what if they had nothing to eat but bacon and beans for an extra week? The sacrifice would be worth it if the photograph served as a peace offering to Henry. A way back into his good graces. "Very well, Mr. Platt."

"Splendid." Mr. Platt lined them up next to the wagon, the boys flanking Carrie. He prepared a slide, draped the cloth over the camera, and admonished them not to move. Caleb stood unsmiling and ramrod straight, but Joe looked up at Carrie just as the flash went off.

The photographer handed her a stub of a pencil and a printed form. "Write down your name and address, and I'll send your photograph as soon as it's done." He waved a hand to indicate the crowded street. "Might take awhile. I've been busy ever since I got here. Lots of folks in town today."

"We're havin' a horse race," Joe told him. "Our friend Griff Rutledge is going to win."

"You don't say." Mr. Platt scanned the crowd, looking for his next customer.

Carrie scribbled on the form and paid the man.

"Thank you kindly," he said, pocketing the form and his fee. "I hope you enjoy the race."

"Can I go to the mercantile now?" Caleb asked.

Carrie smiled. That dime certainly was burning a hole in the boy's pocket. "All right. Take Joe with you."

"Do I have to?"

"Absolutely."

Caleb jerked a thumb at his brother. "Come on then. But don't do anything stupid."

"Meet me outside the bank by noon," Carrie said. "We want to get a good seat for the race."

The boys headed for the mercantile. Carrie took her time

browsing the shop windows, listening to the conversations going on around her. Race Day had drawn a bigger crowd than she'd expected. Outside the dress shop, Mariah stood chatting with Molly Scott. Carrie waved. Mariah returned the wave briefly and resumed her conversation. Stung, Carrie crossed the street. She spotted Daniel and Deborah Patterson, a large picnic basket between them, making their way to the far end of the street, where Sheriff McCracken supervised a small army of young boys. Shovels flashing, they worked to deposit a thick layer of dirt over the brick street.

"Cover those bricks good and proper, boys." The sheriff raised his voice to be heard above the sawing of fiddles and the twang of banjoes coming from an impromptu band near the Hickory Ridge Inn. "We can't have those fancy horses slipping on the bricks and hurting themselves." He looked up and touched the brim of his hat. "Morning, Miz Daly."

"Sheriff."

The train whistle shrieked. Carrie looked around for Griff and Majestic, praying the colt had overcome his fear of the sound. Through the burgeoning crowd, she glimpsed a couple of the other riders leading their horses past the bank to the starting line, even though the race was still two hours away. She pictured Griff off somewhere calming Majestic, preparing him for the race, her excitement muted by the knowledge that after today Griff would have no reason to remain in Hickory Ridge.

Carrie rarely asked God for anything simply because she wanted it. Granny Bell had always said true faith didn't work that way. People were supposed to pray for the gifts of the spirit—grace, compassion, forgiveness—and usually she did. But now, making her way toward the bank, she couldn't help herself. *Lord, if it's all the same to you, give me just a little more time with Griff. A few more moments of happiness.*

"Carrie Daly!" Joe rushed toward her, his slingshot poking from his back pocket, a paper bag bulging with candy clutched tightly in one hand. "Look what all we got—peppermint and sarsaparilla and licorice and I don't know what all. Caleb done ate half of his, but I'm savin' mine till after the race. If Majestic wins, I'm giving him some peppermint. You think he'll like it?"

"My goodness." She smiled at the boy. "Slow down, Joe."

The crowd grew as another train arrived, disgorging people who clogged the street looking for places to sit, opening lunch baskets, getting ready to watch the race. Mr. Platt moved through the crowd, taking more photographs. Carrie watched Sheriff McCracken pose outside his office, one hand on his gun belt. She sent Caleb to fetch their lunch basket from the wagon, and the three of them settled on the steps outside the bank.

Caleb opened the small tin of molasses Carrie had packed and drizzled some over a large piece of cornbread. "Guess who me 'n' Joe saw in the mercantile."

"I have no idea."

"The man from Kentucky that brought his horse for the race. He told Mr. Pruitt that everybody in Tennessee ought to hate Mr. Rutledge because he's from South Carolina." Frowning, Caleb bit into his cornbread. "I don't reckon I understand that."

Dismayed that old political hatreds should mar the day for a couple of innocent boys, Carrie attempted to explain. "You know about President Andrew Jackson, right? He was from right here in Tennessee."

Caleb nodded. "We studied him in school way back when I was little. He ran the British clear out of New Orleans, and he was a famous Indian fighter too."

"That's right. When he was president, one of the men who didn't like the job he was doing was Mr. Calhoun from South Carolina. He and Mr. Jackson fought about one thing and then another all the time."

Joe made a fist and pounded his brother's shoulder. "Sort of like me and Caleb. Except we usually strike hands and make up. Mama makes us."

Carrie smiled. "Too bad she wasn't there to make Mr. Jackson and Mr. Calhoun make up. Some folks around here and in South Carolina too, I suppose, still hold grudges against one another because of those old disagreements. But it has nothing to do with today. All of that happened more than forty years ago."

"Jumping junebugs." Caleb wiped a blob of molasses off his chin. "And you still remember it?"

Carrie didn't know whether to laugh or feel insulted. "I'm not that old. It happened before I was born."

Caleb broke off another handful of cornbread. "Mr. Pruitt said there's some folks in Hickory Ridge that don't like Mr. Rutledge 'cause he plays cards instead of working."

"Mr. Rutledge used to play cards, but he works for Mr. Gilman now, training Majestic."

Carrie brushed Caleb's hair from his eyes and he pulled away. "And we shouldn't judge others."

"No, ma'am. I know that. But Mr. Pruitt said Mr. Rutledge keeps company with the wrong kind of women." Caleb chewed and swallowed. "I don't reckon I understand that either."

Carrie's could well imagine the gossip making the rounds in town today concerning her and Griff Rutledge. Fine. If they wanted to think of her as the wrong kind of woman, so be it. Their attitude said more about them than it did about her. She had done nothing improper. Nothing she should be ashamed of.

She and the boys finished their meal. Caleb took the basket to the wagon and ran off to find his friends. Joe perched on the rail outside the mercantile and dug into his sack of candy.

"Carrie?"

She turned to find Deborah moving awkwardly through the crowd. A couple of men stepped aside for her and tipped their hats.

"Deborah. Hello." The sight of her friend's serene smile lifted Carrie's heart. If only she possessed Deborah's unassailable faith.

"I saw you with the photographer." With her good hand, Deborah clasped her useless one. "He's very persistent, isn't he? Even Daniel finally relented."

"Mr. Platt isn't easily discouraged." Carrie made room on the steps. "Want to watch the race with me?"

"I'd love to, but we can't stay. Mr. Musgrove expired last night and we must call on the family." Deborah nodded and waved to a family of four settling down outside the post office. "It's a long ride out to their place. But at least the weather's nice."

"Too bad you'll miss all the excitement."

"I don't mind. Mrs. Musgrove will need comforting. And going with Daniel on such visits makes me feel useful."

Carrie nodded. How typical of Deborah. Instead of letting her horrific experience break her, she used it as a way to help others. "Mary and I enjoyed your visit last week. We get so few callers at the farm."

Deborah's gaze held Carrie's. "You certainly didn't stay around long. Did you enjoy your afternoon with Mr. Rutledge?"

Carrie blushed. "How did you know—"

Mr. Gilman and the mayor mounted the steps outside the sheriff's office. The banker took up a speaking trumpet and raised his hand for silence. "Ladies and gentlemen. On behalf of Mayor Scott and the entire town of Hickory Ridge, I welcome you to Race Day."

"Oh, there's Daniel." Deborah stood on tiptoe and waved to him across the crush of onlookers. "I must go. Enjoy the race." She patted Carrie's hand. "For your sake, I hope Mr. Rutledge wins."

Carrie watched her friend disappear into the crowd. Caleb and Joe hurried over and plopped down beside her.

The band Mr. Gilman had hired for the occasion played a rousing march as horses and riders made their way to the starting line outside the sheriff's office. Mr. Gilman pointed out the race course. Beginning at the sheriff's office, the horses would race to the far end of the main street, then turn onto the road leading to the park. From there they would race the entire length of the park, following the river, then return to main street, round a set of Mr. Pruitt's empty pickle barrels lined up outside the Verandah, and return to the starting line.

Carrie shaded her eyes and surveyed the crowd lining the course as the banker explained the rules of the race. The entire town, usually so quiet and orderly, was transformed into a noisy sea of color and movement. Out-of-towners in fancy hats and brightly colored silks and farm wives in sunbonnets and faded calicoes stood shoulder to shoulder with businessmen, farmers in rough jeans and work boots, and mill hands smelling of sweat, hair tonic, and sawdust.

Children played along the edges of the crowd, laughing and chasing one another. A few older boys blew on homemade noise-makers, a shrill sound that set a couple of stray dogs to barking. Peddlers moved through the crowd hawking candies and souvenirs. The photographer bustled about, setting up his camera near the finish line. If Griff won, Carrie intended to purchase a photograph, something to hold on to once he was no longer a part of her life. Pushing away the sadness brought on by that prospect, she turned her attention back to the banker.

After acknowledging the visiting dignitaries seated in a special viewing stand at the far end of the street, Mr. Gilman introduced the riders and their horses—two from Maryland, one from Kentucky, and one from Tulip Grove, near Nashville. And, finally, Griff and Majestic. All the horses looked magnificent, their coats gleaming, gaily colored silk ribbons woven into their thick manes, their riders well dressed, with boots buffed to a mirror shine. But Carrie had eyes only for Griff. She hoped he'd seek her out in the crowd, but he kept his head low, his hands relaxed on the reins, all of his attention focused on communicating with his mount. A straggly looking black-and-tan hound trotted into the street, barking and nipping at the horses. The Tulip Grove horse snorted and shied, but Majestic remained calm, his withers quivering in anticipation.

"Ready, gentlemen?" Mr. Gilman called. Griff and the other riders nodded. One of horses whinnied as if in answer, and the people standing nearest Carrie laughed. The sheriff drew his pistol and fired. The shot reverberated along the crowded street. The horses thundered down the dirt track. The crowd rose as one, yelling and cheering.

"Come on, Bold Prince!" A woman in an enormous pink touring hat jumped up and down, jostling Carrie. "Don't let a Tennessee horse beat you."

"Tennessee horses can beat anybody," Caleb yelled. "Run, Majestic."

The horses pounded past the bakery, the barbershop, and the mercantile, a chestnut mare taking the lead. Griff and Majestic were running third, behind the horse from Maryland. Carrie frowned. What was he waiting for?

She craned her neck for a better look as the horses made the turn toward the park. Then the horses and riders were lost from her view as they flew past the gazebo and the cheering crowd. Standing on tiptoe, Carrie clutched her reticule and waited for Griff and Majestic to reappear. At last they returned, hooves flying, bridles rattling as the riders urged them on. Griff glanced to his right and left and urged Majestic into second place as they rounded Mr. Pruitt's pickle barrels.

Suddenly aware that something was wrong, she searched the crowd, then grabbed Caleb's shoulder and yelled above the deafening cheers. "Where's your brother?"

Caleb brushed her hand aside, his eyes never leaving Griff

and Majestic. "Around somewhere. He's all right. Come on, Mr. Rutledge! You can do it."

The horses entered the home stretch. Majestic and the chestnut mare were running neck and neck as they raced past the bank, a blur of black and brown against the brightly dressed crowd.

"Don't move," Carrie told Caleb. "I must find Joe."

She gathered her skirts and worked her way through the crush of onlookers, keeping one eye out for Joe and the other on Griff. The horses sprinted toward the finish line, still running neck and neck. Then Griff leaned low over the Majestic's neck and pulled ahead of the others. A great cheer went up.

A slight movement across the street drew Carrie's attention. She spotted Joe chasing a stray dog, the horses charging toward the finish line. He stopped, pulled his slingshot from his pocket, and took aim.

She pushed frantically through the crowd, praying she would reach him in time. But her legs felt heavy as anvils, her breath came in short gasps. She opened her mouth in a silent scream.

Sitting atop Majestic during the last seconds of the race, Griff felt the familiar exhilaration returning. For a moment it was possible to believe that he was back in South Carolina riding one of his father's favorite Thoroughbreds, basking in a rare look of approval in the old man's eyes.

Now, with a subtle shift of his weight in the saddle, he asked the horse for a little more speed. The colt had a lot more in him, a lot more to give. Griff felt Majestic's effortless stride lengthening beneath him as they covered the final yards of the race, leading by a nose . . . by a head . . .

A tremendous roar went up at the finish line. Griff straightened in the saddle and acknowledged the crowd. The other horses churned up a cloud of dirt behind him. Then Majestic jerked, emitted a terrified neigh, wheeled, reared. And Griff found himself falling.

He felt no pain as his head hit the dirt-covered brick pavement and his shoulder cracked beneath him. Only a blinding light. And then nothing.

TWENTY-FOUR

Pushing her way to the front of the hushed crowd, Carrie saw Sheriff McCracken bending over Griff's still form. One of the other riders caught Majestic's bridle, calmed him, and led him toward Tanner's livery. Joe Stanhope was nowhere in sight. Carrie stood frozen, unable to think or move.

"Where's Doc Spencer?" McCracken yelled. "This man needs help."

Eugenie Spencer hurried through the crowd, the pink silk flowers on her brown leghorn hat fluttering in the breeze. "My husband left for Owl Creek before dawn to deliver Mrs. Patchett's baby. He isn't back yet."

A man in a moth-eaten black wool suit knelt beside Griff. "He's breathing. May have broke some bones, though." He carefully lifted Griff's head. "No blood. I reckon that layer of dirt saved him. But he's going to have a powerful headache when he comes to."

Carrie spoke at last, her voice high and strange. "Sheriff, please get him to his room at the inn so this doctor can look after him properly."

The man glanced up. "Oh, I'm not a doctor, missus. Name's Harlan Wentworth. I used to be the undertaker around here, but I'm over in Knox County now." He jerked a thumb toward Griff.

"I've seen enough bodies in my day to be a pretty good judge of what sort of shape they're in."

Carrie shuddered and looked at the sheriff. "Nevertheless, he must be taken to his room right away."

McCracken removed his hat and wiped his brow with the sleeve of his shirt, the tin star on his chest glittering in the afternoon light. "I'd be glad to take him there, Miz Daly, but I understand he gave up his room this morning. Checked out of the inn and bought a ticket on the evening train. Hotel's plumb full. His room's already taken."

The news that Griff had already made arrangements to leave barely registered with Carrie. For now, he needed her help.

"What about the Verandah? Surely Mrs. Whitcomb will make an exception for a wounded gentleman."

"Verandah's full up too is what I heard. Good news for Maisy Whitcomb, but a piece o' bad luck for Rutledge here."

"Well, he can't lie here in the street like a wounded animal."

"No, ma'am. 'Course not." The sheriff addressed the crowd. "We need somebody to take this man in until he's tended to and fit to travel. Now who has an empty room to spare?"

The people crowding around looked at one another, murmuring and shaking their heads.

Mr. Gilman pushed through the crowd. "I heard the commotion, but the crowd's so thick I couldn't see a thing. After all that planning, I missed the end of the race." He bent over Griff. "What in the Sam Hill happened to you, boy?"

"Horse spooked and throwed 'im." McCracken pushed his hat to the back of his head. "He's out cold. You got room for him out at your house? Every place in town is full."

"So's my house. Me and the missus are playing host to the other horse owners, and Sabrina invited a few of her friends too. I sure do hate it, but we're busting at the seams."

"Mr. Gilman," Carrie said. "This entire event is your doing. You hired Mr. Rutledge to ride Majestic. And now you're unwilling to help him in his hour of need?"

"Not unwilling, ma'am." His voice carried above the hum of voices. "Just out of room." He looked around the hushed crowd. "What about you, Jasper? You've got that extra room."

Jasper Pruitt spat a steam of tobacco juice into the street and shook his head. "Jeanne's mama is stayin' with us. We don't have room either. Besides which, this man's a layabout that's been gamblin' and who knows what all down in Two Creeks. I wouldn't feel safe havin' him under my roof."

Carrie's anger exploded at that. "You people go to church on Sunday and listen to sermon after sermon about helping your fellow man, being the hands and feet of our Savior. And then when an opportunity presents itself to do just that, look what happens."

The banker motioned to the sheriff. "Eli, can't you find a place for him in the jail?"

Carrie frowned. "The jail, Mr. Gilman?"

"Just temporarily, of course. Till we can find someplace better."

She heaved an exasperated sigh. "Sheriff, kindly bring my wagon over here."

"Carrie." Mariah hurried over and whispered in her ear, "What are you doing?"

"Taking him to the farm, of course. I can't leave him here in the street or confined with common criminals." She glanced at Griff, who still lay pale and motionless in the street. "Not after all he's done for us."

Mariah raised her hands in a gesture of surrender and turned away. The sheriff made his way to retrieve Carrie's wagon as Mr. Gilman mounted the steps and addressed the crowd. "Ladies and gentlemen, this man will be all right once he's had medical attention. His accident is an unfortunate blemish on this fine day, but please don't let it interfere with your enjoyment of the rest of the festivities. There's plenty more to see and do before the dance in the park tonight."

The band struck up a lively tune. The crowd murmured and drifted away. Sheriff McCracken drew Carrie's wagon to a stop. He and the undertaker and a couple of burly sawyers lifted Griff into the wagon.

Caleb arrived, red-faced and out of breath. Joe, teary-eyed and dirty, trailed behind his brother, his broken slingshot dangling from his pocket.

The sheriff strode over to his office and returned to press a small brown bottle into Carrie's hand. "This will help the pain. I'll send Doc Spencer out there as soon as he gets back from Owl Creek."

"I'd appreciate it." Carrie allowed the sheriff to help her onto the wagon seat. She picked up the reins and the boys clambered up, their expressions solemn.

"For what it's worth, Miz Daly, I admire what you're doing. I'd have bunked him here in the jail, like Gilman said, but it's crammed with drunks and rowdies. It isn't a fit place for an injured man."

Carrie nodded and turned the wagon for home. As they passed the train station, the whistle blared, reminding her of Majestic. Surely someone would look after the horse. Griff would be more worried about the colt than himself. She guided the wagon around a rut in the road, but she couldn't avoid jostling her injured passenger. Griff moaned. Joe leaned against Carrie and sobbed.

Carrie's anger flared again. "Stop your whimpering, Joe Stanhope. This is all your fault."

"I know it," he blubbered, his thin shoulders shaking. "I was only tryin' to help Griff win the race."

"By shooting that infernal slingshot at Majestic?"

"No. That old hound dog was running for the horses. He

already nipped one of 'em right before the race, and I was scared he'd bite Majestic. I was tryin' to scare him off. But I missed."

"I told you to be careful with that thing. I told you—"

"Stop scolding him." Caleb balled his fists. "It was an accident. He didn't mean to do it."

"He made a decision. Decisions have consequences."

"You're mean," Caleb said. "I hate you."

Carrie bit back a reply. Why did this boy always seem to bring out the worst in her? She drove the rest of the way in silence. When they reached the farm, she sent the boys inside to check on Mary. Then she jumped off the wagon, lifted the bar on the barn door, and drove the wagon inside.

She unhitched Iris and led the mare into her stall. Then she turned her attention to Griff. Until the doctor could come and help her move him, Griff would have to remain where he was. She lifted his head and managed to get a few drops of the laudanum into his mouth, then went inside for blankets.

Mary was awake. Her high, thin voice carried into the hallway. As Carrie gathered blankets, salve, towels, and a washbasin, she heard Caleb describing the crowds, his trip to the mercantile for candy, and the race. "And then Mr. Rutledge fell off, and guess what? Carrie Daly brought him home with us."

Carrie hurried out before she could hear Mary's reaction to that bit of news. Returning to the barn, she removed Griff's boots, covered him with blankets, and slipped a pillow beneath his head.

The medicine had taken effect. He was a dead weight in her arms. She drew a bucket of fresh water from the well and gently washed the dirt from his face. The tiny white scar above his lip was stark white against his tanned skin. A huge bruise bloomed on his cheek, and his forehead was scraped raw.

She smoothed salve onto his scrapes. His eyes fluttered. He tried to speak, but she shushed him. "Don't worry. I'm here."

He fell back against the pillow.

She put a bucket of water and a dipper within his reach. If he woke before the doctor arrived, at least he would have fresh water. She stood beside the wagon for a moment, watching the movement of his closed eyes behind their curtain of thick black lashes and the rise and fall of his chest.

The irony of the situation was not lost on her. Only this morning she had prayed that she might have more time with this man for whom she was beginning to care so deeply. That prayer had been answered.

Unfortunately, Griff was out like a light. She sighed. Maybe she should have been more specific.

Pain traveled along his arm and lodged in his head. His lips and throat felt parched, his tongue swollen and tasting of copper. Every bone ached, every knotted muscle throbbed. His nostrils filled with the scent of hay and manure. Taking deep ragged breaths, he fought against the black fog enveloping his brain and soon was lost in myriad images that seemed so real he could touch them.

He was standing on the piazza of his father's house in early summer. The fecund smells of the low country—pluff mud, fish, salt—filled his nose. He watched the glittering river, framed by the branches of the ancient oaks, snaking toward the sea. Then it was October, and the slaves were digging potatoes, their shovels flashing silver against the brown fields. He was driving his rig down a lane lined with sweet bay and cypress, his sprightly little mare stepping smartly along, with nothing but rice birds and swamp sounds for company. He heard his father's voice, low and urgent, but the words were muffled. He called out, but there was no reply.

A copper-haired angel in blue cradled his head, her breath soft on his ear. Her skin smelled like vanilla and wild jasmine after a low-country rain. He felt light and profoundly peaceful. Astonished to discover that despite all his mistakes he had arrived in heaven, and it wasn't half bad.

He stopped fighting and let the darkness take him.

TWENTY-FIVE

Returning from the barn, Carrie spotted Mary standing at the back door, peering into the late afternoon shadows, a frown creasing her pinched face. Well, it was just too bad. Mary would have to live with the consequences of her son's actions.

Gathering her last bit of strength, Carrie brushed past Mary and entered the kitchen. Caleb and Joe were nowhere in sight. The remnants of a hastily concocted supper littered the table.

"The boys told me what happened at the race today." Mary poured herself a cup of coffee but made no move to offer Carrie one. She slumped at the table in her limp dressing gown, her straw-colored hair tumbling over her shoulders. "I'm sorry Joe caused that horse to throw Mr. Rutledge, but surely you know he can't stay here. It isn't proper."

"He is here. He had no other suitable place to go." Carrie poured herself a cup of coffee and sipped. Bitter as sin and luke-warm to boot.

"Nevertheless, Mr. Rutledge is not the kind of person we want in Hickory Ridge."

"Oh, you mean the person who put food on this table, and paid attention to your children, and rode in a race to benefit the town?" Carrie set her cup down and began stacking the dirty plates.

Otherwise she'd start throwing them at Mary. "I suppose you're exactly right. Surely it takes a terribly indecent and unprincipled person to commit such unspeakable acts."

Despite her illness and fatigue, Mary smiled. "I imagine he was well paid for training and riding that horse."

"As any other man would have been." Carrie poured water into the dishpan and began scrubbing plates.

"I'd expect you to defend him. The whole town knows you're in love with him. Henry would be appalled."

"You have no idea what my brother would—"

"Mama, somebody's coming." Joe pounded down the stairs.

"See who it is, please." Mary raked her hair away from her face. "And tell them I am much too tired for visitors."

Joe peered out the window. "It's the doctor."

"Thank goodness." Carrie dried her hands. "I'll take him out to see Mr. Rutledge."

But Joe opened the front door and ushered the doctor into the parlor. Ennis Spencer removed his hat and nodded. "Mrs. Bell. How are you feeling?"

Mary shook her head. "Tired as ever."

"How about the nausea?"

"The same."

"Any more pain?"

"It comes and goes."

He regarded her over the top of his spectacles. "Then what are you doing up running around?"

"I was just going back to bed."

"Good. If you want this baby, you'll stay there." He turned to Carrie. "Now what's this I hear about Rutledge?"

Carrie recounted the accident and the undertaker's assessment of Griff's condition. "He's lying in my wagon in the barn."

"Let's have a look."

She accompanied the doctor to the barn. Griff had awakened and was leaning against the side of the wagon. He'd obviously tried to drink some water. The front of his shirt was wet, and the dipper lay overturned at his side.

While the doctor probed and prodded and asked a hundred different questions, Carrie brought water and oats for Iris and dragged the wheelbarrow into the stall. Mucking it out, though, was Caleb's job.

"I might be wrong, but I don't think that arm is broken," the doctor told Griff. "Your shoulder's dislocated, and you've got a devil of a sprain. Not to mention a bad concussion."

Griff nodded. "Need to get out of here."

"Nope. You aren't going anywhere until I'm sure there's no damage to your innards."

Griff closed his eyes. "My ship to Australia . . . sails from San Francisco . . . couple of weeks."

"Then it will sail without you, my man. Even if you made it to California in time, you're in no shape for such a long journey." From his bag, the doctor took a small bottle of pills and a tin of salve. He looked up at Carrie. "Do you have anything I can use for a sling?"

"I'll find something."

Inside the house, she rummaged through her belongings, settling on a clean but threadbare sheet that was too far gone for mending. She ripped it into long strips and took them back to the barn. As she approached the door, she heard a long, agonized moan and then Griff's loud "Ahhh!"

She rushed inside to find the doctor positioned behind Griff, both feet braced on the side of the wagon, pulling on Griff's shoulder with all his might. Carrie heard a loud snap, and the doctor released his patient. "There. That should do it."

Carrie handed him the strips of cloth. He expertly fashioned a sling for Griff's injured arm. "You ought not to use that arm for a couple of weeks. Let that shoulder heal. Otherwise it might not ever be quite right."

Griff nodded vaguely, his eyes drifting closed.

"I gave him some more laudanum," the doctor told her. "Did you . . . that is . . . where had you planned on letting this man sleep?"

"I've an extra mattress in the attic. I can bring it out here."

"That'll be fine. In a minute he won't care where he is. Why don't you fetch it, and I'll help him off this wagon."

Minutes later Carrie dragged the mattress into the barn. She covered it with blankets and fluffed the pillow. Then she and the doctor half dragged, half carried Griff off the wagon. Griff barely roused as they settled him on his makeshift bed. After setting his water and dipper within easy reach of his uninjured arm, they closed the door and returned to the yard.

"I admire you, Carrie, taking on another invalid when you've got your hands full with Mary and those boys." Dr. Spencer tossed his medical bag into his rig.

Suddenly dizzy with fatigue, she closed her eyes and massaged her temples. "He needed help, and people seemed reluctant to come to his aid."

He climbed into his rig and picked up the reins. "Folks may have a different view of Mr. Rutledge once the news gets out."

"News?"

"According to the sheriff, Rutledge told Mr. Gilman he intends to donate some of his prize money to the town to hire a teacher for the school."

Carrie felt a small frisson of satisfaction, imagining Mary's reaction to this news. After all the fuss Mary had made about the lack of a teacher in Hickory Ridge, she wouldn't dare criticize the man who had made one possible. "This is good news. Joe will be thrilled."

"It'll make a big difference for the few families we've still got left here." He shook his head. "If this blasted depression goes on for much longer, the entire country will dry up and blow away. But I reckon that's what we get for electing that Yankee Ulysses Grant as president." He tipped his hat and turned the rig around. "I'll be out in a few days to check on Rutledge and on Mary. In the meantime you should keep them both quiet, let them rest."

"Dr. Spencer?"

He looked up. His horse stamped and snuffled.

"Mary's worried that she's seriously ill. Is she? Is the baby—"

"I can't find any medical reason for her complaints. But taking on a new husband, a new home, and then being left with a baby on the way is a lot for any woman to handle. Plain old nervous exhaustion is my best guess."

"My brother had no choice but to look for work elsewhere."

"I'm not blaming him." He shifted on the seat. "Mrs. Bell is too thin. She needs to eat."

"I make meals every day, but mostly she refuses them."

He nodded and flicked the reins. "Do the best you can."

Carrie went inside, exhausted from the long day and from the prospect of preparing for the coming winter. After the first hard frost, it would be hog-killing time. She'd find someone to take care of that horrific chore and set up the smokehouse for curing bacon and ham. Last week she'd noticed a few apples in the orchard. They could be dried and put away. Maybe some of last year's potatoes were still in the hills—if they hadn't rotted dead away. She hadn't had time to look. As long as the cow gave milk and the chickens produced eggs, they could make do until spring.

It would be a struggle. But once Mary's baby came, once Henry was home, life would be infinitely better. All she had to do was hang on a little longer. Then she could move back to town, work for Mrs. Whitcomb again. Or expand her bread-baking enterprise.

She lit the lamp in the kitchen and finished washing the dishes. Maybe it was unrealistic to cling to such hopes. Maybe this life was the only one she'd ever know.

But if that was true, she feared she'd fall into a black pit of despair from which there was no escape.

~

Dear Mary,

At last we got paid. It wasn't as much as we were promised, but Mr. Sullivan, the foreman, says that with so many railways going out of business we're lucky to get anything. I am sending you every bit of it except what I need for food and rent.

Mary, I know you have your heart set on leaving Hickory Ridge and settling here, but Chicago is not the way it looks in the magazines and newspapers. It is full of noise and smoke and steam. The air is black even in the middle of the day, and the city smells like dead pigs. At night the gaslights make everything seem yellow. On my way to work I walk past bars, gambling houses, and worse. It is not a place to raise children. I pray that by the time our baby comes this depression will be over and I can find work in Hickory Ridge again.

Take care of yourself, my dear wife. Kiss the boys for me. Tell them their new papa misses them. And as always, remember me to Carrie.

Your husband, Henry Bell.

P.S. Try not to be sad that we will be apart at Christmas. Think about next year, when we will be together again.

Mary handed the letter to Carrie. "He hasn't even been gone three months, and already he's decided he doesn't like Chicago."

"It does sound dreadful."

"Any place is dreadful when you're poor. Henry is smart. There's no reason why he can't someday become a foreman himself. Then we could live in the better part of town. The boys would have a decent school and get on in life."

Carrie tamped down a surge of anger. Did Mary care anything for Henry at all, or was he simply the means to an end? To avoid another disagreement, she changed the subject.

"The town council is looking for a new teacher for our school." She rose and picked up Mary's breakfast tray. "Thanks to Griff Rutledge."

Mary studied her reflection in her hand mirror. "I will admit, donating his prize money was generous of him. And I appreciate that he's been helping out around here. At least he isn't a complete drain on everyone."

Carrie rolled her eyes. Mary Stanhope had a way of tossing out a compliment with one hand and taking it back with the other. "Speaking of Mr. Rutledge, I must make his breakfast."

"What's he doing this morning?"

"Fixing a hole in the smokehouse roof. Caleb is helping him."

"Caleb is spending entirely too much time with that man."

"Caleb would disagree. Last night he told me Mr. Rutledge is teaching him to whittle. They're making a box for his rock collection."

Mary pinned her hair and set her mirror aside. "So long as he doesn't teach my son to drink and . . . oh." She clapped a hand over her mouth and, with the other, motioned frantically for the chamber pot.

Carrie held Mary's head as she cast up her accounts and collapsed onto the pillows, exhausted and perspiring.

Wordlessly Carrie poured water from the ewer, bathed Mary's face, and took the pot outside to empty it. Shading her eyes with one hand, she looked across the meadow to the smokehouse. Caleb steadied the ladder as Griff climbed down, his arm still in the sling. Griff looked up and raised his good arm in a little wave. She waved back.

Caleb ran over, scattering the chickens, his hair sweaty, his cheeks pink from the sun. "I slopped the hog this morning, then me and Griff fixed the roof. We're hungry."

Carrie smiled as Griff caught up to the boy. "I'll bet you are. Come inside, and I'll make breakfast."

Griff strode onto the porch, smelling of hay and dust and wood shavings, and held the door for her. "After you, ma'am."

While he and Caleb washed up, Carrie sliced the bread she'd baked the day before, fried bacon and eggs, and made a pan of gravy. She poured milk for the boy and coffee for Griff and joined them at the table. This morning's episode in Mary's sickroom had stolen her appetite, but she treasured these quiet moments with Griff. The golden sunrise sliding over the mountains, the sharp autumn air coming through the window, the sounds of chickens in the yard filled her with a sense of contentment. On such mornings it was easy to pretend that this farm was truly her home. That she and Griff belonged to each other.

Griff made short work of his eggs and gravy and settled back with his coffee cup. "Thank you, Carrie. I don't know when I've enjoyed food as much as I have here."

"My brother always said hard work makes food taste better."

Caleb scraped his chair back. "I've got to go. Jimmy D. Washburn is waitin' for me at the river. We're goin' fishing."

"What about Joe?" Carrie sipped her coffee.

"I don't want to take him. He's such a baby."

"Well," Griff said mildly, "do you think it's fair that Mrs. Daly has to do all the work around here and still keep up with your little brother?"

"She's got you to help her."

Griff laughed. "I can fix a roof and chop kindling with one arm, but I'm no good at all at keeping a house or looking after children, even with two."

Caleb started for the door. Carrie stopped him with a hand on his arm. "I do need you to take Joe along. I have a lot of work to do today."

He glared at her, his expression hard, and stomped up the stairs to wake his brother.

Carrie shook her head. "I don't know what to do about Caleb. Everything I ask him to do turns into a battle of wills." She tied on her apron and started clearing the table.

Griff continued to sit, nursing his cup. "I was like that at his age—angry, willful, rebellious. I grew out of it." He grinned. "For the most part. I expect Caleb will too. In the meantime, patience is the order of the day."

Carrie grimaced. "I'm afraid I'm all out of patience." She picked up the milk pitcher. "And out of milk too."

"I can milk Miranda if you like."

"I don't mind doing it. It's one of the less odious chores around here. If you can bring in some more wood, I'd be grateful. The wood box is nearly empty again."

"Consider it done."

"Carrie?" Mary's plaintive voice drifted into the kitchen.

"Go see what she needs," Griff said. "I'll tend to the boys."

Carrie hurried down the hallway. By the time she had helped Mary change her nightdress, Griff and the boys were gone.

Taking up the milk pail, Carrie headed for the barn, where Miranda stood patiently in her stall. The cow seemed to be in no hurry to be milked, so Carrie set aside her pail and went about tidying Griff's bed. In the week since his accident, he hadn't complained once about having to sleep on a thin mattress on the barn floor. In fact, he had sent for his bags from the inn and made himself right at home. Beside his bed was a stack of books, a Bible, and a leather pouch. A pair of gold-rimmed reading glasses lay beside his lantern. Carrie straightened his blankets and caught a faint scent of hair tonic and tobacco. One sock fell from the tangle of blankets. She folded it and left it next to his books.

Miranda shook her head, jangling her bell.

"All right, girl. I'm coming."

Carrie milked the cow and took the fresh milk to the springhouse. For a moment she stood there in the cool dimness, savoring the quiet. Though farm life was never easy, it seemed less trying with Griff by her side. But she couldn't linger here when more work awaited. She pushed open the door and headed up the path to the house.

As she neared the back garden, she heard the sound of a woman crying and stopped short. Land o' Goshen, what was wrong now? She closed her eyes and prayed not to lose her temper with Mary. But when she turned the corner, she saw Rosaleen standing in the shelter of Griff's arms, sobbing as if her heart would break.

The way Griff held her, as if he was familiar with every curve of her body, sent a wave of pure jealousy racing through Carrie. Then she thought of Nate. Had something happened to him? Why else would Rosaleen have driven clear out here?

Torn between worry and curiosity, she ducked into the shadows. It was impossible to return to the house without being seen. And something in Rosaleen's manner suggested that whatever had gone wrong was for Griff's ears only.

In the still of the mountain morning, Rosaleen's voice carried, so Carrie couldn't help overhearing.

"I never thought my sister could give away a baby."

"Are you certain that's what happened?" Griff's voice. Steady and low.

"The Pinkerton detective said so. He said Nola brought her here and dumped her at the orphanage. But now it's closed, and nobody can tell me what happened to her."

"So that's why you came to Hickory Ridge."

Rosaleen sniffed and nodded. "I certainly never expected to see you here."

"That was quite evident the first day I saw you at the Verandah."

"Yes, and you were so mean to me about that loan. But then when I tried to pay it back, you refused. You've changed, Griff. The man I knew would have taken that money and never looked back."

"Maybe," he said, "although back then I was more generous with you than you deserved. But why drive all the way out here to tell me your troubles? Everything was finished between us years ago."

"I know that. But I can't tell Nate why I'm here. He already suspects that I have a secret. If he knew the truth, who knows what he would think of me?"

Carrie's stomach dropped as one by one the pieces of the puzzle clicked into place. A child abandoned at the Hickory Ridge orphanage. Rosaleen's constant probing for information about Hickory Ridge and its past. Her coffee-with-cream skin, and those extraordinary green eyes . . . Carrie had seen those eyes before. She shivered.

"I don't see what I can do that the detectives can't," Griff said.

Carrie peeked around the side of the barn. He was standing apart from her now, arms folded across his chest.

Rosaleen took a handkerchief from her sleeve and dabbed at her nose. "I was hoping for another loan so I can keep looking for them. I've spent my last cent on detectives, and I dare not ask Nate for the money."

"I suppose not."

"I swore I wouldn't leave Hickory Ridge until I knew the truth. And—"

"If they haven't surfaced by now . . ." Griff rubbed his chin. "It's a big country, Rosaleen. You may have to accept that you won't ever know what happened. Too much time has passed."

"So you won't help me."

"I'm trying to help you—by encouraging you to let go of this. Go home. Be a good wife to the bookseller. Perhaps in time—"

Rosaleen whirled around, her bright yellow skirts stirring the dust. "Thanks for nothing, Griff Rutledge."

She disappeared around the side of the house. Moments later Carrie heard the *clop-clop* of hooves as Rosaleen drove away.

Carrie stood in the shadows watching Griff split firewood, her mind reeling. A cold kernel of fear formed in her stomach. Could her suspicions possibly be true? Was Rosaleen Sophie Robillard's mother?

TWENTY-SIX

Mary was sick twice during the afternoon. Carrie was exhausted from cleaning up, helping Mary change her nightdress, and brewing endless cups of slippery elm tea. Joe and Caleb returned from the river covered in mud and smelling like dead fish. Worst of all, at supper, Griff seemed distant and ill at ease.

Carrie watched him from the corner of her eye as she served the boys another helping of fried potatoes. Had she done something to offend him? Or was he troubled by his conversation with Rosaleen? Most certainly he and Rosaleen had once meant something to each other. Did he miss her now? Want her back even though she was wed to Nate? That thought was the most disturbing. Because heaven help her, despite his earlier warnings, she couldn't stop imagining a future with him.

"More coffee, Mr. Rutledge?"

She pushed back her chair, but Griff got to his feet. "Don't get up. I can get it."

Wordlessly he poured himself another cup, refilled hers, and set the pot back on the stove.

"Some pie then."

"No, thank you." He leaned against the door frame sipping his coffee, but his expression said that he was a thousand miles away.

"I want some pie," Joe said. "Me and Caleb are starving."

Carrie gave them their dessert and sent them outside to do their evening chores. Taking her apron from the peg beside the door, she slipped it on and began scraping their plates. Griff grabbed his own plate off the table and raked the remnants of his dinner into the slop pail.

"Thanks, but you don't have to do that."

"Yes, I do." He set his empty cup on the table. "You made my bed this morning. Folded my lost sock too."

She glanced at him. "I was out there anyway, to do the milking."

"I appreciate your bringing me out here when I got hurt. But I don't want you looking after me."

"I don't mind."

His gaze locked on hers. "But I do."

Heat rushed to her face. She had enjoyed the small intimacies his presence afforded. Nursing him in his illness, making his meals, touching the fabric that touched him—all had made her feel closer to him. But now he was pulling away, putting distance between them.

"I've been thinking that in another few days I should go," he said. "My shoulder's much better; my strength is back. I've relied on your good graces much too long."

It wasn't exactly news. Hadn't he intended to leave town on Race Day? Even so, tears misted her eyes. "I suppose you're eager to leave Hickory Ridge. It must seem too tame to a man like you."

He picked up a clean towel and dried the serving platter she had just washed. "I might stay in town awhile longer. I've missed my sailing from San Francisco anyway." He set the platter aside and picked up a plate. "The day I arrived here, Mr. Gilman made me a proposition. Now I've got one for him. And I have a few other bits of business to attend to."

Was Rosaleen one of those bits of business? Carrie didn't dare ask. She needed to talk to someone about her suspicions, but clearly

Griff didn't want her getting close enough to confide in him. The thought was as painful as walking on broken glass. But what had she expected, really?

She scoured the frying pan and set it aside. Granny Bell often said that God's good could be found in everything that happened. That he had a purpose for everything under the sun but that sometimes you had to really look for it. Well, she'd tried to see the purpose in every bad thing that had happened in her life, but her eyes had grown weary with looking.

She forced a smile. "The boys and I will miss having you around. You've made quite an impression on Caleb. He—"

"Carrie Daly." Caleb burst through the door, his eyes wide. "Joe's done gone and set the smokehouse on fire. The door's jammed, and we can't get him out."

Griff tore out of the house, leaving Carrie and Caleb to follow. He sprinted to the barn, grabbed a horse blanket, and soaked it in the water trough beside the barn. Tenting it over his head. he kicked open the smokehouse door and ran inside.

"Caleb, get the water buckets. Hurry." Carrie ran into the barn for the milking pail, filled it at the trough, and doused the flames leaping toward the smokehouse roof. The air filled with the stench of old grease and burning wood. Caleb returned with two buckets, and they took turns throwing water on the fire. A towering wall of hot, blinding smoke rushed toward her, choking her breath.

A section of the roof caved in. Sparks leapt into the darkness.

"Come on, Carrie. We've got to get more water!" Caleb yanked on her sleeve.

She stood motionless, speechless with horror as a wall came down. There was no sense in trying to save the building. The fire had won. She screamed Griff's name.

Caleb began to cry. In the flickering light he looked like an old man, hunched over and defeated. "It's my fault. We were pretendin' to smoke cheroots. Joe didn't mean to do it. He's just a dumb little kid."

Carrie grabbed his shoulders and shook him. "Didn't you learn anything from the last time? Didn't I tell you both not to play with fire? Now Joe and Griff might be dead."

Then she saw a dark shape moving through the thick smoke. Griff emerged, sooty and gasping for breath, holding tightly to Joe. Her knees buckled.

"He's scared half to death," Griff rasped. "But he's all right."

She collapsed onto the ground.

Joe patted her shoulder. "Don't cry, Carrie Daly. Griff saved me." He climbed into her lap and wound both arms around her neck. "I'm all right."

Carrie buried her face in his sooty little shoulder and sobbed. Griff and Caleb hurried back and forth from the well and the trough, pouring more water onto the smoldering ruin until the last of the flames died.

Griff touched her shoulder. "Come inside. Everything's all right now."

He helped her to her feet. Leaving the blanket spread on the fence to dry, he led them into the house.

Carrie turned up the wick in the lamp and examined Joe. He was covered head to toe with a mixture of tears, ashes, and soot. His hands were raw with blisters, but otherwise he was unharmed. Carrie bathed his face, smoothed salve on his burns, and sent him and Caleb to wash up. Then she stole a glance at Griff. His hands and forearms were red and blistered, and he had a nasty scrape on his cheek. His shirt was torn. Carrie longed to tend his wounds, to repair his shirt, but he'd made it clear that her attention wasn't wanted. She handed him the tin of salve. "Thank you for saving Joe. I don't know what I'd have done if . . ."

He nodded, his dark hair falling into his eyes, his expression grave. "I'm sorry I couldn't save your smokehouse too. You're going to need it once that hog is butchered."

She sank onto a chair, suddenly so weary her legs wouldn't support her. "I'll speak to Sage Whiting. He'll know someone at the mill who can rebuild it."

With a quick nod he headed for the barn. Carrie watched him cross the yard, a dark silhouette against the still-smoldering embers, and wiped away bitter tears. Would her troubles never end? She tried so hard to do the right thing, to be the person everyone expected her to be, and yet her whole life consisted of nothing but mourning and ashes.

Griff stripped to the waist and washed away a layer of sweat and soot. His injured shoulder hurt like the devil, his blistered hands throbbed, his raw throat burned. He'd come perilously close to losing Joe. The fire inside the smokehouse was so intense he couldn't see his hand in front of his face. Only the sound of Joe's whimpers guided him to the boy's hiding place in the back corner. He grabbed the child and tossed the wet blanket over them just as the roof caved in. He kicked a hole in the rear wall, and they escaped only moments before the rest of the structure collapsed.

He smoothed salve onto his cheek and hands, toed off his boots, and lay down on the mattress, listening to the scratching of mice in the walls and the low growl of the barn cat chasing after them. His nose filled with the comforting scents of neat's-foot oil, straw, and manure. He was dead tired, but he couldn't stop thinking about Carrie. He could well imagine what he must look like to her, and he didn't like what he saw.

After everything she'd done to help him, he had hurt her, and he regretted that. But he could see that she was already a little in love with him. He had feelings for her too, and that complicated matters considerably.

He couldn't deny the wanderlust that still tugged at him every time the train whistle blew. As appealing as Carrie was, a part of him still wanted to be on that train, exploring new places, unencumbered by duty or love. But the rootlessness that had seemed so attractive to him in his younger days was also beginning to feel like a burden. He could ride the rails from city to city until the tracks gave out, but at the end of the line the truth remained: he belonged nowhere, mattered to no one.

He rubbed a hand over his smoke-stung eyes and turned onto his side, rustling the ticking in the mattress. Somebody would have to build Carrie a new smokehouse. Heaven knew she couldn't afford to pay anyone to do it. She'd insisted on repaying him for the food he'd bought at Pruitt's store, and he was certain there was very little money left to tide her over until more arrived from her brother.

The barn cat, tired of the chase, padded over and settled against his chest. He stroked her head, pondering the way the smallest of decisions could completely alter the course of a man's life and lead to the most complicated circumstances. Every time he planned to leave this town—and Carrie Daly's patchwork family—something else happened to make him stay.

TWENTY-SEVEN

Carrie lit a lamp against the dreary November afternoon and stoked the fire to ward off the chill. Through the kitchen window, she watched Caleb scampering up and down the ladder, taking armloads of shingles up to the smokehouse roof. The building was nearly finished—a fact only slightly more miraculous than the change in Caleb. Thanks to Griff, since the night of the fire, Caleb had become more cooperative and less combative. And that was surely a blessing because, as Mary's confinement dragged on, she became even more irritable and difficult to please.

Carrie set the kettle on the stove to boil and took cups from the cupboard, trying to stave off another wave of sadness. Last week Deborah had visited again, bringing news that Mayor Scott and the town council were almost ready to announce the hiring of a new teacher for the Hickory Ridge school. When that was done, and the last of the smokehouse shingles were nailed into place, Griff would have fewer reasons to stay on in Hickory Ridge.

The kettle shrieked. Carrie set the cups on a tray. A few minutes earlier, Mary had awakened from a long nap, demanding her daily cup of slippery elm tea. Taking up last week's edition of the newspaper, Carrie went down the hall and opened Mary's door.

Her sister-in-law was propped against her pillows, rubbing her swollen belly. She offered Carrie a rare smile that seemed nearly serene. "She's moving around a lot today."

Carrie drew her chair close to the bed and handed Mary a cup of tea. "How do you know it's a girl?"

"Because I asked God for a daughter this time." Mary sipped her tea and closed her eyes. "Haven't you always wanted a little girl to dress in pretty frocks? I declare, my boys can run around in rags and be perfectly happy."

Mary's words were a shot to the heart. Carrie swallowed a sudden tightening in her throat. "If I could have a child, it wouldn't matter if it were a boy or a girl."

The bitter truth ached like a bad bruise. She had neither husband nor children in a world that considered the roles of wife and mother the most important things in a woman's life. But perhaps Frank had been her one chance at real love. She thought of Wyatt and Ada Caldwell. Anyone who spent ten minutes around them could plainly see how much Wyatt adored his wife. She despaired of ever finding another man who would care so deeply for her.

Shaking off her sadness, she unfolded the paper. "Here's the *Chronicle*. Would you like me to read it to you?"

"Only if there are any happy parts. I'm feeling gloomy these days. I wish Henry would write again." Mary sipped her tea. "I don't mind telling you, I am not looking forward to Christmas without him. I dreamed we'd spend it together with the boys . . . and with you too, of course. But now . . ." Her voice trailed away.

Carrie fought a wave of apprehension. It had been weeks since they'd heard from Henry, and she was getting worried. But it wouldn't do any good to upset Mary.

"Here's something amusing." She held the newspaper toward the light. "Thieves broke into the Knoxville Livery and stole two horses. But both were apprehended when the riders, in their haste to make their escape, collided outside the sheriff's office. The horses were unharmed, but one of the thieves suffered a broken arm."

"They ran into each other, trying to get away? Dumb criminals."

"Is there any other kind?"

Mary laughed, and Carrie found herself joining in. She had forgotten how good it felt to share a laugh with someone.

"Thank you, Carrie," Mary said. "I needed that."

She looked so vulnerable that Carrie felt a hitch in her chest. Perhaps Mary missed laughter too. "Would you like me to rub your feet?"

"If you don't mind. They've been so swollen lately."

Carrie rubbed Mary's feet with lavender oil until the afternoon light waned and Mary's eyelids drooped.

"I suppose I should see to supper." Carrie tucked the blanket around Mary's feet and picked up the tea tray. "Would you like me to leave the paper for you?"

"I'm too tired to read. Maybe Mr. Rutledge will want it."

"I expect so."

"Carrie?"

Carrie paused, the tray in her hands. "What do you need?"

"Nothing. I wanted to say thank you for taking care of me and looking after the boys. They can be a handful at times, but they're good boys." She smoothed her covers. "Joe especially loves you. He says you've been reading to him every night before bed. He looks forward to it."

"So do I." Just last night they'd read "Jack and the Beanstalk" again. Joe had leaned his warm little body against her side, his eyes huge with wonder as Carrie read about the brave boy and the fearsome giant. Reading with him reminded her of her own childhood. Somehow sharing stories with Joe made her miss Henry a bit less.

"Shall I bring you some supper?" she asked as she left the room.

"I'm not really hungry. Just see to the boys. And to Mr. Rutledge, of course."

Carrie went to the kitchen to start supper. Darkness fell. Wind whistled through a crack in the windowsill. She lit another lamp, turning up the wick before making a potato soup, thick with fresh cream. She buttered a slice of bread and munched it as she set the table. She should check with Mrs. Whitcomb at the Verandah. Perhaps business had picked up by now and the hotelier would need more bread for her boarders. Though Mrs. Whitcomb paid next to nothing, Carrie was grateful for anything. The last of Henry's money was dwindling fast, and Christmas was coming.

When the soup was done, Carrie opened the back door to call Griff and the boys in, but they had disappeared. Sighing, she grabbed her shawl and hurried across the yard to the half-finished smokehouse.

A thin shaft of light from within spilled across the burned-out grass. She heard Caleb's shout and Griff's deep laughter. Standing on tiptoe, she peered through a narrow opening beside the door.

Griff and the boys were seated around an overturned washtub that held a flickering lantern, a jumbled deck of cards, and a pile of small stones.

"But I don't get it, Griff." Caleb scratched his head. "I thought aces were the best cards in the whole deck."

"Not in triple draw. Deuce to seven, remember?"

"Oh yeah. So a seven is better'n an ace."

"In this game, it sure is."

Joe made an attempt to fan his cards and sent them scattering across the smokehouse floor. "I want three new cards."

Griff grinned. "You can't get any new cards until the first round of betting, Joe. So how many rocks are you willing to bet?"

Joe shrugged. "Three, I guess."

"Three it is." Griff tossed three stones into the pile in the middle of the table. "And I'll see that bet with three of my own." He looked at Caleb, one eyebrow raised. "How about you, son? In or out?"

"I have a question first."

"Sure. Go ahead."

"I'm not saying that I have these cards, but supposin' somebody had a two and a three plus a four, a five, and a six."

"Then that somebody'd be in a fair amount of trouble, my man. Deuce to six is a straight, and in this game that's about as worthless a hand as there can possibly be. Now, how much are you willing to bet?"

Caleb tossed his cards onto the makeshift table. "None, I reckon."

Griff reached over and clapped Caleb's shoulder. "Smart move. Never bet on a losing hand, Caleb, and never bet more than you can afford to lose. Even when you're holding a good hand, there's always the possibility someone else has better cards."

Carrie frowned. Wasn't it hard enough to bring those boys up without Griff's teaching them bad habits? Hickory Ridge was a different place than Charleston. And besides, the boys were too young to learn such things. She'd have to speak to him about that. But not now, in front of the boys. Not when they so obviously adored him.

Clearly, he relished his role as their teacher, and Caleb and Joe basked in his attention. Not wishing to spoil their moment, Carrie retreated to the back porch before calling them in to supper.

Griff ate two bowls of soup and three slices of bread. Between bites, he took turns with Caleb describing their work on the smokehouse. "If this weather holds, we should finish in another few days."

"We appreciate your help." Wary of appearing to serve him, she gave the boys slices of vinegar pie and set the pie tin on the table.

Griff helped himself to a generous slice. "Caleb's a fine worker. His new pa ought to be proud of him."

Joe's fork clattered onto his plate. "Hey, Carrie Daly, guess what?"

"Joe," Griff interrupted. "What did we talk about today?"

"Oh yeah. Sorry." Joe gobbled another bite of pie. "Aunt Carrie, guess what?"

Aunt Carrie. Her heart twisted. How could Griff have known how much the simple honorific would mean to her? She met his gaze over the boy's tousled head, and he winked at her.

"Griff showed us how to play poker."

"Oh?"

"Yes'm. He showed us how to bet and everything. Griff says—"

Caleb thumped Joe's forehead. "Shut up, blabbermouth. We promised not to tell."

Joe frowned. "We promised not to tell Mama. Carr—I mean Aunt Carrie won't care."

Griff's dark eyes glinted with mischief. "Every man ought to know how to swear, ride a horse, play poker, and hold his liquor."

He looked so earnest, so appealing, that despite her disapproval she couldn't stay cross with him. "Undoubtedly very useful skills, Mr. Rutledge, but perhaps better left until the boys are older."

"Caleb already knows how to swear," Joe said. "But I ain't s'posed to tell."

Griff's rich laughter rang out in the small, warm kitchen. Carrie couldn't help wishing their time together could go on forever. But there was nothing more to keep him here in her house. In her life.

Horses' hooves sounded on the road. Moments later came a knock at the door.

"I'll see who it is." Joe jumped up, nearly knocking over his chair, and ran to the door. Carrie and Griff followed.

Dr. Spencer stood on the porch, pressing his hat to his head in the sharp wind. "Hello, Mrs. Daly. May I come in?"

"Of course." Carrie stood aside.

The doctor came in, nodded to Griff. "I was out this way tending to the Patchetts' baby and thought I'd check on Mary before I head home. How is she?"

"Better, I think."

"May I check on her?"

Carrie nodded, and he went in.

"Come away, boys. I need wood and water." Carrie ushered Caleb and Joe down the hall. Griff picked up the newspaper and retired to the parlor.

By the time the boys returned to the house, the doctor had finished his examination. "You're doing a fine job, Mrs. Daly. The baby seems strong enough. But you must keep Mrs. Bell on bed rest and continue encouraging her to eat more."

Joe frowned at the doctor. "When in the Sam Hill is that baby going to come out? It has been in there forever."

Dr. Spencer grinned. "Not too much longer, Joe. I'd say that about seven weeks after Christmas, the baby will make his appearance."

"It better not be a girl. That's all I got to say."

"That's up to the Lord." Dr. Spencer donned his hat and picked up his medical bag. "Oh, some good news today. The town council has convinced Ethan Webster to return to Hickory Ridge as schoolmaster. The school will reopen in January."

Griff appeared in the doorway, newspaper in hand. "This Mr. Webster. Is he any good?"

"He's strict, but very good," Carrie said. "Everyone thought it was a shame when Bea Goldston ran him off all those years ago."

"She was the first schoolteacher in Hickory Ridge," the doctor told Griff. "But not a week after Mr. Webster left, she left town quite unexpectedly too. What was it, Mrs. Daly? Three years ago?"

"Four." Carrie shuddered at the memory of Bea's violent attack on Ada, which had led to the schoolteacher's abrupt departure.

"We hired another teacher, but after the panic of seventy-three she left too. We're much obliged to you, Mr. Rutledge, for providing the means to get Mr. Webster back."

"My pleasure, sir."

"And I'm sorry that not all of our citizens have welcomed you to our town. They're mostly good-hearted. It just takes some folks awhile to warm up to newcomers."

Carrie crossed her arms. It was more than a simple case of warming up to Griff. But he merely shrugged. "I understand. It's all right."

"Well, I ought to be going. Eugenie will be wondering what's become of me." With a nod to Carrie, Dr. Spencer left the house.

Joe danced around the parlor. "We're finally goin' to school."

"I wouldn't be so happy about it if I was you," Caleb said. "Jimmy D. Washburn said old man Webster is mean as a snake. Jimmy D. said Webster takes a cane to you if you don't follow his rules. But he's not the boss of me."

"He is when you are in his classroom," Griff said quietly. "And I'll be very disappointed indeed if I hear that you haven't treated him with respect."

Caleb blushed. "Yes, sir."

"It's late," Carrie told them. "Both of you go on up to bed. And, Joe, don't forget to wash behind your ears. I'll be up later to check."

"Will you read 'Jack and the Beanstalk' again?"

"We'll see. Go on now."

Joe rushed over and threw both arms around her legs, burying his face in her skirts. "Good night, Aunt Carrie."

She stroked his hair. When had she begun to need these children as much as they needed her? "Good night, Joe. You too, Caleb."

He ducked his head and pounded up the stairs.

Carrie returned to the kitchen to finish washing the dishes. Griff followed. She was aware of his sheer size in the small kitchen, the clean soapy smell of his skin. She poured water into the dishpan and scrubbed a bowl harder than was necessary.

"Good news about the school." He picked up a towel and dried a glass.

"Yes. We've been without a teacher for so long, I'm afraid Mr. Webster will find the children have a lot of catching up to do." She scoured the soup pot and set it on the sideboard. "I suppose you're eager to be off at last. We've kept you here much longer than you intended."

"Yes, but it hasn't been at all unpleasant. I've enjoyed the boys."

"They look up to you."

"I'd like to think so." The look in his dark eyes softened. "I've never had anyone look up to me. Philip, my younger brother, always looked to our father, not to me."

"And whom did you admire?"

He shrugged. "I never really looked to anyone until the war. Then it was the other blockade runners I grew to admire. But of course by then I was long past the need for heroes."

"I don't think we ever outgrow our need for heroes."

"Maybe you're right." He smiled down at her, and her heart stuttered. "Who are your heroes, Carrie?"

She considered. "My grandmother Bell. My husband Frank. And Henry, of course. I don't remember very much about my parents. I was still a child when they died."

The kitchen went too quiet.

"I was hoping I might have made that list."

His smile made her stomach drop. Of course she admired him, as much as anyone she knew. She loved everything about him. But now he was leaving her, going away forever. Why tell him how she felt?

A gust of wind blew through the cracked windowsill, guttering the lantern. Griff ran his fingers over the rotted wood and sighed.

"What?" She hung her apron on a peg and dried her hands.

"That needs fixing before it gets any colder."

The sill needed attention, true enough, but an old pillowcase stuffed into the hole would suffice until Henry's return. She studied him beneath her lowered lashes and felt a flutter of hope. Was it possible Griff was looking for a reason to stay?

TWENTY-EIGHT

Griff lit a cheroot and, with a contented sigh, buried himself chin-deep in the steaming bath water. The staff at the Hickory Ridge Inn certainly knew how to take care of a man. Since moving back to town a week ago, he'd enjoyed hot baths, fine meals in the dining room, and an occasional brandy in the gentlemen's smoking room afterward. It made for a peaceful return to town.

Walking away from Carrie, from her farm and those father-hungry boys, had been one of the hardest things he'd ever done. But it was surely for the best. With every trip to town, he'd felt the townsfolk's disapproval not only of him, but of the fact that he was staying at the farm with two women who were neither his kin nor his wife. It wouldn't do for their disapproval to taint Carrie's standing in Hickory Ridge. She would have to live here once he had moved on.

Besides, truth to tell, the weather had turned too cold to continue sleeping in Carrie's barn, and he enjoyed his creature comforts. Still, he missed Carrie and the boys, missed the effort required to keep the farm going. He had forgotten the exhilaration of pure physical labor and the quiet satisfaction of a job well done. He missed seeing Carrie across the table in the evenings, the lantern light turning her hair to burnished copper. The bell-like sound of her rare laughter. There had been no laughter on the morning he left the farm, his few belongings tossed into a rented rig. She waved bravely from the porch as he drove away, one arm wrapped around Joe's shoulder, but he knew her heart felt as empty as his own.

A discreet knock at the door interrupted his thoughts. The valet, a tall, powerfully built colored man wearing a white jacket, stuck his head inside. "More hot water for yuh, Mr. Rutledge?"

"Thank you, Isaiah, but I suppose I ought to get going."

"You goin' back to the bank again this morning?"

"I am indeed." He'd mulled over his plans for weeks now, more energized by the possibilities than by anything since his blockade running days. But his dream was still too fragile to talk about with anyone but the banker.

"I'll get your clothes laid out for yuh."

Griff nodded, and when the man withdrew he sat for a few moments longer before snuffing out his cheroot and reluctantly rising. He wrapped himself in a thick towel, padded down the carpeted hallway of the gentlemen's floor, and returned to his room.

He dressed and perused the latest edition of the Knoxville paper that had been delivered on this morning's breakfast tray. Christmas was only three weeks away, and the paper was full of advertisements for everything from harnesses to chocolates. He thought of Christmases in Charleston—candles everywhere, the tables laden with elaborate centerpieces, glittering crystal and china, and an indecent amount of food. He pictured his father at the head of this year's table, Philip and Susan basking in the happy glow of their upcoming nuptials. He'd have to send a gift, though Philip and Miss Layton were hardly in need of anything.

He turned the page and skimmed the national news. The notorious Boss Tweed had escaped from jail in New York and absconded to Cuba. The Chicago evangelist Dwight L. Moody was attracting great crowds to his revival meetings. And P. T. Barnum was planning a tour with Jumbo, the elephant he'd recently acquired from the Royal Zoological Gardens in London. Griff searched the article for a schedule for the showman's traveling circus. What a treat that would be for Joe and Caleb.

He grinned, remembering their earnest attempts to learn poker. He had long since forgiven Joe for shooting Majestic with the slingshot. Though his shoulder still pained him, the accident had resulted in some of the happiest days he'd known in a long time.

A photograph of a white-stockinged bay colt captured his attention. The headline read, "Kentucky Derby Winner Sold to Mr. William Astor, Jr., for the Sum of $7000." He wondered about the bay's winning time. He hadn't timed Majestic before Race Day, but he had a strong feeling that the sleek black colt could hold his own among the likes of Vagrant. If his plans panned out, maybe one day he'd have a chance to test it.

Downstairs, the lobby clock chimed the hour. Griff folded the paper, picked up his key, and headed for the bank.

⌣

"Aunt Carrie, is Griff coming for Christmas?" Joe stood on a stool in the kitchen, breaking eggs for a raisin cake. The kitchen was warm and fragrant with the smells of spices and wood smoke.

"I don't think so, Joe. I'm sure he has plans of his own."

"Well, did you ask him?"

She stopped stirring. Pale yellow batter dripped from her wooden spoon into the blue crockery bowl. "No, I didn't. We've taken up too much of his time already. Besides, your mother doesn't feel well enough for company."

He sighed and cracked another egg. "It seems like Mama's going to be sick forever."

It felt that way to Carrie too. In the weeks since Griff's move back to town, time had moved at a glacial pace. Her future stretched out before her, an endless string of empty days broken only by the demands of duty to Henry's family. More than once she'd rushed to the door, imaging the sound of hoofbeats on the road. But Griff hadn't visited even once.

Perhaps it was for the best. Every time she looked at him, every time she recalled the sweet heat of their shared kiss, she found it all that much harder to know that the joy he brought to her life was only temporary. Better to sever all ties now.

"Are you finished cracking eggs?" She set her cake tins on the counter, greased them, and dusted them with flour.

"Yes'm." He pushed the bowl toward her. "Are we goin' to the Christmas pageant at that big church tonight?"

"I wish we could. I miss hearing the Christmas story and singing carols, and I miss my friend Deborah. But your mama can't make the trip into town. Besides, it's raining up on the mountain." She glanced out the window at the wild, dark sky. "I won't be surprised if we have a wet night here too."

"Can I go play with Caleb now?"

"Yes, but don't go far. After supper we're going to look for our Christmas tree, and I want to be back before the rain gets here."

"I don't know why we need a tree. Mama said there won't be any presents tomorrow on account of our new papa hasn't sent us any money. Why hasn't he, Aunt Carrie? Doesn't he love us anymore?"

Her chest went tight with sadness and worry. She wrapped her arms around the boy. "Of course he loves us. I don't know why we haven't heard from him either, but I'm sure there's a very good reason."

He shrugged. "It sure won't seem like Christmas without any presents."

He looked so dejected that, for a moment, Carrie was tempted to tell him about the small gifts she'd bought last week. The Verandah had acquired two new residents, prompting Mrs.

Whitcomb to double her order for fresh bread. The money had been just enough to buy a gift for each of the boys. But she wanted to surprise them.

She brushed Joe's hair out of his eyes and made a mental note to give the boy a haircut. "When the baby Jesus was born in the stable, there were no presents for him at first."

"But then the wise men brought gold and stuff."

Carrie smiled. "They did. And I imagine his mother must have thought those presents were another miracle."

"One time Mama said the animals talk on Christmas Eve and it's a miracle. Is that true? Does Miranda talk?"

"I've never personally heard her, but miracles make anything possible."

"I guess. But—"

The teakettle whistled. "Go find Caleb. Tell him supper will be ready in an hour."

Joe ran outside. Carrie finished the cake batter, set the filled tins into the oven, and went to check on Mary. Despite the doctor's orders and Carrie's coaxing, Mary ate hardly anything. Her reticence was irritating. How would she have the strength to deliver the child when the time came?

Carrie peeked into the room. How tranquil and saintly Mary looked in sleep . . . how truculent in every waking hour. Well, having to spend months and months abed was surely a tedious affair. Perhaps seeing the boys enjoying their Christmas presents would improve Mary's mood and her appetite.

Carrie heard hoofbeats on the road and crossed over to the door, her heart thumping. Had Griff come at last? But it was Nate Chastain who reined in and hurried across the yard, his coat flapping in the sharp December wind.

Carrie flung the door wide and ushered him in. "What brings you out this way?"

"I heard things were a little tight for you these days."

She led him into the parlor and tossed a couple of logs onto the fire. Bright sparks flew up with a popping sound. "Oh, Nate, 'tight' hardly begins to describe the situation. We've had no word and not a dime from Henry since October. I'm worried that something awful has happened. In his last letter he said some of the men in the rail yard were nearly ready to riot. What if he's hurt? What if he has lost his job?"

Nate patted her shoulder. "It's worrisome, all right, but don't go borrowing trouble. If Henry was hurt, somebody would have sent word. We ought to hope for the best until there's a reason not to."

From his pocket he drew two small, flat packages wrapped in brown paper. "I brought a couple of books for the boys." He smiled shyly, his eyes suspiciously bright behind his spectacles. "I realize Caleb is not as fond of books as Joe, but they ought to have something for Christmas morning, and these are all I have to give."

Carrie threw both arms around her old friend. "Thank you. And thank Rosaleen for me too."

"Rosaleen's gone."

"What?"

He jammed his hands into his pockets and stared into the flames. "Packed up and bought a train ticket to who knows where. New Orleans most likely." He snapped his fingers. "Just like that."

"Oh, Nate, I am terribly sorry. What are you going to do?"

He shrugged, his expression pitiful as a hen in a hard rain. "Wait for her to come back, I reckon."

"But do you think she will?"

"I haven't a clue. It's obvious she married me only as a means to an end, but what that end is, I can't imagine."

He looked so hurt and bewildered that Carrie told him everything she'd overheard the day Rosaleen came to see Griff. "I'm nearly certain she is Sophie's mother. She came here looking for the girl and needed some way to pay her expenses." She paused, remembering the night Nate and Rosaleen had arrived back in Hickory Ridge after their wedding. "That night, when she passed me on the stairs and said she was sorry, I wasn't sure what she meant, but now—"

Nate was stunned. His face went red as a blister. "She didn't care one iota about books, or me, or about hurting you. It's plain to see that she set her cap for me so I would provide her with a home while she searched for Sophie. And I fell for it." He polished his glasses on his sleeve and put them back on. "Helpless as a fly in a spider's web."

She couldn't bear the look of hurt in his eyes. "I could be wrong. I hope I am wrong. Maybe I shouldn't have told you."

"I have no one but myself to blame." He sighed. "I was tired of being alone in the world. Rosaleen came along, and I didn't think that you would ever . . ." His voice softened. "What happened to us anyway?"

"I don't know, Nate. I suppose we both made promises we couldn't keep."

He stared into the flickering firelight. "Are you going to tell Ada and Wyatt about Rosaleen?"

"I'm not sure what to do. Finding Sophie's mother at this late date would be a shock to everyone. But I keep thinking that the girl deserves to know who her real mother is. Wouldn't it make a difference to Sophie to know the reasons she was abandoned?"

"I'd agree with you if Rosaleen were a different kind of woman. She didn't say a lot about her past. Maybe we're wrong, but I think you should write to Ada. You're her closest friend. Tell her what you suspect. Let her and Wyatt decide whether to tell Sophie her mother may be alive and looking for her."

"That's the other thing." Carrie lit the lamp and turned up the wick. Wind whistled down the mountain and rattled the window panes. "What if I've jumped to the wrong conclusion? What if Rosaleen isn't Sophie's mother after all? Then I've stirred up a hornet's nest for nothing."

"Aunt Carrie?" Caleb burst into the parlor, his nose and cheeks red from the cold. "The cake is burning. And guess who's coming up the road? Griff Rutledge, that's who."

TWENTY-NINE

Nate picked up his hat. "I'll be on my way, Carrie. I hope you all have a happy Christmas."

"Thank you . . . for everything." She placed a hand on his arm. "Try not to worry about Rosaleen. We must pray she comes to her senses eventually."

She and the boys followed Nate onto the porch. Carrie peered into the dusk. Bundled into his winter coat, a bright blue scarf knotted at his throat, Griff stood beside his rented wagon, untying an enormous evergreen. She waved to him. Nate offered Griff a curt nod as he crossed the yard to his horse and rode away.

Griff hauled the tree onto the porch. "I figured the boys might be wanting this."

Joe and Caleb danced around the tree, bright-eyed and rosy-cheeked as English princes.

"Well, just don't stand there, boys," Griff said, "help me get it inside."

Carrie held the door and they dragged the tree into the parlor. Griff went back to the wagon and returned with two short pieces of wood, a hammer, and nails for constructing a tree stand. Soon the tree stood tall and secure in front of the parlor window, filling the room with the smell of fresh cedar.

Memories of other Christmases flooded Carrie's heart. If only her family—her real family—were here now to share in the wonder that was Christmas.

Caleb ran upstairs to fetch the paper garlands he and Joe had been working on for the past week. While Carrie disposed of the ruined raisin cake and Griff made mysterious trips to his wagon, the boys draped the tree with the garlands, a string of buttons, and a small bird's nest. Griff lifted Joe so he could place a shiny tin star at the top. Then Carrie set the table and went to wake Mary.

"Mr. Rutledge has brought Christmas," she whispered when Mary roused herself from sleep. "Do you feel like having supper at the table?"

"Not really. But I want to, for the boys' sake. Can you help me dress?"

Carrie took Mary's best blue dress from the clothes press. It was too tight now; the buttons wouldn't close. But they covered that fact with a new lawn dressing gown Mary had made. Carrie brushed Mary's lank hair, tied it back with a bit of ribbon, and led her to the table.

Griff, who had been admiring the tree with the boys, rose and bowed over Mary's hand. "Mrs. Bell. I'm pleased to see you up and about."

"Thank you." Spotting the tree, Mary let out a little cry of delight. "It's beautiful."

Griff nodded, his expression unusually grave. Something flashed in his dark, expressive eyes. Sorrow? Compassion? A shiver of uneasiness moved through Carrie. But it wouldn't do to let worry spoil this moment.

She clapped her hands. "Time for supper."

They took their places around the table. Carrie nodded to Caleb. They bowed their heads.

"Lord, thank you for Griff and his tree and Aunt Carrie and Mama and for Christmas even though there aren't any presents. Make our new papa come home soon. Amen."

The boys rushed through their meal of fried ham, biscuits, and spiced apples, then hurried to the parlor to admire the tree. Mary, seemingly near tears, picked at her food. Carrie felt like crying too. But at least they had a home, a warm fire, and enough food, even if it wasn't a feast. And Griff was here.

She sipped her coffee, and he smiled at her across the table. Watching him smile was like watching the sunrise over the Smokies, the light beginning soft and tentative before bursting into brilliance. She would miss that smile when he was gone.

"I'm sorry there's nothing sweet," she said. "I burned the cake."

"Don't worry." Griff rose and started toward the door. "Excuse me. I'll be right back."

He went out on a burst of frigid air.

Carrie stacked their plates. "Mary, do you feel well enough to sit in the parlor for a while?"

"I'd like that." Mary caught Carrie's hand as she passed. "Thank you for—"

"You're welcome."

Carrie helped Mary into the parlor and went upstairs to get Nate's presents and the ones she'd bought for the boys. She returned just as Griff walked in with a stack of gaily wrapped packages and a paper sack.

He winked at Joe. "Who wants a present?"

"I do." Joe lunged for a box.

Griff handed each of the boys a box and watched while they opened them—a wooden train set for Joe and an elaborate puzzle for Caleb—then Carrie gave them her presents. Joe grinned when he saw the brightly painted mechanical bank from Jasper Pruitt's mercantile, but Caleb seemed less enthusiastic about his shiny penknife. He tested the blade and fingered the smooth wooden case, his expression sober. "Thanks, Aunt Carrie."

Disappointment welled inside her. "You don't like it?"

"I like it fine. But I was kinda hoping for a rifle."

"You're too young, Caleb," Mary said. "We talked about this before, remember?"

"Yeah, but that was before Papa left. I'm the man of the family till he gets back. I need a gun for going huntin'. And to protect you in case robbers come around."

Mary drew Caleb onto her knees and wrapped her arms around him. "I appreciate that, son, but we don't have to worry about robbers. And Papa will be home soon, just like he promised. You'll see."

Caleb shrugged and stared at the floor. Despite everything he had done to vex her, Carrie couldn't bear the sadness in the boy's eyes. She patted his arm. "Spring will be here before we know it."

"Why don't we sing some carols?" Mary asked. "It is Christmas, after all." She smiled. "I'm sorry we're missing the church program this year. I always looked forward to the singing."

"Me too," Carrie said. "And the pageant. Deborah asked Mrs. Musgrove to help Jeanne Pruitt sew costumes after Mr. Musgrove passed on. Deborah says they're absolutely lovely."

"Maybe we can go next year." Joe looked up from his new train set and grinned. "Maybe Jimmy D. Washburn will play the part of Joseph. Or maybe he'll be an angel."

Caleb snorted and laughed at last. "Jimmy D. an angel? Not likely."

"Well, at least we can sing about angels," Carrie said. She led them through "While Shepherds Watched Their Flocks" and "Angels from the Realms of Glory." Then, when the last note died away, she handed the boys the books Nate had brought for them. Joe immediately curled up before the fire with *Peter Parley's Annual* and studied the lavish illustrations, his other presents forgotten.

Caleb flipped through Hawthorne's *Tanglewood Tales* and set it aside. "I'll read it later."

Once the presents were opened, Carrie settled back with a sigh of satisfaction, but Griff had more surprises. He handed out chocolates and oranges and gave each boy a silver whistle. "But don't go blowing those things inside, boys. You don't want to give the womenfolk a headache."

Joe barely looked up from his book. "Thanks, Mr. Rutledge."

"It was my pleasure, Joe."

Carrie couldn't help smiling as she watched Griff with the boys. What a shame he'd chosen a life that precluded his having a family. He handled Joe and especially Caleb with just the right combination of authority, affection, and respect. He would have made a wonderful father.

"Mr. Rutledge?" Mary reached for her Bible on the side table. "Would you mind? Reading the Christmas story is a tradition in our home."

"I'd be honored, Mrs. Bell."

Settling next to Joe and Caleb, he fished his spectacles from his pocket. He flipped the thin pages back and forth until he found the right passage and began to read. "And it came to pass in those days, that there went out a decree from Caesar Augustus that all the world should be taxed. . . . And Joseph also went up from Galilee . . . to be taxed with Mary his espoused wife, being great with child."

"Like Mama," Joe said, grinning.

Griff nodded solemnly. "Yes."

"Don't interrupt, son," his mother said. "Go ahead, Mr. Rutledge."

"And suddenly there was with the angel a multitude of the heavenly host praising God, and saying, Glory to God in the highest, and on earth peace, good will toward men."

Carrie listened, a familiar tightness in her throat. The story of the coming of the Savior into the world never failed to move her. She thought of Granny Bell, of her lost parents, of Frank, safe now with the Lord, and said a silent prayer for them all.

Closing the Bible, Griff said to Caleb, "Would you put another log on the fire? And excuse your Aunt Carrie and me for a moment?"

Joe looked up from his place on the hearth, his eyes bright with Christmas wonder. "Are you going to kiss her?"

Heat rushed to Carrie's face. She couldn't meet Griff's gaze.

Mary laughed. "That's an impertinent question, son."

"What's impertinent mean?" Joe reached for another chocolate and wiped his fingers on the front of his shirt.

"Never mind. And don't use your shirt as a napkin."

Griff put on his coat. Carrie got hers from the coat tree, and they went out into the darkness. A frigid wind scythed down from the mountain, bringing with it a light, icy rain that needled her cheeks. Griff's horse stamped and snorted in the cold, his breath coming out in small, white clouds.

Carrie looked back at the house. The front windows glowed with light. Hickory smoke billowed from the chimney like exhaust from a train before dissipating into the wind. The boys' faint laughter danced in the air. For a moment, time slipped behind a curtain, and despite Henry's absence and her constant worries, she felt almost happy.

"Carrie." Griff took both her shoulders and turned her to face him. Her heart sped up. "Yes?" Dampness plastered her hair and clung to her eyelashes. She shivered.

He looked into her eyes. "I would rather be keelhauled than to tell you this. I'm afraid I have very bad news."

Her stomach dropped. "Is it Henry? Is he hurt? How bad is it?"

He fished a telegram from his coat pocket and pressed it into her hands. "I was at the mercantile buying toys for the boys when the telegraph operator ran in and handed me this. It came late yesterday, but there was no one to deliver it. She asked if I would do it. Since I know you all."

Carrie went numb. She had no need to read the wire. The truth was written plain across Griff's handsome face. "My brother is dead."

"Yes, honey, he is."

Her knees buckled. Griff caught her, his arms strong and warm around her, and steadied her against his chest. She pressed her cheek against the rough wool of his coat. She couldn't think, couldn't cry. "What—what happened?"

"A terrible accident. According to the railway foreman, a coupling came loose while Henry was unloading boxcars. One rolled over him, crushed him instantly."

She nodded as if it was what she expected. "When?"

"A week or so ago. They had some trouble finding you."

"I see." If she concentrated on practical matters, she wouldn't have to feel the pain of yet another loss. Her mind whirled with the dozens of details to work out, decisions to be made. Should her brother be laid to rest in the country graveyard or on the mountain with Granny Bell? For a while after their parents died, life in the simple cabin above Muddy Hollow had been as calm and peaceful as the mountain itself. Maybe Henry would prefer that. Though the long trip up the winding dirt road would make tending his grave more difficult. But all of that would wait until later. "We must go to Chicago and bring him home."

Griff wiped the rain from his face. "I don't think that will be possible. I did some checking, and from what I understand, unclaimed bodies are sent from the morgue to a hospital where they're . . . um . . . prepared for use in the medical school."

Carrie couldn't stop shaking. How dare they? Henry was not unclaimed. He had a home, a family waiting for him. "Prepared for use? What does that mean?"

He shook his head. "It's better not to know."

"But how can they take a person without permission?"

"Chicago is a big city. A dangerous place. You must understand that several people a day die there or simply disappear without a trace. The authorities can't track down all the kin."

"But Henry worked for a big railway company. Surely they kept records."

"We'll look into that, but I don't want you to get your hopes up. Chances are we won't be able to bring your brother home." He pulled her close. "My dearest girl, I am deeply sorry."

She sagged against him. Never had she felt more alone. Not when the yellow fever took her parents within a week of each other. Not when Granny Bell died. Not even when the awful news came from Shiloh. Each time, Henry had been there to see her through it all. But now . . .

"It's a mistake."

He held her closer, his lips on her hair. The biting wind whipped around the corner. "I wish it were. But we must face the truth."

The tears came then, tears of fear and profound grief. And tears of rage. She had asked so little of God. Why had he abandoned her? Was Henry's death her penalty for flouting convention? For resenting Mary? For wanting too much?

"What am I going to do?"

"We'll figure it out."

He fished a handkerchief from his pocket. She wiped her eyes and looked back toward the house, a tiny island of calm beneath the mountain's great shadow. For the rest of her life she would remember this moment, this sliver of time when she knew what Mary and the boys did not. That their entire world, all their hopes and dreams for the future, had been destroyed.

"We'll tell Mary once the boys are asleep," Griff said. "Waiting a day or two to tell them won't change anything. And then they won't have to remember Christmas as the day they learned their new papa died."

Together they returned to the house. The lantern had burned low. Mary and Joe dozed before the fire. Caleb was engrossed in his book. He looked up, his face rosy with heat, and marked his place with his finger.

Griff placed a hand on the boy's head. "Good book, son?" he asked, his expression full of sorrow.

Caleb nodded as his gaze shifted to Carrie. "What's wrong, Aunt Carrie? You've been crying."

"I'm all right." She nearly choked on the words. She was not all right. She would never be all right. If only there were some way to spare them all from the grief that was coming.

Mary stirred and opened her eyes. "My goodness, I must have nodded off. I'm so sorry, Mr. Rutledge. I'm not a very good hostess."

"You needed the rest." He glanced at the mantel clock. "I didn't realize it was so late."

"Boys?" Mary shook Joe awake. "Time for bed."

Joe roused himself and blinked. "But I'm not tired yet."

Griff lifted Joe into his arms. "Come on, my man. Let's get you tucked in." He nodded to the older boy. "You too, Caleb."

"I'm too old to be tucked in."

Griff smiled. "Maybe you are at that. Nevertheless, it's time you both turned in."

Joe laid his head against Griff's shoulder. "Will you read me a story?"

"Not tonight. It's late."

He disappeared up the stairs with the boys. Waiting for his return, Carrie busied herself picking up their toys, adding a log to the fire.

Mary watched, a frown forming between her brows. "What's the matter with you? You're jumpy as a cat."

Carrie shook her head.

"Did Mr. Rutledge say something to upset you?"

"Mary." Carrie looked at her sister-in-law, wishing she could say something to prepare her for the coming news. But words failed. Her heart turned over. It was true they had never been close, but they both knew what it was like to lose a husband. Frank's death had changed Carrie. She couldn't imagine what it would be like to have it happen twice. Mary would never be the same.

Griff came downstairs and sent Carrie a questioning look. She shook her head.

He sat down beside Mary, his expression calm and grave. "Mrs. Bell."

"No." Mary shook her head. Her eyes filled, and Carrie felt her own tears coming back. "Whatever it is, I don't want to hear it. I can't."

"I know," Griff said gently. "But you must. There was an accident in the rail yard."

Carrie watched Mary's eyes register fear, disbelief, and then horrified acceptance as Griff told her the rest of it. "We thought it best not to tell the boys until after Christmas. Let them have one last day without sadness."

"I suppose that's wise."

Mary didn't weep. She rested one hand on the swell of her belly and gazed at the dancing firelight. Finally she looked up at Carrie, her expression resigned and calm. "I reckon you'll want us out of here, now that your brother is never coming home."

Carrie placed her hand on Mary's arm. "Let's not think about that. Of course you're welcome here. Besides, you couldn't move out now, in your condition, even if you had someplace to go."

Mary's sudden laugher exploded into the room like a gunshot. She bent double, clapped one hand over her mouth, and howled.

"Griff?" Carrie looked up in alarm.

"Hysteria. I've seen it a few times. Have you any smelling salts?"

"No."

"Any liquor?"

"Henry left some whiskey in the cupboard. He used it for when he got the croup."

"Bring it."

Carrie hurried through the dark house to the kitchen. Lighting the lamp, she turned up the wick and rummaged in the cupboard for the spirits and a glass. She carried them to the parlor, where Griff poured a small amount of whisky into the glass.

"Mrs. Bell?" Mary didn't answer. He took her shoulders and shook her, hard. "Mrs. Bell!"

Mary jerked as if waking from a fevered dream and stared at them, unseeing. Griff handed her the glass. "Drink this."

Obedient as a child, Mary drank it down. "There. I suppose that's supposed to make me forget everything."

"I'm afraid you'd have to consume much more than that to reach oblivion," Griff said gently.

"In that case"—she tittered again—"bring me the bottle."

"Mary." Carrie took her sister-in-law's hand. "Come along. You must rest. We have a hard few days ahead of us. The boys will need you to be brave and strong."

"But I'm not brave and strong." She stood, swaying slightly. "That's your department. Good night, Mr. Rutledge."

He bowed. "Please accept my sincere condolences."

"Griff?" Carrie glanced at him as she led Mary from the room.

"Take your time. I'll be right here."

Carrie led Mary to her room and helped her undress. Consumed by grief and dread, Mary moved even more slowly than usual. She crawled into bed and turned her face to the wall.

Carrie fluffed the pillows and drew up the covers. "Are you warm enough?"

Mary's head moved against the pillow. "I don't expect to be warm ever again."

"Listen to me. Once word gets around, all sorts of people will come calling, telling you that they understand how you feel. But they can't, not really." She smoothed Mary's hair away from her face. "Right now you feel as if your life has ended too. You wish it were over, to be spared the unending grief. But one day you will wake up and realize that you slept peacefully through the night, that your heart feels a bit stronger. And one day you will laugh without feeling guilty that Henry is not here to share in it."

Tears leaked from Mary's eyes and ran onto the pillow. "You forget I've already buried one husband. I know all about—"

Carrie rushed on, the words pouring out of her. "You have two boys who need you . . . and Henry's child on the way." She paused. "You're luckier than I was. In this baby, you'll always have a part of Henry. I had nothing of Frank except a few personal belongings returned to me from the battlefield. And my memories."

Mary's hand moved on the coverlet. "Will you wake me in the morning as soon as the boys are up?"

"Yes. We'll go on with Christmas as best we can. And after that, we'll tell them together." She lifted the lamp. "Try to sleep now."

She found Griff in the parlor, tending the fire. The ice-laden wind had picked up, ticking and thumping against the window panes.

"Will Mrs. Bell be all right?" His eyes were very dark, his handsome features troubled.

"She's calm now. I hope she can sleep."

"I should go." He picked up his rain-splotched coat, and they went to the door.

Ice had frozen it shut. Griff wrenched it open. In the feeble lantern light, the yard glistened like a sheet of shattered glass. The horse stood shivering in the bitter wind.

"You can't go all the way back to town in this weather," Carrie said, closing the door. "You can sleep here, in the parlor."

He regarded the narrow settee. "I appreciate it, but truthfully, I'd be more comfortable in the barn." He smiled. "I don't suppose you still have my old mattress."

"It's still out there, next to the extra milk pails. But, Griff, the barn is freezing."

"A manger was good enough for the Savior. I reckon it's good enough for me."

Griff had never really talked about his faith or what it meant to him. Because of his background, she'd assumed he didn't give much thought to God. Perhaps he was a much deeper person than she imagined. "I'll get you some blankets."

Griff led Delilah into the barn, removed the tack, and rubbed her down. He found half a pail of oats and offered them to the ravenous beast, along with a few pitchforks full of hay before rolling out his mattress over a thick layer of more hay. He spread his wool coat out to dry, snuffed the lantern, and crawled into his makeshift bed, pulling another blanket over himself.

Despite the day's exhausting events, he was wide-awake, restless. Reading the Christmas story and seeing Joe and Caleb's brotherly back-and-forth teasing reminded him of when he and Philip had taken their skiff into the marshes and fished all day among the egrets, loggerheads, and alligators. At sunset they returned home sweaty and sunburned, their arms crosshatched with spartina grass scratches, sated with perfect happiness.

Though he and Philip had grown apart as adults, he still retained fond memories of Christmases in Charleston or at River Place. He especially remembered the year he turned fourteen. That year, with

Philip away visiting cousins, his father had presented Griff with his own Thoroughbred, a beautiful little chestnut mare. On that crisp December morning, he tacked her up and rode with his father along the trunk-gate road past the brick rice mill and the clapboard winnowing houses. Even now, if he closed his eyes, he still could see Spanish moss swaying from the branches of the ancient oaks and flocks of birds wheeling over the silvery river.

That day his father had tried, not for the first time, to instill in his elder son a respect for the duties incumbent upon one of his station, for the nuances of Southern honor. Absorbed in getting to know his new mount, Griff half listened, determined not to spoil the day for himself or for his mother. Like other mothers of her social standing, she chose not to interfere with her husband's efforts to mold her firstborn into a younger version of himself. But behind the scenes, she encouraged Griff to follow his heart, listen to his own instincts. Finding her own choices severely limited, she wanted something more for her son.

The barn door slapped in the wind. Griff turned over on his mattress and closed his eyes. Was Carrie still awake? He couldn't forget the look of utter desolation in her eyes, the sag in her shoulders when he delivered the news. He felt terrible for her, for all of them. He hoped that somehow she and Mary could forge ties that would keep the remnants of their fractured family together. Because watching Carrie's relationship with Mary and the boys, fractious as it was at times, had changed him. Made it clear that, in the end, family and God were all that counted.

He listened to the mice scrabbling in the barn and the gruff purr of the resident cat. How was his father getting on? There had been no word from Philip since his brief visit to Hickory Ridge last summer. For all Griff knew, his father might well be dead. The thought chilled him far more than the wind seeping into the barn.

Delilah, restless as he was in the unfamiliar barn, nickered and stirred. Griff quieted her with a soft word. He couldn't leave Hickory Ridge now, not with his business proposition to the banker still pending. Not while Carrie, immersed in grief, needed someone to steady her. But one day soon he'd make a trip to Charleston, try to salvage whatever was left of his family.

He hoped he wouldn't be too late.

THIRTY

Snow began falling around midnight, thin flurries that grew into fat, wet flakes that stuck to the windowpane and piled up on the sill. Cupping her hands to the glass, Carrie peered out at the night-blued snow, listening. Mercifully, Mary and her sons seemed to be asleep.

In the seven long weeks since Christmas, none of them slept very well. Nearing the end of her confinement, Mary was often too uncomfortable to stay in bed and roamed the house all hours. Caleb and Joe, still reeling from the news of Henry's death, woke from nightmares with endless requests for a story or a glass of water. Carrie found their need for constant reassurance exhausting.

She'd dreaded telling them that their new papa would not be coming home, even to be properly mourned, but they'd absorbed the news better than she imagined. She expected tears from Joe, but it was Caleb who cried inconsolably before running out of the house. Joe crawled back beneath his bedcovers with his illustrated book. And now they'd returned to their daily routine and their noisy, rough-and-tumble rivalry. Except for the nightmares, they seemed to have forgotten their grief. Perhaps they hadn't lived with Henry long enough to realize how much they had lost.

But Henry's death was an ever-present source of sadness for Carrie. Tucked into the back of her Bible were two letters from

Patrick Sullivan, Henry's foreman, expressing deep regret at her loss and confirming that in the absence of information about Henry's family, his body had indeed been donated "to medical science."

"You may take comfort," one letter said, "in knowing your loved one will contribute to increased knowledge and better medical care for all."

What comfort was there in having no place to go to mourn Henry? No grave or marker to remind the living of his short years on earth? Perhaps in the spring she would plant a garden of his favorite irises and start a new vine of morning glories on the trellis. Something to remind her that despite her terrible loss, life would go on.

Turning from the window, she crawled beneath the covers and closed her eyes. For now, she had enough food to get them through the rest of the winter. Some of the meat from the pig they had butchered still hung in the new smokehouse. And when word of Henry's death got around town, nearly everyone in Hickory Ridge had come to call, bringing whatever they had to spare—a sack of dried apples or roasted chestnuts, ham and sausages, jars of beans and plums, and enough hummingbird cakes and vinegar pies to stock a good-sized bakery.

But how on earth would she continue supporting Mary and three growing children? Though she and Henry had been largely self-sufficient on the farm, she would still need to buy seeds and pay someone to help with the planting and harvesting. Her bread-baking enterprise alone would never earn enough to buy clothes, shoes, and books for the older boys, medicine and blankets for the baby, and staples such as sugar, flour, and salt.

It had wounded her pride to accept charity from her neighbors. After a life lived mostly on their own, she and Henry had developed an aversion to taking help from anybody. Undoubtedly, some of Mary's contentiousness came from these same feelings. Maybe she and Mary were more alike than she imagined. And maybe Jasper

Pruitt was right and God intended a lesson in humility in all of this. Even so, the problem of providing for a family of five indefinitely would not go away.

Wat Stephens. The mere thought of his name made her shudder. More than once he had bragged to Henry that he was sitting on enough money to buy the Bells' farm with money for a calf left over. Carrie punched the pillow. She would never sell off everything, but Stephens had long had his eye on the twenty acres of Bell land that backed to Owl Creek. Though it pained her to even consider selling a single acre of it, especially to Stephens, the hard truth was that she needed money, and soon.

The parlor clock struck the hour. Carrie drew up her covers and thought of Griff. For the first couple of weeks in January, he'd ridden out to the farm every few days to bring the mail. He never arrived without some small trinket for the boys, chocolate for her and Mary, and news from town. On the last visit, they learned that eleven students had appeared for the opening day of the new term under Mr. Webster and two more new tenants had moved into the Verandah.

Carrie thought of her brief time at the hotel, when she had a job of her own at Nate's bookshop, and life had offered more possibilities. Now there was only one course open to her: looking after Henry's family.

Griff had also said that one of the men who had come to Hickory Ridge for the horse race, a Mr. Blakely from Maryland, had fallen in love with the mountains and was thinking of building a fancy resort just up the rail line from town. That would mean an increased demand for timber and for men who could clear brush, build a road, and construct the resort itself. "If Blakely follows through," Griff told her, his dark eyes alight with excitement, "this could be the beginning of better times for Hickory Ridge." He'd hinted at plans of his own too, but despite Carrie's hopeful urging, he'd been unwilling to share them. "I don't want to say too much till I'm sure."

Lately his visits had grown less frequent. He was busy with his own plans, most likely, but land's sakes, she missed him. Maybe one day soon, he'd—

"Carrie?" Mary's urgent voice drifted up the stairs. "Wake up."

Carrie grabbed her dressing gown and hurried into the hallway. Mary stood at the bottom of the stairs, holding aloft a guttering lamp that cast attenuated shadows on the wall. In the flickering light, her face shone pale as a moonflower.

Carrie raked her hair off her face. "What is it? Leg cramps again?"

"It's time."

Disoriented and exhausted from long nights without sleep, Carrie frowned. "Time?"

"The baby's coming."

"Now?"

"Babies don't consider the clock. They come when they've a mind to." Mary pressed her belly. "I'm going to need your help."

"I'll hitch the wagon and fetch Dr. Spencer."

"It's snowing," Mary said calmly. "And anyway, there isn't ti—oh!"

"I'm coming." Carrie hurried down the stairs. "What should I do?"

She had helped Henry deliver a calf once and, another time, a litter of piglets. But a baby, Henry's baby, was a different matter entirely. What if she made a mistake? Nerves skittered along her spine. *Dear Lord, please help me. Help Mary and this little baby.*

"Help me back to the bed." Mary's face went white with pain. "And whatever you do, don't let the boys come in here. You'll need plenty of warm water. And the knife."

"A knife?"

"To cut the cord, Carrie. And towels. I hope you aren't squeamish at the sight of blood. There might be a lot of it."

Mary seemed preternaturally calm, but Carrie's stomach roiled. She swallowed. "I'd better get the fire going."

Mary gasped as another pain gripped her. "Please hurry."

In the kitchen Carrie shoved kindling into the stove, lit a match and tossed it in, then added a couple of small sticks of wood. The kindling caught, sending gray smoke trailing into the room. She filled the teakettle and a pan of water and set them on the stove.

"Aunt Carrie?"

She jumped at the sound and whirled around. "Caleb?"

"How come you're up?" He blinked. "It's the middle of the night."

"Your mother is having the baby."

His eyes widened. "Don't we need the doc for that? He told me and Joe he has medicine that makes the pain go away."

"Ideally, yes, but there isn't time, so I'm going to help."

He frowned. "You ever helped a baby get born before?"

"No, but I've delivered baby animals, so I sort of know what to expect. And your mother will tell me what to do." She smiled to reassure him. "She brought you and Joe into the world, after all."

"Is she going to die?"

"Of course not. She'll be fine. The baby too. You'll see."

"Jimmy D. Washburn's mother had a baby and she died." A sob caught in his throat.

Carrie opened a cupboard, looking for a towel. "I won't lie to you, Caleb. Sometimes that does happen. But your mother has been in bed all this time, resting, so she'll be strong enough for when the baby comes. You mustn't worry about it."

He nodded and threw both arms around her. "I'm sorry I hit you that time. I'm sorry for showin' Joe how to start a fire and for not mindin' you. I'll try to do better."

She stroked Caleb's mussed hair. "I grew up with a big brother. I know how boys behave."

He pressed his face to her dressing gown. "You don't know what else I done. I chopped up Papa's best fishin' pole."

"Oh, Caleb."

"Ever' time I passed by it in the barn, I thought about him." He looked up at her, his eyes wet. "I figgered if I got rid of it, I could forget all about him, and then maybe I wouldn't feel so bad. But it didn't work."

"No. But I know how you feel."

The kettle shrieked. Carrie made tea and handed him a cup. "I was only a few years younger than you when my parents died. It hurt so bad I wanted to forget them too. But my granny talked about them every day. She told stories about my mama and how she loved to sing and gather the wildflowers that grew all over Muddy Hollow. How my daddy came courting her one time riding on the sorriest old mule Granny'd ever seen."

"He shoulda had a horse like Majestic."

Carrie smiled as she took the kitchen knife from the cupboard. "Pretty soon I started looking forward to Granny's stories. They made me feel closer to my mama and papa." She patted his arm. "It wasn't forgetting that made me feel better. It was remembering."

Caleb sipped his tea and made a face. "You aren't mad at me for chopping up the fishin' pole?"

"I wish you hadn't done it. Henry set a lot of store by that pole. But I understand why you did it." She laid a hand on his shoulder. "Now, I need you to go back upstairs and stay with Joe. Do not come down until I call you. No matter what sounds you hear, you stay put. All right?"

"I guess."

"Not good enough." She draped a towel over her arm and lifted the pot of boiling water from the stove. "I need your solemn promise."

"I promise." He ran from the kitchen.

When Carrie returned to the bedroom, Mary's eyes were bright with pain, her skin shiny with sweat. Her damp gown clung to her thighs.

Carrie set the towel and water aside. "How are you? Is the pain really bad?"

Mary nodded. "Worse than when Caleb and Joe were—ahhh!" She gripped the bedcovers and went rigid until the pain passed. Then she leaned back against the pillow, her breathing ragged, her body limp. "I—I don't think I can take this."

"I know it hurts. But it won't be long until you'll hold Henry's child in your arms. You'll have a part of him back again."

"Yes, but—oh dear God!" Mary clenched her teeth. Rivulets of sweat ran down her face.

Instinctively Carrie gripped Mary's hand. "Hold on. Just a little long—"

The wrinkled, misshapen creature entered the world in a rush. Her hands trembling, Carrie cut the cord and lifted the child, who lay silent and motionless in her arms.

"Carrie?" Mary rasped.

The world receded. Carrie's heart pounded. What to do? She couldn't lose this baby. *Please, God. Please help me.*

"I don't hear a cry," Mary whispered. "The baby's dead, isn't it? And it's my fault."

Carrie felt the child's chest. A heartbeat fluttered, but the skin was turning blue. She blew into the baby's nostrils, tiny puffs of air. Nothing. Holding tightly to the baby, she swung it in a wide arc, back and forth, praying that the rush of air would fill its tiny lungs. Still nothing. Carrie realized she was holding her own breath.

Then, at last, she heard it—a faint mewling sound that quickly grew into a lusty, full-bodied cry. Carrie bathed the tiny child, tears of sadness and relief streaming unchecked down her face. *It's a boy, Henry. Someone to carry on your name. And thank God he's all right.*

She swaddled the child and handed him to his mother. "Mary, here's your son."

"Another boy?"

Carrie smiled. "Henry would bust his buttons if he knew."

Mary squeezed Carrie's hand. "I like to think he does know, somehow."

"Me too." She helped Mary to bathe and change, and left to check the fire in the stove. Now that the child was safely delivered, she was weak with relief and exhaustion but too keyed up to sleep. She made tea and carried a tray to Mary's room.

Mother and child were sleeping. Watching the rise and fall of Mary's breath, Carrie felt her old resentments falling away. They might never be the best of friends, but she and Mary were truly a family now, bound forever by the child they both loved. She wished Mary a peaceful rest, free of the longing for the life that was lost to her now.

Mary's life had not turned out as she wanted. Perhaps no one's did.

Perhaps the secret to a happy life was to want the one you had.

～

The Atlantic lay still and pewter-gray, reflecting the late February sky. Bundled into his overcoat, Griff stood on the battery, watching a fishing boat approach the harbor. His throat tightened. He'd forgotten how much he missed the sights and smells of the low country, the excitement of moonless wartime night voyages aboard the *Nightingale*. He'd missed Charleston too, the way a man misses a well-loved woman.

At one time he had known the city's every nook and cranny—the ornate mansions on Queen and Meeting Streets built with money from rice plantations dotting the banks of the Pee Dee River. The gaming houses, the busy wharf, the elegant theaters. St. Philip's Church, where he attended services as a boy. He recalled countless Sundays spent wedged between his parents and his brother, trussed into scratchy wool suits and stiff boiled collars, tight shoes pinching his feet. He loved the sound of his mother's voice lifted in song, the peaceful hush that descended as the prayers were read, the dust motes swirling in the bright Carolina sunlight, the tantalizing sea smells riding on the sultry breeze coming through the open windows.

But Charleston was a changed place now. St. Philip's bells no longer chimed the hours, having been melted into cannons during the war. Vast stretches of the city from Hassel Street clear up to Tradd had burned to the ground back in sixty-one, leaving a swath of smoking ruins, their insides seared to nothing. Here and there ghostlike shells of homes still stood, reminders of a way of life that was now irrevocably lost. In his opinion, it was this loss, more than any physical ailment, that had sent his father to his sickbed.

He jammed his gloveless hands into his pockets, turned, and walked along Meeting Street toward his father's house. Uncertain of the reception awaiting him after so long an absence, he'd left his bags at the train station. If he was turned away—a distinct possibility—he'd simply head back to Hickory Ridge.

He regretted that he hadn't ridden out to Carrie's place before leaving town. But Philip's telegram, with its terse message, "Come home," had arrived on the same day as his meeting with Gilman at the bank. A trip to Carrie's would have meant missing the evening train and then a two-day wait for the next one. Distracted, he'd scribbled a hasty note to her, intending to leave it with the postmaster, only to find it later in the pocket of his overcoat. Stupid. He hoped Carrie would understand. As uncertain as he was of his welcome in Charleston, he nevertheless wanted a chance to say good-bye to his father. He feared he might already be too late.

Arriving at the Rutledge house, he pushed open the wrought-iron gate, hurried past the tangle of neglected gardens, and climbed the steps to the verandah. Before he could ring the bell, the door opened. There stood his younger brother, bleary-eyed and unshaven.

Philip motioned Griff inside. "Thank God you came. Father has been asking for you."

Griff shucked out of his overcoat and hung it on the hall tree and blew on his hands to warm them. "Then he isn't—"

"Not yet. But soon, I think. Dr. Pettigrew was here yesterday." Philip's voice cracked. "He didn't offer us much hope, I'm afraid."

Griff nodded.

"Susan was here most of the night. I finally sent her home to rest for a while. You need coffee?"

"If it isn't too much trouble." Griff looked around his boyhood home. Nothing, not even the draperies, had changed. On the hall table stood a silver bowl filled with apples. Oil portraits of his mother still hung above the massive fireplace and along the stair landing. A small forest of silver candlesticks crowded the mantel. The furnishings gleamed and smelled faintly of beeswax. His heart ached with loss.

"Is Calpurnia still keeping house for Father?"

"Calpurnia?" Philip led the way to the dining room, where a silver coffee service waited on the marble-topped sideboard. "You have been away a long time, brother. Cal passed on—" He paused while he poured coffee into two bone-china cups—"four or five years ago. Her daughter Daisy comes in a few times a week to tidy up." He handed Griff a cup. "Otherwise, Susan helps me look after things."

Griff sipped the bitter brew. "Susan's a good woman."

"But not good enough for you," Philip said without rancor.

"We wouldn't have been compatible. It has nothing to do with her character. I'm certain you'll be very happy together."

The faint chiming of a bell sounded. Philip set down his cup. "He's awake. Ready to go up?"

Griff nodded, his heart thudding. Stupid to fear his father's opinion at this late date. He wasn't a callow youth of fourteen anymore. He'd made a more than respectable fortune during the war, and he was on the verge of a new enterprise that he found challenging and exciting. By his own measure—which was all any man should care about—he was a success. And yet there was an empty place inside him where his father's approval belonged.

He followed Philip up the curving staircase to his father's room overlooking the summer kitchen and the carriage house where long ago Griff had stolen his first kiss. It seemed now like another life, as if those languorous low-country summers had happened to someone else.

They went in. The curtains were open to the weak winter light. In the grate, a fire leapt and crackled. A small side table was littered with a half-empty water pitcher, a glass, several small brown medicine bottles, a wrinkled handkerchief. A pile of books lay haphazardly on the floor.

"Father?" Philip said softly. "You've been asking for Griff, and here he is."

Their father, wasted and pale, blinked and struggled to sit up. "Griffin?"

Griff moved to the side of the bed. "Hello, Father."

"I—I didn't think you'd come."

"I wanted to see you. It's been a long time."

His father nodded and extended a mottled, clawlike hand. "Good . . . to see you, son."

Despite all the strife between them over the years, Griff's eyes filled. This wizened, helpless shell of a man was the man who had given him life. And now all Griff could think of was the good times. Those years before his father's expectations collided with Griff's own wishes and dreams.

"Sit." Charles Rutledge motioned his eldest son to a chair. "Tell me . . . where . . . have you been?"

"Here and there. Most recently in Tennessee."

"Did you . . . go to that horse race in Kentucky last spring?"

Griff smiled. Horses and horse racing had always been the best thing they shared.

"The Derby." Griff shook his head. "But I rode in a race this past fall. A magnificent colt called Majestic. Sixteen hands high, a wide-rumped, stubborn cuss, but fleet of foot. And a stride like I've never seen before. You'd have loved him."

The squeak of carriage wheels sounded in the street below. Philip rose and looked out. "Susan's back. Will you excuse me, Father?" Philip sought Griff's gaze. "Ring the bell if you need me."

Their father waved him away. When Philip had gone, he turned to Griff. "I'm glad to have a few minutes alone, Griffin. I don't have much time and—" He coughed and motioned for a glass of water. Griff held the glass while his father sipped, the water dribbling down his stubbled chin.

"Maybe you shouldn't try to talk, Father."

"But it's important that you understand why I'm leaving . . . everything to Philip."

The old resentments came rushing back. Anger replaced the pity he'd felt just moments before. But how could he argue with a dying man? "You don't have to explain. What's done is done. And I don't need the Rutledge money. I never wanted it anyway."

"Exactly." The old man's watery blue gaze held Griff's. "You always were the enterprising one. From the time you were small, you had the instincts of a survivor. Philip, on the other hand, needed much more direction."

"And he's more malleable too." The fire had burned low. Griff added another log and tapped it with the poker. "I understand he's going to marry Susan Layton. I suppose I should congratulate you both."

His father sighed. "The joining of family fortunes is a time-honored way of life in the South."

Griff stood with his back to the fire, his hands clasped behind him. "I'm well aware of that. And when I refused to play along with this time-honored tradition, I was disowned."

Charles coughed and sputtered. "Disowned? The way I remember it, you up and left the family, son. And broke your poor mother's heart."

"I'm sorry for that. But you made it clear there was no place for me here."

A pained look crossed the older man's face. "No place . . . is that what you thought? That I was throwing you out?"

"Weren't you?" Even now, the thought burned a hole in his heart. He recalled the years spent in gaming halls, on riverboats, in anonymous cities, heartsick for his roots and alone. His father, so intent upon molding him into the son he wanted, had completely missed the one he actually had.

"I tried to give you what you wanted." The old man picked up the handkerchief from the table and pressed it to his watery eyes. "The freedom to live life on your own terms. It's what your mother urged me to do. But I . . . handled it all wrong. I never intended you to feel unwelcome. Disowned. I never wanted that."

Griff felt his heart crack open. All this time he'd assumed Philip was the favored one and he was the black sheep, misunderstood and unloved. Was it possible that he'd been wrong? That what had looked like indifference was, in fact, his father's way of showing love?

"But, Father, when I left you were so angry with me. So

judgmental. I could see how disappointed you were, and I couldn't bear it."

"Disappointed, yes. Judgmental? Probably." His father paused for breath. "But only because I missed you, son. Philip is not half the horseman you are, nor half the businessman either. I was angry at my loss. Not at you."

"But—"

"In a way, I envied you. But I never stopped loving you. Never stopped trying to find out any bit of news about where you were and how you were getting on."

"I didn't know that."

"In a way it was worse than if you had died. At least then I could have mourned you and . . . made my peace with your absence."

Griff wiped his eyes. That his father loved him enough to give him the costliest gift imaginable—a life unencumbered by the obligations to the plantation and the way of life it engendered—was beyond his comprehension. How in the world had it taken him till now to understand that things are not always as they seem?

"Why didn't you say something, Father? All these years when I thought—"

Tears streamed down the older man's face. "Can you forgive a stubborn, arrogant old fool for getting it all wrong?"

The door opened and Philip came in. "Father? Dr. Pettigrew is here."

Their father frowned and waved one hand. "What for? We all know I'm dying. Tell him to go away. What little time I have left I want to spend with my family. Is that clear?"

"But—"

Griff saw the genuine panic in Philip's eyes. His father was right. Philip would be completely lost when it came to running things. At least Susan would be there to steady him in the days ahead.

"Go on now," their father told his younger son. "If you want . . .

to be useful, tell Susan to bring me up some tea. I'm feeling quite a chill."

Griff took his seat beside the bed. His father fell into sleep, his breathing slow and shallow. In the shadowed room, Griff studied the old man's hollowed cheeks and wrinkled brow and felt a sob catch in his throat. He had completely misjudged everything. Roamed the world in search of what he needed and returned home to find it. He reached down to clasp a gnarled hand. "I forgive you, and I hope you forgive me."

Susan came into the room balancing the ornate silver tea tray Griff remembered from his boyhood, a wedding gift to his mother handed down through generations of Venables. She set it on the table beside the fireplace and turned to Griff, her fingers braided tightly. She looked precisely the way he remembered. Solemn gray eyes, hair coiled into ringlets held away from her face with silver combs. She was tastefully dressed in a simple gray wool gown. A small diamond pin on her shoulder winked in the light.

Griff rose and took both her hands in his. "Dear Susan. How are you?"

"All right." Her eyes filled. "I never expected to see you again."

"I'm a little surprised to be here myself." He squeezed her hands. "You're looking well."

"I'm worried about Philip. He hasn't your strength, Griff. Losing his father, being responsible for the Rutledge holdings—I fear he isn't up to it." She sighed. "Even if you and I hadn't wed, if you and your father had reconciled, at least Philip would have you to rely upon now."

Griff glanced at his sleeping father. "We've made our peace. I only regret it didn't happen sooner."

"Then you'll come home? Help Phillip?"

"I'll help in whatever way I can, but I won't be coming back here. Not permanently anyway. I've made plans back in Hickory

Ridge. Exciting plans. I hope you and Philip will visit next year and take a look."

She spun away. "You're going to throw your life away in some Appalachian backwater? Why, Philip says it's hardly more than a logging camp."

Griff smiled. "Philip wasn't there long enough to appreciate everything it has to offer. It's a small town, true enough, but I can't praise it highly enough."

She searched his face. "A woman deserves the credit for your good opinion of the place, I imagine. I hope she isn't expecting too much from you."

He had no idea what Carrie expected of him, but he intended to find out as soon as possible. Assuming she would still speak to him after his abrupt departure.

Another carriage rattled past. The fire popped and hissed. He glanced out the window.

"I see," Susan said quietly. "You really are in love with her."

The words both surprised and terrified him. But it was true that being around Carrie had softened the hard edges in his heart and given him hope that his life might still be redeemed. That even a man with his past, his passions, could be transformed into the kind of man she deserved.

A slow smile rippled across his face. "I never fully realized it before today. But yes, I believe I am."

THIRTY-ONE

Holding tightly to Iris's bridle, Carrie led the mare from the barn and backed her between the wagon shafts. She struggled with the harness, her fingers stiff in the damp chill of the early March morning. Plumes of gray smoke rose from the adjacent fields where farmers were burning off last winter's stubble in preparation for spring planting. The acrid cloud mixed with the fog still hovering in the valleys and along the mountain ridges. Soon she would have to figure out how to ready her own fields, but that was a problem for another day.

She tightened the martingale and checked the bellyband before returning to the house for the six loaves of bread she'd baked before sunup. Setting them into her wicker basket, she covered the fragrant loaves with clean tea towels and picked up her empty reticule. Thank God Mrs. Whitcomb had doubled her weekly bread order. The money would keep them going for a short while longer. She tried not to think about how they would live until the garden could be planted and harvested or where on earth she would get shoes for Caleb and Joe. Just last week she'd cut a piece of old harness to cover the holes in the soles, but they were growing fast and they wouldn't be able to wear the old ones much longer. And now she must provide for Henry's only son.

Well, this was the task God had given her, and she would do her best to fulfill it. But why did everything have to be so difficult?

"The good Lord never gives us a heavier load than we can tote," Granny Bell had told her more times than she could remember. And perhaps it was true. But she needed help now, celestial or otherwise.

Last night she had reached a painful decision. As reluctant as she was to sell her land, it was her best hope. Besides, with only Caleb and Joe to help her, she couldn't plow, sow, hoe, and harvest it all anyway. She planned to pay Wat Stevens a visit later this morning. Perhaps he was still interested in the section down by Owl Creek.

She thought of Griff. With every passing day, she missed him more acutely. Clearly, he was much too busy to continue looking after her. How could she expect him to? Her family and her troubles were not his responsibility. Still, she couldn't help hoping to run into him in town—not that she had much time to seek him out. Since the baby's arrival, her trips to town lasted only long enough to deliver the bread order to Mrs. Whitcomb and pick up the mail and supplies.

Last week two days of rain had kept her at home, leaving her with too much time to wonder about him, to remember their one kiss, so fraught with heat and longing. Even though she knew they were hopeless and foolish, she couldn't stop her feelings for him. Five minutes in his company could lift her spirits and keep her going for days.

"Carrie?" Mary appeared in the doorway, her hair disheveled, the front of her dressing gown stiff and darkened with milk, the baby asleep on her shoulder. "I'm sorry I overslept. James Henry was fussy half the night. I've barely slept at all. Are the boys up?"

Tamping down her annoyance—she was tired too, after all—Carrie glanced at the clock. "It's nearly eight. They left for school an hour ago."

"Oh." Mary sank onto a chair and shifted the baby to her other shoulder. He began to fuss, and she patted his back till he quieted. "I didn't realize it was that late."

"There's coffee on the stove and leftover biscuits in the oven." Carrie picked up her bread basket. "I must go. Mrs. Whitcomb doesn't like me to be late."

"Surely she understands how busy we are these days."

We? Carrie bit back a retort and retrieved her woolen shawl from the hall tree. "I'll be back this afternoon, after I see Wat Stevens."

Mary nodded. "I've been thinking about that ever since you mentioned it, and I don't think Henry would approve."

"Of course he wouldn't. But he wouldn't approve of our starving to death either." Carrie headed for the door.

"Wait." Mary rose and hurried to her bedroom. Carrie heard her soothing the baby, cooing to him as she laid him down. A drawer rasped open. In a moment Mary returned and handed Carrie a black velvet case closed by a tarnished catch. "Take these. Sell them instead."

Setting down her basket, Carrie opened the case. Nestled inside the satin-lined box were a ruby necklace, a matching bracelet, and a pair of earbobs set in delicate gold filigree. The jewels were quite small, but still . . . She lifted the necklace and watched the blood-red gems catch the light. "They're beautiful. Where in the world did these come from?"

"They were my mother's and her mother's before that. Mother said that my grandmother wore them to dinners at Magnolia Hall before I was born."

"You've had them all this time, while we were practically starving to death, and never said a *word*?"

"Maybe it was selfish of me. But these pieces are all I have left of my family." Mary leaned against the door frame and crossed her arms. "They're as important to me as this land is to you." She sent Carrie a pleading look. "I don't blame you for being angry with me, but try to understand."

Carrie felt her anger soften. She could understand Mary's reluc-tance to part with the last vestiges of her family's history. Everyone needed something to hold on to. Hadn't she kept Frank's letters, her mother's tortoiseshell hair comb, Granny Bell's favorite quilt?

Mary went on. "Last night I realized that if you hadn't come back here to take care of me and the boys, I might not have my baby now. My boys are worth more to me than anything." She picked up the bracelet and draped it over her arm. "Besides, there's no place around here to wear these."

"Exactly." Carrie set the necklace back into its satin nest. "Even if there were, nobody in Hickory Ridge has that kind of money."

"Mr. Gilman has plenty of money, and his wife likes pretty things. Did you see that sapphire pin she wore on her hat at the harvest festival? She told everyone it came from the best store in Nashville. I'm sure it cost a fortune." Mary set the bracelet back in the box and snapped the lid closed. "Take them, Carrie. Sell them for whatever you can get. If Mr. Gilman won't buy them, try Jasper Pruitt at the mercantile."

Carrie ran her fingers over the case. "I can't imagine that Mr. Pruitt will have any use for them, but I'll—"

The baby wailed. Mary scooped him up, and Carrie saw tears standing in her eyes. "Go now," she whispered. "Take them before I change my mind."

Carrie tucked the jewel case into the bread basket, picked up her reticule, and hurried out to the waiting wagon. The fog had burned away, revealing a bright blue sky that lifted her spirits. She climbed up and headed for town.

⁓

A long line of mourners joined Griff, Philip, and Susan at the cemetery. The weather was raw. A sharp wind, heavy with salt, whipped through the churchyard. Standing apart from the knot of mourners at the open gravesite, Griff nodded to the members of Charleston society who had come to pay respects and to a seemingly endless procession of black-clad Rutledge and Venable cousins he hadn't seen since boyhood.

As dirt fell onto their father's polished mahogany coffin, Philip wept openly. He had always been less inhibited than Griff when it came to displays of emotion. What Griff felt, deep in his soul, was a mixture of regret for the years he'd wasted, operating from the false assumption that his father had ceased to love him, and deep gratitude that he had learned the truth before it was too late. Despite the loss, he felt a sense of peace.

The service ended. Griff climbed into the crepe-draped carriage with Philip and Susan, and they returned to the house to greet the other mourners, who arrived with offerings of food and memories of Charles Rutledge. For a while the house hummed with sounds as stories were shared and condolences offered. After the last of the guests departed, several Venable cousins stayed behind to prepare a late lunch for the family. Then, with a flurry of embraces and last words of condolence, they too entered their waiting carriages and drove away.

The three of them sat in the dining room and poked at their food. Philip, his eyes red and swollen from crying, stared into the dancing flames, his fork poised above a plate of ham and grits. Finally he looked across the table at Griff. "Susan told me you aren't planning to come home."

"Charleston hasn't been home for me in a long time. Even during the war, I felt like a stranger here." He drank his tea and set down his cup. "Too restless, I reckon."

Philip nodded. "Still planning your trip to Australia?"

"Not now. I'm staying on in Hickory Ridge."

"And live in that rundown hotel?"

"Not for long." He picked at a small lemon tart. "I'm working on getting my own place. I'm going back there tomorrow, in fact. On the afternoon train."

"So soon? But what about Father's will? The lawyers—"

"It's only a formality, Philip. We both know what it says." He waved one hand, taking in the house and its furnishings. "You're welcome to all of it. I'm perfectly at peace with it."

Philip pushed his plate away. "I daresay you would be, sitting on that fortune from your blockade-running days."

Griff laughed. "I did all right, but the rumors of my vast fortune are highly exaggerated. Luckily, I already have everything I need to be happy."

Philip went to the study and returned with a paper that he held out to Griff. "Here's a list of things Mother wanted you to have. Father insisted that we keep them here until your return."

Griff's throat tightened at the sight of his mother's small, neat handwriting, the ink faded now with age. He hadn't let himself think of her very much in recent years, but now he remembered his mother as the epitome of a Southern lady—submissive, delicate, and except for rare occasions when she attempted to influence her husband's choices, silent to the bone. At nineteen she had married Charles Rutledge and spent her life in the separate sphere of women, an ethereal presence in her sons' lives, but always a loving one.

He scanned the list of silver pieces, jewelry, and personal items. Charlotte Venable Rutledge had wanted Griff to have the small things that meant the most to her. That legacy was more than enough for him.

"You're entitled to it all." Philip poked the fire. "You're the eldest son. Mother left it to you. But I wish you wouldn't take the sapphire and diamond ring." He smiled fondly at Susan. "I have plans for it."

Griff felt a stab of dismay. Father was barely cold and in the ground, and already an argument was brewing. He hated to appear greedy and unaccommodating, but his mother had worn that ring until her death. It was a little piece of her. And the stones reminded him of Carrie's clear blue eyes. Lately he couldn't stop thinking about her.

He shook his head. "I don't want to appear selfish, but I can't part with it." He grinned as an extraordinary thought struck him. "Turns out, I may have plans for it myself."

THIRTY-TWO

"Come on in here, girl." Mrs. Whitcomb held the door open and motioned Carrie into the Verandah's dusty parlor. "Land's sakes, but you're a sight for sore eyes."

Carrie handed the older woman the loaves of bread. She covered the jewelry box with the towel and set the basket aside. "I'm glad to see you too."

Mrs. Whitcomb plopped onto the settee in the parlor and picked up her knitting. "Things haven't been the same around here since you and Rosaleen left."

Carrie's heart jolted. With everything that had happened lately, she hadn't had time to think about Rosaleen. About the near certainty that the woman was Sophie's mother. About the effect such news would have on Sophie and on Ada. About what Nate must be feeling.

"Have you heard from Rosaleen since she left town?"

"Not a blessed word." Mrs. Whitcomb shook her head. "I could wring that woman's neck for the way she treated Nate Chastain. She used him is all. And the poor man is taking it hard." She patted Carrie's hand. "But let's not talk about her. Tell me, how are Mary and the baby?"

"They're well. James Henry is growing like a weed."

Mrs. Whitcomb's knitting needles clicked as she started a new row of stitches. "It's such a shame your poor brother didn't live to see that child. Tell me, Carrie. How are you getting on?"

"To tell you the truth, things are just about as bad as they can be. I'm selling off some land—if Wat Stevens still wants it."

"That's too bad. Henry Bell set a lot of store by that farm of his." She regarded Carrie over the top of her spectacles. "Whatever you do, don't let Wat cheat you, girl. He's a shrewd one. And he has the scruples of a horse trader."

Carrie nodded. "I'm on my way to the bank. I'm hoping Mr. Gilman will advise me on what the land is worth."

Mrs. Whitcomb rose. "That's a smart idea. That man has a heart of stone when it comes to lending money, but he won't steer you wrong. You got time for tea?"

"I'd love some, but I'm afraid I don't have much time. Maybe another day?"

"Whenever you're in town, stop by. My new tenants keep to themselves. It's lonely here since Rachel moved to North Carolina and Lucy lit out for the west."

Carrie smiled at the mention of the irrepressible Lucy. "Is she happy in Montana?"

"I've had only one letter." The innkeeper chuckled. "I reckon that could signify she's either too happy to write or too miserable. But I suspect she's busy. Ranchin' ain't an easy life—as I am sure Ada Caldwell can tell you."

"Ada loves it, though."

"Ada would love any place Wyatt Caldwell hangs his hat. I swear, I never have seen two people more in love than them two. Well, you take care and I'll see you next week. Maybe then you can stay longer."

Leaving the Verandah, Carrie hurried along the sidewalk to the bank, her basket bumping against her hip. When she passed the post office, the clerk tapped on the window and motioned her inside. She pushed open the door.

"Got a package for you, Miz Daly. From that photographer feller up in Buffalo." He handed her a flat envelope. "The one that was here taking pictures of folks during Race Day."

"I remember." Both she and the boys had been in high spirits that day. Amazing how one's life could go from light to darkness in the blink of an eye. She tucked the package into her basket. "Thank you."

"No trouble. And, Miz Daly? I want to say again how sorry I am about Henry. He was a good man."

"Yes, he was." She left the post office and started to the bank.

"Carrie?" Deborah Patterson hobbled toward her, her good arm outstretched in greeting. "I tried to catch you at the Verandah just now, but you'd already left."

Carrie clasped her friend's good hand. They'd seen too little of each other these past weeks. "How are you?"

"Very well. It's Mr. Chastain I'm worried about."

"What's the matter with Nate? Is he ill?" With a start she realized she hadn't seen him since Christmas. Not even when Henry died. Odd indeed.

Deborah drew her onto the bench outside the barbershop. "He's fine in body, as far as I know. It's the dear man's spirit I'm worried about." She nodded to a farm wife headed for the mercantile. "For a while after his wife took off, he started coming to church every Sunday. But he hasn't been to services in nearly a month."

"Neither have I. I know I should. Mary and I take turns reading Scripture on Sundays, but it isn't the same."

"No one expected you to come so far in the middle of winter, especially with a little baby." Deborah patted Carrie's hand. "Besides, our Lord says that when two or three gather in his name, he's there too. But now that the weather is improving—"

The train whistle sounded. Mr. Gilman drove up to the bank and got out of his rig. Carrie clasped Deborah's hand. "I'd love to talk longer, but I have business at the bank."

Deborah nodded. "I wish you'd go see Mr. Chastain. He needs a friend."

"I will. Soon."

"But he's hurting now. Please say you'll go, just for a moment."

Carrie studied Deborah's face. How did she retain such love and trust in God when life had given her every reason not to? "All right. I'll go now. Before I see Mr. Gilman."

"I knew you would." Deborah smiled and stood. "I must go. Daniel's waiting for me to help ready the church for Sunday's service. He's surely wondering what happened to me."

She waved and headed up the street. Carrie picked up her basket and crossed to the bookshop. The door bell chimed softly as she went in. She glanced around. The curtain was drawn against the light. Books lay in untidy piles against the walls. The shelves held a jumble of books, chipped coffee mugs, papers, flattened cartons, and empty sacks. Half of the hand-lettered labels she'd made were missing. She stared, sick with disbelief. All her work, destroyed.

"Nate?" Standing on tiptoe, she peered into the gloom.

He shuffled to the counter, India at his heels. He fumbled in his pocket for his spectacles and put them on. "Carrie. What do you want?"

"I don't want anything. I was in town and realized I hadn't seen you for a while. How have you been?"

He waved one hand. "What do you think?"

She wanted to cry. "Oh, Nate, what has happened to you?"

"Rosaleen Dupree happened to me, that's what."

"I take it she hasn't come back."

"No, and I hope she doesn't." He indicated a thick stack of papers on the desk beneath the window. "Can't make heads or tails of my account books. And money is missing from my bank account too."

"You don't think she stole it?"

"Maybe she paid off my creditors with it, but I sure can't find a record of that."

"Well, if she didn't pay them, you'll hear about it sooner or later." She opened the curtain, tidied a stack of books, and brushed at the dusty counters with her fingers. What a mess.

"Leave it." Nate covered her hand with his own. "I have coffee in the back. Want some?"

Deborah was right. Nate needed her. Mr. Gilman—and Wat Stevens—would wait. "All right."

He filled their cups and they sat by the window, she in the chair, he perched on the corner of the desk. She couldn't help noticing the dark circles beneath his eyes. He'd lost weight too.

He glanced at her basket. "Still baking bread for Mrs. Whitcomb?"

"Yes. I delivered an order this morning."

"I'm sorry about Henry. I should have paid you a call." He gulped his coffee. "I don't know why I didn't."

"That's all right. Deborah Patterson delivered the ham you sent. I appreciate it, Nate."

He nodded. "I should have done more to help you. Not that I have any money, but there are other things—"

"You don't owe me anything."

He toyed with his empty cup. "Do you ever regret the way things turned out? Between us, I mean."

She scooped India into her lap. "The night you brought Rosaleen to the Verandah—"

"I made a mess of telling you about the marriage. I've regretted it ever since."

"It was a shock. But then I realized that the plans we made grew out of other people's expectations rather than our own."

"I thought that too, at first. But now I realize how deeply I cared for you. I reckon I made a mess of telling you that too."

"Yes, you did." She smiled. "But really, it's all right. I suppose I took you for granted too."

He nodded. "It's dreadful, isn't it? Being without the person you love. I never understood just how much you missed Frank, but now—"

He took her hand, and alarm bells sounded in her head. Was he about to kiss her? She set India onto the floor and stood. "Nate, you mustn't—"

"Carrie?"

"You're married now. And I—"

"I know. You're in love with Rutledge. I saw it in your face the day Henry and Mary got married. Whatever chance I might have had with you disappeared the day he got off the train."

"I was going to say that I hope you won't let Rosaleen's absence ruin the good life you built here. That I treasure you as the good and dear friend you've always been. As I hope you will continue to be."

"I see." He blinked as if waking from a dream and picked up their cups. "Well. Just . . . look at this place, will you? I reckon I'd best get to work. Get the ledger sorted out."

"I wish I had time to help."

"Nope. You saved my bacon once, and I let all your hard work go to waste. It's time to stop feeling sorry for myself and get on with things." He smiled, looking more like the old Nate. "Friends?"

"Always." She kissed his cheek and picked up her basket. "I should go."

Five minutes later she was seated across from Mr. Gilman. He listened intently while she outlined her plan to sell off some land.

"I need some advice on what to charge."

He rubbed one hand across his face. "That's a hard question. Bea Goldston sold off her land in Two Creeks for six dollars an acre.

But that was before this depression got so bad. These days there are plenty of folks who already have more land than they know what to do with. No sense in farming it with prices as low as they are."

"I see." She opened the jewel case and set it on his desk. "Then I need to sell these. We—Mary and I—thought they'd make a nice present for Mrs. Gilman."

He picked up the bracelet and turned it toward the light coming through his office window. "It's a nice little trinket."

"A trinket? These have been in Mary Stanhope's family for three generations."

He fingered one of the earbobs. "That doesn't make them worth anything."

"But they're rubies. Set in gold. They must be worth something."

He fished a pair of spectacles from his pocket and put them on. He placed the necklace on his white handkerchief, unfastened the clasp, and turned it over. He picked up his letter opener and made a tiny mark on the clasp. A sliver of the metal curled onto the handkerchief. He pointed. "See, underneath this gold plate is plain old tin."

"But the rubies—"

"Are made of colored paste. I'm sorry. These are worthless."

Fakes. She swallowed. "Are you sure?"

He returned the jewels to the case. "Over the years I've bought more than a few baubles for my missus. I've learned how to tell imitations from the real thing."

She rose. "I won't keep you any longer."

"There's one thing you might consider if you want to sell that land to Stevens."

"I don't *want* to sell it, but I have four other mouths to feed. Besides, you said the land is worthless."

"No, I said a farmer might not need it for crops. Rumor has it that plans to build a resort here just might work out. That Blakely fellow from Baltimore is keen on the idea. If he decides to build, that land will be worth ten times what it is today . . ."

She saw him hesitate. "But?"

"It might be years before the resort is actually built. Wat Stevens is no fool, though. He knows what that land will be worth then." He steepled his fingers and smiled up at her. "Sounds to me as if you can't afford to wait. You need cash right now."

"Yes. Desperately. I can't earn enough baking bread."

"Stevens can afford to buy that land and hold on to it. If the resort comes in, he can sell it off and make a tidy profit. If it doesn't, he's still sitting on some of the finest farmland in the county. When this depression ends, he'll double his yield. If it was me, I'd ask ten dollars an acre. Firm."

"Ten dollars?" It was a fortune.

"He can afford it. Don't let him tell you any different." His voice softened. "I'm real sorry about that jewelry."

She left the bank and headed for the Stevens farm. Situated on a winding dirt road halfway between town and the lumber mill, it lay in a broad valley bordering the river. A series of wooden fences marked the boundaries and led upward to the Stevenses' log farmhouse.

Carrie halted the wagon in the side yard and climbed down. The smell of burning fields teased her nose. In the distance, Wat Stevens walked behind a team of plodding horses, plowing up a cloud of black dust.

She rounded the house. Mrs. Stevens, a faded woman in a brown dress and a threadbare blue apron, was out back slopping hogs. They grunted and rooted in the long wooden trough near the barn. A line of laundry flapped in the March wind.

"Carrie Daly." Mrs. Stevens set the slop bucket aside and pushed her sunbonnet off her head. "Ain't seen you in a coon's age. What brings you clear out here?"

"I need to speak to your husband. If he can spare the time."

"What about?"

"Last year he asked my brother about buying some land."

"Then maybe your brother ought to be the one doing the talking."

"My brother is dead."

The woman frowned. "Henry Bell is dead? How in the world—"

"An accident in the rail yard." Briefly Carrie filled her in. "We didn't know about it until Christmas."

"Well, if that don't beat all." She shook her head. "Living way out here, we're the last to know anything. I sure am sorry to hear it."

She put her fingers in her mouth and emitted a piercing whistle that reverberated across the valley. Wat halted the team and looked up. His wife motioned him over.

He took off his hat and wiped his face with a crumpled bandanna. "Miz Daly."

"Henry Bell went and got himself killed in Chicago," Wat's wife informed him. "It happened clear back in December, and we must be the last people in the county to know about it. I declare, Wat Stevens, you have got to do something to get us another preacher. Without church on Sundays, we don't hear about anything."

Wat squinted at Carrie. "That's real bad news, all right. But you didn't come all this way just to tell us about it."

"I'm going in the house to get us something to drink," Mrs. Stevens said. "My mouth is dry as dirt."

Carrie watched her go. Her own mouth felt dry too. Bargaining with Wat Stevens would not be easy. But there was no sense in beating around the bush. "Last year you were interested in buying the twenty acres we own down by Owl Creek. Now that my brother is gone, the farm is too much for me to handle. I'm wondering if you're still interested."

"Maybe." He leaned against a fence post, crossed his ankles, and studied her through narrowed eyes. "How much you askin' for it?"

"Twelve dollars an acre."

"Twelve . . . what on earth have you been swilling? There ain't a tract of land in this whole county worth that kind of money."

"Maybe not now, but I'm sure you've heard about the resort coming to town."

"I've heard *maybe* there's a resort coming to town. That's a big difference."

"But suppose it does happen? You could sell that land for twice what I'm asking."

"Then why are you willing to let it go?"

"My brother is dead. I have to support his sickly wife and three growing children. I can't plant it all, and I can't afford to wait." She crossed her arms. "It's the best bottomland in the county. You know it's worth it."

"I wouldn't buy heaven itself for twelve dollars an acre."

Carrie waited. Surely he would make a counter offer. Whether Henry sold off a corn crop, a sow, or a wagon, he always started at a price higher than he was willing to accept. Bargaining was an expected part of doing business. But as the silence stretched out, broken only by the song of the little finches flitting through the hedgerow, she grew worried. What if she had squandered her best chance to sell the land at any price?

"Nine dollars an acre," Wat said at last.

"But Mr. Gilman said—"

"I wouldn't listen to him I if was you. I ain't never met a banker yet I could trust. They all got bad reputations. Maybe he meant well, but twelve dollars an acre is outrageous. I'd be the laughing stock of the county if I paid that much for farmland in times like these." He kicked at a dirt clod. "Now I've made you a fair offer. You can take it or not."

"That land is worth ten dollars an acre, resort or no resort. It'll be worth more when the depression ends."

"Gilman said that, did he?"

"It's only common sense, Mr. Stevens. But I can see you are not willing to make a fair deal. Perhaps someone else will be amenable to my price." She headed for the wagon, determined not to let her disappointment show. She wouldn't be cheated out of her birthright. She'd find some other way to make ends meet.

"All right." Wat caught up to her. "Ten dollars an acre. To help out a couple of widows and a bunch of children. Come on in, and we'll write up a bill of sale. We can meet on Friday to sign the deed and transfer the money."

Carrie followed him into the house in a daze. She had done it. Two hundred dollars would be enough to keep the farm going for a very long time.

Wat pulled out a chair and scribbled out a bill of sale, then he and Carrie both signed it. Mrs. Stevens served buttermilk and slices of chess pie. Carrie finished both and rose.

The Stevenses followed her outside. Carrie climbed into the wagon. "Shall we say ten o'clock on Friday, Mr. Stevens?"

"As good a time as any, I reckon."

"See you then." She headed back to town in high spirits. At the Hickory Ridge Inn, she stopped to find Griff. Maybe he would be too busy to take time for her, but she was so relieved to have sold her land that she was unable to contain her good news.

The clerk looked up when she entered the lobby. "Help you, Mrs. Daly?"

"I would like to speak to Mr. Griffin Rutledge."

"So would I. But he isn't here."

"Oh. Do you know when he'll be back?"

The clerk snorted. "I'm not sure he'll be back. He's been gone for more'n two weeks, and he left here owing me for his room. Just up and left in the middle of the night." He shook his head. "I knew he was no good the minute I laid eyes on him."

Carrie leaned against the counter. Griff had left without even saying good-bye? "Surely there's a good explanation."

"'Course there is. He's a no-good gambler who comes and goes like the wind. Well, nothing I can do 'cept wait to see if he turns up. What was it you wanted to talk to him about? You want to leave a message in case he shows?"

Numb with disappointment, Carrie shook her head. What a fool she'd been. For a while it had felt as if she and Griff were already a team. Despite his recent absence, she had let herself believe that something strong and real had formed between them. But it hadn't meant a thing.

She left the inn, climbed onto the wagon, and shook the reins. The tears came then . . . because Nate was right. She loved Griff Rutledge. With everything that was in her, she loved him.

If only he could love her too.

It wasn't as if he hadn't warned her. But she'd plunged headlong into a relationship with him anyway, willing to risk heartbreak for a few months of feeling wanted and admired. What did she expect would happen? For all she knew he might have headed to Australia. Or gone after his old friend Rosaleen.

It didn't matter. Griff was not the settling-down kind of man, no matter how hard she pretended otherwise. Her dream was over. And she had only herself to blame.

THIRTY-THREE

An hour late, the train huffed into Hickory Ridge, the whistle shriek-
ing. Griff hauled his bags up the narrow aisle of the gentlemen's car.
He glanced at the railway clock and groaned. Gilman would be furious at having to wait.

He left his bags at the inn, apologized to the irate clerk for
his abrupt departure, and settled his outstanding bill. A generous
tip improved the clerk's mood considerably, and Griff extracted a
promise that a hot bath and fresh linens would await his return.
After a quick freshening up and a change of shirts, he picked up
his rig at Tanner's livery and headed for the Gilmans' place, eager
to seal the deal before the banker changed his mind.

Passing the mercantile, he thought about Carrie. How that
woman had changed him. A solitary life devoid of commitment
no longer appealed to him. His brief time at the farm with her
had awakened him to the joys of family life. Carrie was a natural
mother. He could see that in the way she dealt with Joe and Caleb,
not the easiest boys he'd ever met. She knew not only how to keep
a house but to make it a home. At the Bell farm, he'd felt a sense of
peace that otherwise eluded him.

Farther along the street, he smelled bread baking and grinned
to himself. Carrie Daly was the best baker in the county, to boot.

His mouth watered at the memory of breakfasts in her cozy kitchen when the entire room smelled wonderfully of biscuits and warm strawberry jam.

She was pretty too, with those sapphire eyes and russet curls. There was nothing he didn't like about her. The memory of their kiss seared his heart. During the long journey from South Carolina, he'd imagined growing old with her. Watching the years change her face, walking with her across their own piece of land, knowing they belonged to each other. Maybe it was all a sentimental dream. Maybe she wouldn't even speak to him after his unexplained absence. But he couldn't help how he felt.

The question was whether a woman of such strong principles could overlook his past. He hadn't told her about his connection to Rosaleen. Perhaps when she knew, she'd refuse to have anything further to do with him. But he wouldn't lie to her. If they were to have a future together, he wanted to begin with a clean slate, no secrets between them.

The day after his father's funeral, he'd gone to the telegraph office, intending to send Carrie a wire. He stood there for half an hour, composing message after message. But no matter how he tried to explain himself, the terse language of a telegram seemed wrong.

He hadn't prayed for himself in a long time, but as the horse *clop-clopped* toward the Gilmans' place, he asked God to give him the right heart and the right words to win the woman he loved.

⁓

Mary and the baby were sleeping. Carrie moved through the house quietly, grateful that the boys had not yet returned from school. Though her worries about money soon would be a thing of the past, she still grieved her lost dream. She had no future with Griff. Her future was here, looking after this cobbled-together family.

She removed her shawl and hat, and went upstairs to change her dress. Through the window, she glimpsed a tiny sprig of green among the brown vines on the trellis. The morning glory she'd given up for dead was coming back to life. How beautiful it had looked last summer on Henry's wedding day.

That day she'd asked God for the grace to accept Mary and the boys into her family. Perhaps Henry's death, and Griff's absence, were his way of answering her prayer. She thought of Deborah, of her friend's willingness to submit herself wholly to God even in the direst of situations. Could Carrie do that? She was tired of struggling, of carrying burdens too heavy for her heart and her head. She perched on the edge of her bed and closed her eyes.

This wasn't exactly the way I pictured my future, Lord, but I trust you with all that I have and all that I am. I surrender to your will.

Downstairs the door burst open and Joe raced in, yelling at the top of his lungs. She hurried down the stairs, a finger to her lips. "Shhh. Don't wake your mama and the baby."

"Sorry." Joe thrust a book into her hands. "I can read it all by myself. Mr. Webster says I'm one of the best readers in the whole class." He jerked his thumb at his brother. "An' he said Caleb is best at arithmetic. Can I read you the raindrops poem?"

Carrie smiled and smoothed his hair. "After supper. Right now I need firewood and water. Iris needs feeding, and poor Miranda needs milking."

Caleb tossed his books onto the settee. "Don't worry, Aunt Carrie, I'll take care of it."

"What are we havin' for supper anyway?" Joe asked. "I'm hungry."

"If you'll fetch that ham out of the smokehouse, I'll fry some up and make the gravy you like."

Joe's eyes widened. "Ham? I thought we were savin' it for when Griff Rutledge comes for supper."

"Mr. Rutledge has gone away." She tried to smile, but tears threatened. "Besides, this is a special occasion. You brought home a book to read all by yourself."

He nodded. "Yes'm. I'm right proud of it, all right, but I still wish Griff was here."

She sent them out to do their chores and went to the kitchen to peel potatoes. At least now she could buy all the food they needed. And seed for planting. And shoes for the boys, perhaps a few bolts of fabric. Since the baby, Mary's figure had grown softer, rounder. Her old clothes barely fit anymore, and the boys needed new shirts for school.

"Carrie?" Mary came into the kitchen and took a stack of plates from the shelf. "What happened in town? Did Mr. Gilman buy my jewels?"

Carrie paused in her preparations. Should she tell Mary the gems were worthless or preserve the illusion? Granny Bell always said honesty was the best policy. But really, why tell Mary the truth when it would only hurt her? "He didn't buy them, but it's all right. I sold twenty acres of land to Wat Stevens. We'll sign the papers on Friday."

Mary nodded, her expression sober. "I'm sorry you had to sell off part of this farm, but honestly? I'm glad to have my jewels, even if I never wear them again."

"Our photograph arrived," Carrie said, eager to leave the subject of the fake jewels. "I left it on the table in the parlor."

Mary hurried to get it and came back smiling. "It's wonderful. Look at how grown-up my sweet boys look. I only wish Henry'd had the chance to see it."

Carrie sliced the potatoes into a pot of cold water. "At least the boys will have it as a reminder of Race Day."

Mary grinned. "Griff Rutledge will enjoy it too, especially when he sees it in the silver frame he gave me."

"He has left town." Carrie worked to keep her voice steady.

"The clerk at the inn told me he skipped out without a single word." She lifted the cast iron skillet onto the stove and dropped in a dollop of lard. "I don't expect to see Griff Rutledge ever again."

Mary seemed stunned into silence. Momentarily. "Well, it's for the best if you ask me. He isn't husband material. It's too bad you let Nate Chastain get away. Now, there's a steady man for you." Mary set the plates on the table and went to get James Henry, who had begun to cry. "Deborah Patterson said poor Nate is grieving himself to death over that no-good Rosaleen Dupree."

"I saw him in town today. He's made his peace with the situation and is getting back to the business of running his shop."

While Mary tended to the baby, Carrie fried the potatoes. Joe and Caleb tromped into the kitchen with the ham and a pail of fresh milk. Carrie sliced off a few pieces of ham and fried them, made gravy, and took half a vinegar pie from the pie safe.

After supper, Carrie washed the dishes while Mary nursed James Henry, and Caleb and Joe bent over their lessons. She waited patiently while Joe read the poem about the raindrops, helped Caleb with a problem in long division, and at last returned to her room to write her long-delayed letter to Ada Caldwell. She couldn't keep secret her suspicions about Rosaleen Dupree any longer. For Sophie's sake, she hoped Rosaleen was not the girl's mother. What kind of woman would give away a child, deliberately trap a man into marriage, and then abandon him?

She sat at her dressing table and pulled out her writing box. What was Rosaleen's connection to Griff? He hadn't volunteered the information and really, it wasn't any of her business. Besides, what did it matter now? She always loved the wrong person . . . or loved too late . . . or not at all. Obviously, love was not what God had in mind for her.

She dipped her pen into the inkwell and began to write. Outside, pale spring light leaked out of the sky. Deep shadows slid along the distant mountains and into the valley. A flock of sparrows swept past her window in a smear of brown and settled into the trees. She sighed, a sense of peace mingling with her melancholy.

Downstairs a commotion erupted, followed by footsteps pounding up the stairs. Joe burst into her room and ran to the window. "Aunt Carrie! Aunt Carrie! Somebody's coming."

THIRTY-FOUR

Joe pushed past Carrie and pressed his nose to her bedroom window. "See? Somebody *is* coming."

She looked out. A horse and rider cantered through the trees and onto the shadowed road leading to their house. Despite herself, hope fluttered in her chest. She capped her ink bottle and followed Joe downstairs. He raced ahead and threw open the door, waking James Henry, who began to wail.

Griff reined in and strode across the yard. Caleb left his books on the kitchen table and followed Joe outside. "Hey, Mr. Rutledge. You brought Majestic."

"Can we give him a treat?" Joe asked, wrapping his arms tightly around Griff's legs. "I missed you something awful. Where in the Sam Hill have you been?"

"It's long story, son." Griff laughed and extricated himself from the boy's grasp. He handed Joe an apple for the horse. "Maybe you boys can keep Majestic company while I talk to your Aunt Carrie."

He looked at her then, his dark eyes alive and questioning. "May I come in?"

She wanted to shout for joy and fling herself into his arms, but she nodded, hiding the intense yearning building inside her. "Of course. Please come in."

She stood aside while he entered. From Mary's room came the soft sounds of a lullaby. A grin stole across Griff's handsome face. "That's a lovely sound, isn't it? A mother crooning to her child."

"Yes." She was as full of questions as Joe. Where *had* Griff been all these weeks? Why had he left Hickory Ridge without saying good-bye? And why was he here now . . . with Mr. Gilman's prize Thoroughbred?

In the parlor he took off his coat and draped it over the back of a chair. He added a log to the fire and motioned Carrie to sit beside him. In the soft light his face looked boyish and uncertain. She perched on the edge of the settee, trying to maintain distance, but his nearness was impossible to ignore. She remembered the warmth of his lips on hers, the steady strength of his arms encircling her.

He cleared his throat. "I've so much to tell you that I scarcely know where to begin."

"I know you've been away. I was told that you left quite suddenly."

He nodded. "My brother, Philip, wired that our father was near death. I thought I should go to Charleston at once."

"Of course. Is your father—"

"Expired the morning after I arrived. I wrote you a note the day I left and then forgot to leave it with the postmaster. It was thoughtless of me, and I sincerely apologize."

"I was confused when I found out you'd left town, but I do understand. And I'm sorry about your father."

He gripped her hand and stared into the fire. "So am I. It turns out that I'd misunderstood him completely these many years. I'm thankful I had the chance to learn the truth. It freed me to go ahead with the plans I'd been making here." He paused, his eyes searching her face. "I want to share those plans with you, if you're willing. Will you come with me?"

"Now? It's nearly dark."

"I know a shortcut, and I hope you'll think the trip is worth it."

He looked so full of excitement and hope that nothing could have kept her from him. "Let me tell Mary we're going."

He grinned and grabbed his coat. "I'll get the boys back inside. Don't forget your wrap. It's chilly out tonight."

Carrie knocked on Mary's door and made her explanation as brief as possible. "I won't be out late."

Mary cradled James Henry and shook her head. "People will talk."

"Maybe they will, but you know something? I'm so happy to see Griff Rutledge that I don't care one whit about idle gossip."

"Obviously. You've mooned over him since the day you first laid eyes on him. You've always cared more for your own wishes than for the good of others."

Carrie kept her voice low. "How dare you say that? After all I've done for you and your children."

Without waiting for further argument, she grabbed her hat and shawl from the hall tree and went outside. "Joe and Caleb, please go inside and finish your lessons. Mr. Rutledge and I are going out for a little while."

"Can't we go too?" Joe asked.

"Not this time, son," Griff said. "Go on now, and mind your aunt Carrie."

The boys shuffled inside and closed the door. Griff swung into the saddle and held out his hand. Carrie gave him her hand, placed her foot in the stirrup, and vaulted into the saddle behind him.

"All set?" He turned Majestic toward the road.

"Yes." She wrapped her arms tightly around his waist, rested her cheek against his back, and breathed in his scent, a mixture of wool, hay, and horses. Her irritation at Mary melted away like a spring snowfall. She felt like a princess in one of Joe's fairy tales, swept away on horseback. Whatever Griff wanted her to see could not surpass this moment, riding through the growing darkness with him and Majestic.

Griff urged the colt into a gentle canter. They left the road and cut through a stand of red cedar and old oaks, following a broken-down fence bordering the woods. The chilly spring air cooled her face. Overhead the moon rose full and bright, and the stars—shards of pure white light—glittered in the indigo sky.

They exited the woods. Ahead, shining white in the moon-light, was the Gilmans' place. Every window glowed with yellow light that spread in rectangles across the broad expanse of lawn. Across the meadow stood the barn, lit by a single lantern.

"Here we are."

"Mr. Gilman's? Are you training for another race?"

Griff dismounted and held out his arms for her. She slid from the saddle and into his strong embrace. He cupped her cheek in his hand. "Carrie."

Tears started behind her eyes. "I thought you'd left for good," she whispered. "I thought I'd never see you again."

He brushed a strand of hair from her face. "You won't get rid of me that easily. I talked Gilman into selling me a piece of this place. I plan on settling down here."

"But what about Australia? What about—"

"You've changed me, Carrie. You've spoiled me for any kind of life except the one I plan to build here."

He had changed her too. Before Griff, she'd lived a life of quiet duty, resigned to being alone. He had allowed her to hope that perhaps one day she could live a life of joy. She wanted to tell him how she felt, but her heart was too full.

Griff offered his arm. "Come on. Let me show you."

They crossed the meadow and came upon a small cottage, well hidden from the main road. Moonlight spilled across the wide front porch and illuminated a small garden at the side of the house.

"It isn't much now," Griff said, "but I plan on fixing it up, building on a better kitchen at the back. Maybe expanding the garden too. There's already a good well out back, and a dandy creek for fishing, and thirty acres for raising and training Majestic's offspring."

Carrie stared up at him, scarcely able to take it all in.

"Bought him too." Griff's pride was evident. "Cost me a king's ransom, but he's worth every penny. In a few years I'll have one of the best horse farms in the South. Maybe I'll eventually produce a Kentucky Derby winner."

"That's wonderful. But I'm surprised Mr. Gilman was willing to part with Majestic."

"Horses are in my blood, Carrie. Breeding them, training them, racing them is what I was always meant to do. Gilman understands that. That's why he was willing to wait until I could get my funds from London. Besides, it isn't as if he can't see Majestic anytime he wants."

"I'm so glad. I know you'll make this into a wonderful place. Maybe one day Hickory Ridge will be famous because of you."

"I don't care about that. I've already got everything I could hope for. There's only one thing missing." He drew her close, and her heart kicked inside her chest. She could barely breathe. Here at last was everything she'd ever wanted, right in front of her.

"While I was away I realized I'd loved you from the first day we met," he said. "But I had nothing to offer you then."

"Your heart is more than enough."

"You'll marry me then?"

"Yes, Griff. I will."

He clasped her hands, a serious expression in his eyes. "Then there's something else I need to clear up. About Rosaleen—"

Of course she wondered about the connection between them, but why spoil this moment of perfect happiness? "It doesn't matter now."

"It matters to me. I won't begin a marriage with questions and secrets between us."

"All right." She drew her shawl tightly about her shoulders and leaned against the rail fence.

"We met in a gaming parlor in New Orleans shortly after the war. She was the prettiest little thing I'd ever seen. Smart as a whip too. She beat me three straight hands of triple draw before her luck ran out and she left the game. When I left that night, she was standing in the street, crying. Told me she had no place to sleep, nothing to eat. Said she was heading over to Madame Rochard's sporting house to earn a few dollars. I felt sorry for her, a beautiful young girl, down on her luck and desperate enough to—" He shook his head. "I gave her twenty dollars and told her to stay away from cards and forget about working for the madam."

"Were you . . . did you love her, Griff?" Painful as it was, she had to know.

"For a time. She was beautiful, flirtatious, exotic looking—the qualities that appeal to a young man. Every man in New Orleans who ever met her was smitten. I suppose that was part of the attraction too, that she had chosen me. I was proud to squire her about to the theater and dinners. But—"

"But she didn't give up cards."

"No, and she wasn't exactly a stranger at the madam's place either."

Shock and revulsion moved through her. She prayed Rosaleen had no connection to Sophie Robillard Caldwell.

"One morning as I was leaving my hotel, I saw Rosaleen in the company of a man I knew from the poker tables. He was three times her age and richer than Croesus. Turns out they'd known each other for a while and were running their own little moneymaking scheme. Her tears were all an act, a play for sympathy."

"She wasn't really desperate for money?"

"Not by a long shot." He rubbed the small scar on his upper lip. "Like a fool, I tried to convince the old goat to stay away from her and got a punch in the face for my trouble. A month or so later she admitted to her trickery with old Croesus, said he'd left her high and dry, her sister was sick, and she needed a loan. I named an exorbitant interest rate to discourage her, but she called my bluff and signed a promissory note, and I gave her the cash."

He shook his head and reached up to scratch Majestic's ear. "Over the years the interest compounded into a considerable sum. Then last spring, funds from my bank in London were delayed and I ran a little short of cash myself. I went to New Orleans to collect what she owed me, but Rosaleen was long gone. So I hired Pinkerton's to find her."

"And you found her here, at the Verandah."

"Yes. In the end I forgave the debt, but I'm finished rescuing that woman from her own bad choices. Rosaleen wouldn't know the truth if it rose up and bit her. She's told so many stories, I doubt if she remembers which are true and which aren't." He brushed a twig from her shoulder and smiled into her eyes.

"I'm glad you told me."

"I hope you haven't changed your mind about me."

"For trying to help someone you thought was in trouble? Never." She looped her arm through his. Relief, joy, and gratitude welled up inside her. "You're stuck with me now."

Griff kissed her soundly. Carrie wound her arms around him and kissed him back, tears leaking from her eyes.

Griff looked dazed, as if he couldn't believe his good fortune. "Imagine me, of all people, about to become an old married man." He threw back his head and laughed. "Carrie darling, isn't life amazing?"

THIRTY-FIVE

Amazing, Carrie decided as she stirred batter for a cake, didn't begin to describe the turn her life had taken. The two months since Griff's proposal had passed in a blur.

First she'd taken her blue satin dress to Jeanne Pruitt to have a lace overlay attached and wired Ada Caldwell the news: "Marrying Griff. Need wedding hat." Then she finalized the sale of the land to Wat Stevens and deeded the rest of the farm to James Henry, under Mary's trusteeship until he came of age. Giving up her long-time home was bittersweet, but in her heart of hearts she knew it was what Henry would have wanted. The Bell farm, though diminished in size, would go on.

Perhaps it was knowing she would always have a place to live that had softened Mary's attitude toward Griff. Upon learning of the impending wedding, she insisted on hosting it at the farm, then set about cleaning and polishing with an energy Carrie hadn't known she possessed. Now the windows in the parlor, draped with freshly washed and ironed curtains, sparkled. The wooden floor gleamed. Joe and Caleb had pounded the rugs till they looked almost new.

Best of all, folks in Hickory Ridge were gradually coming to accept Griff. Perhaps the fact that he bought a piece of land, linking his future with theirs, had changed their minds. Perhaps they finally appreciated his role in effecting Mr. Webster's return to the school. Last week, even Jasper Pruitt had allowed that maybe Rutledge was all right, despite his past.

Carrie had changed too. Slowly but surely, God had given her the grace she'd prayed for, turning her old feelings of resentment and resignation into gratitude and joy, gradually molding her into the woman he wanted her to be. She would always feel a certain amount of guilt that she and Henry had never patched up their last disagreement. She would always regret that he'd died not knowing how hard she tried to do the right thing. But God's forgiveness was larger than her own doubts. She could honestly say she was at peace with the world.

A shout drew her attention. Through the window she watched Joe and Caleb playing in the warm May sunshine and smiled at their unbridled enthusiasm. How deeply she loved them now.

A wagon jostled up the road. Carrie set down her mixing bowl and went outside.

"Nate?"

He stopped the wagon and jumped down. "Hello, Carrie."

She couldn't help feeling a bit uncomfortable. She had seen him only in passing since their last meeting at the bookshop, and the memory of that encounter still lingered. "What brings you out here?"

"Package came for you on last night's train. I was at the station to pick up a shipment of books, and I couldn't help noticing it's from Ada Caldwell. I figured it might be important."

"My hat." She took the package and ran her fingers over it. "And not a moment too soon either. I was beginning to worry that it might not get here in time. Thank you, Nate. It was thoughtful of you to bring it all this way."

He shrugged. "I was coming this way anyhow. Don't know if you've heard—Wat Stevens has put up the money for a new preacher out at the church."

Carrie smiled. "I suppose Mrs. Stevens finally wore him down."

"I reckon so. Anyway, the new reverend will be here a week from Sunday, and I'm cleaning up the church a little bit. It's been vacant a long while."

"Too long." She toyed with the string on her package. "How are you, Nate? How are things at the shop?"

"Mostly sorted out. Your visit that day was a pure blessing to me. It made me realize I can't keep thinking about the mistakes I made and pining for what might have been." He smiled down at her. "I just received a copy of Melville's new book about his trip to the Holy Land. The first volume anyway. I'll set it aside for you if you like."

"I'd love that."

A long silence fell between them. Finally, Nate said, "Reckon I ought to get going."

"Well, thank you again."

"Good luck to you, Carrie girl. If anyone deserves to be happy, it's you."

"Oh, Nate, you deserve happiness too. I only wish Rosaleen—"

"Me too." He climbed onto the wagon and picked up the reins.

"Will I see you tomorrow? You're invited, you know."

He hesitated. "I appreciate it, but . . . I don't think so. I'm pretty busy at the shop. I hope you understand."

He turned the wagon and drove away. She took the box inside and lifted the lid. Ada's letter rested on top of the hat.

Dearest Carrie,

Wyatt and I couldn't be more pleased with your wonderful news. I only wish we could come to Hickory Ridge for the wedding, but I have some exciting news of my own. A new baby is on the way, due in October. Wyatt is beside himself with wanting another son, and though she won't say so, I think Sophie is glad too.

Thank you for your letter about Rosaleen Dupree. Wyatt and I have decided not to say anything to Sophie until we're sure. Wyatt has begun discreet inquiries, and we will certainly let you and Griff know if there is any news. In the meantime, I don't wish this situation to mar the happiness you so richly deserve.

When I remember you as I first knew you back in seventy-one, so bottled up and burdened by grief, so resigned to a life without love, to know now that you have at last found your match reminds me again of God's infinite wisdom, mercy, and love. Be happy, Carrie dear. Wyatt and I look forward to another visit to Hickory Ridge once our new little Caldwell is safely delivered. Perhaps we'll visit next year when, who knows, you might be awaiting a child of your own.

Your Ada

Carrie lifted the hat from its paper nest, a typical Ada Wentworth confection of lace, feathers, and ribbon, perfect for a wedding. She tried it on before her mirror, smiling at the memory of the first hat Ada had made for her. Who could have predicted back then that Ada would one day make her wedding hat too?

A feeling of quiet peace stole into her heart. Even amidst sorrow and loss, God had blessed her beyond all imagining. And tomorrow, she would become Griff Rutledge's wife.

⁓

"Carrie? Are you ready?" Mary stuck her head into the room. "Mr. Rutledge is here with the Pattersons. Deborah is beside herself, waiting to see you. And Mr. Rutledge's brother is here too."

Carrie smiled. Yesterday evening she and Griff had met Philip's train, and the three of them had enjoyed dinner at the inn. Though

Philip Rutledge lacked his elder brother's confident charm, Carrie liked him at once.

"Come in," she told Mary. "Can you help me with these buttons?"

Mary swept in wearing the dark blue lace frock she'd worn for her wedding to Henry. Thanks to Jeanne Pruitt's skillful remodeling, it fit again, and now Mary looked much as she had before so much travail overtook them. Her fingers worked the tiny buttons on Carrie's dress. "There. You look like a princess."

"I feel like one." Carrie twirled around and picked up her hat. "People say God moves in mysterious ways without really thinking about what that means, but I am proof of the truth of that." She pinned her hat into place and fluffed out the ribbon. "I never thought that coming back here when my heart really wasn't in it would lead me to the love of my life."

Mary's gaze held Carrie's. "God has changed us both."

Two sets of feet thundered along the hallway, then Caleb and Joe burst into the room. Caleb stopped short and stared at his aunt. "Aunt Carrie, is that you? Holy smokes, you're beautiful."

Carrie grinned. "Try not to act so surprised."

Joe looked up at her, his little face scrubbed and shining. "I'm not surprised. I always knew you're prettier'n a speckled pup."

Carrie and Mary laughed.

"When are we going to eat that cake?" Joe asked. "I'm so hungry I'm about to faint dead away."

"It won't be long now." Carrie dropped a kiss on his head. "You and Caleb go tell Mr. Rutledge I'll be right down."

After they left, Mary took a small package from her pocket and handed it to Carrie. "I want you to have these."

Carrie unwrapped the ruby earbobs and felt a stab of guilt. Should she have told Mary the truth about their value? But what purpose would it serve to disillusion her?

"I know they aren't valuable," Mary said quietly.

"But how—"

"After you brought them back from Mr. Gilman's, I noticed a small scratch on the clasp of the necklace. I tried buffing it out, and more of the gold leaf came off. That was when I realized they were only imitations."

"But they're still important to you."

"Yes." Mary waved one hand. "I don't blame you if you don't want to wear them. But I wanted to give you something, and they're all I have to give."

"Of course I want to wear them. They're beautiful." Leaning toward the mirror, Carrie fastened them in place and watched them catch the light. "Thank you, Mary. Maybe one day my daughter will wear them."

Mary nodded toward the door. "You'd better get down there. Don't keep Mr. Rutledge waiting."

Carrie descended the staircase. In the parlor Griff stood next to Daniel Patterson, looking up at her with such devotion in his dark eyes that her throat closed up. Deborah, her eyes bright with tears, smiled as Carrie walked toward her groom. Mary followed Carrie down the stairs and stood next to Deborah. Joe and Caleb crowded in next to Philip.

Daniel opened his Bible and motioned to Griff. "Take ahold of her hand, sir."

Griff smiled and clasped both her hands in his warm grip, sending his strength and his love flowing into her.

"Griffin Rutledge, do you take this woman, Caroline Louise Bell Daly, to be your wedded wife? To love her all the days of your life?"

"You bet I do." Griff's eyes never left her face.

The preacher grinned. "Caroline Louise Bell Daly, do you take Griffin Rutledge to be your wedded husband? To love him all the days of your life?"

Carrie nodded. "I do."

Griff let go of her hands and took a ring from his pocket. "My darling Caroline, this ring has been in my family for generations. I give it to you as a token of my faith and devotion."

The gold glittered, the sapphire and diamonds sparkled in the spring sunlight streaming through the parlor window. Griff slipped it onto her finger.

The preacher began a prayer, but Carrie's heart was already full to overflowing with love and praise for the Father who had given her beauty for ashes, the oil of joy for mourning. Who had poured out upon them all the full measure of his grace.

ABOUT THE AUTHOR

A native of west Tennessee, Dorothy Love makes her home in the Texas hill country with her husband and their two golden retrievers. An accomplished author in the secular market, Dorothy made her debut in Christian fiction with the Hickory Ridge novels.

A NOTE FROM THE AUTHOR

Dear Readers,

Thank you so much for visiting Hickory Ridge again. I hope you enjoyed renewing your acquaintance with Ada and Wyatt Caldwell, whose story is told in the first Hickory Ridge novel, *Beyond All Measure*. And I hope Carrie's search for true love and abiding grace leaves you inspired and entertained.

Much of my reader mail comes from people wanting to know which parts of my novels are fact and which are fiction. The town of Hickory Ridge, while firmly rooted in a real location in the southern Appalachians, is the product of my imagination, as are all of my characters. But the economic conditions portrayed in *Beauty for Ashes* are all too real. The panic of 1873, which was caused in large part by unbridled expansion of the railways, resulted in a prolonged economic depression that was keenly felt across the South.

The disposition of Henry's body, as insensitive and horrifying as it seems, is a reflection of actual conditions in Chicago toward the end of the nineteenth century. The details regarding Southern blockade runners during the Civil War are true as well.

Some years ago I spent a lot of time in and around Charleston, South Carolina, researching a novel for young readers and fell hopelessly in love with the Carolina low country. Creating the character of Charlestonian Griff Rutledge provided an excuse to revisit all of the things I love about that very special place. I hope that reading this novel has given you a sense of its beauty and the pull it exerts upon everyone who is lucky enough to spend time there.

One of the best things about being an author is receiving mail from readers. I love hearing from you either through my website, www.Dorothylovebooks.com, or by snail mail to Thomas Nelson, P.O. Box 141000, Nashville, TN, 37214, Attention: Author Mail. Or join me and my friends on Facebook for the latest news, announcements, and fun.

You're cordially invited back to Hickory Ridge next year when Sophie Robillard, the beautiful little orphan you first met in *Beyond All Measure*, returns to Hickory Ridge as a young woman set upon making a name for herself in the newspaper world, and discovers some surprising secrets about her past.

Until then, may His face shine upon you and give you peace.

Dorothy

READING GROUP GUIDE

1. How does the title of the novel, *Beauty for Ashes*, relate to Carrie and Griff? To Deborah? To Mary?
2. Hickory Ridge is a small town tucked beneath the mountains. How does geography influence the townsfolk's customs and attitudes? What role does geography play in defining your city or town?
3. Griff and Carrie both experience great loneliness in their lives. How do they cope with it?
4. Carrie tells Caleb that it was not forgetting that helped her heal after a great loss, but remembering. Do you agree or disagree? Why?
5. After Mary's baby is born, Carrie muses that people's lives rarely turn out as they planned and that the secret of happiness is to want the life one has. Do you agree or disagree?
6. In Charleston Griff realizes he has spent years roaming the world looking for what he needed, then returned home to find it. Have you ever had a similar experience? How did it change your view of yourself or the world?
7. On her visit to Hickory Ridge, Ada Caldwell tells Carrie to pray "the prayer that never fails." What prayer, above all others, sustains you?
8. Deborah believes Carrie is frightened by the thought of complete surrender to God. What causes us to be fearful of such a commitment? What are its implications?
9. Near the end of the story, Mary realizes God has changed her and Carrie. How does each woman grow and change over the course of the story?
10. Carrie's friends disapprove of her relationship with Griff. Have you ever had to choose between keeping someone's approval and following your heart?